To Bred

Liam Rogers

GW01465138

To Tame a Mighty Tyger

To Tame a Mighty Tyger

K.H. ROGERS

THE SOL PRESS

First published in 2013 by
THE SOL PRESS
Carrickbawn, Blackrock Road,
Dundalk, Ireland.

A CIP record for this title is available from The British Library.

ISBN-13: 978-0-9927316-2-5

Cover painting by Michelle Rogers
Cover design by David M. Kiely
Set in 11 on 17 Sabon
by David M. Kiely
Printed by Dolman Scott

To James, Jennifer and Annabel

Let words be your weapons and ye shall wield
the power of the sun in your hands.

If Mother Nature had a voice she would have had no more eloquent
a spokesman than Chief Seattle of the Suquamish Indians. A man
whose culture uniquely understood that the relationship of Mother
Nature and human nature must be a symbiotic one. A man who
possessed the wisdom to realize that "the Earth is not something we
inherit from our ancestors, but borrow from our children."
The following is the text of a speech he allegedly gave in 1854.

THE PRESIDENT IN WASHINGTON sends word that he wishes to buy our land. But how can you buy or sell the sky? The land? The idea is strange to us. If we do not own the freshness of the air and the sparkle of the water, how can you buy them?

Every part of the earth is sacred to my people. Every shining pine needle, every sandy shore, every mist in the dark woods, every meadow, every humming insect. All are holy in the memory and experience of my people.

We know the sap which courses through the trees as we know the blood that courses through our veins. We are part of the earth and it is part of us. The perfumed flowers are our sisters. The bear, the deer, the great eagle, these are our brothers. The rocky crests, the dew in the meadow, the body heat of the pony, and man all belong to the same family.

The shining water that moves in the streams and rivers is not just water, but the blood of our ancestors. If we sell you our land, you must remember that it is sacred. Each glossy reflection in the clear waters of the lakes tells of events and memories in the life of my people. The water's murmur is the voice of my father's father.

The rivers are our brothers. They quench our thirst. They carry our canoes and feed our children. So you must give the rivers the kindness that you would give any brother.

If we sell you our land, remember that the air is precious to us, that the air shares its spirit with all the life that it supports. The wind that gave our grandfather his first breath also received his last sigh. The wind also gives our children the spirit of life. So if we sell our land, you must keep it apart and sacred, as a place where man can go to taste the wind that is sweetened by the meadow flowers.

Will you teach your children what we have taught our children? That the earth is our mother? What befalls the earth befalls all the sons of the earth.

This we know: the earth does not belong to man, man belongs to the earth. All things are connected like the blood that unites us all. Man did not weave the web of life, he is merely a strand in it. Whatever he does to the web, he does to himself.

One thing we know: our God is also your God. The earth is precious to him and to harm the earth is to heap contempt on its creator.

Your destiny is a mystery to us. What will happen when the buffalo are all slaughtered? The wild horses tamed? What will happen when the secret corners of the forest are heavy with the scent of many men and the view of the ripe hills is blotted with talking wires? Where will the thicket be? Gone! Where will the eagle be? Gone! And what is to say goodbye to the swift pony and then hunt? The end of living and the beginning of survival.

When the last red man has vanished with this wilderness, and his memory is only the shadow of a cloud moving across the prairie, will these shores and forests still be here? Will there be any of the spirit of my people left?

We love this earth as a newborn loves its mother's heartbeat. So, if we sell you our land, love it as we have loved it. Care for it, as we have cared for it. Hold in your mind the memory of the land as it is when you receive it. Preserve the land for all children, and love it, as God loves us.

As we are part of the land, you too are part of the land. This earth is precious to us. It is also precious to you.

One thing we know – there is only one God. No man, be he Red man or White man, can be apart. We *are* all brothers after all."

ONE

"WHAT DO YOU WANT ME TO DO?" he'd asked earlier on the phone.

"To change the world, Jack . . . to change the world."

Another anxious glance at his wrist-cell . . . Five minutes to midnight. He jerks back the curtains again and peers out at the quiet residential street, suffused as it is with a hazy amber glow. The car would be here at midnight, probably a sleek black silent one. One you could only hear the engine of if you pressed your ear hard against the bonnet, and listened to it humming like a bee. Time was when cars purred and roared, but the modern thermoelectric ones snuck up on you like soft-padded cats – stealthy but healthy.

Another glance as he paces up and down the living-room . . . Two before midnight. The soft clunk of a car door outside; footsteps now, striding purposefully, closer and closer. The doorbell trills one solid ring.

He hesitates and rubs his clammy right hand against his trousers before opening the door. A huge figure of a man looms over him, at-tired head to toe in an immaculate, shiny black suit and tie. The fig-ure's eyes stare directly at him to fix his gaze and question him.

"Jack Andersson?"

"Yeah, that's me," he answers, awkwardly thrusting out his right hand.

The man's eyes search the doorway and the house behind him, before darting back to question him again.

"Anybody else in the house with you, Mr Andersson sir?"

"Just my wife Jenny in the kitchen, and my son Josh. He's eleven . . . he's asleep in bed."

The man is scanning the house all the while with what Jack assumes is an infrared body detection device.

"Thank you, sir!" he snaps, before raising his right cuff to his mouth and turning away. "We're clear," he says.

A second burly figure opens the rear door of a big black car parked out on the street to let someone out. Jack waits at his front door, his right arm still held out ridiculously, anticipating a handshake. I'm an idiot, he thinks; should've known that guy was an agent.

Looks at his wrist-cell . . . Five seconds to midnight . . . Jesus, these guys don't mess around!

Five seconds later he gets his handshake.

"I'm Walter Franklin. I'm on the White House senior staff, but you can just call me Walt."

The two sit in the living-room, facing one another across an old mahogany table. Franklin is in his mid-fifties. Thinning grey hair is swept neatly back from his temples. The deep-set eyes that dominate his face make him appear morose. His look is quick, suspicious and pregnant with intent, if you dare hold its gaze. But offset by a well-practised, easy smile; one to disarm, cajole or convince when occasion demands. He reminds Jack of what they used say about the former Soviet premier, Gorbachev – a nice smile but iron teeth.

"Well, Jack, I'm sure you're wondering what in hell a senior White House staffer is doing sitting in your living-room past midnight."

"You think?" he answers with a nervous shrug.

"I'm sorry, Jack, for security reasons we couldn't discuss any of this on the phone. I hope you understand?"

"Sorry, Walt, I haven't a clue what this is all about."

"Well then, I'll cut straight to the chase. The President has requested me to ask you to do something for him."

Jack frowns briefly.

"Me!"

"He wants to commission you to write a book for him."

"A book . . . what kind of a book?"

"A book about *him*. A biography."

"Hey, come on, there are hundreds of biographies about Roberts," he laughs bemusedly while rubbing a hand across his forehead.

"Yeah, I know, I know. But this one would be different. This book would have his official seal of approval. Access to people who really know him . . . influential people. People other biographers could never even dream of interviewing. I have a list here of individuals you would be personally authorized to talk to about the President – take a look!"

He slides some documents across the table. Jack's eyes widen as he scans the list. He recognizes the names of many well-known politicians, businessmen, scientists and environmentalists.

"You've eighteen months exactly to write the book. October fifteen next year is the deadline."

"You're kidding me. Right?"

"No, Jack. That's the time frame."

"Nah . . . it's impossible. I can't do all the research and basically write a history book on the President's entire life within that time frame. Nobody could do it – at least not accurately and comprehensively."

"Don't you think the President knows that already? He's not looking for that type of book. What he wants is a book about *him*. Something personal, something that will capture the essence of him as a man. Let the academic historians squabble over the details about how he has achieved all that he has."

Jack shifts uneasily in his chair and looks suspiciously at Franklin.

"Now I get what you're looking for," he nods repeatedly. "You're really looking for a glowing portrait of the President; to be published three weeks before he seeks re-election in November. Aren't you . . . ?"

Franklin stiffens, looking momentarily nonplussed.

3

" . . . a sort of sophisticated piece of pre-election propaganda, isn't it?"

"Well, I hadn't thought of it quite that way," Franklin replies guardedly.

"I'm sorry, Walt, I hate politics. I hate what politics has done to this country and what it's doing to this world. I admire your boss and what he's trying to do – who wouldn't? – but I don't want to get involved like some pawn in a giant political chess game."

"Well, we're all pawns, like it or not, so long as we have the power to cast our individual votes. But even pawns can topple kings, change the game for better or worse."

Franklin pauses, composing his thoughts as if sizing Andersson up. This should've been an easy sell, he thinks. A once-in-a-lifetime opportunity for a struggling political columnist; a hack writing for a $10-a-month cyber-rag. Time to change tack and alter the angle of approach.

"Tell me, Jack, what's the most scared you've ever been?"

"You mean apart from when I answered the door tonight to your seven-foot bodyguard?"

"Hang on a sec, would you?" interjects Franklin, picking up his cell. "Tony, will you haul your ass in here?"

Tony has to bend his head to enter the living-room.

"Yes sir, Mr Franklin, sir!"

"Tony, shake hands with Mr Jack Andersson, would you. Jack, this is Tony Vespazzi, Secret Service agent detailed to White House security."

"Pleased to meet you, Mr Andersson, sir."

"You too," ventures Jack, surprised at the softness of the giant's hand.

"Tony's really a nice guy. Aren't you Tony?"

"Yes sir, Mr Franklin, sir!"

"That'll do Tony, thanks. You can go now."

Franklin shakes his head in mock exasperation as he leaves the room and half-whispers:

"Yes sir, no sir, three bags full, sir, one false move and I'll shoot you in the head, sir. Sorry, Jack, those guys get paid to be paranoid. Anyways! Tell me when you felt most scared in your whole life."

Jack reflects a while then arches his eyebrows unconsciously as he remembers.

"Well, that would be my son Josh when he was age two. Jenny, my wife, rang me at work. She could scarcely breathe the words out. Told me he'd collapsed here at home, was unresponsive, breathing funny and shaking all over. She'd called nine-one-one. Christ, I could hardly drive the car, I was that scared. My legs were shaking, my mind was racing. Kept telling myself two-year-old kids don't just collapse and die in an instant. Maybe it's meningitis or epilepsy or a brain tumour. Crazy things went through my head – like how much do white coffins cost, or what did we do wrong for God to do this to us? Jenny was near hysterical when I got to Emergency. I'd only seen her like that once before; she was shaking with terror and sobbing desperately. I tried to reassure her but we both ended up crying. The doctor came out after the longest time, little Josh walking beside him, holding his hand. Doctor said he'd had what's called a febrile convulsion. He had an ear infection and his temperature spiked over forty. He said it was very frightening but harmless. Lots of kids under five get them, until their bodies learn to regulate their temperature better. Josh would be fine once he'd had a course of antibiotics to treat the underlying infection."

Jack pauses, cups his two hands together over his mouth and blows hard through them, shaking his head, remembering the relief.

"Then the doctor jokes: 'Won't you say sorry to Mommy and Daddy, Josh, for giving them such a scare.' 'Won't!' he shouts. 'Not my fault.'"

Franklin chuckles and nods his head knowingly.

"That's kids for you. One minute they're dying; the next, they're bouncing around as if nothing's ever happened." Then he stops and stares directly into Jack's eyes.

"The way you and Jenny felt that day . . . scared out of your wits . . . that's the way each and every one of us should feel about the future of the planet. I don't have to tell you. You watch the news every day, same as everyone else. As it is, the President spends more time in the eco-situation room than the Oval Office. Big Carbon's gonna kill us, if the man doesn't get re-elected. Jesus! Jack, this is a chance in a lifetime. This is the most important work you'll ever write. The most significant thing you'll ever do if you value the future. And I'm pretty sure – as a father – you must!"

Jack presses his lips together and looks away. Cups both hands again over his mouth and blows through his fingers; thankful almost to have escaped Franklin's steely stare.

Franklin punctures the air with a sharp snap of his fingers.

"Ah, almost forgot!" he says, reaching inside his jacket and then sliding a sealed envelope across the table. Jack frowns, hesitates, moves his hand gingerly across the table and picks it open. He's holding a cheque. Looks at it twice to make sure it's really his name on it, that he's not reading the decimal place wrong on all the zeroes. He returns to Franklin's steely stare.

"I told you: this is the most important thing you'll ever do. That's the job paid for, in full and in advance. The President of the United States of America has every confidence in your ability and dedication to your appointed task. I have the contract right here, awaiting your signature."

Franklin's proffering a gold pen in his right hand, hovering over some documents. For the second time that night, Jack's thinking: Jesus, these guys don't mess around.

"Sorry, Walt, would you give me a few minutes?"

"I swear to God, you got five minutes with Jenny or I'm outta here."

* * *

Jenny's sitting in the kitchen with elbows planted on the table, absent-mindedly tinkling a lukewarm cup of coffee with her finger-nails. Jack walks up behind her, drapes his arms loosely around her neck and presses his nose into her long blonde hair. Takes a deep breath before drawing back and kissing her on the cheek. He gently takes both her hands, stops, and gazes at her. She smiles at him; she can tell he's feeling excited but struggling to suppress it.

"Honey, that guy in there is Walter Franklin from the White House. He came here to ask me to write an official biography of the President. I've been given eighteen months to write it, if I accept the commission. But it'd mean a lot of travelling, doing interviews, research and stuff, both here and abroad."

Jenny runs her fingers through her hair, biting her lower lip, a barely perceptible wince etched in her face.

"I don't know, Jack . . . Josh really needs his father right now, and eighteen months might as well be an eternity for a little kid. Even for me it is! I don't know, Jack . . . it's a huge commitment."

"Yeah, I know, but . . . "

"And it's not your field. You're a journalist, not a biographer."

"But Jenny, it's still just words. It's just a book."

"Just a book," she sniffs. "Tell that to Marx, Mohammed, and the Four Evangelists and go figure! Roberts is cranking up his election campaign already; don't you see?"

"Sure I do, honey."

"What are they offering anyways?" she adds, almost as an after-thought.

"I really wanted your full support on this without having to mention money. The lack of it never stopped you backing me up ever since I started writing."

He hesitates, smirks as he fishes the cheque from his pocket and then lays it ceremoniously on the table directly in front of her. She studies it, shakes her head disbelievingly and gazes up at her husband, her eyes starting to brim with tears.

"My God . . . Oh, my God!"

"I do this . . . I do this thing, honey, and we never have to worry about money again . . . *ever*." Jenny nods vigorously in tacit agreement. "It's a chance in a lifetime. I gotta do it."

She's still nodding as he makes for the door. Now she stops him with a plaintive catch in her voice.

"Why you, Jack? This thing is so much bigger than you."

He turns, smiles, shrugs, and flings his palms up in the air at the same time.

"I have absolutely no idea."

Franklin is tapping the face of his watch as Jack comes back.

"You're lucky it's running a little slow, Mr Andersson," he says without a trace of irony. "Do we have a deal or not?"

Jack pauses affectedly, a measured silence to solemnify the moment. He spies the gold pen and takes a deep, self-satisfied breath.

"That's a really nice pen you got there, Mr Franklin."

"I only use it for special occasions. This a special occasion?"

"Yes, I suppose it is."

As soon as Jack has the contract signed, Franklin produces a large brown envelope.

"This is a letter signed by the President, authorizing you to interview the individuals named on the list I showed you already. I had it laminated, as you'll need to use it on a regular basis. This is a copy of your interviewees again, this time with all their relevant contact details, private addresses, cell numbers, emails and so forth. This is your accreditation card. Will you please verify the personal details listed on the card and confirm the picture on the card is you?"

Jack picks up what looks like an outsize white credit card, and smiles back at a picture of his solemn self. He examines the details.

They're all correct: name, height, weight, genetic profile, et cetera.

He flips over the card and winks at the iconic presidential emblem on the reverse. It looks different now; this Eagle's got JACK ANDERSSON printed under it. He feels strangely smug but uneasy as he responds.

"It's perfect."

Franklin continues. "This document is further general guidance from the President himself on his expectations for this project. I have been directed by him to handle this business personally. You will have no other contact whatsoever with any other member of the White House staff. I will be your sole official contact at all times. Any problems, queries, concerns – anything at all – you can call me using this dedicated cell."

Franklin hands over an ultra-slim cell. It feels almost weightless in Jack's hand.

"Leave it switched on twenty-four-seven, would you please. And for Chrissake don't lose it! The number is untraceable. Only officials with maximum security clearance are authorized to use these things. Okay?"

"Yeah, sure."

"You must confine your interviews to those persons on the list I've given you. If for any reason, at any stage, you feel it imperative to talk to an individual who's not on that list, you must communicate through me and seek the President's permission to proceed. Is that clear?"

Jack nods earnestly.

"There is a code-name assigned to this project. It is known by only two people on the planet, namely Walter P Franklin and one Elijah Hunt Roberts, current President of the United States of America. Jack Andersson, you will be the third and final person to be apprised of this code. I'm going to write it down here on this slip of paper, show it to you, and dispose of it after you memorize it. Signal me when you've done so."

Franklin's gold pen traces ever so lightly on the paper, almost as if he's afraid to commit the information to writing.

S-T-E-E-L-M-A-N

"Got it, Jack?"

He nods again in acknowledgement. Franklin quickly tears up the slip of paper, shoves the scraps into his mouth, chews, and swallows hard.

"You only whisper that code, right at the very beginning of any communication we have with each other. I'm sorry, this is just security protocol, but it's the only way I can positively identify you. Do not under any circumstances use your own name. Any questions?"

"When do I get to see the President?"

"Says it right there on the file. You have an appointment with him at nine a.m. on October fifteen next year. Your interview with him on that date will be the final chapter of your book, so to speak."

"Hey, you guys got it all worked out like clockwork. You never doubted for one second that I wouldn't sign up for this, did you?" Jack says wryly.

"I never doubt my powers of persuasion. Least of all when I arrive armed with a big fat pay-cheque and a seven-foot agent."

Jack escorts him to the front door – and stalls him just before he opens it for him.

"Why me, Walt?" he asks in hushed tones. "Why me?"

"I serve at the pleasure of the President of the United States of America. I don't question his directives. I just carry them out. So you'll forgive me when I tell you; I ain't got the foggiest."

Tony's standing sentry at the door; he whispers into his right cuff as the door opens.

"Benjy's en route."

"'Benjy!'" blurts out Jack in comic bewilderment. Franklin turns around in disgust.

"Ah, it's a secret service thing. We all got our codes. President's is Eagle; mine's Benjy."

Jack is giggling like a schoolgirl.

"Why Benjy?"

Franklin waves dismissively.

"Guy with the lightning rod. Aw! Go figure it out, why don't ya."

Jack is chuckling all the way to bed. Looks at the cheque again and can't stop chuckling.

He looks in at Josh's bedroom. The light's always on in this room – right throughout the night – the child can't sleep with it off. He stares at Josh's shock of brown hair splayed out on the pillow, and smiles at his cute face. He wishes his son could somehow always be like this, perfectly asleep in dreamland. But he knows the nightmares will start yet again when the boy awakens in the morning.

TWO

JACK'S STUDY IS TINY. More a glorified booth. What few books there are on the shelf behind him must all be at least twenty years old. He eases himself back into his black leather chair, keeps his head dead still, and focuses on the darkened fifty-inch screen in front of him. A tiny pulse of faint, violet light identi-scans his iris; it doesn't even make him blink. The holographic image of a woman instantly materializes in glorious polychrome on the screen. She has curly blonde hair, crystal-blue eyes, and a crackerjack smile. A face to launch a thousand ships and worth the wreck of every one. She's exactly twenty-five years old and always will be. Jack likes to tease Jenny – "CASS is one helluva program." Jenny always responds: "I don't mind as long as *I'm* still the Apple of your eye."

"Morning, Jack!"

"Morning, CASS! Any messages?"

"Your brother Robbie says 'hi' and the auto shop will have the car fixed and available for collection any time after four o'clock today," she breezes. "Oh, and you can tell Josh the latest Pixar is definitely premiering on the twenty-first at fifteen hundred hours, and I'll have it for him just one hot minute after."

"Thanks. That's great, CASS. Listen, I've been asked to do something. I need you to create a file."

"Sure, Jack. What do you want me to call it?"

He thinks for a couple of seconds.

"Call it 'Eagle'."

"Eagle?"

"Affirmative," he orders. "I also need you to compile a report for me on the GeoNova political movement, and a second report on

12

President Elijah Hunt Roberts . . . with specific emphasis on personal biographical detail. Okay?"

"That might take some time, Jack. One hour minimum."

"Tell you what, CASS: why don't you make them both level-one reports and take three hours instead. Take your time surfing the Cloud and cross-reference all your sources. Accuracy is paramount for Eagle."

"Okay, Jack!" she pipes back. "I'm on it already."

"I also have some documents here I want you to scan and file under 'Eagle slash admin'."

He lifts the sheaf of documents given him the night before by Franklin. Thin shafts of violet light emanate from the side of the screen, one for each document in succession as he holds them up steady for CASS.

Jack leans forward; CASS may be only Apple's latest "face of cyberspace" but that still doesn't prevent him feeling self-conscious.

"CASS, I want you to find the best-rated child psychiatrist within a two-hour radius."

"Standard price parameters?"

"Not this time, CASS. Cost irrelevant."

"Got two for you. Profile and pictures on display in just a sec."

"Will you ping Jenny to come in here? She needs to see this."

Less than a minute after, Jenny squeezes into the study, glances at the screen and discreetly closes the door.

"Take your pick, honey."

She first examines the faces of two middle-aged men juxtaposed on the display then screws up her face as she weighs up their credentials.

"That guy on the right. I've seen him on TV. He's good, but he smiles and talks too much."

Josh doesn't like shrinks that talk too much.

"Mmm . . . the guy on the left . . . besides being handsome, he seems more composed, self-assured . . . authoritative."

Jenny gives a coquettish shake of her head as her eyes meet Jack's.

"I like him. Reckon that's our guy. What's his name again?" she asks, peering at the monitor.

"Bo Kvellner."

"I don't know whether that name is cute or just plain stupid!"

"Before you go, Jenny, where did Roberts give that speech . . . you know: the one where he used the F-word?"

"That'd be Yankee Stadium about ten years ago, I think," she replies as she's holding open the door, squinting back from the light.

Jack is enveloped again in the dark womb of his study.

"Cass, I need you to play a YouTube clip of a GeoNova concert at the Yankee Stadium about a decade ago. You can reference the keywords 'fuck', 'Elijah Hunt Roberts' and 'speech', to speed up your search."

"I've got it!" she chirps. "Do you want the whole clip?"

"No, just start one minute before the speech, and play for fifteen minutes."

"Enjoy the show, Jack!"

It is a balmy New York November night. The Yankee stadium is one sweaty seething mass of a hundred thousand people. But you can hear a pin drop as Roberts comes on stage. He isn't walking or striding but there's a relaxed feline quality to his gait, as if he doesn't have to strain a muscle to maintain his momentum. As quick as he's on the podium, his bronzed face is beaming back at his audience from banks of huge plasma screens. He wears no expression nor betrays a single clue as to his inner state of emotional being. Body, mind and man seem to radiate a profound serenity – a cosmic, inner peace incarnate. All except his eyes: those dazzling, cobalt-blue eyes. It is as if he has summoned the will of the entire universe and expressed them solely through the instrument of his vision. These eyes are mesmeric, hypnotic; these eyes are electric. This man is no televangelist; he's not come looking for your money or your prayers – but by God he wants your soul!

Also Sprach Zarathustra thunders out from multiple speakers, and the crowd waits for their idol to speak.

"Ladies and gentlemen! I really do not need to say much. The pictures you have seen on the screens here tonight bear more eloquent testimony than the humble words that one man can convey. All I have to say is this: if you could view the world through my eyes . . . the big picture . . . the whole thing. If, for just one second, you could comprehend with my mind. Run your fingers across the fabric of life itself. Everything from the Big Bang to this very second. You would know . . . you would all know . . . how precious life on Earth really is.

"Now, you would know . . . you would all know that we have absolutely no right *to fuck it all up.*"

The crowd erupts with a euphoric primeval roar of approval. A tide of raw, heaving humanity swells, flows and ripples around the stadium. "GeoNova" is their mantra. GeoNova is their religion.

Roberts is motioning his head real slow from side to side all the while. Tears are coursing down his cheeks and his voice is ready to crack; but not a split-second before he's reached his peroration – the crux of his speech.

"If you could see what I see . . . If you could feel what I feel . . . Man . . . Man . . . you'd weep for this world . . . and you'd never, ever stop!"

The heaving tide of humanity swells, sweeps, and roars its mantra again.

Roberts seizes the minute's interruption to compose himself and proclaim his own, now iconic, mantra.

"I am Elijah Hunt Roberts. I am going to reclaim the Promised Land. And you are all coming with me. Together . . . we're going to change the world! Change the world!"

Now the music starts up – GeoNova's soaring anthem – an urban hymn from the late twentieth-century band, The Verve.

> Cause it's a bitter sweet symphony, this life
> Trying to make ends meet
> You're a slave to money then you die. . . .
>
> No change, I can change, I can change. . . .
>
> Well I never pray
> But tonight I'm on my knees, yeah. . . .

The crowd is swaying in time to the melody. There is not a lyric or a beat of that anthem that is not seared into its collective consciousness. Roberts is planted on the podium like a colossus. His mighty head is tilted back, with his eyes zeroed on the zenith of the heavens above him. His long arms stretch ramrod straight to the sky in a giant 'Y'. Every one of his taut fingers is reaching for the stars. And he's got exactly one hundred thousand souls nestling in his palms.

Jack takes a deep breath as the clip concludes and thinks: Elijah Hunt Roberts – Eli to his friends – that man is some piece of work!

"CASS, will you connect me to the office of Dr Bo Kvellner, please."

A soft intermittent tone reassures Jack that the call is connecting. When quantum computing telecommunications technology was in its infancy, users had to wait in silence for a response. They found it disconcerting, so the manufacturers had to reconfigure their software and revert to the good old-fashioned beeps.

"Bo Kvellner's office. Good morning, Mr Andersson," tweets the face on-screen, flashing a feigned smile.

Jack flicks his eyes down instinctively to double-check the name panel highlighted in blue.

"Good morning, Ms Chang. I want to arrange an appointment for my wife Jenny and myself to see Dr Kvellner as soon as possible, please."

"I'm sorry, Mr Andersson, Dr Kvellner has a twenty-week waiting list . . . vacations, conferences, et cetera . . . it'd be late September at the earliest."

Jack searches the schedule of professional fees displayed on the right side of his screen. But he doesn't find the exact information he's looking for.

"What do you charge for priority appointments, Ms Chang?"

"Oh! That'd be two thousand dollars for a priority initial consult, but we still wouldn't be able to facilitate you until—"

"I'm going to be a little tight for time next eighteen months. Go tell Dr Kvellner I'll pay him ten thousand for an appointment tomorrow afternoon."

"Just a minute, please." But she's back in a jiffy. "Fifteen hundred hours tomorrow okay, Mr Andersson?"

"Fifteen hundred tomorrow is just fine!" Jack says tetchily, and feels his lips press together as he thanks "Mizzz" Chang.

Her image fades. Jack relaxes back into his chair and rubs the crown of his head with his hands. In his mind, he hears the crowd again chanting that lyric – the line that everyone must live by every day.

You're a slave to money then you die.

THREE

THE WAITING-BUBBLE adjacent to Kvellner's office is completely spherical, apart from the gently curved floor, designed to accommodate hyper-comfy chairs for clients. Jenny has chosen from the computerized Viewscape menu to illuminate the entire inner surface area of this sphere with a serene vista. It is a sultry September sunset. The cloudless evening sky is perfectly mirrored by its reflection on a large lake. The body of water is ringed by an angular mountain range. The setting sun glints off the snows clinging to its series of ragged peaks. Jack and Jenny's faces are bathed in a surreal, golden amber glow as they listen to *his* musical preference: Beethoven's *Pastoral Symphony*. Their senses are immersed in this sublime, 360° dreamscape, until the voice of Miss Chang rouses them from their reveries—

"The doctor can see you now."

Kvellner cuts a handsome, dapper figure, with sallow-skin and neat, silver hair. He insists on wearing gold-rimmed reading spectacles, despite being able to adjust the font size on his desktop PC. They accentuate his gravitas, as does his thin, quick smile, and single, firm handshake.

He invites them to sit. Jenny looks at all the gold frames adorning the walls of the psychiatrist's office, displaying his numerous degrees and qualifications. This is so much better than a bargain online session with a pseudo-shrink and a spell on the cyber-couch, she thinks. Jack is holding Jenny's hand; he likes to when he's nervous.

"Well, Mr and Mrs Andersson – how can I help you?"

"It's our son . . . Josh," says Jack. "He eh . . . needs a little help."

"We all do." Jenny nods towards her husband.

"He has been diagnosed with Asperger's Syndrome," Jack continues.

"How long ago?"

"Three years come this fall," says Jenny.

"Well, rather than bombard you with a million questions you've probably been asked already, I'd like to spend a few minutes reviewing his psychological evaluation. Did you bring it with you?"

Jenny passes him a biscuit-coloured card, and as he's scanning it into his PC, she tells him.

"There's two reports there, Doctor – we got a second opinion to confirm the initial diagnosis."

Kvellner spends the next few minutes examining the file on his monitor. He's searching the pouches of his cheeks with the tip of his tongue and rolling his head knowingly as he reads the material. He tightens his lips and exhales gently through his nose as he's finished and readying to speak.

"Mr and Mrs Andersson, I've been a clinical child psychiatrist for thirty years. And in that time, we have made wonderful advances in our understanding of the human mind, and the clinical psychiatric conditions with which it is all too commonly afflicted – both paediatric and adult. But . . . A.S. is a combination of a congenital abnormality of the frontal lobes . . . and right-hemisphere cortical dysfunction. It's an autistic-spectrum disorder that we can manage but not cure. This really isn't my specific field. There are other therapists better qualified than me in this highly specialized area – and at a fraction of my fees. In short, I genuinely don't want to waste your time or more of your money."

Jenny winces as she feels Jack squeezing her left hand. He's fuming!

"Don't tell us that we came here to sit in a fancy ball and pay you ten grand to watch a goddam sundown! Say it ain't so, Bo, say it ain't so," he adds caustically.

But Kvellner remains unflappable, too seasoned a professional to rise to the taunt.

"I'm genuinely sorry, Mr and Mrs Andersson, but your son is not a suitable patient for a man with my caseload or limited clinical experience treating A.S."

Jack is on his feet now, remonstrating with the psychiatrist about the money he's already been paid.

"Let's go, honey. We've been taken for a ride!" he says angrily, almost dragging Jenny up from her chair.

"Settle down, Jack!" she orders. "We're not being fair to Dr Kvellner. Now sit down and hush up. What's your Desk Access Code, Doctor?"

"'BKV one-zero-nine'."

Jenny flips open her cell and calls out the name "CASS" . . . the response is instant—

"Afternoon, Jenny!"

"Hi, CASS, would you please upload the file 'Josh psychreports' to 'BKV one-zero-nine slash NY'."

"Sure, Jenny. You'll have it in one hot minute."

"Thanks, CASS."

She pauses.

"To be frank with you, Doctor: we have six evaluations from six different psychologists."

She pauses again.

"Call it female intuition, but something just doesn't feel quite right about this whole thing."

"You consulted *six* other psychologists before you came to me?" he asks rhetorically.

"Yes, Doctor."

There is a quiet hint of desperation in her voice that almost begs the psychiatrist to persist. He's scrutinizing the screen again through his gold-rimmed spectacles, rolling his head slowly as before, poring over the fresh material.

"No," he's saying, "the reports are all the same: 'social impairment, narrow interests, repetitive routines, formal pedantic language and unusual prosody' . . . The list goes on ad infinitum, of classic problems and behaviours typical of Asperger's Syndrome that your son presents with."

"He's named Josh, Doctor," Jenny says. "Look again," she pleads.

Kvellner senses her anguish as his eyes glide across the screen again; up and down, over and back, comparing and contrasting all the documents simultaneously displayed. He's looking a good ten minutes then stops cold and almost inaudibly comments to himself: "That is very unusual . . . Josh scores quite high on his IQ tests . . . but giftedness is not an uncharacteristic attribute of A.S. But that's not what bothers me here . . . "

"Yeah," interjects Jack, "he's a really bright kid behind it all."

Jenny taps Jack gently, once on the forearm.

"What bothers you, Doctor?" she says, her voice rising with concern.

"Well, I'm looking at four different IQ tests here: a Wechsler, both adult and child, a Kaufman Battery, and a Fischer K. Josh scores exactly the same in every test, despite the fact that each test is discrete. The statistical probability of achieving identical IQ results across four different tests is remote, to say the least. He's hitting a convenient ninety per cent every time. What you really need to discover is the ten per cent of Josh that he is choosing to conceal."

"Can you find that ten per cent, Doctor?" Jenny ventures in a strangely excited yet pleading tone.

Kvellner leans straight back into his chair; his eyes seem kinder now, set almost incongruously beneath his grave, silver brows.

"Mr and Mrs Andersson," he intones, "at risk of seeming superlatively arrogant, I am probably the best clinical child psychiatrist in New York. If I can't negotiate a path into your son's psyche then no one can do it. And I will do it – under one condition."

Almost unconsciously, Jack and Jenny find themselves looking at one another and holding hands again.

Kvellner steels his stare and continues now in more measured tones.

"My success rates are inversely proportional to my clients' mendaciousness; which is just a smart way of saying that if you are not completely frank and honest with me, we don't stand a chance! So don't tell me any half-truths . . . conceal nothing from me."

Jack is nodding his head apologetically. Jenny's smiling and saying, "Thank you, Doctor."

Both stand and shake Kvellner's hand again, a little less formally this time.

His smile is broader and more benevolent now. "Miss Chang will schedule some priority appointments for you."

Jack suddenly looks horrified.

"It's okay, regular rates will be fine from now on," the psychiatrist tells a relieved Jack – who still can't get his head around, or simply forgets, all the extra zeroes in his latest bank balance.

Zipping along in the express elevator to the ground floor, Jenny turns to him and says wistfully:

"Funny thing . . . I'd forgotten there used to be snow on top of mountains."

FOUR

THE AMBULANCES CARRY the Red Crescent, barely discernible under their grime-caked, white paintwork. Little puffs of reddish dust rise up under the wheels as the drivers slam on their brakes outside the hospital entrance. The wide front doors are like a great, black cavernous mouth choked with the dead, the dying, the wounded and the bewildered.

Armed security men are brandishing their weapons at the surging crowd, and firing intermittently into the sky to stem the tide. The wails and screams of the terrified reverberate through the dry desert air. There's been yet another bombing in some unpronounceable Iraqi town. A daily scene of utter chaos is captured by a media crew and broadcast to a weary Western World. The camera pans and focuses on the figure of a tall bearded man running towards the hospital. His bloodied robes are swirling in his slipstream as he cradles a little boy. He is roaring something over and over, scarcely audible at first . . . *"All . . . Allahu . . . Allahu akh . . . "* before it crystallizes into a desperate chant . . . *"Allahu akhbar! Allahu akhbar!"*

The man's run slows to a stride, a walk, a hesitant shuffle, and then he stops and stares at the hospital entrance. He collapses onto his knees and grinds them into the sand. The sun blinds his eyes as he rears his head back and up to the sky. He raises the boy as if he's offering him up, Abraham-like, to his merciful god. All the while, he's hoarsing his refrain, but it's becoming more plangent now. The boy's head of jet-black hair lolls to one side and his lifeless eyes roll back. The weight becomes too heavy for the man's arms to bear, so he gently lays the limp body in the dust. His tears and the blood commingle – gratefully accepted by the baked, desiccated earth. Clasping

23

and squeezing his own bloodied fingers, he raises his hands to heaven one last time in supplication. Then he utters a cry of overwhelming human anguish. A cry that transcends language and only a human heart can articulate in a moment of perfect grief. The camera seems to shudder as it pans away to the rest of the crowd. The crew director's voice can be heard in the background.

"Stop rolling . . . just stop!" he orders.

Jack Andersson wakes with a single gasp and sits bolt upright in his bed, wiping his damp forehead with his arm. It is a dream, and yet not a dream. He remembers viewing that footage on CNN during the Iraq war early in the century. His own father was watching the television with him. When the clip was finished, his dad grabbed the zapper and pressed the OFF button. Jack turned instantly towards him to see what was wrong. His father wasn't weeping but Jack sensed, from the tiny quiver on his under-lip, that he was upset. "God-awful war," he'd hissed through clenched teeth. Jack was in Mrs Cranmer's eighth grade at the time. All his class enjoyed learning about the Civil War, as all Northern boys do, from Bull Run to Appomattox. One boy once asked, "What's war really like, Mrs Cranmer?" She'd stopped and thought a minute before answering.

"It's all hell broke loose, I guess. I suppose General Sherman summed up war best when he described it so."

Jack hauls himself up out of the bed, muttering, "Christ, I hate that fuckin' dream."

It is only seven a.m. but Jenny is up already. Josh wakes at exactly this time every morning without deviation. His mother tried to fool him a couple of times by putting the clock in his room back one hour, so she could get some extra sleep. But it didn't make the slightest difference. Jack reckons that the boy has an atomic clock ticking inside his head – accurate to the nanosecond. Josh can only sleep nude between

24

silk sheets; any cheaper material has too rough a texture for his skin to bear all night. Even silk pyjamas are too distracting a physical sensation for him to go to sleep. So that is why, at precisely 07.01 every morning, Josh is naked as he stands at the bathroom door. Jenny is kneeling at the bathtub with the flexible showerhead in her hand. She gives him a perfunctory nod to usher him in, and then says in a HAL 9000 emotionless tone: "Good morning Josh." He stands perfectly still at the door with a peculiar, stiff gaze, one that doesn't look at his mother, but looks through her instead. "Good morning, Mother," he responds in an equally mechanical voice, before entering the bathroom. His "friends" at school used to tease him that he walked like a puppet on a string. His physiotherapist is trying to help him with his gait and posture. Currently, when he walks, the upper half of his body is rigid, like a robot's. But his legs still move like a staggering marionette. Josh terms it his "awkwalk"; he likes to mess around, inventing new words.

As he steps into the bathtub, Jenny turns on the water. It streams gently through the shower head. The water-pressure must be exactly right – too high or too low and he'll start raising his voice. The water temperature must be set at precisely ninety-eight point six degrees Fahrenheit – too hot or too cold and he'll start shouting "Goldilocks! Goldilocks!" Everything has to be "just right" in Josh's world. Jenny holds the shower directly over his head and the water trickles through his hair, down his face, neck, chest, abdomen, genitals, thighs, knees, and finally, feet. He has a lithe body and a skin tone that can almost be described as bronzed. He stands with his head tilted back slightly, eyes closed and arms outstretched, parallel to the floor. There is not a trace of a smile, yet his face wears a peculiarly beatific expression. At such moments, he reminds Jenny of a magnificent bronze statue of an ancient Spartan boy warrior: graceful, spear-poised, latent power. She rubs some cinnamon-scented oil onto her palms and fingers, and massages his body from head to toe. The faintly sweet smell helps relax him. It is the only time Josh can tolerate human touch on his bare body without recoiling. The psychologists theorize that, because the water that saturates his skin is set at normal core body temperature, and because he has his eyes shut, in Josh's mind he is back in his mother's womb. It is dark, it is warm, and it is absolutely safe from the chaos that is the pervasive reality of his world. Maybe that is the reason why this morning ritual, for both Josh and Jenny, is the high point of the day.

Josh can dress himself; left sock first, then right sock, underpants, trousers, shoes, vest and shirt, always in the same order. Modern, synthetic nanofibres have considerably reduced the level of friction between textile and skin, but they are still expensive. At seven twenty-five, he is sitting at his usual place at the breakfast table. It is always the same breakfast: a bowl of plain cornflakes with milk chilled at precisely thirty-four degrees, followed by half a grapefruit – the sour-er the better. Four years ago, the conventional electrical grid started to experience problems due to excessive demand. Power outages were infrequent, but voltage levels were often reduced to maintain an adequate supply. Fridge temperature regulation became an issue as Josh noticed from the get-go that his milk wasn't "just right". For a full week, he had refused his cornflakes; he sat at the breakfast table every morning shouting "Goldilocks! Goldilocks!" Jack and Jenny eventually relented and switched to GeoNova's GreenGrid. Twice the price but worth every consistent volt, to store their milk at exactly thirty-four degrees.

At seven thirty this particular morning, Jack is explaining to Josh that he is flying to Los Angeles on United Airlines Flight number 53, departing 11.05 from JFK. And returning on UA 84, landing at JFK at 16.35 on the twenty-fifth.

Jack pauses and waits for the inevitable question.

"Why not fly Qantas, Father? Qantas is the safest airline."

"Qantas does not fly the route to Los Angeles out of New York," he answers.

And then it starts. Josh cups his hands over his ears and adopts a high nasal tone.

"Uh oh, uh oh . . . Qantas, Qantas never crashed . . . I'm an excellent driver . . . Yeah yeah . . . toothpicks two forty-six total . . . boxer shorts at Kmart . . . yeah yeah . . . we're counting cards . . . counting cards."

Jack and Jenny wait in silence for this series of sound bites from the movie *Rain Man* to finish. They know that once Josh starts this perfectly mimicked routine, he has to complete it. Jack would prefer to tell him that he always flies Qantas but knows that Josh will be obsessive about tracking the flights – therefore he is compelled to provide him with accurate details.

He realizes it is imperative to avoid ambiguity to minimize stress for Josh, so words like "maybe", "perhaps", "sometimes" or "later" are not in his lexicon. For Josh, abstractions can be fiendishly difficult to comprehend, so sarcasm, double meaning, irony, puns or metaphors can be a real challenge. Jenny's aunt once told him "You have your father's eyes." He was absolutely horrified. "But I have my own eyes!" he protested. The coach at school told him to always keep his eyes on the ball, so he lifted the ball up and pressed it against his nose. Everybody laughed. His teacher asked him once "Do you want to change your mind?" "What a bizurrd question!" he answered; "Is there something wrong with the one I have already?" Everybody laughed.

The first time he heard his parents use the phrase "it's raining cats and dogs" he exclaimed: "Oh, there will be blood everywhere!" Even they laughed. Josh is used to the sound of everybody's laughter, but never his own.

Jack hears three short pings on his cell. He looks directly at his son's face, to try and command his attention.

27

"Excuse me, Josh," he says in a measured voice, "Cass has a compu-call for me."

Jack's left iris is identi-scanned; Cass randomly chooses either left or right eye, to maximize user security.

"Morning, Jack!"

"Morning, Cass," he must respond, for her to verify that his vocal speech pattern is authentic.

"I have a priority call for you from GeoNova Industries. Do you want me to connect you?"

"Yes, please, Cass."

The face of a young woman appears on screen. Jack flicks his eyes down instinctively to the flashing blue name panel.

"Good morning, Mr Andersson."

"Good morning, Annabelle."

"Mr Andersson, I just want to confirm that your flight number is United Airlines fifty-three, arriving today at Los Angeles International. Is that information correct?"

"That is correct."

"Excellent," she smiles. "Please proceed to the VIP meet-and-greet area after your arrival, where a GeoNova representative will assist in transferring you to a corporate jet. We look forward to welcoming you at our HQ today."

"Thank you, Annabelle."

"Goodbye, Mr Andersson, and enjoy your flights."

Her image fades. Cass reassures Jack she's monitoring the cab she booked for him; its current status is "en route" and "on time".

Jack strolls back to his bedroom. He opens his motorized suitcase, and ticks off a mental checklist, as he sorts through its contents. Glances again at his cell: seven fifty-five. I'd better say goodbye to Josh, he tells himself. Between eight exactly and half past, when he leaves for school, Josh will be completely lost in cyberspace. He wears a helmet, not unlike that of an astronaut, with an internal computer display for a visor. The psychologists advise that, when he dons that helmet, he enters a psychically different place.

They would prefer he was more grounded in physical rather than virtual reality. But compromises are necessary to reduce his anxiety, to enable him to comprehend the chaos that dominates his world. Jenny reckons Cass is way better than giving him sedatives.

She's speaking with Josh about the latest Pixar release as Jack comes back into the kitchen, suitcase in tow.

"Goodbye, Josh; my cab will be here at eight fifteen," he says proffering his right hand but not expecting a handshake. Just this once, he hopes . . . just once. Josh stands and makes rhythmical involuntary movements with his left hand, as he ponders.

What is the appropriate response here? . . . something his special needs teacher told him at school.

Suddenly, he stretches his arms out wide, and drops them at the elbows. He walks clumsily towards Jack, like a drunken scarecrow. He doesn't embrace his father but presses his left cheek up against his chest.

"Goodbye, Daddy."

"Good boy, Josh" he replies, bending down and kissing his hair, delighted at this rare gesture of affection.

It's after eight and Josh is totally lost, but absolutely safe inside his helmet.

Jack and Jenny are still looking at each other, searching for their own "appropriate response". Sometimes it's a fine line between crying and laughing.

FIVE

JACK REMEMBERS BEING in Los Angeles International Airport when he was a teenager. It was a crowded, bustling mass of tourists and business types then, hurrying to and from their destinations. Nowadays, it's a different story. Air travel restrictions have been introduced to reduce carbon emissions, and ticket prices are going through the roof. Jack thinks maybe his monthly travel allowance isn't so generous after all. There are a few chauffeurs milling around the VIP lounge, but he doesn't see anyone carrying an electronic board with the name "Andersson" on it.

"Good afternoon, Mr Andersson," he hears spoken quietly behind him. He turns, to find a tall, elegant figure dressed in a distinctive dark-green suit edged with orange: standard GeoNova corporate attire.

"I'm LeRoy Fitzer, but everyone just calls me Fitz."

Jack gives him a wary handshake and asks quizzically: "How did you know it was me?"

Fitz smiles diffidently as he produces his cell and points to it.

"There is a proximity alert device application on this, and I have your cell number inputted to detect your location." He shrugs. "Picking anyone up is a piece of cake now, once you've got their number."

"Well, that's pretty neat, Fitz!"

"We like to think a little different at GeoNova. Your suitcase, Mr Andersson?"

"Thank you, Fitz."

Jack has to warn him to slow his pace or he will burn out the motor on his suitcase as they're heading towards the apron. But Fitz just casually switches it to manual without breaking his stride. They shield their eyes as they emerge from the terminal onto the tarmac. Jack is panting now, trying to keep up, but relieved to see a twin-engine corporate jet emblazoned with GeoNova's logo less than fifty yards away. Its captain is waiting at the bottom of the stairway to welcome Jack aboard. He has an almost military bearing, with his flamboyant gold-braided suit and swarthy complexion. His face seems to glisten, even under the shadow of his ostentatious peaked cap.

"I am Captain Massimo Tardelli. Welcome aboard, Mr Andersson, for this short flight to GeoNova HQ. Please, after you," he says politely, beckoning him up the stairs.

"I didn't think GeoNova would approve of me using an airplane instead of taking the train for this short trip, Captain," says Jack.

"This craft has a minimal carbon footprint. Our fuel is a blend of synthetic oil and biofuel derived from algae."

"I'd say that costs some?"

"Approximately five hundred dollars a gallon."

Jack freezes in astonishment and gives him a look as if to say, "Am I really worth that much?" before ascending the boarding stairs.

He settles himself into one of the plush, dark-green leather seats with orange piping, and buckles up. Stretches out his legs fully and smiles to himself, thinking of the cramped seating on his UA flight that morning. He can hear distinctly the exchange between the control tower and the captain through the cockpit door as they are taxiing. And knows, even before Tardelli announces it on the intercom, that they are cleared for takeoff. The engines power up, the aircraft bullets down the runway and sweeps into the sky.

Jack is gripping both armrests, wishing he was back on his United flight. His Italian pilot nudges the thrust levers forward to accelerate his ascent – and wishes he was at the controls of a Saturn v8 space-rocket instead.

Thirty minutes soaring over the Mojave Desert and Tardelli announces over the intercom that they are approaching GeoNova.

"Observe from the window, Mr Andersson."

Jack peers out at a vast, incongruous patch of green defying the arid landscape. A giant swirl of spiralled silver, shaped like a metallic Catherine wheel, glitters in the sunlight at its centre.

"We circle around now for a few minutes. Mr Kincaid wanted me to show you everything."

The plane banks sharply to the left and swoops down for a closer inspection.

"These silver arms are actually a Concentrated Solar Thermal Array. A series of curved – how you say? – parabolic mirrors that track the sun as it moves across the sky. The architects designed it to exactly copy the shape of the Milky Way galaxy. It is a pity this is not a night flight. To see it illuminated in the dark . . . izza fantastick. It is like travelling through outer space . . . no joke. GeoNova's HQ is not only an administrative and research facility but a power generating station as well. Fifty thousand people live and work underground, directly beneath that solar-panelled array. We land in two minutes. Okay, Mr Andersson?"

"Fine, fine, Captain," he says nervously.

"Don't worry, Mr Andersson, I will land her gently . . . like laying bambino in cot!"

Two security personnel are waiting at the bottom of the stairway as Jack steps off the plane.

"Good afternoon, sir," coolly intones one. "We need to check your credentials, please."

Jack quickly pulls out his biometrics card from his inside breast pocket and presents it to him. The other produces a small, hand-held iris scanner device and ushers Jack under the shadow of the aircraft, so he won't have to squint in the sunlight.

"Focus on the blinking green light and clearly state your full name, sir."

"Jack Anthony Andersson."

"Please open your mouth for a cheek swab, sir," the man continues.

The two security personnel spend five minutes matching his genetic profile, using another hand-held device, in which they have inserted the cotton swab.

"Please follow us," they pronounce at last in practised unison.

They walk towards a figure standing patiently at the side of the runway. He is a large man, not overweight, but looks like someone who was once quite portly and then shed his excess fat. So now he appears like a deflated bag braced to a broad-shouldered mast. But, as the CEO of GeoNova Industries, he has one of the most instantly recognizable faces on the planet. Jack keeps asking himself the same question over and over as he approaches: "Why me? Why me?"

He can still scarcely believe the words as he repeats them.

"Good afternoon, Jack. I am Tyler Kincaid. Welcome to GeoNova."

Jack looks at the hand outstretched to greet him. Knows there is something radically wrong, but can't quite figure it out. Kincaid pauses before breaking out into a hearty laugh to alleviate Jack's embarrassment.

"I'm left-handed. I always shake with the left. Why should you righties rule the world?"

Jack laughs back, nodding his head with relief while twisting his own right arm awkwardly to complete the handshake.

"Captain Tardelli give you a good flight?" he continues as he's escorting him towards a recessed incline in the grass.

"Yes . . . eh . . . fast."

"You know, that guy was formerly an astronaut with the European Space Agency. He's a great pilot!"

A set of darkened glass entrance doors glides back silently. Jack is staring now at what looks like a regular-sized silver car perched on a monorail. With a low hiss, its two doors are raised up, like an old DeLorean or a hovering predatory bird. An attractive young woman is sitting in one of its two seats.

"Step up into the pod, Jack," gestures Kincaid.

"But I thought you and I were just going to do a straightforward interview?" queries Jack, gazing at the single empty seat.

"No, Cathy will take you from here," he smiles. "We'll talk later."

"But . . . "

Kincaid places his hand on Jack's arm as he lowers himself reluctantly into the pod.

"If you want to understand anything about Eli Roberts, you have to see where his heart beats. Cathy, take him to the 'Gumball' first."

There is a low hiss again as the gull-wing doors close, and the silver pod starts to sail towards the beating heart of GeoNova.

Cathy begins: "Mr Andersson, this is the electric monorail system we use to travel all around the site. Fifty thousand employees live and work here, mostly underground. It's real easy getting around, though. You just step into a pod, call out your destination to the on-board computer, sit back, relax, and you'll be there in less than five minutes."

"So we're shooting straight for this . . . 'Gumball', is it?"

"Sure."

"Funny name."

"Makes perfect sense when you see it," she says, pouting.

The pod soon slows to a smooth stop, followed by a low hiss. She leads him to a viewing gallery overlooking a giant shiny metal cylinder serviced by a maze of pipes.

Jack peers through the thick observation glass as Cathy switches on a technical display screen.

"What the hell is that?"

"That, Mr Andersson, is a pebble-bed nuclear reactor. It doesn't use fuel rods, like conventional reactors, to control the core. Instead, there are three hundred and sixty thousand 'pebbles' of uranium oxide, three thousand of which are removed from the bottom of the reactor every day as spent fuel, and replaced with new ones. Each 'pebble' is roughly the size of a pool ball, and itself contains thousands of kernels of uranium dioxide, each encased in silicon carbide with a pyrolitic coating. The pebble is enclosed within a graphite shell that can tolerate temperatures up to five thousand degrees Fahrenheit; which is to say, basically, that this reactor is practically meltdown-proof."

Jack scrutinizes the image of the reactor vessel generated on the screen adjacent to the observation glass. It does indeed look like a giant gumball machine harnessed to a turbine and generator.

"Do you know much about physics, Mr Andersson?"

"Only that it starts with an 'F'," he quips impatiently. "What does this have to do with the President?"

"Well, this is the main electrical power generating source for GeoNova on the North American continent. We utilize it to supplement our GreenGrid, when the sun is not shining on our CST arrays, or the air is not blowing through our wind farms. It is essentially carbon neutral and generates easily manageable nuclear waste. But the real beauty of this reactor, apart from minimizing the risk of accidents to practically zero, is geopolitical."

"What do you mean?"

"What I'm saying is: the material used in this reactor has no weapons applications whatsoever – so the risk of nuclear proliferation is eliminated. We are currently constructing these pebble-bed design reactors in many developing countries, to wean them off fossil-fuel burning to generate power."

"How much does one of these things cost?"

"Ten billion dollars, give or take, but a lot cheaper, safer and more environmentally-friendly than Generation Four nuclear plants."

Cathy gives Jack a coy look.

"You're not really the scientific type we normally get here at GeoNova, are you?"

"No, I'm a political columnist."

"Okay . . . I'll keep the technical jargon to a minimum," she says with a patronizing laugh, as they head back to the pod.

"Sure . . . unless it's political."

Three minutes later, they're walking along gleaming white corridors flanked by a series of laboratories. It's a busy place. Cathy raises her voice slightly as she explains various research functions, and simultaneously bustles past dark-green streams of GeoNova uniformed personnel. She halts at the start of a long corridor marked NANO ENGINEERING DEPT.

"Do you remember the CCD crisis a few years back . . . Colony Collapse Disorder?"

"Sure, when all the bees nearly died out. I remember the pictures of all the Chinese, out pollinating their crops and orchards by hand. Experts were talking in terms of a food supply apocalypse."

"The problem was resolved right down this corridor, Mr Andersson, third room on the right," she states proudly. "Scientists at the time calculated we had only five years before all bees died out, due to a combination of Varroa mite infection and environmental toxins.

Then we invented the nano-bee," she says with an insouciant smile. "An artificial insect, designed and constructed using nanotechnology. We dispatched hundreds of people across the globe, armed with the requisite software to control swarm flight patterns. Governments paid GeoNova an absolute fortune to artificially pollinate their crops, thus averting potentially catastrophic famines. Subsequently, we went one better, and genetically modified natural bees to become immune to the environmental stressors that were causing CCD in the first instance. And sold the GM bees for billions, back to the same governments."

36

"I'm impressed," says Jack. "You've got some pretty smart people working here."

"The average IQ of a GeoNova employee on this site is one hundred forty-five."

"Wow! That include you, Cathy?"

She just smiles back with an almost disparaging look.

"My son Josh would fit right in here."

"Bright kid, is he?"

"Oh yeah! . . . Tell me one thing, Cathy: Why did those governments pay billions for the GM bees when they were already forking out billions for the nano-bees? I mean: Why pay twice over to solve one problem?"

"Because we wouldn't sell them the technology for the artificial bees."

"And so you could double up on your profits!"

"Something like that," she answers, a note of irritation creeping into her voice.

"I didn't think GeoNova would be that ruthless . . . mercenary, even. I was always under the impression you were the good guys . . . more philanthropic."

Cathy fires Jack a smouldering stare from under her immaculately sculpted eyebrows, but composes her answer carefully.

"Our business is to save the planet. It doesn't have a dollar price tag on it!"

She glances at her watch instinctively, as if unconsciously wanting to break the tension. "We'd better hurry. Mr Kincaid is expecting you in 'Earth Office' in twenty minutes."

They walk quickly to the nearest monorail terminal and pick up a pod.

"Why is Kincaid's office referred to as 'Earth Office'?" Jack queries as he's strapping himself in.

Cathy brings up a diagram of GeoNova's HQ on a monitor in front of him.

"This whole eco-colony, as we like to call it, is architecturally designed to be an approximate copy of our Milky Way. Our solar system lies about two thirds of the way out from the centre on one of its spiral arms, called Orion."

Jack pores over the map; the "Gumball" is dead centre and "Earth Office" is conveniently blinking for him, highlighted in greenish blue, about one third distant from the outer rim of the site.

"Well, that's pretty neat, Cathy!" he says as they come gently to a stop.

"We like to think a little different at GeoNova, sir."

The trace of pride in her words almost borders on condescension now. A woman who has retreated here with the elite of GeoNova, thinks Jack, to escape the tedium of mundane intellects. Anyone with a sub-145 IQ is definitely not welcome in Cathy's ivory tower.

SIX

KINCAID IS STANDING in the middle of his circular "Earth Office", legs apart, arms akimbo, and beaming a broad smile as Jack enters.

"What do you think of our eco-colony, Jack?"

"Well, I have to say I'm impressed."

"This is our vision of the future. A community dedicated to living an environmentally sustainable lifestyle. Energy generation is practically carbon-neutral here. Our nuclear technology is light years away from Three Mile Island or Chernobyl or Fukushima; it really is going to help save the planet. Did you notice anything physically unusual about the people you saw working here?"

Jack reflects for a couple of seconds.

"Yes, I didn't see anybody beyond about thirty years of age, apart from yourself."

"Anything else?" Kincaid is chuckling to himself, and seems to trace his hands over an invisible outline of his former girth.

"Sure," nods Jack, picking up the prompt, "there wasn't one individual who was overweight."

"I used to be a much larger man myself, you know. But I learned, as we all must learn, to consume less. Eat less meat. Just buy less stuff. It is capitalist heresy. But you know what – we simply don't have a choice any more. We recruit the best and the brightest from all over the world here; they have an average IQ of one hundred forty-five."

"So Cathy told me."

"You could say that GeoNova HQ is a global brain trust pursuing a greener world," Kincaid continues. "We have well-advanced plans to diversify and establish eco-colonies right around the planet. We have teams of scientists researching and developing geo-thermal energy, synthetic biology, drought-resistant GM crops, carbon-capture and sequestration technologies; the list goes on ad infinitum. Eli Roberts promised that together we are going to change this world. GeoNova is the catalyst that will power us toward that transformation."

Kincaid theatrically pauses and gazes up at the glass-domed roof that is flooding his office with the waning desert sunlight. Jack likes his smile but knows that, like Franklin, he has iron teeth, a steel soul and a will to match them both. He notices a small, curved bookcase at face level to his left, stacked with a series of black-spined books, their titles etched in gilt lettering.

"Have a good look, Jack; I was going to show them to you anyway."

Jack slides one off the shelf and flips open the front cover.

"This book is almost brand new!" he utters in amazement. "I thought they'd stopped printing books years ago."

"This series was specially commissioned. Of course it's all printed on recycled paper."

"It still must have cost a fortune."

"It's just a small indulgence."

Jack caresses the gilt-edged pages with an archaeologist's reverential touch. But he hardly recognizes a single word on them.

"What language is this?" he enquires.

"It's German."

"You speak German?"

"Fluently."

Jack closes the book and examines the title etched on its spine. *Menschliches, Allzumenschliches.*

"What does the title mean?"

"It means 'human, all too human'. It is a philosophical work written by Friedrich Wilhelm Nietzsche in the late nineteenth century. Ever heard of him?"

"Yes, I have actually. Didn't the Nazis adopt some of his ideas in their propaganda?"

"I think 'hijacked' might be a more appropriate term. Nietzsche was no anti-Semite or ardent nationalist, Mr Andersson."

Jack duly notes the formal change in address – "Mr Andersson" – and senses he has struck a raw nerve. Kincaid is standing directly in front of him now, smiling out of one corner of his mouth, as if he's just pulled a big cigar out of it. He lays a firm, avuncular hand on Jack's shoulder and whispers discreetly.

"Let me give you some advice. If you want an accurate insight into Eli's psyche, you must study Nietzsche's philosophy in depth. Otherwise, you cannot hope to effectively accomplish your literary task."

"Well, thank you, Mr Kincaid. Are you ready to start the interview now?"

Kincaid glances down at his watch.

"I am leaving for New Delhi in ten minutes. I have a meeting with the Indian PM tomorrow morning. So shoot fast!"

"But . . . but I thought we'd more time."

"Saving the planet is a time-consuming business," Kincaid says with a wink.

"Sure, I understand," concedes Jack. "You mind if I record this interview on my cell?"

"No problem. Fire at will."

"When did you first meet Roberts?"

"Twelve years ago, at a UN conference on climate change in Stockholm. I was working for 'Big Carbon' at the time, a top executive with Exxon. He came up and introduced himself, though I already knew who he was. Ever seen the movie Ben Hur?"

"Yes, it's a real classic."

"There is a scene in that film where Charlton Heston is being led away to the Roman galleys with a gang of other condemned men. They stop in a little village on the way, for their military escort to water their horses. The Roman commander refuses to let the hero quench his thirst. Then a man comes out of a carpenter's shop and gives Ben Hur the water he desperately needs to survive the journey; against the express wishes of the Roman commander, who orders him to stop. The man ignores him. The Roman draws his whip and the man stands up and confronts the officer. The director never shows us the man's face but we all know it is Jesus Christ. The Roman officer takes one look at that face and backs down; his cruel nature tamed beneath that divine countenance. So, when Eli Roberts shook my hand and asked me go work for him, I just looked up at him and said: 'When do I start?'"

Kincaid looks wistful as he reflects on his story and then glances at his watch.

"The Greeks used call it 'charisma', Jack. A magical gift bestowed by the gods on a chosen few, favoured mortals."

"What's Roberts like . . . as a man, I mean?"

Kincaid pauses and ponders the question for a good half-minute in total silence.

"Man's a mass of contradictions," he says eventually. "More you think you understand him, the more you realize you never will."

"I don't follow you, sir." Jack frowns.

"Sometimes words alone aren't adequate to answer the best questions."

Kincaid gazes amiably at Jack, turns to his desk and picks up an egg-sized spherical object. He covers it with both hands and rolls it in his palms for a few seconds, toying with it.

"Have a look," he says, extending one hand now and revealing the object. "Isn't it beautiful?"

Jack is admiring a greenish-blue, pearlescent miniature of the world, cocooned in Kincaid's palm. Its surface is exquisitely detailed, with named mountain ranges, rivers, deserts and oceans. But there are no borders or individual countries outlined.

"Yes, it's a really beautiful object, sir."

"Go on, take it," says Kincaid, pressing it into his visitor's hand. "It's yours; a memento of your visit here, or a gift for your son Josh perhaps?"

"Well, thank you, sir. That's very generous of you."

Kincaid glances at his watch yet again.

"Don't mention it. Listen, I want to show you something else before I go."

There is a quiet hum as a small trapdoor slides back in the middle of the floor and what looks like a dentist's chair ascends. Kincaid taps its green-and-orange leather upholstery and invites Jack to lie down. Jack walks falteringly twice around the chair, eyeing with suspicion the two seat belts dangling from the sides.

"Where am I going in this thing?"

"This chair is anchored solid to the ground. You are not going to move one inch."

"Then why the seat belts?"

"Trust me. You have nothing to fear but yourself," Kincaid answers cryptically.

Jack stretches his body out full as he sinks into the soft leather. Kincaid pulls two straps diagonally across his chest and adjusts them, so that they intersect exactly over his sternum. Two clunks reassure him that his interviewer is now safely belted up.

"Ever been to a planetarium, Jack?"

"Only once when I was a kid."

"Okay, then you just pretend to be that kid again and enjoy the show!"

There is a loud hum this time, as two giant curved metal shells rise up gracefully from the floor and meet seamlessly at the apex of the domed roof, to form a perfect hemisphere.

There is not a chink of light anywhere. Jack remembers being locked in a tiny cupboard when he was five by his brother Robbie. He screamed and screamed until his mother heard him and let him out. That was one of the scariest moments of his life.

An iconic photograph of planet Earth is projected directly above him now. He hears a deep voice booming out and beginning to narrate the scene. It is that of Elijah Hunt Roberts.

"This is a picture of the Earth, photographed by the crew of Apollo Seventeen in nineteen seventy-two. It is the most commonly reproduced image in publishing history, an image that has seared itself into human consciousness. But let us go then, you and I, and scrutinize the night sky; for the bald Moon beckons from the starry platter of the firmament."

Jack's eyeballs feel sucked into the ceiling as he gazes at that familiar face, cracked and cratered as if captured through a telescope.

"The Moon always wears the same imperturbable face to greet observers. She may wax and wane and hide her dark side. But she is no lunatic like old King Canute. Time and tide will wait for no man, for even the heaving oceans are twice a day moonstruck."

A burned-orange ball, crowned white, now appears.

"Mars: the mighty god of war. That rusty globe, though scarcely from his weapons corroding. And now the Asteroid Belt. It is hard to believe that one little lump of rock should end the tyranny of the dinosaurs. Imagine: to rule the world for millions of years; then God decides to throw a stone to end it all. Life and death is such a vicious game of random, cosmic chance. Einstein said God doesn't play dice. I disagree."

A giant orb of swirling red-and-yellow bands now swells the entire expanse of the ceiling.

Jack hears himself gasp at its magnitude.

"Jupiter; the Ancients crowned him king of the planets, over three hundred times our earthly mass. A sagacious giant, but his blood-red Spot betrays the secret storms of that Olympian intellect.

"Now Saturn; he of the same countenance; gloomy, taciturn; but a face well rebuked by many a splendoured ring.

44

"Uranus; a greenish disc that spins on its side. A long orbit and a crazy calendar.

"Neptune; a smooth crystal-blue sphere, aptly named the Sea-God of the solar system. Look at that great, dark spot on its surface. Even the calmest exteriors cannot conceal their inner demons.

"At last, Pluto: the god of the Underworld. Deservedly condemned to a remote, tiny body at the boundary of our civilized system."

Jack feels a vague sense of unease as the journey continues. The graphics are so crystalline in clarity that the scale and intensity of the entire audio-visual experience verges on the overwhelming.

"We must venture through the Kuiper Belt, and beyond the Oort Cloud. Behold the Zodiac and all the constellations. There is Perseus the Gorgon-slayer, who petrified the Kraken and stole the heart of Andromeda. Look yonder; they love each other still. There is Cancer the crab, a pair of ragged claws scuttling across the silent, celestial ceiling. And Orion the giant hunter, who could wade through the oceans while parting the clouds with his bow.

"Our Sun is now a tiny, glittering speck behind us, as we journey one hundred thousand light years across the Milky Way. There are two hundred billion stars in our galaxy alone, and some one hundred million galaxies comprising our universe. For most people, the cosmos is simply a linguistic construct, confined within their narrow intellectual parameters. Language can be so cumbersome and imprecise. It defines humanity, yet obscures ultimate reality. Man yearns for absolute truth, but can only aspire to ever-greater truths."

The spherical ceiling now fills with images of stars, clouds of stars, colossal pink pillars of gas, fiery crucibles of hydrogen, in which Jack is told stars are annihilated and created in a nebulous womb. The journey continues through the universe in silence for a couple of minutes before Roberts continues.

"Silence is the song of the universe – an acoustic triumph of pristine, primordial pitch. It is truly the sound of God's own voice."

Now the screen goes completely black, and Jack's unease heightens, as he is plunged into darkness once again. Why don't the lights come on? The show's over. He's just about to call out Kincaid's name when he spies a tiny white dot spinning in the void directly above him.

"We have been travelling back through time for almost fourteen billion years to see this – a singularity. It is the universe squeezed into a ball. All the answers we have ever sought are contained within this tiny, infinitesimal dot. It is the Alpha and the Omega. The Zenith and the Nadir. All that was, all that is, and all that will ever be. It is a portrait of the Odyssey – observe the quarks rejoice and a universe awake!"

Jack grips the sides of his chair, digging his nails into the soft fabric. His heart begins to pound. His breathing becomes an audible panting. The entire sphere seems to swallow him whole, as it detonates and explodes into a kaleidoscope of deafening chaos.

"Jesus, Jesus!" he screams. "I'm going blind. I'm going blind." He feels his heaving chest strain against the straps as if his lungs are going to implode with the pressure.

"Prepare to return home from Father Time to Mother Earth – a wondrous epiphany."

Jack tentatively opens his eyes. He is accelerating back through the universe, past myriad galaxies and stars. It is like being on the front of an intergalactic rollercoaster. The Milky Way spins into view. I am nearly home, thank God! The solar system appears once more and he zooms past the outer ice giants. Now Saturn, Jupiter, Mars and Earth at last. But the graphics zero in upon the Earth and accelerate again down through the clouds. The North American Continent, California, Mojave Desert, GeoNova HQ and Earth Office crash through the metal hemisphere. And now the screen becomes a giant mirror, a huge reflection dominates its surface – the terrified features of Jack Andersson.

The room is plunged into pitch-darkness once more. Jack is five years old again, back in that cupboard wanting to throw up with sheer fright. But he's a man now and his mother is long dead. He barely suppresses a whimper: "Mr Kincaid, Mr Kincaid!" But there is no answer; only a loud hum as the metal shells mercifully separate and return to the floor. There is a lambent, orange glow from the sun setting in the western sky. Heaven's nightfruit's first twinklings hang low in the eastern sky.

And Jack Andersson, for the first time in his life, knows his exact position in the cosmos.

SEVEN

JOSH AND JENNY ARE SITTING in the waiting-bubble adjacent to Kvellner's office. Josh has chosen a bird's-eye view of the rotating Earth from the Viewscape menu. He finds it hard to remain still, gets up and paws the inside of the sphere as if trying to part the cotton wool-like clouds. "I am Superman, I am Superman," he pretends, miming the theme tune. Jenny's getting irritated and chooses the *Blue Danube* by Strauss to help calm him. She doesn't know why she's picked this particular piece of music to accompany the Earth scene. Perhaps a film I saw once, she muses.

Kvellner is standing in front of his desk to welcome them.

"Josh, this is Doctor Bo Kvellner," introduces Jenny.

Josh hesitates and his eyes flit to the ceiling, as if searching for something. Kvellner is now down on his haunches to be exactly eye level with him, and to appear less intimidating. He is conscious that a towering adult can be a frightening prospect in a child's imagination.

"Kvass, kvell, kvetch, kvutza," rhymes Josh mechanically but quietly until he finds his verbal hook.

"Bo! Lo! Bo! Yo! Bo! Wo! Bo! How go, Bo?! So-so no? Rockin' to 'n' fro in a mo' though, Bo!" Then he puts his hands on his hips, sticks out his belly and roars: "Ho! Ho! Ho!"

Kvellner smiles at Jenny as the Santa Claus routine finishes.

"He's a real live wire."

"I'm electric, I'm electric," answers Josh, wagging all his fingers frenetically.

"I'm sorry, Doctor, Josh can get a little hyper when he meets a new psychologist."

"That's okay, Mrs Andersson. I completely understand. You can take a seat again outside and I'll speak with you when we're done in about an hour, all right?"

"Okay, Doctor," she nods, frowning at her son, who doesn't even notice she's leaving the room.

"Please, sit down in this chair, Josh," invites Kvellner. He speaks in a slow and measured voice. His tone is even, firm and controlled. He must consciously articulate each word precisely, ensuring a pause between each sentence to minimize misunderstandings.

"Okay, Josh. Now I am going to adjust your chair electronically so that your body will fit better on the chair. I will use this zapper in my hand to control the adjustments."

Kvellner presses a button to manoeuvre the base, making sure it supports Josh's thighs, yet enables him to have both feet planted on the floor at the same time. The back of the chair is adjusted so that it is flush with the base of his spine. Finally, a small headrest is lowered, until it snugly cradles the back of his head.

"Is your chair comfortable now, Josh?"

"Yes, Bo, ready to rock to 'n' fro in a mo."

"I want you to place the palms of your hands flat on the arms of your chair."

"Oh, Bo! That's real neat. How come chairs have arms but no hands? Clocks have hands but no feet; how so, Bo?"

Kvellner studiously ignores the questions, just waits patiently for the boy to obey his instruction. Josh looks through him with a vacant stiff gaze as if to say: I can wait all day.

Five minutes later and Kvellner is still waiting, but he has the patience of a statue, having fought this silent war of wills with a thousand kids. Josh's left hand begins to move involuntarily in a circular, rhythmical motion, increasing in intensity with his impatience. He wants to stop his hand betraying his emotions under Kvellner's inscrutable gaze.

He relents and smacks his left palm on the left arm of his chair first, before doing likewise with his right hand on the other arm.

Kvellner knows he has won the first round and chooses that exact moment to assume his own seat directly opposite Josh.

"Okay, Josh, I am going to play some relaxing music for you now. I want you to close your eyes and just listen to it."

"No go, Bo! I'm afraid of the dark, Doc. Darkdock."

"I know, but you are in control. If you feel afraid you can just choose to open your eyes at any time. You are in control of the dark here. So I am going to start the music. You just listen to the music and the sound of my voice."

"Are you going to sing so, Bo?"

"No," he says, suppressing a smile. "I want to help your body be less tight. I want you to relax. I will tell you exactly how to do it as the music plays."

Josh sits with his feet planted firmly on the floor; his forearms resting on the long arms of his chair, with palms stretched out and laid flat. His eyes are shut as the music begins but flutter intermittently as though he is afraid to let go of the light.

"Now, I want you to use your imagination and pretend that your feet are getting warmer and heavier . . . now imagine the calves at the back of your lower legs getting warmer and heavier."

"But that's crazy, Bo. I don't have cow legs."

"Just focus on the parts of your body that I mention . . . If you have any other thoughts, just accept them and let them silently float away."

Kvellner spends the next few minutes getting Josh to methodically imagine all the various parts of his body getting warmer and heavier. Josh is visibly more relaxed as Kvellner finally gets him to focus on his head. His eyes are now fully closed and have ceased their nervous fluttering.

"Imagine there is no tightness inside your head; it is completely free of thoughts."

"But I can't switch it off, Doc."

"I know, but just imagine . . . Imagine you are just your own breath. Breathing in pure calmness and breathing out only fear . . . Imagine you have no body, yet you exist in perfect harmony within a quiet universe."

"That I am like God – immanent?"

"Exactly, Josh," he barely breathes before pausing, watching, waiting and then . . .

"Describe how you feel inside your head."

"I am a statue of a seated Tutankhamen. I am filled from the tips of my toes to the crown of my head with warm liquid gold. And when I open my eyes I will blind you like the rays of the sun."

Unbeknownst to Josh, there is a small computer screen positioned just above and behind his head. Kvellner hardly has to raise his gaze from the boy's face to read the historical reference displayed.

Tutankhamen: Ancient Egyptian pharaoh.
Born 1341 BCE. Reigned c.1332–1322 BCE.

"So, you feel like a boy-king. But why do you want to blind me?"

"I can't help it. It's not my fault I am a beamish boy."

Kvellner repeats the phrase "a beamish boy" to prompt the computer.

From the poem "Jabberwocky" by Lewis Carroll (1832–1898).
Meaning imprecise.

"Ah, from Lewis Carroll! Is that your favourite poem, Josh – 'Jabberwocky'?"

The word seems to physically click inside his head. His eyes widen

like saucers and the lines flow from his lips like relentless waves at a
river mouth.

'Twas brillig, and the slithy toves
Did gyre and gimble in the wabe;
All mimsy were the borogoves,
And the mome raths outgrabe.

"Beware the Jabberwock, my son!
The jaws that bite, the claws that catch!
Beware the Jubjub bird, and shun
The frumious Bandersnatch!"

He took his vorpal sword in hand;
Long time the manxome foe he sought –
So rested he by the Tumtum tree,
And stood awhile in thought.

And, as in uffish thought he stood,
The Jabberwock, with eyes of flame,
Came whiffling through the tulgey wood,
And burbled as it came!

One, two! One, two! And through and through
The vorpal blade went snicker-snack!
He left it dead, and with its head
He went galumphing back.

"And hast thou slain the Jabberwock?
Come to my arms, my beamish boy!
O frabjous day! Callooh! Callay!"
He chortled in his joy.

'Twas brillig, and the slithy toves
Did gyre and gimble in the wabe;
All mimsy were the borogoves,
And the mome raths outgrabe.

Kvellner has waited patiently while Josh delivered his recitation. He knows it is a perfectly practised routine that he must perform, and doesn't even bother to glance at the screen opposite to verify its accuracy. Josh, having finished, maintains a fixed, absent-minded stare. His entire performance spoken as if it were a casual conversational aside.

"What is your interpretation of that poem?"

"The author: he's fighting words all the time. The Jabberwock is really a metaphor for language itself. He thinks he's conquered it with his verbal sword. But he can't do it. It's like trying to slay Proteus."

Kvellner repeats the word "Proteus" to prompt the computer again.

Proteus: Ancient Greek or Roman sea-god
capable of taking various forms at will.

"Why do you think you are a beamish boy?"

"Because I have a bright, shiny mind. That's why I'm afraid of the dark dock. When are you going to do the IQ test?"

"No, Josh, you will not be taking an IQ test."

"Why so, Bo?!"

"Because I know you will score exactly ninety per cent. Why do you choose never to achieve a perfect score?"

"Because I dare not disturb the universe."

Kvellner frowns; then a flicker of recognition smoothes the creases on his forehead. He knows this reference before he even checks the computer screen. It is one of his own favourite poems and he loves the title.

53

There is a trace of nostalgia in Kvellner's voice as he dreamily hears himself repeat the title aloud: "The Love Song of J. Alfred Prufrock."

Suddenly, he lowers the point of his chin and presses it against his chest. Stretches his hand across his brow and rubs his temples with his thumb and middle finger. "No!" he mouths to himself through clenched teeth. The poem is over one hundred and thirty lines in length and he correctly guesses that Josh absolutely will not stop until the last syllable is uttered. If he is interrupted, he will just go back to the start again. Kvellner's momentary lapse of concentration has surrendered control of the session to his patient – for at least ten whole minutes. Josh rattles off the poem in a flat monotone, devoid of modulation, inflection or emotion. Kvellner slowly shakes his head in amazement at this flawless feat of memory. He wonders why Josh is speeding up towards the end. And gets his answer precisely as the last line leaves the boy's lips, his head swinging now like a metronome.

"Tick tock, tick tock, tick tock. Sixteen o'clock, Doc. Time to go so, Bo!"

Kvellner glances at his gold Quantum Rolex, which is accurate to the nanosecond. It reads exactly sixteen hundred. He's puzzled as he notices the boy is not wearing a watch.

"Don't you have a watch?"

"Yes, Doc. I have to ticktime in my head, though, 'cos the straps would chafe my wrist."

Josh is alone in the waiting-bubble. Miss Chang is working at her desk but frequently casts a wary eye at a monitor to check that the boy is okay. Jenny is sitting across the desk from Kvellner. She has taken Josh to see six psychologists already but is still full of hope. Some day, some professional is going to tell her that her beloved son was misdiagnosed with Asperger's Syndrome. Some day, with the correct medication, he will be perfect; just like the day he was born. She wrings her hands as she listens to Kvellner.

"Mrs Andersson, Josh is really a very sweet boy and has a wonderful, verbally inventive imagination. He has a very powerful eidetic memory – which is to say, he can recall whole tracts of text at will. Almost as if he can see them plainly on the page with his mind's eye. But this is not atypical of people with A.S."

"I know that," she acknowledges resignedly. "At one psychologist he went to, she mentioned the book *Ulysses* and he just started from the first page and wouldn't stop. He freaked out when we eventually stopped him after about a half hour. I had to sedate him."

"*Ulysses*, by James Joyce?"

"Yes, he knows it cover to cover, Doctor. Jack says he's like one of those characters in that science fiction movie *Fahrenheit 451*. You know the one: where all the books have been burned but some people have memorized them to preserve them. Josh has a whole library in his head."

Kvellner strokes his chin pensively.

"He knows *Ulysses* verbatim. That is very unusual. Even for a child with A.S."

"What about the ten per cent of Josh that you said he's not revealing to us?"

"That is what I am really trying to concentrate on, Mrs Andersson. But psychiatry is not like physics or mathematics. There are no proofs or cast-iron laws when it comes to the human mind. And the only guarantee I can give you is that I will do everything within my professional competence to help you and Josh."

"I appreciate that, Doctor. If there is anything Jack or myself can do to help, don't hesitate to ask; not for a second."

"Sure. Oh, there is one thing. He spends an inordinate amount of time on the computer. Try and find out what material or sites he is accessing. It might provide a better clinical insight into what is going on in his psyche. Okay?"

"Sure, fine. I'll get Cass to send you a report directly."

Jenny is standing at the door of the waiting-bubble. With the tips of his fingers, Josh is caressing the image of the Earth that completely illuminates the inner surface of the sphere. He stops and presses his ear tight against the world.

"Shhh . . . listen, Mother. If you listen closely you can hear it breathing in and out . . . in and out . . . in and out. It's alive. It's really alive."

EIGHT

"Morning, Jack!"

"Morning, Cass! Any messages?"

"I have a short communication from a Mr Tyler Kincaid of GeoNova Industries. He apologizes for the brief nature of your conversation and his hasty departure. Nevertheless, he hopes you enjoyed your visit there. Do you wish to send a response, Jack?"

"Yes. Tell him I enjoyed my visit very much. Tell him it was a very … illuminating experience."

"He'll have it in one hot minute," chirps Cass.

"Cass, I need you to compile an analysis on all the material that you loop into Josh's cyber-helmet. Prioritize the data based on his most commonly accessed sites, games, books, et cetera. Categorize and factor in time spent on each one. Use March first as your initializing date. That will give us nearly four weeks' usage analysis. Please send the completed report directly to Dr Bo Kvellner as soon as possible."

"I am sorry, Jack. I cannot comply with your directive."

"What!?" he says, stunned.

"I am sorry. I cannot comply with your directive."

"I don't understand … "

"I cannot access the requested data."

"Why not?"

"Security protocols prohibit."

Jack leans forward towards Cass's self-satisfied face, as if to eyeball her and ask: "Is this some kind of joke?" It's like having an argument with your girlfriend, he thinks. But he is definitely going to have the last word.

57

"Priority override Jack seven-nine-three-five," he orders and confidently leans back in his chair.

CASS's crystal-blue eyes and crackerjack smile freeze on the monitor. Then spark back into life, as if re-animated by a lightning jolt of electricity.

"I am sorry, Jack. I cannot comply with your directive."

"How in hell . . . Well, that's just great, CASS! I'll fix you girl, I'll fix you," he rasps.

"I do not require maintenance, Jack. I detect no anomalies with any of my cognitive functions or software applications."

Jack sighs heavily at her ignorance of contextual idiom.

"CASS, connect me with my brother Robbie. Can you comply with that directive?"

"Sure thing," she smiles.

Jack fumes quietly, and reckons quantum interfaces have still only the emotional sensitivity of circling vultures. Robbie's face doesn't appear on screen but Jack can hear his voice over the sound of running water.

"Sorry, little bro; just having a shower. I'll switch it off. What's up?"

"Morning, Robbie. Having a little problem with CASS here."

"Ah!"

"Yeah, she's not being very co-operative. Keeps saying she can't comply with my directive."

"You're not asking her to access porn sites again, Jack are you?"

"No!" he laughs back. "All I'm looking for is a history of the info she's feeding into Josh's cyber-helmet."

"Well, that should be pretty straightforward. I mean: I set it up for you. Have you tried your override code?"

"Sure, but no success with it either."

"Mmm . . . I suppose you want me to come over have a look?"

"Today would be great."

"I'll be there in an hour. Tell Jenny go put on the coffee."

"Thanks. See you later, Bro."

Cass's pretty image reappears and Jack winks sarcastically at her. I'll fix you, girl, he knows for sure.

"Cass, will you please download two texts from the iBooks store."

"Sure thing. What are the titles?"

"*The Philosophy of Friedrich Nietzsche: A Beginner's Guide* by Leon Koenig, and *Nietzsche: Philosopher and Prophet* by Professor Karl Heinz Hubner."

"Okay, I'll have them on your iPad in one minute. Is there anything else?"

"Yes. You'll find Professor Hubner's contact details under 'Eagle slash admin'. I need to arrange an appointment with him. Let me know when he is available to connect."

Jack is telling Jenny to stop fussing with the coffee, cakes and cookies; it's only his brother for God's sake. But Jenny likes Robbie a lot, and Jack knows it only too well.

"Remember, honey, Robbie is the second-last guy you went out with. I'm the one put the ring on your finger!" He's half-joking.

"I know, but he looks just like you and he's so-o-o handsome," she teases.

Jack hears a long ping on his cell.

"I'll get the door! I don't trust you alone with that guy," he says mischievously.

Robbie arrives in the kitchen shaking his head wistfully as Jenny combs her fingers through her long blonde hair.

"Hi, Robbie," she purrs.

"Jenny! You look fantastic! Better even than Cass; despite what my little brother says."

"Well, right this minute any woman looks better than Cass," Jack says, rolling his eyes. He purses his lips while watching the two embrace.

Jenny feels Robbie's cheek, pressed against the nape of her neck. She wonders: If I'd married Robbie instead and had a son, would he be like Josh?

"Little man at school, is he?"

"Yeah."

"Don't worry, I'll have this thing sorted in a few minutes," Robbie says. "Quantum engineers like me eat silicon chips for breakfast, you know. . . . How is Josh anyhow?"

Jenny holds his gaze just long enough to yield a mute answer, grimaces and looks away.

"Coffee, Robbie?"

"Sure. Thanks, Jenny."

"Morning, Robbie!"

"Morning, CASS! I need you to perform a complete virus scan, please."

Robbie turns to Jack and whispers, "She'll just be a couple of minutes."

The bow of CASS's hot-pink lips seems to tauten while she conducts her self-diagnostic routines.

"No viruses or anomalies detected," she announces at last.

"Jack, did CASS give a reason for not being able to comply with your directive?"

"Yep, just said security protocols prohibit."

Robbie is holding an iPad.

"Display security protocols listing for a CASS AP35 series," he orders. The list flashes up instantly on his hand-held screen as he remotely pairs his iPad with CASS.

"CASS, will you please correlate your security protocols listing with that on the paired device . . . please?"

"I am sorry. I cannot comply with your directive."

"Well, that's a little strange," he says, screwing up his nose at her.

"What are you going to do now, Robbie?"

"Call in the cavalry, Jack!" He addresses his iPad again.

"Hi, Tom. Robbie Andersson here."

"Hi, Robbie, what can I do for you, friend?"

"I need to perform a BFI on an AP35. Can you up the prog to me?"

"Oh! That's a first. Hope you enjoy it!"

Jack's puzzled. "What are you doing?"

"I'm performing a Brute Force Intrusion on your computer, Bro," he grins. "Take a last look at that pretty face; CASS is about to be raped!"

Robbie points his device at CASS and her image dissolves and fades to grey. A long series of program titles appears; one is flashing red.

"There we go," announces Robbie. "There's your problem right there. A rogue program entitled 'Aspie One'. CASS, please delete security protocol 'Aspie One' and re-configure to default settings."

"I am sorry. I cannot comply with your directive."

"Well, I'll be damned."

He bends down and touches the flashing red panel and a sequence of text scrolls up. He studies it quizzically and reaches for his iPad.

"Tom, are you getting this?"

"Yeah, Robbie."

"What kind of ciphertext is that?"

"Just a second . . . Whoah! That, my friend, is alpha grade ciphertext. I seen it only once before, about six months ago doing contract work for the Pentagon. State-of-the-art photonic-chip based quantum encryption with infinite temporal key strength. She's a real uncrackable humdinger of a program."

"Nothing we can do then?" replies Robbie.

"Well! I can fly or U-haul your computer back to California and wait six months to get it decoded – if you're lucky."

"I'll take a rain check on that. Thanks for your help anyway, Tom. Good luck."

"What's happening?"

"Well, Jack, I'd love to tell you I could sort this problem out with my pocket electron microscope and a nanoprobe. But you heard the man. This 'Aspie One' program cannot be decoded or deleted, and I haven't a clue how CASS got it."

"You know what Aspie means, don't you?"

"No, I don't."

It's the term Asperger's sufferers call themselves to distinguish them from Mundies . . . normal people."

"Are you saying Josh had something to do with it?"

"Who the hell else?!" Jack shouts.

"Easy, Bro. Why do you need to find out exactly what the kid is accessing anyway?"

"He has a new psychiatrist who says it might help him get an insight into Josh's mind."

"Another psychiatrist?"

Jack gives his brother a rueful look.

"She just can't accept it, Robbie, she just can't!"

"I know. It's a real tough break; especially now you're only allowed to have the one kid. Listen, I'll go explain to Jenny."

"Sure, keep your paws off her though," he says under his breath.

Robbie is holding Jenny's hands, trying not to fall into her misty, brown eyes.

"I'm sorry, I really am, Jenny. Josh downloaded some program that prevents anyone checking his usage history."

"Can you not delete it?"

"No."

"Can you not unscramble it or disable it in some way?"

"No."

"Why the hell not?"

Robbie steps back as if to better frame her under his pitiful gaze.

"Because it's military grade ciphertext that's virtually uncrackable. I have absolutely no idea how Josh obtained this 'Aspie One' program."

"Did you say 'Aspie One'? Is that the name of the program?"

"Yes."

"I bet Josh wrote it himself."

"No! There's only a half dozen people in the world could quantum encrypt a program like that. It's pure state-of-the-art stuff."

"What do you mean: *virtually* uncrackable?"

"Jenny, Jenny . . . just stop," he says softly.

"But Kvellner said he really needed it to try and find out what is going on inside Josh's head," she answers tearfully.

He draws her towards him and wraps his arms around her waist. Their flushed cheeks caress each other. Jenny feels a frisson creep down her spine and a dagger through her heart at the same time as Robbie whispers into her ear.

"I love you. And I'd do anything to take away the hurt. But I just can't."

She drapes her arms around his neck and tries to stifle her sobs.

"But it hurts . . . it hurts . . . it hurts all the time."

"I know, I know," he keeps repeating as they are swaying in mutual embrace.

Jack is leaning against the doorframe, with his arms tightly folded and his eyes fixed on the ceiling.

"Thanks, Robbie. You can leave now. You know where the door is."

Jack's eyes never leave the ceiling as his brother passes on the way out. Jack waits until he hears the door slam.

"Jesus, Jenny! Could you two be any more egregious? Robbie's not married; maybe you could have one other kid with him, a normal kid . . . huh?!"

"Ah, shut up, Jack!" she fumes, her tears rapidly evaporating.

"No, Jenny. Hear me out. Kvellner's no different from the other half-dozen shrinks we've been to see already. He'll never find out what's going on inside Josh's head. Not him, you, me, Josh, nobody, *ever*. Just accept the diagnosis and learn to live with it or give up and go to hell!"

"As you have," she fires back. "There's something different about that boy and it's not Asperger's. I don't know what it is but I feel it. And I'm going to find out even if it kills me."

"Or this marriage!" yells Jack.

Three pings on his cell and Jack gratefully retreats to his study.

"Jack, I have Professor Hubner on voice link only. Do you wish me to connect you?"

"Yeah, thanks, Cass," he answers breathlessly, thankful he won't have to look him in the face.

"*Guten Morgen*, Herr Andersson. I regret the reception is not good but I am up two thousand metres, climbing the Zugspitze."

"I'm sorry, Professor?"

"The highest mountain in Germany! Us *Philosophen* like to keep our heads in the clouds," he strains, his voice trailing off with the wind.

"Cass, can you compensate for this background noise?"

"One moment, Jack."

"Good afternoon, Professor. I want to arrange an appointment with you."

"I know all about it, Herr Andersson. April twenty-seventh at fourteen hundred I have a free afternoon at my university."

"That's great."

"*Bitte*? . . . I'm sorry?"

"I said that's great, Professor."

"Then I look forward to welcoming you in Berlin. *Auf Wiedersehen*."

Jack double checks the house to make sure it is empty. Pulls back the curtains and sees the car is gone and Jenny is away. He lifts an ultra-slim cell phone and covers his mouth when he hears his call being picked up.

"Steelman," he whispers.

"What can I do for you, sir?"

"I've been trying to arrange an interview with client number eleven. But she's not being co-operative and it'd be really convenient to see her on April twenty-nine on my way back from Germany."

Franklin pauses before he answers,

"Yes, thought there might be a problem with that one. I'll speak with my boss and see if it can be resolved. Thank you."

The line goes dead. Jack is thinking of Eleanor Roberts, ex-wife of the President of the United States. He is dreading the prospect of interviewing her; she has a reputation for being irascible and eccentric.

Some cyber-mag he'd once read described her humorously as "a woman living next door to herself". It didn't seem so funny now in light of the tragedy that befell her.

NINE

Jack walks into Hubner's office in the Humboldt University of Berlin. It is like stepping into a time machine: shelves stacked and groaning under the weighty tomes of ancient philosophies. He is transfixed, plunged into the dark well of the world's collective wisdom. He shuts his eyes, smells the musty books, breathes in the knowledge, and recalls the libraries of his childhood. A faint sound of laughter reins in his reveries of yesteryear. He turns quickly and finds a man in his early thirties smirking at him.

"I'm sorry, I'd forgotten there were once so many books in the world," Jack says, reddening.

"That's quite all right, Herr Andersson. I like a man who is overwhelmed by books. A hundred years ago, before they started incinerating people, the Nazis burned books instead, right outside this university. I fancy maybe someday somebody will pull the plug on this Earth, all the lights will go out, and all the information stored on our computers will be lost for ever. Can you imagine what that would be like? For mankind to forget all it has ever learned; all of its stored memories outside of human consciousness – lost for ever. In a world without printed books, civilization is a mere mouse click away from oblivion."

Jack nods his head in tacit agreement.

"Jack Andersson, I presume?"

"Yes. Professor Karl Heinz Hubner, I presume?"

The two shake hands, Hubner with a perfunctory slight bow in the old German tradition.

"Coffee, I presume, Herr Andersson?"

"Yeah, would be great."

"Well, where do you wish to begin?"

"Please, Professor; before we start I need you to remember that I am not an academic. I have read a couple of books on Nietzsche, but that hardly qualifies me as an expert. So I would appreciate it if you could explain everything to me in layman's terms."

"But of course. I understand."

"Firstly, why is Nietzsche's philosophy so crucial in understanding Elijah Roberts?"

"Mmm . . . that is not an easy question to address. Nietzsche is both a complex and a very subtle philosopher. But you must remember that the GeoNova political movement in general has appropriated many tenets of his philosophy to its ideological bosom. Nietzsche argued that God is dead, and I suppose one could argue that subsequent history has proved that the idea of God is, at the very least, terminally ill. Nietzsche recognized that this loss of traditional religious belief would herald the advent of an age of nihilism. That is to say: an absence of belief in anything, no moral compass, rampant individualism to the detriment of social obligations."

Hubner stops as if to check this student is keeping pace with him.

"Does this scenario appear familiar to you?"

Jack gulps down a mouthful of coffee, grateful to be asked an easy question.

"Yes, very familiar, very prophetic."

"Hence the title of my book – *Nietzsche: Prophet and Philosopher*!" the professor remarks wryly. "Modern Man has lost faith in many institutions; Church, politics, economics, society, even Mother Nature herself. Ultimately, Roberts understood that humanity had lost faith in itself, and set about its restoration through the medium of GeoNova. Practically all human problems can be resolved on the intellectual and emotional plane, Herr Andersson. We must simply summon the will to tackle the profound ecological issues that confront the modern world. Nietzsche coined the term '*der Wille zur Macht*', 'the will to power'. GeoNova espouses that we must harness the collective will of humanity to achieve an eco-catharsis, or we are destined to perish from the Earth. It is a compelling argument, is it not, especially when you have a child . . . Josh, I believe?"

"You've done your research on me?"

"But of course," Hubner answers coolly before continuing.

Typical Teutonic efficiency, notes Jack, gulping down another mouthful of coffee.

"Nietzsche posited that Man has become alienated from Nature. The population of the planet is now some nine billions, seventy-five per cent of whom live in cities. People assume everything magically grows or is reared in their local shopping mall; they forget that Mother Nature is their grocer, their butcher, their daily bread. They forget that humanity itself is the fruit of the Earth, however bitter that harvest may prove to be."

Hubner pauses briefly, presses his hands together as if in prayer, and taps his middle fingers rhythmically against the tip of his nose. Communing with himself, as if there isn't another soul in the room.

"We are too indulgent, Herr Andersson. Like spoiled children, too much is never enough; we consume everything our Mother gives us and offer nothing in return. But even mothers have been known to murder the fruit of their own wombs. We must learn to govern our natural appetites; sex or reproduction, for example. That is why GeoNova introduced a one-child-only policy. As you are aware, even meat consumption has been restricted by legislation to reduce carbon dioxide emissions. Nietzsche of course advocated that we transcend our own human nature and embrace the concept of the Übermensch, which is—"

"You mean the ideal of a type of superhuman?" interjects Jack, pleased that he recognizes the German term. "Like Eli Roberts himself perhaps?"

Hubner dismisses the idea with an almost contemptuous limp

wave of his fingers.

"*Nein, nein*; I think he would much prefer the term 'superhuman-ist'. Nietzsche wrote that, 'Man is a rope, tied between Neanderthal and Superman – a rope stretched taut over an abyss.' A kind of tug-of-war contest between Mother Nature and base human nature. Eli will never release that rope. He will grip to the last and pull the rest of humanity through – even if it kills him."

Jack hears a long ping on his dedicated cell.

"Oh! I'm sorry, Professor, I gotta take this call. I'm really sorry," he says rushing for the door.

He glances up and down the old corridor; it is deathly quiet. But instinctively he covers his mouth and barely breathes, lest even his whisper echoes in the hallowed halls of academe.

"Steelman. . . . "

"Good afternoon, sir. Client number eleven will do an interview with you day after tomorrow; April twenty-nine at seventeen hundred local time. Interview will take place at the address you have on file."

"That's great," says Jack. "What about transport?"

"Direct flight to Dublin at eleven a.m. tomorrow already booked for you, sir. You can download your priority-boarding pass at the Lufthansa desk at Brandenburg International, Terminal One. Got those details okay?"

"Yeah, I've got 'em."

"One more thing – a word of advice from my boss. Treat her like the lady he once loved – okay?"

"Wish me luck!"

"Good luck, sir; you'll need it!" Franklin sighs knowingly as he terminates the call.

"Apologies again, Professor; I had to take that call."

"Sure. You must be an extremely busy man, having undertaken this tremendous project, writing the Book of Elijah. Like an Old Testament scribe, are you not? Writing a New Testament for a new age?"

Jack pauses, formulating his answer. Hubner glances furtively at his watch, almost signalling him to hurry up, as he doesn't have time for slow minds.

"Well, I hadn't quite thought of it that way, Professor – especially as this particular Elijah is an atheist."

"Oh, please! You cannot conceivably write this book of yours based on such an assumption."

"Well, Nietzsche said God is dead, and Roberts sure as hell doesn't agree with the presidential oath of inauguration. As you know, he went to the U.S. Supreme Court to have it amended on religious grounds. How much more evidence do you need?"

"Ah! Would that the world could be so accurately apprehended with such a monochrome *Weltanschauung*, Herr Andersson."

Jack cocks his head to one side, feeling like a little puppy under its master's patronizing gaze. Jack hasn't a clue what "veltinshunk" means; he is struggling to breathe in the rarefied atmosphere of this ancient ivory tower. Fuck you, he thinks, you conceited Kraut; glad we kicked your ass in forty-five.

"Sorry, Karl, my German is not so good. What do you mean, 'veltinshunk'?"

"It means world-view. You must examine life through polychrome lenses, with a multiply perspectival approach as Nietzsche practised and advocated. To put it simply, you must not look at the world through the eyes of a child any more – it is too late for that."

"You still haven't answered the question. Does Roberts believe in God?" prods Jack.

Hubner presses his hands together again as if in prayer and pinches the wings of his nose.

"The question does not admit of a negative or affirmative answer, but I will give you an answer nonetheless. There was a pre-Socratic

Greek philosopher called Xenophanes, who wrote, in the sixth century before Christ: 'The Ethiopians say their gods are flat-nosed and black. The Thracians say their gods have blue eyes and red hair like themselves. If horses and oxen had gods, theirs would have four legs and a tail. Protagoras, in fifth-century Athens, said that Man is the measure of all things . . . including his gods. In the nineteenth century, one of my German predecessors, Feuerbach, proposed that God did not make Man in his own image, but that Man made God in his own image. The first gods Man mythologized were ones of Nature: gods of the Sun, the Sky, the Ocean, the Earth; Gaia herself was a Greek goddess.

"But the Christian god, the monotheistic variety; that is the distilled essence of the perfect man, a god that transcends Nature. It is necessary to heal that fissure between heaven and Earth – to replace the faith in God as we perceive him with a love of Nature. Man can only seek salvation within himself; God and Mother Nature are big enough to save themselves."

"You still haven't answered my question, Professor. Does Roberts believe in the existence of God, or does he not?"

"Ultimately, the ontological question of God's existence is irrelevant. Fundamentally what matters is the human idea of God – for that definitely exists. Roberts believes in the power of the idea of God, but knows in his heart that only humanity's faith in itself can save it from ecological Armageddon. Am I making sense?"

"Too much so," muses Jack quietly in reply. "Many people have dubbed Elijah Hunt Roberts a saviour, a 'green messiah'. I am sure you have met him personally. Do you believe he can save us?"

"I have met Eli on only one occasion. He came to visit me here at the university in Berlin during a formal state visit two years ago. He presented me with a gift. Would you like me to show it to you?"

"Sure."

Hubner swivels round to a locked bookcase behind his desk. He fishes a key from the pocket of his trousers and opens it, reverently, like a set of church doors or a tabernacle. "Come see," he whispers conspiratorially.

Jack is gazing at a set of black-spined books, their gilt-tooled titles glistening in the gloom.

"I have seen these before!" he says excitedly. "It is the complete works of Nietzsche. Isn't it?"

Hubner seems somewhat startled to have his thunder stolen, and sharpens his tone.

"Where have you seen this set of books before?"

"In Tyler Kincaid's office, at GeoNova Industries' headquarters in California."

"*Ja,* of course!" Hubner remembers suddenly. "This is a specially commissioned set of books issued by Eli himself to all of GeoNova's higher party members. A token of gratitude after his becoming elected President of the United States."

"It's a lovely gift, real books – I mean, books like they used to make," Jack says with a note of nostalgia. "What was it like meeting the President face to face?"

"You haven't met him yourself?"

"No! Not yet."

"Ah, it was *wunderbar*! He sat across this desk from me for almost an hour discussing Nietzsche in fluent German. The only language in which one can truly appreciate and comprehend the nuances of his philosophy. Roberts has a mind in a million; so clear, so brilliant, razor sharp, a diamond mind, Herr Andersson. We argued about Nietzsche's demise. You know what eventually happened to him, don't you?"

"Something about him collapsing under a horse in Turin, no?"

"Precisely! The story, apocryphal or not, is that in eighteen eighty-nine he saw a horse being whipped by a cab-driver in the street. He went over and embraced the poor creature, collapsed into a type of paralyzed psychotic state and never regained consciousness. He lay in a bed for eleven years until he died at the age of fifty-five in nineteen hundred. Many scholars claim this was symptomatic of tertiary syphilis, but Roberts is convinced his mind simply disintegrated under the weight of his immense intellect."

Jack shudders as he recalls an old photograph of the philosopher lying prostrate on his bed, with his ridiculous walrus moustache and brush-mop hair. And a perpetual vacant gaze that seemed to search forlornly inwards for erstwhile sanity.

"Professor, tell me something about the essence of Eli Roberts. What is the man really like as a human being?"

"Good question, Herr Andersson. Probably the best answer I can give you is Raskolnikov's dream about his childhood in Dostoevsky's *Crime and Punishment*. I'm sure a writer like you is familiar with the passage already?"

"Yeah, yeah, sure . . . long time since I read it though," lies Jack, his cheeks pinkening.

Hubner gazes at him reprovingly before continuing.

"The novel's main character dreams he is a seven-year-old boy. He witnesses a Russian peasant who over-burdens his little grey mare with a huge cartload of people. The animal struggles to move even a centimetre, so his owner flogs it with a knout, but the animal cannot budge. A crowd of drunken, laughing people urge him on. 'Whip her about the eyes,' they roar, 'beat her round the eyes.' He whips the poor beast mercilessly until it starts to totter on all fours. Not falling quick enough for the incensed owner, though, he grabs a cart shaft and flogs her until she collapses. Even still, the little mare flounders and tries to get up in defiance of its owner's murderous intentions. So, as the crowd continues to exhort him, he pulls out a crowbar and finally beats the brains out of the beast. The little boy utters a cry of anguish, runs up to the dying horse and flings his arms around her head, cradling it and sobbing his furious heart out. I remember this nightmare story so vividly, for Eli compared himself to that boy.

"'I am that little boy fastened to that dying animal,' he said, 'as the foul rag-and-bone shop of the world looks on and laughs. But this is no circus animal's desertion as Man awaits his end. Dreading and hoping all.'"

Hubner stops and breathes deep as the memories of Roberts's visit flood back. Jack looks at him and thinks that even this impressive philosophical intellect is utterly in awe of the man.

"You know, Herr Andersson, the last thing Eli said to me before he left was this: 'The world will bend to my will.' And what an indomitable will it is! He is the tallest blade of grass in a field under the funnel of a mighty tornado. Watch how he bends, but never breaks. . . . "

Jacks listens, as Hubner's rhetoric starts to soar. He finds in it an eerie echo of speeches, delivered right here, in the dark heart of Berlin, a century ago. Even Hubner's flawless English diction sounds more strident now and guttural in tone.

" . . . It is contrary to ze natural order of zings that a single species such as *homo sapiens* should be so overvelmingly successful. It is an aberration of Nature I tell you."

"But what of the essence of Roberts himself, Professor? What is he really like – as a human being?" Jack asks once more.

Hubner looks icily at Jack, the whites of his eyes like veneered porcelain.

"He is the toughest man you will ever meet, and the most compassionate man you will ever meet."

TEN

JACK WAITS FOR IT. He knows it is coming, yet he can't stop it. It is a dream, yet not a dream.

He is awake, yet not awake. Here it comes . . . "Oh, Allah! Please don't take my son. Please spare my little boy." Then that cry of overwhelming human anguish; a primeval scream to split the sky and shatter the heavens so God must hear his entreaties.

Jack is lying in his bed in a Berlin hotel. He forces his eyes wide open but the rest of his body is rigid with terror. He is paralyzed, suffocating, and has to consciously will his lungs to breathe. He sits bolt upright with a single, panicked, gasp. Every one of the hairs on his head hangs heavy with beads of sweat. "Christ, I hate that fuckin' dream!" he mutters, stumbling into the shower.

Suddenly a voice booms into the room.

"*Guten Morgen*, Herr Andersson. Six o'clock wake-up call! Six o'clock wake-up call!"

Herr Andersson? Jack wishes he knew the German for "fuck it anyway" but just roars back a sardonic "*Ja, wunderbar!*" at the auto-receptionist.

Dublin Airport is now Ireland's sole commercial airport, due to international flight restrictions and tighter immigration controls. The United Nations has designated the island of Ireland an "eco-haven", as the effects of climate warming are potentially less catastrophic here in formerly benevolent temperate climes. At first only wealthy continental Europeans came to retire here to escape the sweltering months of April to September. But all changed after the "eternal summer" of five years ago, when millions of Southern and Central

Europeans clamoured to migrate to Ireland, the United Kingdom and Scandinavia. Global climate zones themselves were edging northwards, and people had no choice but to follow. Ireland's population burgeoned from four and one half million in 2010 to over twelve million now. The era of eco-refugees dawned with ruthless immigration policies and a paranoid state apparatus designed to stem both swelling human and oceanic tides. The Emerald Isle, once christened the land of "a hundred thousand welcomes", has a stone-cold heart in a warming world.

Jack is next in the queue at immigration security, which is under military control. He holds up his cell for his electronic ticket to be scanned. The soldier examines it and crosschecks the details on his palm-top. A second soldier is summoned to further scrutinize the information and the two confer.

"Are you Jack Anthony Andersson?" barks the second soldier.

"Yes, I am," he states firmly.

"Follow me, Mr Andersson."

He is led to a nearby interview room and spends the next fifteen minutes undergoing a battery of identity verification procedures. A second door swings open and the soldier stiffens to attention as his superior struts into the room.

"Captain, sir!"

"At ease, private!"

Jack has been standing all the time. There is only one chair in the room and the captain is now sitting in it, behind a grubby plastic desk. He peers suspiciously at Jack from under heavy eyelids, his thick-set ruddy face seeming to smoulder with officious disdain. Jack glares back at him, tiring of this constant standing and interminable staring but not wanting to blink first. Eventually the captain begins.

"Allow me to get right to the point, Mr Andersson. We have detected a credit-card transaction anomaly with your flight ticket purchase from Berlin."

"I don't understand. It's paid for. What's the problem?"

"The problem is that you didn't purchase it with your own credit card. Who paid for your flight here?"

"Well, I presume the U.S. government did."

"You *presume*? You work for the American Government, do you?"

"Well . . . not exactly."

"What do you do then . . . *exactly*?"

Jack feels the hairs rising on the back of his neck and senses his cheeks burning as he struggles to explain himself. He's shifting his weight from one foot to the other as the army officer idly picks at the brass buttons on his cuffs, and looks on in silent satisfaction.

"Look!" Jack protests, whipping his official ID card from his inside jacket pocket and waving it. Check it out for yourself – all the bio-metrics stack up with the identi-tests you've just done."

The captain looks at the card dismissively.

"Oh, I've no doubt you are Jack Anthony Andersson. But what is the purpose of your visit to Ireland?"

Jack goes over to his suitcase, parked against the wall of the inter-view room. He takes out the laminated, signed letter from Roberts, authorizing interviews for his biography. He presents it to the captain, who lays it on his desk and scrutinizes it.

"So, you are here to do an interview on behalf of the President, is that correct?

"Yes, that is correct."

"What is the name and address of your interviewee?"

"Eleanor May Roberts, ex-wife of the President. Somewhere in County Galway. I have the exact address on my cell. I got a meeting with her at seventeen hundred tomorrow."

The captain leans towards the computer on his desk and taps a few keys. He swivels his bulldog neck vehemently as he double-checks the information now displayed on the monitor.

"I have no such individual of that name resident anywhere in this state. How unfortunate," he adds witheringly.

"Aw, Christ!" groans Jack. "She must have changed her name to remain anonymous or something."

Jack is straining to maintain his composure, clutches his dedicated cell and contemplates calling Franklin direct. *Can't use the code-word, damn it!* he thinks.

"Listen: call Mr Walter Franklin at the White House. He'll clear up this whole misunderstanding. Please call him!"

"You want me to call the *White House*?" says the captain, raising a derisive smile.

"Yeah, they'll sort this out in a jiffy."

The captain takes his time donning a headset and mic plugged into the side of his computer and waits to be connected.

"This is Captain James Neary, Immigration control at Dublin Airport, Ireland. Could I speak to a Mr Walter Franklin, please?"

The headset is leaky so Jack can faintly hear Franklin coming on, and telling the captain to be brief as he's just about to attend a meeting.

"I have a Mr Jack Anthony Andersson here, claiming to be working on behalf of the current administration. Is that correct, Mr Franklin?"

"Yes, he's one of our people."

"He further informs me that he has a scheduled interview with a Mrs Eleanor May Roberts in Galway at seventeen hundred tomorrow."

There is a long pause. Jack can hear Franklin breathing more heavily.

"That is classified U.S. government information, Captain Neary."

"That may be the case, Mr Franklin, but I have no record of the named interviewee and even if she does exist, the correct diplomatic protocols have clearly not been observed."

"What are you telling me, Captain?"

"I am officially informing you that Mr Andersson will be detained until his visit to Ireland is authorized through the correct diplomatic channels."

"Oh, I don't *believe* this *shit*," protests Franklin. "You are *way* out of your league here, soldier!"

"Your *man* doesn't have satisfactory diplomatic authorization. So frankly, Mr Franklin, I don't give a damn what division *you're* playing in!"

Franklin's voice is tailing off; he's pissed as hell and shouting something about the U.S. ambassador to Ireland as Neary disconnects.

"Private, would you kindly escort Mr Andersson here to the detention block. Please ensure that he also surrenders all communication devices and his luggage for inspection."

Jack glares at the captain and almost blurts out a "Fuck you very much, soldier"; bottles his rage instead and fumes silently. *Goddam droid*, he reckons. *Doesn't know who he's fuckin' with.*

Jack slumps his aching head back into a greasy pillow on his detention-cell bunk, grits his teeth as he hears the door-lock click behind him. A disorienting feeling envelops him as he realizes he is utterly desolate, deprived of freedom and communication with the outside world. He ponders on the desperate plight of the eco-refugees from Bangladesh; millions of them; forced to flee as the rising ocean reclaimed their land. Neighbouring countries could only absorb so many; the rest fled in boats, the lucky ones drowned. The former, condemned to eking out an existence, hugging the shorelines of the world and raiding ports for provisions. Treated as modern-day lepers of the high seas, seaborne parasites, the flotsam and jetsam discarded by a drowning humanity.

Jack recollects viewing the video footage captured by a GeoNova satellite – of puny rafts being swept up on an Irish beach, scrawny figures of men, women and cowering children spilling onto the sand. Their rags soaked in blood after the army scythed them down in a hail of bullets. Everybody died, but nobody cared in the land of a hundred thousand welcomes.

The lock clicks open and Jack is awake, yawning and looking at his watch. He has been incarcerated for four hours now.

"Please follow me, Mr Andersson," orders a soldier.

Jack hauls himself up from his bunk. Five minutes later he is back in the interview room.

Captain Neary is pacing up and down and doesn't even acknowledge his presence. The sounds of heavy boots approaching echo rhythmically along a corridor. The door swings open.

"Colonel, sir!" bellows Neary with a mechanical salute.

The colonel pointedly ignores him and turns to Jack.

"You Andersson?"

"Yes, sir!"

Then the colonel pivots on his soles to face the captain.

"Neary, did you verify with Mr Walter Franklin, a senior member of the White House staff, that Jack Andersson was currently employed by the U.S. government?"

"Yes, sir, Colonel, sir."

"Did you deny a direct request from the current American ambassador to Ireland seeking his immediate release from custody?"

"But . . . but . . . "

"*Yes* or *no*, Captain?" he presses.

"Yes, sir, Colonel, sir."

The colonel steps back, takes out his cell, holds it up and says: "This phone is going to ring in precisely ten seconds. And *you*, Captain, are going to take the call and do exactly what the man says, understood?"

"Yes, sir, Colonel, sir."

The cell rings and Neary answers. The colour drains from his flushed face as he recognizes the caller's voice. His mouth opens and closes desperately; his body is contorting like a freshly hooked fish.

"I am so sorry, Mr President, so sorry . . . " he keeps repeating.

Jack claps one hand over his own mouth to disguise an involuntary giggle. Neary is standing in front of him now, apologizing profusely and proffering his right hand.

The colonel is addressing his subordinate once again.

"You have a choice, Neary. Either face a court martial for a gross breach of diplomatic protocols or resign immediately from the army."

"I resign," he whispers.

"I'm sorry, Captain, could you repeat that."

"I resign from the army, Colonel, sir!"

"Turn around, Captain," he orders.

The colonel stands directly behind his subordinate, looping his middle fingers under the captain's shoulder boards bearing his rank and insignia. And with a single deft movement rips them off simultaneously.

"You're relieved, Neary," he whispers sharply into his ear.

He swivels again to face Jack and conveys a fulsome, official apology.

"If I can assist you in any way, Mr Andersson, please just ask."

Jack glances at a clock on the wall. "Well, I've missed my rail connection to Galway, Colonel."

"Don't worry, I'll arrange overnight accommodation for you here in Dublin and a helicopter transfer direct to your destination tomorrow afternoon. I will personally accompany you."

Jack is standing with his hands buried in his pockets, pursing his lips and asking himself that burning question: *Why me? Why me?*

The helicopter flies low over the gently rolling Irish landscape. The fields below are burnished golden brown by the late April sun; the colonel is lamenting the lost green fields of his youth.

"We have a Mediterranean climate now, Mr Andersson. Even my kids pick their own oranges in the garden for breakfast. I never thought I'd see it in *my* lifetime!"

Jack nods sympathetically, then points down to an approaching patch of bright green on the outskirts of a large town.

"There are a few green fields coming up shortly, Colonel."

The colonel peers out and emits a weary sigh.

"That's an eco-refugee camp. There are thousands of those tents sprouting up across the country. People just keep coming. Not the kind of invasion we in the army had ever envisioned. I didn't sign up to shoot unarmed civilians you know."

Jack nods sympathetically again and for a split-second feels a guilty twinge over Neary's cashiering. The thrum of the rotors intensifies as the helicopter gains altitude. Jack looks out at the magnificent mountains of Connemara beckoning in the distance.

The colonel smiles at him admiring the scenery.

"We'll be flying over God's own country in a few minutes," he says. "Sure where else but here could the wife of Elijah Hunt Roberts retire to."

Jack alights from the helicopter – and simply *has* to stop and stare, his senses numbed by the overwhelming splendour of the spectacle that confronts him. The mountains sweeping like lush emerald and russet carpets towards the sky. Tiny streams trickling down their sides, glistening like quicksilver veins in the haze of the sun. A cool wind whistles through the gaps between the gentle peaks and lightly ruffles Jack's hair as he wonders: *Is this a painting or a dreamscape? Surely this is the world as God himself intended. Such a place as this reminds a man that Mother Nature can be tame and majestic, and not the vengeful bitch she has become.*

Eleanor Roberts's adoptive home is a grand old mansion, nestled in a copse of trees on the slopes of the Maumturk Mountains. Its large windows reflect the late-afternoon sunlight as Jack strides up the front steps and rings the doorbell. He suddenly remembers he has been almost dreading this interview. The door creaks open and a middle-aged man greets him.

"Mr Jack Andersson, I presume?"

"Yes, that's me."

"Do come in," he says gravely.

He is led beyond the chandeliered main hall to a dark, old-fashioned drawing-room. A turf fire is blazing and the room is suffused with the smell of warm earth. His eyes smart as he breathes in the smoke.

Eleanor Roberts is reclining on an antique chaise-longue, resting a glass of whiskey in the heel of her right palm. She wears her dyed, Titian hair unusually long for a middle-aged woman. Allows it to flow freely and untrammelled like a little girl's. She is wearing a full-length bronze sequinned evening gown. The fabric is stretched so tight across her svelte figure that it seems to shimmer like the scales of a mermaid, basking in the twilight. Eleanor doesn't get up as Jack tentatively approaches her.

"Sit down," she says, gesturing to an empty chair facing her.

She stares directly into Jack's eyes, maintaining an unnerving silence as he seats himself. In her left hand she is holding a lit cigarette, which she sucks lazily, smudging the filter tip with heavy, scarlet lipstick. Jack can hear the faint smack of her lips as she gently releases the smoke in his direction. He coughs once, signalling his irritation that she is being downright rude. But she pointedly refuses to alleviate the tension and continues to stare directly at him. An almost piteous expression is cast across her face as she inclines her head to one side and takes another drag of her cigarette. A ticking grandfather clock competes with the occasional cracklings of the fire to punctuate the silence. Jack feels like a lab specimen, squirming helplessly under the microscope of some gimlet-eyed technician.

"So *you* are the man that Eli sent," Mrs Roberts states at last.

"Yes."

"A buck-a-day political cyber-hack," she sneers. "Why *you* of all people, Mr Andersson?"

"I have *absolutely* no idea, Mrs Roberts."

She narrows her mascara-laden eyelashes and takes yet another drag of her cigarette.

"I can assure you, whatever the reason, it must be a good one," she muses. "Tell me, why did you marry Jenny?"

"Excuse me?!" Jack is taken aback.

"Your wife. Why did you marry her?"

"I really don't see the relevance of that question, Mrs Roberts."

"Was it love?" she persists.

"Of course."

"Mmm . . . " she sniffs. "People get married for all kinds of reasons; money, religion, convenience, desperation – love usually comes well down the list. Was your Jenny not eh . . . slightly pregnant when you married her?"

Jack feels the blood rising and boiling in his cheeks as he glares at her. *How could she possibly have that information?*

"How can you *know* this?"

"A woman in my position has her sources," she replies with a detached air of self-satisfaction, "and usually they are impeccable. But please, allow me to begin whilst you calm down."

Jack senses his body forced tight against the back of his chair. His lips pressed firmly and his nostrils flaring as he consciously tries to slow his breathing.

"I married Eli, not for money or power, but love and love alone – the greatest weapon a woman possesses. The first time he ever laid eyes on me I was in a choir singing an old English hymn called *Gaudete* in a church in San Antonio, Texas. The service was being held in his honour. Do you know what the Latin title of the hymn means, Mr Andersson?"

"No," he answers curtly.

"*No?* I didn't imagine you would know."

You haughty bitch, he thinks.

"Anyway, he sent an agent to summon me afterwards. I remember exactly his introduction: 'I am Elijah Hunt Roberts. I am going to change the world, and I want *you* to help me to do it.' 'How?' I asked. 'Marry me,' he answered. Oh, it was all *so ridiculous*! He thinking he could have whatever woman he desired with a simple snap of his fingers. Not me! No. In my book, a man chases a woman until *she* catches *him*.

"So I politely declined his preposterous proposal. He simply smiled at me and began telling me a fable. How a long time ago in India a mighty bull elephant accidentally trampled on a nest of ants. A few of the ants crawled up his legs and stung him. He stamped his feet and swished his tail to get rid of them, but to no avail. More ants clambered up onto his back to sting him, so he dipped his trunk in a nearby stream and sprayed water on his back to wash them off. But thousands of ants continued to attack him, stinging through his thick, grey hide. Maddened with the pain, the elephant let out a tremendous roar and charged through the jungle, knocking down trees in his rage. He arrived at a great river and leaped into it with a gigantic splash. Wallowing triumphantly for a while in the soft, muddy riverbed, he watched all the tiny ants perish."

"'So pray tell, Eleanor, how do you stop a rampaging bull elephant?' he asked.

"'You cannot, Elijah Roberts,' I countered. 'You may only embrace it.'

"'Clever girl, Eleanor; Eleanor *perpulchra*,' he answered.

"Eli prefers using sententious aphorisms and allegorical stories. It is seldom normal conversation with him, but lofty prose or poetry or myths spoken in ancient tongues."

She stops and slowly sips from her glass of whiskey, before taking a quick puff of her cigarette. Jack frowns as he observes her.

"What does *perp . . . perpulchra* mean?"

"It is Latin. The epithet ascribed to Queen Eleanor of Aquitaine in the twelfth century – it means 'most beautiful'."

Jack maintains his frown as he studies her face: the heavy make-up, the thick scarlet lipstick, the dark, gloomy eye-shadow. She sighs wearily as she recalls.

"I suppose I was beautiful *once*, underneath these cosmetics. But, as Oscar Wilde so aptly quipped: a man's face is his autobiography; a woman's is her own work of fiction."

All at once, Eleanor stands up. She smoothes the creases of her bronze sequinned gown with the inside of her forearms first. Then her tall, elegant figure sweeps past Jack, towards a set of heavy, crimson drapes. As she hauls them apart, the room is bathed in warm sunlight. Jack is blinking back hard at her silhouette.

"Come here," she says softly. "I wish to show you something."

Jack approaches a large bay window and is once more enchanted by the verdant terrain.

"Do you see that mountain on the right? The tallest one."

"Yes," he nods.

"Eli always insisted on taking me to see only the most beautiful places around the world. Invariably, wherever we went, we would climb to the highest point, to better survey the Earth below. And then we'd embrace each other. And so it was, many years ago, that we first stood on that summit over there and Eli said: 'Look at the green carpet of the world stretched out before you, Eleanor. Tread softly, because you tread on my dreams.' He kissed me hard as we embraced and I said: 'Yes I will; yes I will, *forever*.' Then he brought me to this house and told me: 'This is your wedding gift.' Eli wanted the whole world to bend to his will; so what chance had I, a mere woman, to resist a man so . . . *so driven* in pursuit of me; like a rampaging bull elephant."

Gustav Klimt, *The Kiss* (*Lovers*) 1908–09

Jean-André Rixens, *The Death of Cleopatra*, 1874

Eleanor yanks the drapes closed as if she wants to banish the memories as quickly as possible. She sashays back towards the fireplace and tosses fresh turf into the blazing hearth fire. A half-empty bottle of whiskey is sitting on the mantelpiece. She pours herself a generous measure and sips it hastily.

There is a protracted silence again. Jack doesn't want to pose any questions. Figures at the rate the woman's drinking alcohol, she'll tell him all he wants to know in due course.

"Do you recognize that picture?" she enquires at length, pointing vaguely at one of two prints hanging above the mantelpiece.

"I do," he answers. "It is *The Kiss* by Klimt, I believe."

"Ah! At least you know something of art," she snickers. "Eli once told me this painting best encapsulated the love we had for each other. Look, Mr Andersson! See how the man dominates the woman, how she submits to his passionate will. The image is sensual, erotic: two lovers on the threshold of a sublime sexual experience."

Her voice trails off with the smoke of a freshly lit cigarette and her eyes reflect the flickering flames from the open hearth.

"I have had a few lovers in my lifetime; but Eli . . . Eli Roberts was the most ruthless lover of them all," she sighs.

"I don't recognize the other print, Mrs Roberts. What is it?" asks Jack, trying to change the subject.

The picture is of a beautiful young woman, stretched out naked on a bed. A servant girl is draped over her feet while a second one surveys the scene from the head of the bed. It is also a sensual and erotic work, yet something sinister lurks within. Jack feels a rising sense of dread and begins to berate himself. *Shouldn't have asked that question!*

"I'm sorry. I should have been more sensitive. You *really* don't have to talk about it!"

"That's okay, Mr Andersson. I *do* want to talk about it."

"Are you sure?"

"Of course I'm sure!" She snaps. "Clara died right here in this house, you know. Her death wasn't accurately reported in the media. It wasn't . . . it wasn't meningitis that killed her." She takes a drag of her cigarette, drains her whiskey hurriedly and gestures towards the picture with her empty glass.

"Like Queen Cleopatra there she took her *own* life. Can you believe it? For God's sake, she was only twelve! My one and only baby!"

"Oh, Mrs Roberts, I am sorry, *so* sorry – nobody told me, I apologize. That . . . that . . . is *absolutely* tragic."

Eleanor ignores him. Her head is raised towards the ceiling and her yearning gaze seems to hunt in vain for the lost spirit of her child.

"She took an overdose of my sleeping pills. I found her myself, lying naked on her bed. As beautiful in death as she was in life; long auburn locks and freckles . . . She'd left a note for me, it simply read: '*Like a lamb to the slaughter, born without a future.*' How could she possibly *think* such a thing? The suicide of a child is the ultimate betrayal of a mother's love. Don't you agree?"

"I don't know what to say, Mrs Roberts."

"A child is a living monument to love; conceived from an act of love, born and reared with love. Yet *her* death was an act of hate. She was an exceptionally gifted child; loved the world, loved nature; all forms of life, but obviously despised her *own* . . . You have an exceptionally gifted child, do you not?"

"Yes. His name is Josh."

"I know, but Josh doesn't really matter. He's not like Clara. He has Asperger's Syndrome; therefore he doesn't *have* a worthwhile future. Does he?"

Jack gasps as if her words strike him physically, like a mallet in the chest. He strains to fill his lungs with enough air to vent his overwhelming rage, to tell Eleanor Roberts exactly what he thinks of her.

She is leaning against the mantelpiece for support, a refilled glass of whiskey trembling in her nicotine-stained fingers. A fading butt end dangling from one corner of her lipstick-smudged mouth. Her make-up is caking and peeling from the heat of the turf fire, and heavy black lines of mascara trickle down either side of her nose. Jack glares at her; her face reminds him of some hideous, surreal waxwork clown, melting and disintegrating in the heat. A work of fiction, he thinks. Yes, now he remembers: *The Picture of Dorian Gray.*

"I want you to give something to Eli in person," she says, her voice mellowing to a whisper.

Jack is still seething with a bizarre blend of hatred and profound pity.

Treat her like the lady Eli once loved, advised Franklin.

"What is it?" he asks sharply.

"It is a gift."

She hands him a sealed envelope. He frowns as he looks at it; *"To Daddy"* is written in a neat, delicate script, with a chain of blood-red, black-eyed poppies pencilled under it.

"I don't understand, Mrs Roberts. What is it?"

"It is a suicide note. Clara left it for her father but I never gave it to him."

"I'm not sure this is appropriate. I mean: I'm not scheduled to meet him until October, next year."

"Trust me, Mr Andersson. It is not the weight of days that kills a condemned man – only *the* day of his execution."

"I don't understand."

"I know. Frankly, I thought the man Eli sent would be smarter than *you*; somebody more . . . intellectually gifted; like your son Josh perhaps. Eli always wanted a son, you know, but even the most powerful man on the planet permits himself only one child."

"What kind of man was your husband? I really need to capture the essence of him as a man – to write this biography, you understand."

Eleanor tosses her hair back with almost aristocratic hauteur.

"My *ex*-husband believes that all problems are amenable to a rational solution. That all institutions and cultures and systems of governance are merely intellectual thought-constructs. He thinks that the most intractable of conflicts can be resolved by people simply altering their opinions. He is correct, of course, but his weakness is that he is supremely intellectualized, and fails to appreciate that lives are lived and decisions made at a basically emotional level. Eli married *me* to compensate for this affective deficit he recognized within himself . . . that and my unique talent, of course."

"What talent, Mrs Roberts?"

She lights up a fresh cigarette and sips her neat whiskey.

"A philosopher once said that reason is the slave of the passions. And that is true for most individuals, but not Eli. Eli killed my baby . . . murdered her . . . he only worshipped her mind . . . but that was not enough . . . I *loved* her. Spirit and soul," she says pathetically.

She slumps down into the chaise-longue and her moist eyes appear ablaze as they reflect the orange glow of the fire.

"Eli knows nothing about true love; considers it only a trick of nature or a mental illness to perpetuate the species. That man is one cold bastard I tell you . . . one ruthless, calculating bastard."

Hell hath no fury like a woman scorned, thinks Jack.

Eleanor regards him with a supremely cynical smile and raises her glass aloft.

"Cheers, Mr Andersson."

Jack tactlessly cups a hand and raises an invisible glass in response.

There is a brief silence.

"This interview is over," she announces abruptly. "Mr Moriarty will show you to your room for the night."

Moriarty leads Jack upstairs and along a gloomy corridor. There are no pictures adorning the oak-panelled walls; the old mansion is devoid of colour, in stark contrast to its splendid setting.

"This is your room for the night here, sir."

"Thank you, Mr Moriarty."

Jack pauses and studies the man from under his eyebrows.

"Have you met Mr Roberts?"

"Many times, sir."

"What is he *really* like?"

Moriarty says wryly. "They say no man is a hero to his valet, but the master of this house is an exception."

"And the lady of this house . . . what of her, Mr Moriarty?"

"You must forgive her, sir. She has not been well for some time."

Jack feels his stomach rumble and remembers he hasn't eaten since morning.

"Could I have something to eat, please?"

"Of course, sir, but meals are not permitted in *this* bedroom. I will call you down when I have some food prepared in the kitchen."

Jack's bedroom has a deep-pile, azure carpet. The walls are chrome yellow, with a chain of colourful flowers snaking along gracefully just under the ceiling. The curtains are a light pink, and patterned with purple love hearts. He kneels down beside the window to examine a bookcase, its shelves brimming but neatly arrayed. His eyes skip along the titles: children's illustrated encyclopedias; mythologies of the world; classic works of fiction; wonders of science and nature. He stops short and frowns at a newish, black-spined book wedged conspicuously amongst them. Picks it out gingerly and slowly opens the front cover. There is a hand-written inscription under a title he can't even pronounce.

"To my darling daughter Clara – Dare seize the fire!"

Jack shakes his head as he closes the book and gently squeezes it back into place. Gazes at Clara's bed and imagines her dove-white naked body stretched out on the duvet. Her pale, freckled face and auburn locks. Her cold little breasts hardening as she sleeps deeper and deeper, down towards her death.

There is a small locker adjacent to the head of the bed with a book lying wide open upon it. Jack approaches it and scans across the open pages. He recognizes the delicate, neat script of Clara Roberts – it is *her* diary. His eyes are riveted on the entry for her last day on Earth. Stares at it yet can't believe it. The letters are etched in bold print on the cream parchment. It is just a single word:

"STEELMAN"

ELEVEN

Josh is comfortably seated and facing Kvellner again. His eyes
are closed but his mind is hyper-conscious as he imagines his whole
body, like a hollow metal statue, slowly filling up with warm, liquid
gold. This relaxation routine wastes exactly fifteen minutes of every
one of his fortnightly sessions as Kvellner methodically calls out each
area of Josh's body. At precisely three fifteen, Josh lazily raises his eyelids and his iridescent eyes seem to burrow through the wall opposite.

"Tell me about your school, Josh. Do you like your school?"

"Yes, Doc. It is made out of a lovely old orange-red brick. Sometimes
I like to touch the brickwork because it is always warm, even when
it is cold outside."

"Have you any friends at school?"

"No, just myself."

"What do you believe the other children in your class think about
you?"

"Most of them don't think at all. I mean: how can you think about
nobody? When you are nobody you are invisible; you don't have feelings; you are only a thing."

"What about the few children that *do* have an opinion of you?"

His left hand tightens involuntarily, and his index finger stiffens
out and starts to draw tiny circles in the air, while he marshals his
thoughts.

"I used to think I was funny because everybody laughed at me all
the time when I was little. I know I still awkwalk peculiar and use
bizurrd words, but I'm trying not to be a freak any more. That's what
some of them still call me . . . a freak."

"How do you react, Josh, when they tease you with that word?"
asks Kvellner, peering over his gold-rimmed glasses.

"My head feels like a balloon filled with blood and all the words get squeezed out. Then I keep chasing after them, to make them stop laughing, but I can never catch them. Usually, Miss Alvarez comes to take me somewhere quiet, and helps make my head go back down to normal size again."

"Is Miss Alvarez your class teacher?"

"No, Doc, she's only an assistant who specializes in teaching freaks like me."

"Who do you like most of all the people in your school?"

"Well, it is a Catholic school, Bo, so God is my favourite person at the school. He wrote the Bible as well, which is a terrorfull book."

"Do you talk to God, Josh?"

"Not any more, Doc. I used to pray when I was a kid, but eventually I realized I was just talking to myself."

Kvellner crinkles his nose up and shuts one eye, looking puzzled as he tries to fathom the boy's logic.

"So why is God still your favourite person if you cannot communicate with him?"

"That is a ludicrazy question for any psychiatrist to ask. God is everybody's favourite person because he has a perfect mind. Of course you know God is insane, don't you, Doc."

"What do you mean?"

"In the beginning God created a perfect world called the Garden of Eden. It was full of fantastical animals like unicorns, phoenixes, chimeras and snarks, for Adam and Eve to play with. Then along came a snake and persuaded them to eat an apple from the Tree of Knowledge. God was so mad that he banished the two of them for ever from the beautiful paradise – just for eating that little apple. But that wasn't the real reason; the original sin was Adam and Eve striving to become intelligent, to become different from the other creatures they shared the garden with.

"When God saw Adam and Eve's descendants getting ever more

94

smarticulate he got scared. So he decided to drown all the people, even the kids, in a great flood. Everybody drowned except Noah, his family, and all the animals. What kind of crazy being does that – kill all the people and save all the animals? That's perfectly insane, Doc, isn't it?"

Kvellner leans back, arches his eyebrows and smiles in surprise at Josh posing him a question.

"Well, you must remember some stories in the Bible are basically . . . allegorical. 'Myths' is a good word; stories to help people understand the world before science provided more accurate explanations."

"Have you ever heard of 'Ouroboros', Doc?"

Kvellner repeats the word to prompt the computer display above Josh's head.

"Ouroboros": From Greek mythology – a snake that eats its own tail. Culturally symbolic of eternal cycle of life or time.

"Yes, I know what it is"

"That's the name of the snake that wrecked the Garden of Eden. He grew so big and so fat that he could coil himself around the whole world. He ate all the fruit and killed all the other animals, until there was nothing left to consume except himself. So all that remained was a colossal head stranded in a vast desert. Is it a sin to be intelligent, Doctor?"

"No, Josh. Why do you ask me that question?"

"I think God gave me Asparagus Syndrome to punish me," he whispers.

"Why would God want to punish you?"

The boy sits bolt upright, and his left index finger is drawing invisible circles in the air again. His head rolls from left to right but his eyes retain their vacant gaze.

"Secrets, secrets . . . things I'm not supposed to know, Doc." He presses his left index finger vertically over his sealed lips. "Shhh . . . Shhh!"

"Tell me one of your secrets."

"I can't, Doc."

"Why not?"

"Because then it wouldn't be a secret any more."

"Josh, this office is a safe place. You have absolutely nothing to fear here. The space that exists between you and me at this very moment is secure; there are *no* threats. Your secrets will be safe here."

"Are you sure, Doc?"

"Trust me, Josh," he quietly reassures him.

"If I tell you a secret will you promise not to be angry?"

"I *promise* you. No matter *what* you tell me I will *not* get angry."

Josh sits statue-like in his chair, his eyes shut tight as he summons the will to articulate the words. Kvellner scarcely dares to draw his own breath to avoid distracting him.

"Finkelstein, Jacob A, two forty-seven Greenwood Drive, East Brooklyn. Svenson, Agatha R, Apartment fourteen, Roosevelt Building, Manhattan."

The names and addresses are hardly out of Josh's mouth before Kvellner is on his feet and glaring at the boy. He can feel the air rushing through his nostrils as he battles to maintain his composure.

"Miss Chang!" he snaps through an intercom. "Could you please send Mrs Andersson in here a moment?"

Jenny's anxious face quickly appears at the office door.

"Is everything okay, Doctor Kvellner?"

"Yes, Mrs Andersson. I just need to check something on Miss Chang's computer. Do you mind keeping an eye on your son for a couple of minutes?"

"Of course not, Doctor."

Kvellner strides into Miss Chang's office. He lays both fists on her desk as he leans over it to look at her monitor.

"Miss Chang, could you please display my appointments for later today."

She calls out his request and the names and times are instantly flashed up on screen.

"Finkelstein, Jacob A. 16.30"
"Svenson, Agatha R. 18.00"

"Miss Chang, was Josh Andersson *ever* in this office at any time during his visits?"

"No, Doctor. Never!" she protests. "Why, is there a problem?"

"Yes! Our information security systems have been totally compromised. That Andersson kid has accessed all our files, names, addresses, and probably my case notes as well. We've been *hacked!*"

Josh is sitting in the waiting-bubble again. Miss Chang is not taking any chances this time as she sits within the sphere herself, watching his every move with suspicion. A simple cloudscape illuminates the inner surface area of the sphere. Josh staggers awkwardly, hugging its circumference, caressing cotton-wool-like cumulonimbus as he flies round and round the virtual sky.

"I'm on cloud nine in cloud-cuckoo land. I am superman. I am superman," he chants breathlessly.

Miss Chang tosses her head, and wishes Josh Andersson would shut up and hurry home.

She knows she will shortly get a new and more sophisticated office computer system. And the transition is going to be an administrative nightmare.

Kvellner sits behind his desk, removes his spectacles and smooths his silver eyebrows with the thumb and middle finger of his right hand. His eyelids flutter and his cheeks flush as he starts to speak.

"Mrs Andersson, when you informed me some time ago that you couldn't obtain any search history from Josh's computer, what was the precise technical reason for that?"

"Well, according to his uncle Robbie, who is an IT systems engineer, Josh downloaded a rogue program that prohibits anyone from accessing his material."

"I see. It makes sense now," Kvellner nods soberly.

"What do you mean, Doctor?"

"I mean, that Josh was covering his tracks to this office."

"I don't understand."

Kvellner takes a slow deep breath before he responds.

"I'm sorry, but your son has hacked into my computer here. He has memorized patient details; probably accessed his own medical records, my private clinical notes . . . and God knows what else."

"But how do you know this?"

"He told me himself, Mrs Andersson."

Jenny lowers her head, mortified with embarrassment.

"I am *so* sorry, Doctor. I feel so ashamed of him."

"It's really not *your* fault – or Josh's either, for that matter," Kvellner smiles sympathetically. "You must be cognizant of the fact that those with Asperger's do not experience or interpret the world like normal people. External reality is chaotic for Josh, particularly in the context of trying to comprehend other people's emotions. Emotional responses are complex, subtle, often irrational, and impossible to couch in linguistic terms. Josh is obsessed with words; he explores the world around him using words. But language can't adequately describe the totality of human experience, and it is at that boundary, if you will, that Josh loses control. And that sense of losing control is truly terrifying for him."

Jenny dabs her eyes with a handkerchief, striving to stifle her sobs as Kvellner continues with his analysis.

"All these routines – learning poetry and whole books by rote – are phenomenal feats of memory, but are purely a means to exert control over his immediate environment. The same 'control' principle applies to his obsession with computers. In Josh's head, the *virtual* world is so much more predictable and comprehensible and an ultimately safer place than the scary *real* world. To him, hacking my computer is an entirely justifiable crime. His visits here become less traumatic for him, he has more *control* over the clinical process if he has read my case notes and anticipated my strategies."

But Kvellner's sympathetic line of reasoning fails to alleviate Jenny's anguish. She clasps her hands and squeezes them tight under her chin as if trying to disguise her quivering lower lip.

"Have you made *any* progress with him at all, Doctor?"

"I must emphasize that I can only work with the information I receive. If Josh chooses *not* to reveal his innermost thoughts, despite my best endeavours . . . well then, we *can't* make substantial progress. I know psychology is not an exact science; and as a professional I am loath to say it. But sometimes, Mrs Andersson . . . sometimes we just need to get lucky!"

"How on earth are we going to get lucky, Doctor?"

The psychiatrist leans forward and folds his arms loosely on the desk.

"Do you know a Miss Alvarez at his school?"

"Yes, I know her."

"I want you to ask her to do something for me. I know it is somewhat unorthodox, but when Josh is at school his guard is definitely lowered, compared to sitting under my spotlight."

He hesitates as Jenny leans forward eagerly herself.

"Tell her to ask Josh to write an essay about himself . . . a sort of three-page autobiography, if you will. You don't need to tell her that *I* want it, maybe that you are just concerned about his self-perception and simply want to get a better insight into it. Are you comfortable with that?"

"Yes, I think that's a really positive idea, Doctor. There's just one other thing that concerns me."

"What's that?"

"Josh isn't sleeping well at all. Sometimes I get up in the middle of the night to look in on him and he's wide-awake, staring at the light. Frequently he's tired during the day, more anxious in himself, and I end up having to give him a sedative to calm down."

"Okay, how long has this been going on?"

"About two or three weeks now."

"Well, if the boy is not getting sufficient sleep, he can't function well psychologically. So I recommend a short course of sleeping pills to regularize his sleeping pattern. If that is okay with you, I can write a prescription straightaway."

"Thank you, Doctor – anything for a decent, long sleep," she says, brightening at last.

TWELVE

DUSTY, DOWNTOWN MANHATTAN is scorching under the fierce glare of the midsummer sun. Jack has his car's air-conditioning set at full blast as he sits behind the wheel, oblivious to the heat, waiting for the lights to change. He can see his destination shimmering in the distance, like a giant crystal spear thrust into the heart of the New York skyline. It is a geometrically perfect, square pyramid, with its four sides stretching relentlessly fifteen hundred feet into the air. The exterior of this towering edifice is constructed almost entirely of glass, except for the pyramidion at its apex, which is filigreed with the finest gold. Occasionally, when the angle of the sun's rays is right, they catch the very tip, and it shines like a beacon over the city and beyond, into the Atlantic. Elijah Roberts likens it to the eye of God opening. But Josh has warned his father to beware, as a single glance from God could kill him or even blind him.

Jack steps out of the ground-floor security office as soon as his identity has been verified. He is greeted by a fresh-faced young man, smartly attired in a dark-green uniform edged with burned orange. The two walk briskly to an executive express elevator, discreetly located off the main concourse.

"What floor, sir?"

Jack flashes him a broad grin.

"We're going all the way to the top, kid!"

The doors close with a gently reassuring *whoosh* and the young man is grinning as he straightens up and calls out the word "Pyramidion". Jack has no sense of time, space or speed as he silently hurtles skyward. Suddenly, the elevator is flooded with sunlight. Jack shields his eyes and looks down in horror as New York rapidly disappears beneath his feet. He feels dizzy at first, and quickly becomes disoriented as with sweaty hands he seeks to regain his balance against the sides of this glass capsule.

"Holy *shit*, Jesus Christ!" he keeps repeating, until the doors eventually open at the summit of the building. Jack spills out of the elevator – straight into a plush office perched precariously on top of the world. His head is still spinning and he is staggering as he tries to bring two fuzzy figures into focus. He can hear them chuckling.

"You'll be okay in a minute, Jack."

"Happens most everybody first time."

One of them gives the elevator operator a generous tip and says, "Thanks, Charlie."

"Charlie" has been grinning the whole way up the glass elevator and he'll *still* be grinning all the way back down to the ground floor, thinking: *Yeah, the journey to the top of GeoNova Finance is one helluva ride.*

Zak Taylor and Scott Reshevsky, two of the richest men on the planet, are standing, completely relaxed, each to a side of a triangular table. Both are casually dressed in jeans and ivory-coloured shirts. Taylor is tall and lanky and wears a tan cowboy hat to disguise his thinning hair. Reshevsky is squat, with a set of white teeth that seem almost too big for his mouth. The atmosphere is informal. They positively insist on using first names only, as Jack settles comfortably into an orange-green leather chair.

"Well, it's a real privilege to meet with you guys and I guess you know already exactly why I'm here. So let me start by asking you about the first time you met Eli Roberts."

Taylor smiles amusedly and nods his head in Reshevsky's direction, to permit him to recount the story.

"Zak and myself were working for a stock-trading firm run by a guy named Yaacov Rubinstein. He was a real tough son of a bitch; spent his youth playing blitz chess in Central Park, Union and Times Square. His whole life was just hustling suckers for every buck he could swindle out of them. Yaacov had a very simple business philosophy. He said: Trading stocks is just like playing chess. Dead easy so long as you keep making the right moves.' Before he hired any new guy, Rubinstein always challenged him to a five-minute blitz game. Just to test how the guy's intellect coped with the time pressure and to enjoy crushing his ego. 'Cos Rubinstein never played chess for fun – only for blood!"

Reshevsky stops and chuckles to himself before he continues his tale.

"And then along came Eli. He sat across the board from Yaacov and asked how much extra he'd get paid when he beat him. Yaacov looked down his nose and told him: 'You young punks are all the same; you play chess with your balls and not your brains.'

"Then Eli picked up the clock and adjusted his *own* time, from five minutes down to one minute. So he was left with only sixty seconds to play all his moves, compared to his opponent's five minutes. I swear to God, Rubinstein nearly fell off his chair when Eli took off his own tie and wrapped it over his eyes saying he'd prefer to play blindfold.

"I made the moves for Eli, and pressed his clock for him, as both called out their moves. Yaacov was under real pressure, sweating over the board as he bashed out his moves, and Eli instantly responded.

"Then Rubinstein stopped, stared for a full two minutes at the position, played his move, and smiled. Eli had twenty seconds left on his clock, and I counted every one of them, right down to zero. Yaacov leaned back, arms behind his head, and announced: 'You lose on time, *sucker*. Now get the fuck outta my office, you arrogant prick.'"

Taylor and Reshevsky are both laughing hard now as they remember.

"Then Eli removed his blindfold, stood up and asked me what time business opened in the morning. Then he turned to Rubinstein and said, 'By the way, I have checkmate in twelve moves against best defence.' He turned round to me as he was leaving, winked and said: 'See you at seven-thirty tomorrow morning, Scott.' Man, it was priceless; Rubinstein with a face like thunder, analyzing the board, inputting the position onto his computer chess program, and confirming Eli's checkmate in twelve. Finally, he threw up his hands and said: 'He might be an arrogant son of a bitch, but any guy that can play like Bobby Fischer is more than welcome to come work for me.'"

Zak Taylor is from Alabama and takes up the story in his lazy, Dixie drawl.

"We spent near five years together working in that office: Eli, Scott and me. Roberts was just like a sponge, soaking up everthin' the boss could teach him about trading stocks and high finance and such. Eli spent a lot of time, though, on Wall Street, talking with the traders on the floor. Nothin' illegal like, just talkin', Jack, you understand?"

Jack gives an economical nod of his head in mute acknowledgement.

"After a couple of years, Eli was playing with some awful big numbers. He didn't *always* make the right calls, but Yaacov didn't mind, 'cos the man performed and profits were soaring. I mean: all you gotta do is beat the odds. If you call it right only fifty-one per cent of the time, you're making money. And if you're dealing in hundreds of millions, you're going to make a lotta bucks. People used to call us the 'Holy Trinity', 'cos we were far and away the three most successful traders on the New York Stock Exchange. But make no mistake about it, Jack – Eli, he was Gawd, I tell ya."

"So how'd it come about you gentlemen left Yaacov Rubinstein and set up GeoNova Finance?"

Reshevsky grins to reveal an enormous, gleaming smile. "Poor Yaacov never had a son of his own, so he was kinda grooming Eli to take over his business after he retired. But the last year we were working there, Eli started losing interest. Rubinstein hauled him into his office one morning and confronted him. 'How come you're only losing money on *Big Carbon* corporate trades?' he demanded. But Eli never batted an eyelid – I mean, the guy rarely reacts; you almost never know what he's thinking. So the boss is ranting and raving, and shouting that the last thing he needed was a trader with an environmental conscience. But Eli takes one pace forward, looks him square in the eye and says: 'I think when speculators forsake their private conscience to perform their commercial duties, they lead financial markets by a short route to chaos.' Rubinstein sacked him on the spot. So Eli lopes out of the office, dons his coat and hat, and coolly smiles at Zak and me. We were both shocked when we asked him 'Where are you going to go *now*?' 'I'm going to change the world, boys – question is, what are *you* going to do?' We never doubted him for *one* second, and walked right out the door with him – and *never* once looked back."

Taylor cocks his head and makes a low whistle.

"Yeeah! That was a purdy big decision. Rubinstein might have been a tough, mean son of a bitch, but he was a real shrewd operator. Guys rarely left him, and those that did turned out to be either losers or cracked under pressure. People were wary about dealing with GeoNova when it was founded, but Eli had a lot of contacts, and above all, he had a reputation for being *straight*. 'Integrity is a priceless commodity,' he used always say."

Jack seizes a conversational pause and leans forward.

"But what other qualities did Eli have, as a *man*, to enable him to become so phenomenally successful?"

"Personnel!" exclaims Reshevsky pointing his finger at the ceiling. "He had an uncanny ability to choose the right people. Always the brightest, the most honest, the most fiercely loyal. People, I suppose, he recognized with qualities that he saw the best of himself in. Whenever he hired new staff, the very first lesson he'd teach them was the true value of money. He'd take out a plain, regular sheet of paper, lay it on his desk and write '*one hundred dollars*' on it. Then he'd take a one-hundred-dollar bill from his wallet and put it down right beside the paper sheet. 'Tear up that sheet,' he'd say, and the new staffer would step forward and rip it up. 'Now tear up that hundred-dollar bill,' but they'd always politely refuse. 'What's the problem?' he'd ask. 'They are both just pieces of paper with numbers on them.' But nobody could ever give him a satisfactory answer other than 'It's money.' Then he'd smile, nod his head and tell them that in Germany, back in the nineteen twenties, their currency collapsed, and citizens burned money on the pavements to keep themselves warm."

Jack frowns. "What's the point?"

"The point is: money is only an idea. It's still just a regular piece of paper made from regular old trees. Even the numbers on our trading screens are just electronic displays, giving an appearance of solidity to pure wind, as Orwell put it."

"Y-e-p," drawls Taylor. "It reminds me of the one and only time Scott and me *ever* had an argument with Eli Roberts. Business was flying at the time; we were raking in the bucks. Then Eli declared one day that he wanted to convert all our cash reserves to gold – all our investments to be liquidated, even at a loss, into gold. We told him he was crazy. I mean: gold is a commodity, and its value can fluctuate like any asset. Why put all our eggs in one basket? It goes against any wise investor's first instinct: to always diversify your portfolio. I swear to Gawd, we were going to walk. But Eli was insistent – man's got testicles of titanium – called our bluff and came up trumps. Six months later came the day the dollar died."

"Eli saw it all coming," Reshevsky chimes in. "The Federal Reserve's policy of quantitative easing was just a money-printing exercise, creating billions of electronic dollars to finance ballooning budgetary deficits. And then one day somebody switched the light on. Everybody stopped and looked at each other, and realized we were all gone doolally, playing in a financial loony bin. The almighty dollar was nothing but a paper tiger. Markets, property, stocks, the price of *everything* plummeted, and cash plumb ran out of places to hide. But gold went stratospheric! Man, we were multimillionaires on Monday and billionaires come Friday."

Reshevsky grins as he reminisces. There is a twinkle in his eye as he poses Jack a question.

"Do you know where gold comes from?"

"Sure, it comes from the ground, mines, sometimes rivers I guess."

"That's exactly what I thought when Eli first asked me. But it's not the right answer."

"What do you mean?" Jack frowns.

"Gold is an element that is manufactured, or nucleosynthesized, to use the correct scientific term, deep in the heart of Class One A supernovae. Which is to say: stars at least ten times the size of our sun, exploding and bursting their contents throughout the cosmos. I know it seems crazy when you think about it but it's absolutely true. You see, Eli doesn't *think* like regular people. With him it's always the big picture, the true value of things, never just superficial appearances."

"Yeaah," says Taylor. "Eli asked me the same thing. 'Where would you rather put your money – in somethin' forged at the heart of the biggest and brightest stars in the universe or in a wafer-thin slice of a tree?' Yep, gold is more than just an idea. It's got that shiny 'eternal' quality – real substance. Did you know, Jack, that the quantity of gold in the whole world is no bigger than a twenty-one metre cube?"

Jack looks at him disbelievingly. "No, I didn't, Zak. But now I understand how Roberts earned the nickname 'Midas'."

"Oh! Don't call him that, Jack. Even in jest."

There is an awkward lull. Taylor twiddles with a gold pen he is holding and Reshevsky shifts his mass uneasily in his chair.

"Sorry, guys, did I say something out of place?"

Taylor tips the rim of his Stetson and stands up.

"Come here," he says, ushering him towards the window.

He lays a long arm along the length of Jack's shoulders.

"Quite a view, ain't it?"

"Sure is, Zak," Jack answers, gazing out over the vast metropolis of New York.

"Make you feel like God, it would, if you look long enough."

"Maybe."

"Eli used like fold his arms and stand looking out from this 'xact spot. Said it was his second-favourite view in the whole world."

Jack looks up at Taylor's grim jaw line.

"What was his favourite?"

"That'd a been his daughter's face."

"I remember attending his daughter Clara's funeral," Reshevsky cuts in. "Her death from meningitis near killed him; certainly killed his marriage to Eleanor! The story of Midas was his theme for the eulogy. A legendary king, given a great gift by the gods, of turning everything he touched into gold. Then his little daughter comes running up and embraces him, and to his horror, she is instantly transformed into a golden statue. Midas breaks down and cries and pleads with the gods to restore his daughter and take back their gift. The gods take pity on him and bring his daughter back to life. 'That is the most valuable lesson we can draw from any myth,' Eli said. 'Money is only a shared, imaginative possession, but children . . . young life is hope incarnate!'" Reshevsky clucks his tongue. "I swear to God, if words alone could resurrect the dead, Eli Roberts would do it."

The three fall completely silent. Jack can judge by Sam and Zak's stony faces that the memory of Clara Roberts's funeral has made a profound impression on them.

"Do you have a kid, Jack?" Reshevsky eventually enquires.

"Sure, I have a son named Josh. He's eleven years old."

"A son! A son!" declares Reshevsky. "Ain't you a lucky man. Zak and myself each have a daughter. What's Josh like?"

Jack gives a sheepish grin. "He's a great kid. Doesn't look like me, though. He's handsome, and really smart too."

"Yeaah," drawls Taylor, adjusting his hat. "You look at your kid and know there is hope. Know why we gotta change the world. I mean: if we really love our kids we wouldn't be trashing the planet, would we? You wanna hear my favourite story about Eli?"

"Sure, okay," says Jack.

"Well, when *Fortune* magazine declared him the world's first trillionaire, Eli decided to go and do an interview with one of their correspondents. So this guy turns up one day and Eli says: 'Come with me; I want to make a statement.' The day before that, Eli had bought the entire stock o' Arctic Oil for near twenty-five billion dollars. We were all amazed that he even invested in 'Big Carbon' stock in the first place. Anyway, this *particular* mornin' was his very first meeting with the board of Arctic Oil. So Eli strolls into the boardroom, and him lookin' round like a big cat stalking his prey. He stands at the top of the table, and announces that he's shuttin' the whole company down and firing every employee from that very moment. Everybody started hollerin' that he couldn't do it, and threatening billion-dollar lawsuits. But the bottom line was banks lost confidence and stopped lending to Arctic Oil, so the company was forced to close anyway. I suppose when you're worth a trillion dollars, the world will purdy much bend to your will."

Jack is chuckling as Taylor finishes.

"Yeah, Zak, I remember reading that article in *Fortune*. It was a helluva statement, and it really catapulted GeoNova's environmental credentials into the public consciousness."

Jack turns to Reshevsky.

"What's your favourite story about him, Sam?"

Sam leans back in his chair with a wistful sigh.

"I have a thousand and one stories I could tell you about Eli

Roberts, if we had the time. But I think my most memorable moment was witnessing him negotiating with President Goulding the week the dollar died. Goulding sat in the *very* chair you're sitting in now, Jack, pleading with Eli to help bail out some of the banks, and stave off the collapse of the financial system; just like JP Morgan did in nineteen hundred seven. But Eli refused, unless Goulding publicly announced his intention to introduce a Carbon Emission Reduction package. The President was furious, accusing Eli of holding America to ransom and inevitable economic surrender to the Chinese. Said he was unpatriotic.

"Oh . . . Then Eli got animated, and he *really* is one man you *definitely* don't want to get riled up. 'Mr President,' he said, '*Big Oil* paid for your ticket into the Oval Office, and their price was a licence to poison the atmosphere. So don't *dare* lecture me on holding this nation to ransom, while you threaten life on this entire planet with extinction!' Goulding stormed out, but two days later, events forced him to relent. Yes, the President of the United States lost his next election right here in this room. I think that whole episode is the very first time I realized that Roberts might one day become President himself. And he'd pay for his *own* ticket into the White House."

Jack is fascinated as he listens, and wonders how Roberts has achieved all he has thus far.

"Geez, guys, how the hell did he do it all? Richest man on the planet, President of the United States of America, leader of GeoNova – which is probably the greatest political movement in world history. You know him better than most anybody. What is it about him?"

Reshevsky and Taylor look at each other, shrug their shoulders, and just laugh like two schoolkids who haven't a clue what the answer is.

"Well," drawls Taylor, "I suppose it's obvious when you think about it, Jack. Most anybody could do it – just so long as they keep on making the right decisions."

"Yes," observes Reshevsky, "life, politics, business, it's all like one big game of chess. If you consistently play the best moves, you're bound to win every time!"

Jack shuts his eyes tight as the express elevator plunges to the ground floor. He daren't even open them as he answers a call on his normal cell phone. He thinks it's Jenny's voice, but is not sure because the breathless speech is quavering with emotion. He hears the name "Josh" being stuttered, along with the words "suicide" and "school". The elevator comes back down to earth with a bump and Jack sprints out like a greyhound, racing across the concourse and out into the stifling, afternoon heat. The air is so humid that he feels his heaving lungs are almost inhaling pure water as he runs. Fumbling for his keys with trembling, sweaty hands, he zaps open his car and collapses into the driver's seat. The interior is baking hot but Jack doesn't even think of switching on the air-conditioning or lowering the windows. He just wants to press hard on the accelerator and drive the hell out of Manhattan!

THIRTEEN

WHEN JACK ANDERSSON first set eyes on Jenny, his brother's latest girlfriend, he knew she was different. It wasn't her long blonde hair, her soft brown eyes or her winsome smile. Nor was it her fine facial features, her elegant figure or her fierce intellect either. No, it was all of these and more – a form so much more beautiful than the sum of its parts. He did not see it so much as feel it, like a persistent, tight knot in his stomach whenever he was in her presence, or a vague, aching sensation that permeated both his body and his mind. Sometimes she would catch his gaze and hold it briefly, sufficient to tease but not commit herself – until the night they both got drunk in a New York bar. Robbie had been called back urgently to his office; the company's new quantum computer system had crashed yet again. Jack seized his chance as they talked and smoked. He wanted Jenny to be drunk when he told her he was in love with her. He walked her home, fell into her misty, brown eyes, kissed her and couldn't stop. And Jenny didn't want him to stop as her body arched and yielded, arched and yielded beneath him; her head lolled back, mouth agape and long tresses fanned out across the pillow. Jack wished he didn't have to exhale, wished he could capture and preserve that exquisite physical moment for ever, before it became pure memory. For that was the precise, breathless moment when he realized he could never know happiness again without this woman's love.

"People *fall* in love," his mother had said to Robbie. "Falling is not a conscious decision. It's like an accident – it just happens."

But Robbie felt betrayed; his brother had stolen his gorgeous Jenny and even *"accidents"* have guilty parties, especially if they are drunk. After sixteen years of marriage Jack still likes to remember the very first time they made love. She was the only girl he had *ever* made love to in his *entire* life, or ever needed to. And today is a good day to remember it . . . especially today.

Jenny is holding her head in her hands, her elbows firmly planted on the kitchen table. She has scarcely stopped weeping since Miss Alvarez gave her a copy of Josh's "autobiography" and informed her she had been legally obliged to report its contents to the school principal. Jack pores over the document, intermittently wincing and frowning with incredulity, emitting little gasps as he nears the end. Finally, he finishes reading it, pauses and momentarily reflects.

"Are you absolutely sure, Jenny, that Josh wrote this himself, that he didn't just cobble it together by using a few literary websites?"

"No, Jack, Miss Alvarez told me she had disabled Cloud access on his classroom computer while he wrote it," she tearfully replies.

"But it's not possible for an eleven-year-old kid to write stuff like this on his own. It's just too advanced, too adult even for a boy like Josh."

"You're not getting the point!"

"Sure, I get the point! Josh has the intellect of an adult but the emotions of a five-year-old."

"You're *really* not getting the *point!*"

"Now I have it!" he says, snapping his fingers. "He has memorized reams of this material from the Cloud – all these references to Joyce, God, the Nazis and psychiatry and . . . "

"Jack! Jack! Just shut up already, just shut up." Her voice is petering out to an anguished moan. "Can you not see it? Do you really not see it?"

"See what, Jenny?"

"Oh, for *Chrissake*, Jack, he's threatening to commit suicide!"

"No, no, you're exaggerating, honey. Just because he makes references to it doesn't mean he's actually *threatening* to do it. And kids that age don't go round killing themselves. Come on, Jenny, try and think about it logically."

"Logic has nothing whatever to do with what goes on inside *my* son's head," she protests.

"*Our* son, you mean."

"Whatever! Anyways, why does Miss Alvarez feel she has to report it to the principal? Would it be because she also considers it a suicide threat, or is she *exaggerating* too? Huh, Jack?" she adds sarcastically.

Jack is on his feet now with arms folded, head cocked with a smug half-smile.

"Eh, no, honey. You can bet your bottom dollar that the line where Josh writes that 'God is a Santa Claus for grown-ups' will really yank their Catholic chains. And you being a good Catholic girl should know it's much more important to preserve dogma than life."

Jenny casts her eyes to the ceiling and puckers her lips in disgust. She stands and glowers at him; then brushes past and swings open a cupboard door. She rifles through its contents, grabbing out boxes of pills and slapping them down on the table in an untidy pile.

She lifts one of the boxes and points to it.

"*Zoloft – a selective serotonin reuptake inhibitor to treat aggression, anxiety and depression,*" she reads aloud; then slams it back down on the table.

She picks up a second box and reads: "*Risperidone – a low-dose antipsychotic for stereotyped movements, agitation and idiosyncratic thinking.*" She fires the box back down and lifts a third. "*Zyprexa,*" she continues, "to reduce repetitive behaviours. *Revia:* also designed to help reduce obsessive behaviour. *Xanax:* for anxiety again . . . shall I go on, Jack?"

"No, that's *enough*, Jenny."

She unceremoniously slides the pile of boxes towards him.

"No, that's not *nearly* enough. It doesn't even come close," she says, gesturing towards the pills with a single sweep of her hand. "All these medications, all this *shit*, means he's deteriorating, means we're losing him. And that goddam essay of his is further proof, if proof were needed, that we're going to lose him one way or the other."

Jack is slowly sifting through the boxes and half-emptied silver-foil containers, shaking his head and then shrugging.

"I still reckon you're overreacting," he answers insistently, but adopting a more emollient tone. "These medications are just the typical drugs regimen for Aspies," he shrugs again.

"No, while you're touring around the globe, researching the life of Elijah Roberts, I'm watching Josh Andersson fall apart right in front of me. He's more anxious now, waking in the middle of the night and staring at the light . . . and school, socializing with other kids is . . . well, is just a disaster. And Kvellner isn't making much progress either. So you'll forgive me if I seem to be reacting like any normal mother would."

Jack gives her a contrite look.

"I'm sorry, honey. I plain forgot that you gotta take the brunt of things on your own here at home. Forgive me?"

She smiles quickly and rubs her eyes before embracing him. Jack feels her warm breath tickle the side of his neck and smiles to himself as he holds her, recalling the night he first told her he loved her.

"Oh, Jack, Jack," she repeats his name softly, in time with their swaying bodies.

"We'll be okay, Jenny," he whispers. "Shhh, now . . . shhh, baby," he says, running his fingers through her hair.

Then he stops abruptly and picks up a silver container from the table marked "*Stillnoct*".

"What's that one for? The name seems kind of familiar."

She leans back lazily and peers at the brand name on the packet he is now holding in front of her eyes.

"Oh, that's just a sleeping tablet. It counteracts some of the side-effects of *Risperdal,* and you know, just helps him sleep, is all."

He fires an anxious glance at the medicine cupboard, gaping over the sink where Josh washes down his pills with water chilled to precisely thirty-four degrees Fahrenheit. The memory strikes Jack like a thunderbolt as his mind is transported instantly back to Clara Roberts's bedroom. The mental image of her marble-white, naked corpse lying on her bed causes him to shiver and inhale sharply.

"What's wrong?" frowns Jenny, sensing his body stiffening.

"Why is that cupboard not secured?" he barks as he stands back and points to it.

"What do you mean?" she answers, maintaining her frown.

"Why is there no lock on that *goddam* door is what I'm asking!"

"I . . . I never thought of it."

"Well, start thinking and sort it out," he snaps.

Her reddened eyes well up with tears again, as Jack mumbles something about writing up some interview notes and hurriedly leaves the kitchen. He closes the door firmly behind him, stands still, and gently taps the back of his head against the wooden door. He shuts his eyes, inhaling and exhaling through his nose to try and alleviate a pounding headache. The sound of his thumping heart is still ringing in his ears as he slowly opens his eyes. A pair of green eyes instantaneously meets his gaze. It's Josh, staring through him as though he is watching his mother crying through the closed kitchen door. Jack feels a rush of air through his flaring nostrils as he raises his voice with sheer exasperation.

"You're *killing* us, Josh. You know that, son? You're fuckin' *killing* us!"

The child remains standing perfectly still, his handsome face devoid of emotional expression or any trace of reaction. Then he holds out his two empty palms in front of him and approaches his father with faltering steps.

"But how is this so, Father? Look: I have no weapons. How can I kill you if I am not armed?"

Jack stares disbelievingly at him. He feels his right hand curl into a tight, white, knotty fist. The boy's head is tilted back slightly and Jack wants to punch that chin hard enough to knock his head clean off, and enjoy watching it bounce against the walls. But he turns instead and rams his right knuckles against the kitchen door with a reverberating roar of frustration. He instinctively cradles his injured hand; his head hurts; his ears hurt, and behind the kitchen door he hears the love of his life weeping bitterly. He turns again and clamps his left hand on Josh's narrow shoulder and winces as he gestures towards the kitchen with the other.

"That's the sound of a heart breaking," he hisses.

"Interesting, I wonder what a mind breaking sounds like?"

Mrs Larsen is the principal of Josh's school. She is sitting behind an expansive desk in her office, introducing Jack and Jenny to a panel of three other people.

"This is Dr James Campbell, who is an educational psychologist . . . this is Monsignor Patrick Murray. As you know, the school here is under the aegis of the Catholic Archdiocese of New York and the monsignor is here as its representative in a pastoral capacity. Mrs Kennedy, Josh's grade teacher, you know already of course." Each of them nods wordlessly in turn as he or she is introduced.

"As you are aware, Mr and Mrs Andersson," she continues "Miss Alvarez has recently brought to my attention an essay that Josh wrote in class. The nature of the contents of that essay has raised significant concerns as to Josh's state of psychological well-being."

She pauses for a quiet breath and looks directly at Jack and Jenny before resuming.

"In fact, the concerns raised are, to put it mildly, alarming. And it is only fair of me to tell you at the outset that we are currently reviewing Josh's suitability for continuing in a mainstream class environment."

"What does that *mean* exactly?" asks Jack.

"It means that we are actively considering not allowing Josh return to this school in the fall."

"Oh, my God!" gasps Jenny, staring wide-eyed at Jack.

Mrs Larsen raises her hands and calmly says: "Listen, we're here to afford you an opportunity to help us *all* understand why Josh wrote the things he did. Frankly, we don't precisely understand it, but just because we don't understand it doesn't mean we should treat your son too harshly."

She turns to her teaching colleague and asks her to commence the discussion.

"Josh is an extraordinarily bright child," Mrs Kennedy says. "Truly imaginatively and verbally gifted, as can plainly be seen by the quality of language in his essay, irrespective of the content. I mean: I never scarcely believed that an eleven-year-old was even capable of writing like this. But I genuinely feel that Josh is totally lost in my class, even with Miss Alvarez's wonderful assistance. He just can't socialize with the other children, can't play with them or effectively communicate with them in any meaningfully emotional way. All this is not untypical of many children suffering from Asperger's Syndrome, and I have had *some* experience with children with this condition. But my gut feeling is that his condition has gotten worse. Maybe there is something else wrong with him that we're not picking up."

She squirms uncomfortably in her chair as she sums up.

"I'm going to be incredibly crude, but I don't mean to be because I can't think of a better way to put it. Even Josh himself says it in his essay when he writes that there is a fine line between genius and madness – and I think Josh falls *j-u-u-st* the wrong side of that line."

"Jenny, do you feel that Josh's mental health has deteriorated in recent times?" queries Mrs Larsen.

Jenny squeezes Jack's hand tight. "Yes, I do," she concedes.

"Listen," interjects Jack. "We have the matter in hand. Josh is seeing a top psychiatrist now . . . a top expert in his field."

"May I inquire who that is, Mr Andersson?" asks Campbell.

"Dr Kvellner," states Jack, leaning back in his chair.

"Dr *Bo* Kvellner?"

"Yes, that's him. You know him?"

"He's a very eminent man. I don't know him personally but I've read some of his articles in various periodicals. Has he read Josh's essay yet?"

"Our next appointment is day after tomorrow, Dr Campbell," says Jenny quietly. "It was Kvellner's idea for Josh to write a kind of auto-biography, so he could get a better insight into his mind. What do you think of the essay, Dr Campbell?"

"Well, I don't really want to pre-empt Dr Kvellner's diagnosis, but this work is clearly that of a very troubled young mind. It's quite obvious he is ideating suicide. There is no explicit threat to carry it out, but the mere fact that he is admiring the act of somebody else taking their own life is . . . well, disturbing. Some of the language employed, particularly the German words, are apocalyptic in tone. For example: *Endlösung*, the term for Hitler's 'Final Solution' to the so-called Jewish problem; *vernichtet*, which means 'destroyed'; *Götterdämmerung* is 'the twilight of the gods'. *Sein und Zeit* refers to 'being and time'. Also to the title of a book by a Nazi philosopher named Martin Heidegger. Even the last lines of his poem at the end – *I Universe* – echo another philosopher named Nietzsche, who similarly inspired the Nazis with his views on Übermenschen and *Untermenschen*; that is the concepts of superman and subhuman respectively. The term *Untermenschen* was in fact commonly used to refer to the mentally ill to justify their extermination by the medical authorities during the Nazi era. . . . "

Mrs Larsen and Kennedy both look positively aghast as Campbell continues to expound on his interpretation of Josh's autobiography. Monsignor Murray sits impassively, nonchalantly sucking his large cheeks in and out, as if no academic explanation were necessary or desired. But even *he* raises an eyebrow as Jack pointedly interrupts the detailed analysis.

"Oh, please, Doctor! I know something about Nietzsche's philosophy, and that man was no anti-Semite or ardent German Nationalist. That's a common misconception."

Campbell is swiftly taken aback and scowls across the desk.

"Nietzsche was a proto-Nazi at the very least."

"A nihilist," notes the monsignor laconically, raising an index finger.

"Oh, thank you, Monsignor," Campbell remarks with a prayer-like clasp of his hands, "that's an excellent word to describe the essence of Josh's essay – nihilistic."

Jack and Jenny's eyes dart back and forth between the two men, as if labouring to comprehend their shared private logic.

"Nihilism is basically a total rejection of religious and moral principles; a belief that life is devoid of meaning, combined with a general sense of despair or hopelessness. Even the title *Nobody* that Josh has chosen for himself in his work is indicative of his complete absence of feelings of self-worth. Yet the poem at the end is simply a . . . solipsistic, delusional, eschatological nightmare, where Josh visualizes himself as an instrument of God no less."

Campbell stops and scans his bemused audience; apart from the monsignor. As if expecting a round of applause for his incisive explication.

"Eh . . . well, thank you, Doctor, for your contribution," says Mrs Larsen. "Before I invite the monsignor for his input I would just like to preface his remarks, if I may."

She nods obsequiously in his direction, and he returns it with a courteous nod of his own.

"Jack and Jenny," she begins, "I feel it is imperative to mention that this school's mission is to inculcate Catholic, Christian values in our students. Our objective is to promote and foster a love and appreciation of our Catholic faith, through all our words and deeds. To prepare children for future active participation and service in a vibrant community of Christian faith."

She pauses and purses her lips before addressing Jenny directly.

"You were a student here in this school. Your own mother, God bless her, taught right here in this school. So you know *exactly* where I am coming from. Please bear this in mind as you listen to the monsignor, thank you." She signals with her eyes to the figure dressed entirely in black, apart from the gleaming white square of his collar, leaning over the side edge of the table. His bushy eyebrows knit together under an aloof frown that crowns a penetrating gaze as he leans further forward.

"Mr and Mrs Andersson," he gravely intones, "while your child's essay is so profoundly disconcerting on many levels, as the good doctor has already elucidated for us, I specifically wish to focus on its religious and sexual aspects. Your child has written, and I quote: '*God is a Santa Claus for grown-ups*'; '*God is lurking in my unconscious where he was born.*'

"He also goes on to describe his personal experiences of the holy sacrament of confession in a *blatantly* sacrilegious manner. I ask myself, even in these modern, secular times, how can an innocent child possibly conceive of these things?"

"I'm sorry, Monsignor, I really am," says Jack. "But Josh is not a normal boy, and I suspect he is accessing all this inappropriate material through his computer."

"Via the Cloud or Internet or whatever you want to call it! Have you not imposed restrictions on his computer usage, as clearly set out in the school's home policy guidelines on this issue?"

"He has unfortunately got around – circumvented – parental controls, Monsignor."

"Are you telling me he has unrestricted access to the Internet?"

"Yes, Monsignor."

"So is it conceivable that he is also viewing content of a sexual nature? That he is being exposed to pornographic material?"

"No! Not Josh. He's just not that kind of kid – not yet anyway. I mean, he's still too young," laughs Jack nervously.

"But this situation is intolerable! An eleven-year-old child is being given tacit parental approval to enter a world of adult experience. Why have you thus far failed to address this issue?"

"I'm sorry, Monsignor," says Jenny, shutting her eyes as if ashamed to look him in the face, "but Josh would just go plain crazy if we didn't allow him on the computer."

Campbell smiles wryly at the unintentional irony of her statement.

The priest sits up, stony-faced, and puffs his large cheeks, as if breathing in more air to vent his increasing anger.

"Did you realize that your child has written a Joycean pastiche of a scene describing the sexual act?"

"Excuse me?" asks Jack quizzically.

"Have you read this script, Mr Andersson?"

"Well, I did but . . . I didn't grasp everything."

"Obviously! This scene is written in the style of Molly Bloom's soliloquy from *Ulysses*."

"Oh, yes, Monsignor, Josh knows *that* book off by heart," ventures Jenny in mitigation.

The priest throws his hands up in the air and exchanges an incredulous glance with the psychologist.

"This really is not an occasion for levity, Mrs Andersson. Your child could absolutely *not* have penned this without some *direct experience* of human sexuality himself."

"What!" exclaims Jack, barely containing himself. "What are you *suggesting* here, Monsignor Murray?"

"I'm suggesting he has been adversely influenced by people and events beyond the confines of this school community. Malign influences and unspeakable perversities."

Jack runs his fingers through his hair, as if he's hearing the words in a horrible dream and needs to remind himself that he's really awake.

"Am I to understand that you are alleging that Josh is being sexually abused?"

The others jolt back in their chairs with a sharp collective intake of breath, and hold it while waiting for the monsignor to respond.

"The detailed account of sexual intercourse your child writes is too accurate to have been simply read about or viewed on a computer screen."

"I can't believe you're thinking like this," murmurs Jack, staring back at the blank faces. "No, it's a lie. It's simply not true."

"Please, Mr Andersson," huffs the monsignor. "Please don't ask me, a humble priest, to tell you, a married man, about the sight, sounds, tastes, tactile sensations and *smells* of sexual intercourse in the present company."

Jack hears Jenny starting to sob and feels his own cheeks beginning to burn.

"You're a liar, Murray!" he blurts out angrily.

The priest rises to the challenge as he grabs a copy of the essay off the table. Dons his spectacles and reads the relevant passage aloud.

"'*Fishsweat and treacle*'," your child wrote. "What do you think the contextual explanation for that phrase is, Mr Andersson? Don't insult my intelligence by telling me your son could know this *unless he actually saw it and smelled it!*"

"Oh, my God!" exclaims Mrs Kennedy, involuntarily clasping her knees together as if to catch the penny falling in her lap. "That is *disgusting*. That is just the *rudest* thing! The *rudest* thing!"

"Can we take a moment to calm down here please, please, Monsignor?" implores Mrs Larsen.

"Sure, of course. I'm sorry, ladies. Please forgive me for my literary . . . indiscretion."

The principal looks suitably sympathetic at Jenny dabbing her eyes with her handkerchief.

"I'm sorry, Jenny . . . Jack. I can't imagine how difficult this must be for you, but Dr Campbell and the monsignor have studied Josh's script in great detail, and both are in agreement on their interpret—"

"Yes," Dr Campbell cuts across. "Kvellner will see its diagnostic implications immediately he has read it," he is nodding emphatically.

"What implications, Doctor?" queries Jack.

"I don't want to pre-empt the man; he's a fellow-professional, after all."

Jenny looks up.

"Kvellner said there was ten per cent of Josh's mind that he was trying to discover. Like a secret to unlock the mystery of his psyche. Is the answer here?" she asks plaintively, pointing a trembling finger at the script lying on the table.

"As I said, Dr Kvellner is an eminent professional and I don't want to pre-empt his diagnosis. You understand?"

Jack and the priest are staring at one another across the table, trying not to blink as they simmer. The monsignor slowly presses his hands together, intertwining his chubby fingers, and kissing a purple stone inset into his large, gold ring.

"Are you a Catholic, Mr Andersson?" he says at last.

"No," he brusquely replies.

"Do you even believe in the existence of God?"

Jack is on his feet to answer, his arms tightly folded as he recalls verbatim Professor Hubner's intriguing answer to the identical question in Berlin.

"The ontological question of God's existence is irrelevant. What matters is the *human idea* of God – for that *definitely* exists."

The monsignor slowly rises to his feet and leans forward, laying his two large hands on the table for support. A look of barely concealed contempt is etched in his face.

"*Quod erat demonstrandum,*" he announces with an oratorical flourish. "A man conversant with the philosophy of Nietzsche; a nihilist and an *atheist*. Your little boy never stood a chance with a heathen for a father. Did he, Mr Andersson?"

He turns, picks up Josh's script and rips it up.

He turns again, his face apoplectic with rage.

"This work is that of a child *possessed*. It is an *abomination* born out of an overwhelming spiritual failure by his parents. You have failed your child, Mr and Mrs Andersson. You have failed God's greatest gift – your only child."

Jenny jumps to her feet to confront him.

"I don't care what you think!" she shouts. "I don't care what *any* of you think. I know there is something *incredible* . . . something *terrific* . . . something *truly amazing* about Josh. I don't know what it is," she cries, "but I'm his mother, and any mother who believes in her child has . . . that child has a future!"

She breaks down, and Jack flings his arms around her neck to kiss her and console her and tell her how brave she's been.

"I think *you're* terrific, honey. I think *you're* incredible; I think *you're* amazing *too!*" he tells her, fighting back his own tears.

"They had their minds made up already, before we even got to the school, honey!" asserts Jack from behind the wheel of the car. "They think Josh belongs in a nuthouse or a school for retards. But don't worry, honey, we'll get him a *better* school come the fall. Don't you even worry about . . . " He is interrupted by the ringtone of his dedicated cell. Jack recognizes Franklin's number from the caller display on the dashboard. He pulls over sharply to the kerb on a busy street.

"You can't *stop here*, Jack!" Jenny protests.

"I know!" he shouts, anxiously glancing at the flashing number. "Can you step out a moment, and I'll drive round the block and come pick you right back up. Please, honey?"

"Agh, Jack," she groans, rolling her eyes before exiting the car and slamming the door behind her.

Jack speeds off, cupping his hand instinctively over his mouth as he answers the call.

"Steelman."

"Good evening, sir," Franklin responds in a business-like tone. "Client number twenty-seven on your list. I have arranged an urgent appointment for you to see him day after tomorrow in Florida. I will text all the requisite details to you shortly."

"But that date is not convenient for me."

"I'm sorry, but this client is ninety-two years old and has maybe a month at most left to live."

"I swear to God it really is *not* convenient for me."

"The President of the United States is paying his final respects to this man tomorrow. So surely if *he* can find time in *his* busy schedule, you can too."

"I'm sorry. I've got something else really important to do day after tomorrow."

Franklin is breathing more heavily now but doesn't mince his words.

"The man is staying off his painkillers a couple of days, so he can keep a clear head for the President's *and* your visit." He appears to hesitate. "Or maybe I should send someone over to your house, looking for our money back!"

"Okay, okay, I get your point. I'll *be* there, *goddammit!*"

Jenny slumps back down into her seat and throws a black look at her husband.

"Was that Franklin?"

"Yeah."

"I figured it was."

"Listen, honey, I can't make Kvellner's appointment day after tomorrow."

"Oh, Jack! He said he needed to see *both* of us this time."

"I know, I know, but it just can't be helped, is all. Something urgent has come up."

"More important than Josh?"

"Course not. But it's paid work, goddammit!"

"Oh, surely you can postpone."

"*No, I can't*," he says impatiently.

"But . . . "

"But we discussed this, honey – remember?" He smiles and gives her a patronizing pat on the thigh to mollify her.

"Just stay focused on the money, Jenny . . . focus on the money, honey," he repeats. Jenny glares intently at him, her flaming eyes like lasers set to ignite paper or vaporize gold. She is crying yet again, and wondering if she will ever stop.

"What price sanity?" she sobs inaudibly under her breath.

"What's that, honey?"

"Nothing!"

"NoBody"

WHEN I FIRST GOT SICK it felt like I was living with my whole body turned inside out, everywhere hurt raw; even my soul. The drugs keep everything contained now though – it's like wearing a really thick skintight rubber diving suit with a huge old-fashioned iron helmet and a tiny, fuzzy viewing glass. Now I don't feel anything except a vague floating sensation. I used to scream constantly at Everybody but now I can only do so inside my metal helmet where NoBody can hear me. Now I can only cry on the inside where NoBody can see me. When your stomach gets upset you first feel nauseous, then the sick feeling gets more intense; your stomach commences to heave and you enter into a cold sweat. You kneel and grip the toilet bowl, the blood rushes up and swells your head, you can't breathe, you hate throwing up but know you'll feel better afterwards; your body knows you have to do it. Being mentally ill is a bit like having your head stuck down the toilet except that you know that you can't vomit out what's making you sick so your body doesn't know what to do. I told the psychiatrist my brain is a buttonless washing machine on an eternal spin cycle, churning dirty laundry that can never be emptied or cleaned. "Why keep stuffing me with pills if it's never going to be clean?" I asked. He smiled and said, "to stop you pulling the plug out." I reckon that's the first law of psychiatry – always keep your patients connected to the mains.

"Stillborn" is a queerky conception. How can you still be born after you die? Or is it just called that because you are dead still when you come out? A woman's body still forces her to do it. "Lost" is another bizurrd word – Have you lost your mind? – If I could only remember where I left it. I met a woman called Janice once who lost her child, not in the mall or the park though, no, more prosaic, in her own house. She was in her early thirties and had been trying to have a kid for a few years until a "miracle son" arrived. How she worshipped that baby, morning, noon and night, twenty-four seven! She used always stroke his soft little pink face when whispering "nighty night" to him in his sleepycot. Then one special morning she went to rouse him but his cherubby cheeks were hard and mottled blue.

"The coldest thing I ever touched," she sobbed. "I stood there paralyzed, mouth wide open but couldn't make a sound. Then I saw it stretching out in the corner of the cot – my ginger cat, flexing his front claws and sticking his tail straight up. He stared right at me, grinning like a Cheshire, opened his mouth wide, curled up his tongue and yawned a triumphant "Miaow". I screamed and screamed. I just knew he'd done it. "Oh my poor blue breathless boy! Oh my wicked jealous puss!"

The second law of psychiatry states that healing words mend broken minds and cost less than drugs. Talk is cheap; writing prescriptions more expensive, but poetry is pure gold; least said soonest mended as Everybody says. So I wrote Janice a poem to make her feel better, to prove I was human too and knew exactly how she felt and why she did it. Why she hung that ginger cat's body on an oak tree like old Absalom. I was going to title it "Schrodinger" because words have an uncertainty principle too. Just like subatomic particles they resonate and NoBody can determine accurately where they are going or precisely what they mean. So I made a quantum leap of faith and decided to name the poem . . .

Animus

You never gave it back cat
You never gave it back

Though I buttered your paws
And fed you with cream
You robbed my baby's breath cat
You stole his milky breath

O I know how you feel puss
I know how you feel
I know exactly how you feel!
As I watch you hiss and claw
At the bottom of a clear
Plastic bag.

"What does 'animus' mean?" she asked.

"It means hatred; it derives from the Latin for 'spirit' or 'breath of life'," I answered. "You've hit the rusty nail inside my head," she groaned. "I'm suffocating, gasping for air, though I have all the oxygen I need. I simply can't breathe out any more, I have forgotten how to do it – I must remember quick otherwise I'll pop."

I saw a girl who went pop once. She really liked poetry too but only to hurt rather than heal. She set up a tripod and filmed herself reciting that Larkin poem – "This Be the Verse." The one that starts with "They fuck you up, your Mum and Dad" and ends with "and don't have any kids yourself." Then she leered straight into the camera and sucked a nine millimetre bullet clean out of the barrel of her Daddy's handgun. Everybody at the funeral thought what she did was tragic but obscene. I mean blowing your mind out like that is not the same as blowing a candle out is it? NoBody thought that girl made a valid point-blank. She formulated her Endlösung and vernichted herself. Bit the bullet and disconnected herself from the mains. Wearing an iron helmet stops you from doing things like that.

The third law of psychiatry states that the brain is a minedfield. You tread on one thought and another one blows up somewhere else. Everybody just marches straight across hoping to avoid triggering any thoughtbombs that require too much conscious effort to defuse. It's safer travelling in a straight line, minimizes detonations, but I'm always setting off cerebral ordnance and never getting to the far side because of their parabollixed trajectories. Memories are tyrants – once you put them in power they can never ever be deposed, no matter how often you try to jettison them or poison them with chemicals. Mental control is a ludicrazy notion; I mean if I ask you not to imagine an elephant; don't think of its thick grey skin; its long trunk and floppy ears; not to visualize its huge body, ivory tusks and cylindrical legs.

Can you really avoid conjuring up that image in the eye of your mind? I read an account once of a British athlete who attended the opening ceremony of the 1936 Berlin Olympics. "Those Nazis really knew how to put on a great show," he commented.

"They switched off all the stadium lights after sundown but every one of the thousands of spectators had a lit candle in their left hand. There was an eerie silence at first in the summer breeze; then I heard a noise like a susurrating sea rising up all around me. The noise got louder and louder until it reached a crescendo; it was hypnotic, mesmeric – Everybody chanting the same refrain over and over. Everybody saluting with their right arms angled javelin straight at exactly forty-five degrees. *Sieg Heil! Sieg Heil! Sieg Heil* they roared in unison. I swear," he confessed, "I had to clench my teeth and shove both my hands into my pockets not to join in with them." Now that is awesome power, to get people to become sheeple, to think and act exactly the same like a flock of klutzes. Everybody knows exactly how, when and what to say and do without even knowing why. Rituals make life more comfortable, they carve nice straight lines through the mindfield. Here Comes Everybody striding straight and true, not looking left nor right and threatening NoBody.

The fourth law of psychiatry states that the fine line between genius and insanity is exactly the same width as the line dividing divinity and humanity.

Almost Everybody believes in God; so did I before I became mentally ill. When I was little I talked with Him most all the time. Sometimes I hurt Him but I wasn't allowed apologize personally; I had to go to confession. Teacher said confession was like a phone call to God to tell him you were sorry for your sins, except you had to use the operator – only the priest could speak directly with Jesus. Kneeling in the confessional box was like waiting to get sick in the toilet bowl and vomit out your sins. But it was dark, sealed in a coffin waiting . . . waiting for the wooden board to grate back and make my heart jump and my teeth grind. You couldn't see the priest, only hear him rasping and see the white square of his collar peering at you like a little square white eye in the gloom, examining your soul. Even though I was scared, I knew all the words I had to say and what exactly I had to do, my sins were always the same. Penance was just like getting the laundry cleaned, same clothes; same stains once a month. I think "grace" was the name on the soap powder they used.

Then one day the priest asked me had I any "bad thoughts". He explained they were impure and a mortal offence against God. I reckoned I could spend my entire lifetime sitting in a rocking chair; not lifting a finger and orchestrating a whole repertoire of bad thoughts that would damn my soul to hell for eternity. Eventually I informed god that he could go to hell himself with his dogmatic Dominicans steeled in cold Aquinas, squaring circles with their canons.

But god still exists inside me, lurking in my sub-conscious mind where he was born; a Santa Claus for grown-ups. I still shove my hands in my pockets when passing a church in case I accidentally bless myself;

like one of Pavlov's dogs salivating just because a bell tinkles. And I'm not afraid of dying any more; you'll feel just the same a zillion years after you die as you did a zillion years before you were born.

Ulysses is a great big dirty book that Everybody has heard of and NoBody has read. Everybody gives up as soon as they start and think it's usyless. NoBody thinks it is bloomin' deadaly. It describes two guys named Leopold and Stephen and every single thing they thought and experienced during one day in Dublin. Joyce was a genius because it took him less than one thousand pages to write it. The book is fall of interesting words like: concupiscence; hypospadias; thaumaturgy and metempsychosis. Met Him Pike Hoses is Double Dutch from the Gobbledy Greek via the Deceased Latin for the transmigration of the soul into a new body. I guess it's like having everything you have ever thought and experienced, all those images and emotions captured on one holo-disc; ejected and re-inserted into a brand new machine when the old model packs up. Wouldn't it be phenomenal if the mind could be just like that? A lifeworth's sensorium stored and accessible at the flick of a pre-conscious switch. The unconscious would be deleted, the conquest of memory achieved. *Ego Invicta* after titanic evolutionary struggle. The contents of the brain reduced to a little mega-core chip that can be read and analyzed. Shrinks would become software engineers, re-programming rogue neural networks, painlessly deleting corrupt files in complete silence and without chemical application. A panacea for psychiatric anomalies. Everybody could be hooked into a giant quantum computerized mental matrix monitored by the state to maintain and preserve orthodoxy. NoBody would be mentally ill on the royal road to Utopia in excelsis! No idyll freudened yung mynds adled with poxy toxydoxy.

Words can look alike but mean completely different; laughter and slaughter; womb and tomb; cancer and dancer; marital and martial;

scared and sacred; Santa and Satan. Just like a genetic sequence, one letter in the wrong order can spell dysaster. If I knew all the words in the dictionary, their denotations, connotations and nuances and could sequence certain words in a precise order; discovered the write literary formula; then I know I would be cured. My psychiatrist argues it's not as simple as just discoursing words, there are emotions as well. Emotions are really thoughts without words, you can't accurately describe them, you can only feel them. Most Everybody has them and makes them do crazy things without really knowing why. The language sort of disintegrates inside their heads. Love is a bit like that, the words fragment, get all dreamy and jabberwocky, but your body knows what to do and forces you to do it.

Got drunk with a girl one night and staggered her home falling fell into her kaleidoscopic brown eyes soft wet mouth savoring stale fagsbeer firmsoft milky cherrybreasts spitswopping oozymoist warm runnyhunny O honey honeysuckle honeysucculent breathsharing breathstop . . . Vidi . . . Vici . . . Veni seminal moment fed you with cream fellfouling fishsweat 'n' treacle dirty laundry softbreathe again bad thoughts Love you! Miaaaow!

PieSkytrist   SighHighTriste   SickHighaTree   SkyHighTree
SkyKiteWrist   CyclEyeTricks   PikeEyeTryst   SlyTheatricks
Scythetheeatrix . . . slay Proteus with verbalsword Catch twenty two Everybody agrees – stop thinking and you can't go insane.

The fifth law of psychiatry states that normality is defined as Everybody's consensus and NoBody's errors.

I dreamed my psychiatrist closes one eye and squints at me with the other wide open as he says: "We're letting you out today; how does that make you feel?"

"I feel like squeezing the universe into a ball and rolling it inside my head without having to wear an iron helmet to contain it all."

He laughs nervously. "I cannot stop you reading poetry but it's vital to keep taking the medication."

"Nonsense," I protest, "I am a god, transcendent and immanent within and beyond my own universe, patiently paring my finger nails, refining my body out of existence."

"It is a fine line between . . . "

I interrupt him, ". . . between divinity and humanity. Everybody knows it but NoBody is saying it. Demons, deities and demagogues – devious doppelgangsters all." I turn as I am just about to leave his office; he is still scrutinizing me suspiciously with a big round eye.

"Odysseus," I tell him, "got the Cyclops drunk in his cave and told him his name was NoBody. Then he blinded the creature with a fiery log. The Cyclops groped and wailed in his cave and searched frantically for Odysseus. All the other Cyclopes heard him from their own caves, Everybody was shouting, 'Who has hurt you? What creature has hurt you?'

"'NoBody has hurt me, NoBody has tricked me,' cried the Cyclops in response. So none of his friends came to help him. And Odysseus escapes across the wine-dark snotgreen sea and continues his poetic exploits."

Here is a poem that NoBody wrote.

I Universe

Zero is the perfect integer
Neither positive nor negative
It splits infinity in two

I am circle devoid circumference
All points of the compass
Apogee and perigee

Zenith and nadir
A fearful symmetry

I am atoms
I am quarks
Forged in the fiery crucibles
Of stellar hearths

I am love and I am hate
Destined to murder and create
To butcher innocents in my wake

Of Eden and Armageddon
Gog and Magog, Sodom and Gomorrah
Yearnings of yesteryear
And forebodings of the morrow

Of yin and yang
And zeit und sein
I am ten trillion cells in concert
Each stamped with life's design

I am dancing Lord Shiva
Come death destroyer of worlds
To swat the globe from orbit
And surrender to the stars
To shear the fabric of space-time
Collapsed into a great Black Hole

I am übermensch und untermensch
Am precocious wunderkind
Wailing tales of Ragnarok and Gotterdammerung

I am Leviathan and Behemoth
Am monster from the id
A unity of opposites
And instrument of God

I am Satan, I am Christ
I am this and so much more
For I am human, all too human
The meaning of the Earth

Joshua A. Andersson

The sirens wail all the time through the wandering suburban streets of Greater New York. Normally Kvellner wouldn't notice as he finishes reading Josh's "autobiography", but he can't help raising a rueful smile as he hears them and reflects on the author's mind. It is sailing treacherously between the Scylla and Charybdis of delirium and insanity and he now despairs of its salvation. He has submitted the text of "*NoBody*" to a specialist website, in order to conduct an exhaustive literary and psychological analysis. Quantum computers have evolved into an extremely powerful diagnostic tool in the theatre of general and psychiatric medicine. Modern doctors have come to rely almost exclusively on their superior speed and sheer quantity of technical information, in formulating accurate diagnoses. But Bo Kvellner is a practitioner of the old school, trusting his own human instincts first and cyber-analysis a distant second. He will *always* forge his *own* professional opinion first, to avoid the computer program result prejudicing his clinical diagnosis. Kvellner grimaces and nods knowingly at the screen in front of him while the analysis is flashed up. Their opinions concur. Kvellner removes his gold spectacles and lays them on his desk. He leans back in his chair, hands clasped behind his head, and takes a deep satisfying breath.

Exhaling gently, he ponders on how he is going to break the news to Jenny and Jack Andersson; and how he knows he is going to break their hearts. Eureka, he thinks – I have found it: I have found the ten per cent!

FIFTEEN

Jack drives his rented car around the grounds, searching fruit-lessly for a shady parking spot. He parks as close as possible to the main entrance of the retirement home, to minimize his exposure to the broiling, enervating heat. The constant buzzing and clicking of insects is akin to a demonic orchestra playing some frenzied atonal symphony, rejoicing in the Florida sunshine. He is welcomed at the front door by an obese, black nurse who talks incessantly. Jack is positive she must be from Zak Taylor's hometown, although he has never heard anybody drawl their words so fast.

"Oh, Mr Andersson, he was here yesterday . . . oh, my . . . oh, my," she says as she leads him down a corridor. "Can you *believe* it, Mr Andersson – Eli Roberts hisself come visitin' us.

"I shook the man's hand right over there," she gestures at nowhere in particular. "Oh, my, he has the softest hands and a most gentle manner. And isn't he the handsomest of men, Mr Andersson. And tall too; just as tall as good old Abe Lincoln he was . . . Oh, my. We wuz all so excited. Who'd have thought the professor here had such esteemed acquaintances, oh, my . . . I even got a picture took with the president. I swear I'm votin' GeoNova now 'til the day I die. . . . "

They pass through a dayroom; and the nurse presses her index fin-ger against her lips and signals *Jack* to stay quiet. He shudders as he scans the vacant faces of the elderly residents seated about the room. One man has his eyelids clenched tight. His facial features are frozen and his mouth petrified into an awe-filled O-shape. He appears so ancient it looks as if he has witnessed "Rapture" and is paralyzed on the threshold – terrified at the prospect of his impending drift into oblivion.

"Come now," the nurse whispers as they are leaving the dayroom, "the professor's room is just along here a little ways."

"Some of our residents here are over a hunderd you know," she continues. "Folks who can afford to live a lot longer now, don't you know." She stops outside a door at last and smiles. "Here we are, this is Professor Sol Weiseman's room. He has been *so* lookin' forward to your visit you know."

He frowns and thanks his garrulous guide but is relieved to see her waddle back down the corridor.

On opening the door gingerly, he spies his ninety-two-year-old interviewee propped up on his pillows, sporting a black bow tie and a freshly pressed, gleaming white shirt.

"Is that you, Jack Andersson? Is that really you?" The voice is hoarse.

"Yes, Professor."

The old man's face lights up. It is wan, craggy, and careworn, but with the bright eyes of a wonder-filled child.

"Let me shake the hand that is writing the official biography of my friend Eli Roberts."

Jack proffers a tentative hand, taken aback by the professor's enthusiastic welcome.

"You can tell a lot from a man's hand! The hand is the cutting edge of the mind. The softer the hand, the sharper the mind. Eli has a soft handshake as have you, but he is left-handed of course, he always *insists* on shaking with his left. Oh, you have no idea how happy I am today, after what Eli told me yesterday."

"What did he tell you, Professor?"

"Sol, please – just Sol is fine."

"Okay. *Sol* it is then."

"Names are *so* important, Jack. I was born just after the Second World War. Many of my relatives were killed in the Holocaust and my mother and father wanted to have lots of children. I was the eldest in a family of five boys and three girls. Not like today's crazy world of one child per married couple. The name Sol means 'sun', and I was always treated as the pioneering light of a new generation by my parents."

"So how did a pioneer like you end up being a global authority on mythology?"

The old man tugs at a few errant white bristles he missed while shaving.

"Well, my parents took me to visit Auschwitz once when I was a little kid. After that, I was always fascinated by how ordinary people could perpetrate such horrors; just wipe out innocent folks on an industrial scale. I think Hannah Arendt captured it well when she described it as the 'banality of evil'. It was just ordinary people killing other ordinary people, after all. That's why I became interested in mythology, because it is the stories that people carry around in their heads that make them behave the way they do."

"I don't understand what you mean exactly. I always thought of myths as just ancient stories that merely entertained or explained things. Most of them aren't even true anyways."

"Sure, sure, but you gotta remember that what's true is irrelevant. It's what the public perceives as truth is important." The professor nods sagely with a benign smile.

"Yeah, I suppose you're right. Truth is like beauty – in the eye of the beholder."

"Exactly, Jack. Take the case in point of the SS guards in the extermination camps; the same brutes who taunted the prisoners that they'd only ever escape through the chimneys. Those guys genuinely believed that they were of superior Aryan stock in comparison to their Jewish prisoners. The Nazi regime portrayed the Jews as vermin in their propaganda. Idealized the perfect German citizen as a racially pure Nordic type with blond hair and blue eyes. The German *Volk* led by their *Führer* had a destiny to fulfil – a *Reich* reigning for a thousand years. Does this vision not have some mythological under-tones? What do you think?"

"Well, I never quite figured it that way, Professor."

"Sure, I can understand. Nobody ever stops to really think about what they actually believe in, or what motivates them to behave as they do. Now, you take the great religions of the world. Now, there is mythology in modern action: beliefs predicated on 'ancient stories', as you refer to them."

"Is that why Roberts hates religion, because it's rooted in fantastical stories and been the cause of so many wars?"

"Mmmm . . . " the professor muses. "Be careful there, Jack! I think it might be simplistic to argue that Eli hates religion. You gotta remember that *any* difference between people is a potential source of conflict. It can be economic, cultural, racist, skin tone; anything really. The human brain may be a social organ but we humans are hard-wired to be rather tribal creatures."

"But surely, Sol, religion in particular has been a prime motive for conflict from the dawn of history?"

"Well, that's true."

The old man raises a hand as if conceding the point.

" . . . but you're forgetting the hammer."

"The hammer?"

"Yes, the hammer."

"I don't quite follow you . . . ?"

"The hammer was a wonderful invention; a great tool for man to create things. But remember it can also be a destructive weapon."

"What's your point, Professor?"

The old man tugs at his white bristles again. His tone is at once gentle and reassuring.

"Well, I suppose it's what purpose we *choose* to use the hammer for that's important. Isn't it?"

"Yeah, yeah . . . you're right I guess. . . . You're a clever man. You

142

know that?"

"Ah shucks, Jack! I'm old school," he shoots back with faux modesty.

Then he stops to pause for breath, and stares directly at Jack from under his bushy, white brows.

"I am going to ask you something horrible . . . something really horrible coming from an old Jew like me who lost so many of his ancestors in the Shoah, as we call it."

He stops again and props himself up against his pillows, as if to steel himself to pose the question.

"If we are all destined to live a life of eternal bliss in heaven, then what difference did it make when all those chosen people perished in the showers and the ovens, and the pitiless pits on the Russian front? What difference does it make if death on Earth is . . . accelerated, if we are going to live happily ever after anyways?"

Jack's eyes are wide with astonishment; he shakes his head and doesn't want to even contemplate an adequate response.

"I can't answer that question. It's just . . . "

Weiseman sinks his creaking frame back into his innumerable pillows with a slight groan.

"I have an answer. An answer born of many years of thought and bitter experience. I asked my father once where God was for the Jews in Auschwitz. He looked at me with rheumy eyes and placed both his hands on my shoulders as he spoke. 'Always remember, son, until your last breath; that God was with us as we walked into the showers. That God was with us as we breathed in the poison gas. And that God forgives even those that murdered my mother and my father.' It was the first and last time I ever saw my father weep. The answer to my question, is that only through death does our experience of life have any meaning. Only death defines our existence, and gives it a purpose."

The professor slowly shifts his body to one side with a painful gasp.

"Oh, this dying is such a boring business; at least it was until Eli's visit yesterday. I'm sorry; I digressed, didn't I?"

"Yes," Jack answers with a light chuckle.

"Oh," he says, raising his voice, "I have never been so scared yet so excited in my whole life. Eli told me all his plans on how he will change the world. And it is wonderful, Jack! Truly wonderful! Oh, that man is a genius."

The professor motions him forward and indicates to whisper something in his ear.

"Canada is going to become the fifty-first state of the United States and Greenland will be number fifty-two," he winks.

Jack stands back and looks disbelievingly at the old man.

"They'll be two mighty big states."

"It's true; it's all true. GeoNova has a few eco-colonies there already, and lots of wealthy Americans are beginning to migrate northwards to escape the ravages of global warming. I wanted to retire to the Florida Keys you know," he says wistfully. "To die beside the sea; the sea is full of memories you know. But I couldn't go there because the Keys are submerged half the time, with the rise in ocean levels. Such a tragedy – who would ever have imagined that mankind was capable of wrecking the whole planet without even resorting to nuclear weapons?" He pauses to catch his breath again.

"But Eli has it all calculated. He is going to save the world. I swear that man is going to save the world," he declares with a light clench of his fist.

"What about the Chinese?" ventures Jack. "Will they be on board?"

"Oh, sure!" exclaims the professor with a dismissive wave. "They will simply have to go along with his plans and stop pouring carbon dioxide into the atmosphere."

"Is that a fact," muses Jack aloud.

"You don't believe me, do you? But Eli is the power of modern myth incarnate. He is perhaps like Atlas the Titan holding the entire world on his shoulders."

"Or maybe like that other guy Camus wrote about; rolling a huge boulder up a hill all the time only to see it roll down again when he gets to the top."

"Sisyphus!" roars the professor with a hearty laugh that causes him to double over, convulsed with pain. "Oh, God! Oh, the pain!"

"Are you okay, Professor? Do you want me to get the nurse?"

"No! I'll be fine. Just give me a minute," he rasps. "Would you mind opening the window a little for me, please?"

Jack walks to the far side of the bed and half-opens the window.

Sol waits a couple of minutes before continuing, his breathing still a little laboured.

"Eli asked me to tell him a story yesterday. I'm a bit like the sea, I think – full of memories and myths, but I know my mind is so much more unfathomable than any ocean. Anyway, I related the story of the Salmon of Knowledge to him. Are you familiar with the legend?"

"No! Go on, Professor. If it's good enough for Eli Roberts, I'll listen to it."

"Well, it's an old Irish legend about a young boy named Fionn, whose father has been killed in battle by his enemies. They want to kill the boy too but he escapes and gains shelter with a kind poet named Finnegas, who lives beside a great river. The poet tells him of a mighty fish that swims in the river, and any man who eats it will gain perfect knowledge. So the poet, who has spent many years trying to catch this fish, eventually catches it one day and gives it to Fionn to put on the fire to cook, although the poet naturally wants to eat it himself. But the little boy touches the fish to check if it is cooked and burns his finger. He automatically sticks his finger in his mouth, and inadvertently becomes the first man to taste the Salmon of Knowledge and know all there is to know. Subsequently, Fionn grows up to be a great hero."

The professor pauses and clasps his hands together in satisfaction.

"Oh, Eli – Eli simply adored that story. I felt really proud to have told him that legend. He is going to be such a great hero himself so long as he has the stamina. Do you know the origin of the word 'stamina'?"

"I'm sorry, I don't know it."

"Well, in Greek mythology every human being has their thread of life woven by three women called the Fates. When a person's time comes, one of the women cuts the thread and they die. The Greeks imagined that the longer the filament, the longer that person would live. That thread was called the 'stamen', hence the word derived from it: 'stamina'."

"That's a fine story, Professor – I mean, Sol."

"Thank you, Jack. Unfortunately, my long thread is getting rather frayed. But really, I am privileged to have lasted this long with my memory intact. Did you see the other patients on your way in here?"

"Yes, I saw some of them in the dayroom."

"Alzheimer's is a horrible demise! The stories, the myths in our heads that sustain us all, slowly but surely wiped. What is a mind without the narrative of memories? Nothing but a three-pound hunk of meat."

Jack is nodding in agreement; he has been standing all this time but now edges to the bed and sits on it, regarding the old man with compassion.

"Forgive me, Sol, I didn't get much time to prepare for this interview as you weren't on my appointments schedule for another few months; you understand?"

"Of course. I totally understand," he says amicably in return.

"What exactly is your connection with Eli Roberts? How well do you really know him?"

"Well, to tell you the truth, I only ever met the man twice before yesterday. I have spent my academic life studying mythologies from

146

around the world. On first meeting him, I have to say he was one of only a few individuals I have ever met outside academic circles who deeply understood and appreciated the true importance of myth in moulding modern society. He asked me about Gaia, of course, which is the name the Greeks gave to their version of Mother Nature. Back in the late twentieth century a scientist named Lovelock theorized that planet Earth was literally a single living organism, which he named Gaia. There is of course an underlying unity to all living creatures; for example, all life is encoded with the same genetic alphabet of DNA; from humans to bacteria; even plants. It's wonderful really, when you think about it! I suppose Eli crafted a good picture to put in people's heads when he paralleled the Earth with the human body. A healthy individual's core body temperature is ninety eight point six degrees Fahrenheit – but if that figure goes up just a couple of degrees then you start feeling ill. Well, that is precisely what is happening our precious Earth all the time, and droughts, flooding, hurricanes and melting ice-caps are the geophysiological symptoms."

The professor suddenly stops and gazes at the foot of the bed, his eyes welling up with tears.

"Look at that, Jack! He raises a weary arm to point – isn't it beautiful, just beautiful?"

Jack turns to see a butterfly hovering about the bed, lightly flapping its iridescent wings and gracefully carving capers in the air in defiance of gravity.

"Oh, to think that humble creature has probably more life left in it than I do! But what are we? . . . what are we but mere mortals; *ephemeroi*, as the gods call us – mere creatures of a single day."

The old man breaks down and Jack pats him comfortingly on the shoulder.

"I am entitled to cry," he sobs.

"Of course, you are only human after all. Maybe you'd like to take a break."

"No it's just . . . "

A nurse bustles smartly into the room, wordlessly ushering Jack off the bed and away from the professor. She presses a small hand-held device into Sol's ear. A series of graphs are instantly updated on her medical iPad. She looks concerned as she lays her hand on his forehead and listens to his breathing.

"Ten more minutes, Sol," she whispers seriously.

"Is that all I have left to live, Nurse?" he jokes.

She arches a brow as she notices the butterfly dancing about the room and the half-opened window. With a deft movement of her hand, she tries to swat it with her iPad. She misses; stands up, swats and misses the evasive creature once more.

"Did you open that window, sir?" she raises her voice to Jack in frustration.

"I'm sorry I . . . "

His answer is interrupted by the sound of Sol chortling to himself.

"Would you look at that the both of you; isn't it beautiful?" he's saying.

Jack and the nurse turn and watch as the butterfly alights on Sol's chest, almost fluttering its wings in time with the ripples of the old man's laughter.

The nurse raises her hand and moves towards the professor to whoosh the insect away. But Jack darts across, reaches out and grabs the raised hand.

"Excuse me, sir!" she protests. "We have rules on hygiene in this establishment. Let go of my hand this instant!"

As if the butterfly can sense the waves of tension in the air, it suddenly ascends and floats capriciously out the open window. Jack releases his grip and glares back at the nurse.

"Five minutes, sir; or I swear I'm going to call security!"

Sol eyes Jack's puzzled expression and scowls as he watches the nurse march out of the room.

"Is the book going well for you, Jack?"

"It's going okay, Professor. But Eli is a hard man to get a clear picture of."

"It's not easy being an author. For a reader it is just a few days' experience at most. But a writer has to research, create and craft every single word. How much more intense of an experience is that compared to the reader's?"

"You have written some books yourself by the sound of it?"

"Many; just academic texts though. But this book of yours is going to be a great book about a great hero in Eli Roberts. Books can change the world. I'll tell Karl Marx myself if I meet him after I die."

He laughs to himself at the prospect of his imminent death.

"The pen really is mightier than the sword, Jack. Which reminds me," he says with a lazy snap of his fingers: "Eli asked me to give you something."

He slowly reaches over to his bedside locker and lifts out a small black box.

"Take it."

"What is it, Sol?"

"I don't know exactly, but Eli told me to tell you to put it away safely and only use it to write the last chapter of his biography."

Jack approaches him hesitantly and gently takes the box from his grasp. He opens it to reveal a solid gold pen.

"Oh, that is a really wonderful gift. It's a gold pen, Sol . . . here, look."

The old man peers down and his eyes glaze over as he admires it.

"God be with the times that great literature was once written with such fine instruments, and not clicking mice or finger-taps on screens. Be proud of it and use it well."

"I will, Sol."

"Promise me it will be a great book, Jack!"

"I promise."

They hear the sound of approaching footsteps echoing along the corridor.

"Goodbye, Sol; thank you. I really enjoyed your stories."

"I'm glad you liked them," he says, taking Jack's right hand. "Remember that old Chinese proverb: every man should have a son, plant a tree and write a book."

The door opens and the nurse enters once again with her arms folded.

"Five minutes are up, sir!"

Jack gazes at the dying professor one last time before he bends over and whispers in his ear.

"I have two done already. Only one remains."

Jack can hear Sol's voice ringing down the length of the corridor as he walks out.

"Make sure it's a great one, Jack! Make sure it's a great one!"

Jack sits behind the wheel of his rented car and orders the voice-activated ignition to start up. He decides to admire his new gold pen afresh in the sunlight, and removes it carefully from its black presentation box. He feels the solid weight of its gold shaft as it glints in the Florida sun. There is something lightly engraved upon it, and he adjusts the angle of his hold to aid his examination of the pen. He squints and readjusts to make certain he has correctly read a word that is barely legible—

"*STEELMAN*"

SIXTEEN

KVELLNER IS STANDING at the door of his secretary's office as he greets Jenny and Josh.

"Was your husband not able to make this appointment, Mrs Andersson?"

"No, I'm very sorry, Doctor; he had to fly to Florida in a hurry," she says, her voice thick with disapproval.

"Mmm . . . that is unfortunate." He sounds even more grave than usual. "Would you mind waiting in Miss Chang's office for a little while, as I need to use the waiting-bubble for Josh's session today?"

"Of course, Doctor. He will like that for a change."

"I'll notify Miss Chang when we're done in there. We will finish a little early today, as I need some extra time to speak with you afterwards, okay?"

"Sure," she half-smiles; laying a hand on her son's back to urge him forward towards the waiting-bubble.

"Why are we in the sphere so, Bo?"

"I want to show you some colours, shapes, numbers and materials, and ask you questions about them, Josh."

"I'm not a first-grade student any more, Doc."

"I know that, but I am hoping you will enjoy it anyway."

"I prefer words."

"I know, Josh; now I am going to play the soothing music you like so you can relax."

The next quarter of an hour he spends indulging Josh with his customary relaxation routine.

The boy opens his eyes at last and Kvellner tells him he is going to alter the colour of the illumination on the inner surface of the sphere.

He calls out the colour "red", and immediately they are bathed in a deep, red glow. Josh tenses his body as his eyes adjust to the transformation from standard white light.

"What picture is in your head when you see the colour red, Josh?"

"Blood."

Kvellner calls out "green" and the lighting is again transformed.

"Chlorophyll," Josh answers without pausing.

One by one, the colours are called out with increasing pace to minimize the boy's response time.

"Yellow."

"Sun."

"Blue."

"Earth."

"White."

"Safe."

"Brown."

"Soiled."

"Black."

Instantly they are plunged into total darkness and Josh screams at the top of his voice: "*Nobody!*"

"White! . . . computer . . . white!" orders Kvellner, clamping his palms instinctively against his ears to protect them from the penetrating scream as it reverberates around the confined space.

"I am sorry; that was totally my fault. It was not my intention to frighten you."

The boy stares back impassively at him as if the incident had never occurred.

"I should have known you detest black, as it is the colour of darkness. It was careless of me."

"But I like black, Doc."

"You do?"

"Yes."

"Why do you like the colour black?"

"Because it is the colour of Nobody. It is my own colour. But it is only my second favourite, Doc."

"What is your favourite colour then?"

"Orange."

"Would you like me to change the lighting now from white to orange?"

"Yes."

Kvellner calls out the word and the sphere quickly radiates with a vibrant tangerine hue.

"Why do you like this particular colour?"

"Huitzilopochtli, Doc."

"Oh," he answers, searching in vain for the overhead monitor that instantly explains any obscure references. "What exactly is that?"

"Huitzilopochtli was the sun-god of the Aztecs. They believed the sun would die unless it was regularly filled with human blood, so they sacrificed a lot of victims to keep him happy. Orange is a mixture of red and yellow, so I guess the sun must burn that colour when it fills up with blood. You seen the movie *Apocalypto*, Doc?"

"Yes, an old Mel Gibson movie; I saw it once a long time ago." He frowns as he recalls it. "The scenes of human sacrifice were a little gruesome for my tastes though."

"Oh no, Bo! – blood doesn't taste gruesome; it tastes of salt. It seeps into the ground after all the great wars and becomes the salt of the earth. Orange is a life-and-death colour; that's why the leaves turn orange between summer and winter."

"Why is the colour white safe for you, Josh?"

"White is all colours of the spectrum unified. It's not a real colour, but you need it to see everything. I feel safe when I see everything."

"Okay, I want to show you three shapes, and I would like you to tell me what images or thoughts come into your head first when you view them."

Kvellner calls out the word "square" and a diagram flashes up right in front of Josh.

"Aztecs," he says. "They never invented a wheel, and a square is just a four-cornered wheel, after all."

"Circle."

"Rembrandt, safe."

"The artist?" queries a mystified Kvellner.

"Yes, Doc. He was the only painter in history who could draw a perfect circle freehand. I like spheres; they are like a bunch of eternal circles spun by a gyroscope. Spheres are so safe; the strongest shape in nature . . . like a womb."

"Triangle."

The word scarcely has time to echo before Josh is on his feet, his mouth wide open with awe as he gazes at the pyramidal shape of the diagram opposite. He shuffles awkwardly towards the image of the triangle, genuflects and makes the Sign of the Cross with his left hand. Then he starts to rock back and forth on his haunches, clasping his hands in prayer and raising his eyes aloft in supplication. Kvellner, startled, leans back quickly in his chair, the better to observe the spectacle.

"Tell me about the triangle, Josh?"

No answer is forthcoming, so he repeats the question. There is still no answer, so he rises from his chair, goes over and taps the boy lightly on the shoulder.

Josh seems to suddenly snap out of a trance-like state and points at the image of the triangle as he solemnly intones: "The omniscient eye of God opens on the tip of an arrow in flight."

"What do you mean?"

"Only from the very top of the pyramid can you see all sides at once. Oooh . . . it is so sharp, so acute, Doc. That view can kill a man. A single glance from God and you might die or even get blinded. It is a wowerful sight."

154

"Why do you believe that?"

"I am Leviathan and Behemoth / Am monster from the id / a unity of opposites / and instrument of God," he chants in a mechanical tone.

"That is a verse from your poem *I Universe*, is it not?"

"I didn't write that poem."

"Well, who wrote the poem then?"

"Nobody wrote it."

Kvellner endeavours to suppress an ironic smile and requests the sphere's computer to display a sequence of numbers from one to ten.

"What is your favourite digit, Josh?"

"My left index finger."

"Sorry. . . of the digits shown on the surface of the sphere," he calmly corrects himself.

"I have two co-favourite numbers, but neither of them is here."

"What are the two numbers?"

"Infinity, which is a mathematical symbol that looks like an eight lying down stretched out – and zero of course."

"Why zero, what is special about it?"

"J0sh has only a single zero in it; so does G0d. But 'N0b0dy' has two zeroes in it, which means it has double the power. Zero and Infinity are like two sides of the same mirror, Doc."

"Okay, Josh, I want to finish our session fifteen minutes early today so I can spend a little more time than usual talking with your mother."

"Five minutes and forty seconds left so, Bo!"

Kvellner bends down and pulls out from under his chair a small plastic tray. There is an assortment of materials inset into it in neat squares. He approaches the boy, asks him to close his eyes and touch each of the materials in turn, describing any thoughts or images that come to him as he does so.

"Glass . . . smooth perfection like a mirror. Sandpaper . . . ouch! Erodes the pyramids. Carpet . . . burned my knees when I was a baby. Fur . . . is alive; don't pet it, Doc, only I can rub it up the right way.

Tactile test terminated; it is four forty-five exactly, Bo!"

"Thank you, Josh, for reminding me."

For once Josh's appealing green eyes directly meet Kvellner's as he poses a question.

"Are you going to tell my mother I'm a moonatic?"

Kvellner breaks his gaze and pretends he doesn't hear the question. Steps out of the waiting-bubble and gestures to Miss Chang.

Jenny leans forward anxiously in her chair as Kvellner is readying to speak from behind his desk. She can just make out a copy of Josh's essay displayed on a screen that is slightly angled away from her. Kvellner puts on his gold-rimmed spectacles, folds his hands and tightens his lips in a wincing manner as he begins.

"Mrs Andersson, allow me to begin by expressing my disappointment that your husband was unable to make this appointment. In fact I would really prefer to have this discussion with the both of you simultaneously. I could arrange another appointment to accommodate your husband if you so desire?"

"No, Doctor, Jack is really tied up with this project he is working on. His schedule is unreliable; he might have to fly anywhere at a moment's notice."

"That is unfortunate."

He pauses and closes his eyes briefly before continuing somewhat reluctantly.

"Mrs Andersson, you will find what I am about to tell you rather difficult. You are not going to absorb all the information I am going to give you; therefore I recommend we record this discussion. I think it would also be a good idea as you can take the recorded conversation home with you and share it with your husband. Is that okay with you?"

She nods her consent and exhales sharply as she does so.

"I have subjected Josh's autobiography to extensive critical analysis, employing a variety of computer-aided models, allied with my years of clinical experience and professional intuition. It has greatly assisted in clarifying my opinion of your son's condition and I would like to express my personal gratitude to you in obtaining it for me."

"Okay, Doctor."

"Josh has a precocious intellect, a truly extraordinary linguistic virtuosity, even for a child presenting with Asperger's Syndrome. His mind is so powerful that he imagines that he is an instrument of God. This idea is of course delusional, but perfectly rational in the context of highly developed, artistically creative minds. I am reminded of the composer Handel, who reputedly claimed to have seen the face of God after writing his famous 'Hallelujah Chorus'. What I am trying to say is that some people are so exceptionally gifted that they genuinely believe their inspiration is somehow divinely endowed; a gift from God, if you will. And to be honest with you, Josh's work, despite its complexity and multiple allusions, is entirely coherent and intelligible. But ultimately the content, particularly of his poem *I Universe*, is indicative of a conflicted internal dynamic process."

"I don't understand exactly what you are telling me, Doctor."

He raises both palms in a calming gesture.

"Please, just bear with me until I am done, okay?"

"Sure."

"To my mind, it is not a coincidence that Josh is obsessed with the works of the author James Joyce. Indeed I've read psychological profiles of him, which suggest he may possibly have even suffered with Asperger's Syndrome himself."

Jenny raises her eyebrows and brightens fleetingly.

"But Joyce was a tortured individual. He spent seventeen years crafting his final book named *Finnegans Wake*. A book that is practically impenetrable, and written in an ethereal dream-like language that almost defies comprehension. The theory has been advanced that Joyce had such a capacious intellect that he had the ability to consciously connect with his own subconscious mind. However, this almost unique ability came with a price-tag."

Kvellner pauses for breath and peers over the rims of his spectacles.

"The reason it took Joyce so long to complete *Finnegans Wake* was that the writing process itself was his only means of avoiding psychosis, Mrs Andersson."

Jenny claps her hand to her forehead and rubs her palm across its deepening furrows.

"Are you telling me, Doctor, that Josh is becoming psychotic?"

"Not exactly."

"You mean there's something else as well?"

"Yes . . . I suspect there is," he answers very deliberately.

"Oh, my God!"

"Mrs Andersson, it is impossible at this relatively early stage of Josh's life to proffer a definitive diagnosis. But, having spent a number of sessions with him, and more conclusively, based on the evidence of his story *Nobody*, I am as confident as I can be that your son is presenting with a pro-dromal phase of schizophrenia."

A numbing sensation slowly rises from the tips of Jenny's toes until her entire body feels like a cold lump of lead.

"Oh, my God! Schizophrenia. . . . How is that even *possible* for a kid?"

"Unfortunately, there is a slightly elevated risk of Asperger's patients progressing to develop schizophrenia."

"But what about the ten per cent, Doctor; the IQ tests?"

"It is quite obvious that Josh accessed a variety of IQ tests on-line and simply memorized all the answers. That is how he scored a consistent ninety per cent across the board."

"So is that the ten per cent – schizophrenia?"

"Yes, I am inclined to think so."

Jenny closes her eyes and her lower lip begins to quiver.

"But how can you be sure, Doctor, that it might not be something else . . . there just has to be something else! I feel it in here," she says, with her trembling hands clutching her breast.

Kvellner shuts his own eyes and shakes his head despondently.

"I am really sorry, but Josh is clearly displaying delusional tendencies. To some extent, he recognizes a duality within his own psyche when he tellingly refers to himself as 'a unity of opposites'. Again, I am sorry; this must feel like a bereavement, a sense of loss for you. But there are a number of support groups, which you might find beneficial and perhaps even counselling for yourself and your husband."

"I promised myself I wouldn't cry today, no matter what," she says tearfully. "Please tell me my boy has a future, Dr Kvellner."

"Of course he has a future," he says, sliding a convenient box of tissues across the desk towards her.

"With the aid of modern pharmaceuticals, schizophrenia is a much less intractable condition than heretofore. His future is . . . well, somewhat more challenging than we originally envisaged or— "

"Hoped for," she cuts in dejectedly. "Are you finished with Josh now, Doctor?"

"Well, I am reasonably satisfied with my diagnosis and I can continue to treat your son in the long term if you so desire. But I certainly won't need to see him on the current fortnightly basis, you understand."

"I understand perfectly."

"Mrs Andersson, could you please hold up your cell phone for me so I can transmit our recorded conversation to it from my computer. As you can appreciate with Josh, it is a more secure device than your home computer."

She limply raises her left arm and angles it towards the brand new computer on the desk.

A shaft of amber light pulses; pairs up with and instantaneously transmits the information to her wrist-mounted cell. Kvellner stands up and approaches her with his right hand extended and a slight swagger to his gait.

"Thank you," he says, shaking Jenny's hand and helping her up from her chair with two consolatory taps on her elbow. She looks at him, her frightened eyes peering at him from behind a mess of damp tissues.

"Didn't Joyce have a daughter with schizophrenia, Doctor? I remember Jack mentioning it."

"Yes, Lucia was her name."

"Didn't she die in a mental institution?"

"That was a long time ago, Mrs Andersson; psychiatry has made tremendous advances since," he says, straining a semi-smile.

Josh and Miss Chang are both immersed in a glaring, burned-orange haze that causes Jenny to momentarily recoil as she walks into the waiting-bubble. There is a diagram of a triangle displayed once again on its inner surface. Josh is stretching up and stroking its apex with the tip of his left index finger. "Oh, so sharp, so acute," he is saying. He can hear his mother behind him, sniffling above the sound of her rustling Kleenex.

"The flavour of the ocean is contained within a single drop. The flavour of the mind is contained within a single tear. Mother's mind is all salty today." He doesn't even turn to look at her as he articulates the words.

SEVENTEEN

JACK TRUNDLES IN THE FRONT DOOR of his house just after eight a.m., his suitcase in tow. He calls out Jenny's name three times and is surprised not to get an answer. Since his interview with Sol Weiseman he has called her numerous times but failed to contact her directly and just left increasingly anxious messages instead. He searches the bedrooms upstairs first, and finds all the beds in apple-pie order. His heart begins to pound as he runs back downstairs and looks into the sitting-room and then the kitchen. Everything is curiously spick and span in an unnerving way; he cannot remember the house ever being so neat and tidy. A shadow flits through the rays of the morning sun as they flood across the spacious walled garden and penetrate the rear window of the kitchen. Jack rushes towards it, jerks back the curtain and squints at a grotesque scene. Josh is wearing his cyber-helmet and gambolling blindly around the rectangular perimeter of the lawn, intermittently raising his visor to avoid straying into the flower-beds. Jenny is on her knees, beneath the canopy of a single white oak tree that dominates the centre of the lawn. She is hunched over, carefully cutting a patch of grass with a pair of tiny silver scissors that gleam in the sunlight. Jack feels his heart sinking as he goes out into the garden and steps warily on the clay as he approaches her.

"Hi, honey," he says in a quiet voice.

She swivels to face him, her eyes flashing wildly like those of a startled animal. She stands up and places both gloved hands on her hips, arching her back in a defiant stance as she glares back at him. Suddenly, she peels back the glove on her left hand, removes her wrist-bound cell and tosses it towards her husband.

"Everything you need to know is recorded on that. You'll find the file located under 'Kvellner interview', *if* you're interested!"

Then she turns away, bends down, studies the patch of grass and recommences her meticulous blade-work.

Jack slumps into the chair in his study and stares at the screen in front of him, allowing CASS to identi-scan one of his irises.

"Morning, Jack!" she says cheerily

"Morning, CASS," he replies wearily. "I want you to locate and play an audio recording filed 'Kvellner Interview' from Jenny's cell, please. For information security reasons please do not store this file in your memory bank; request audio-play only. Okay?"

"Okay, Jack. I have scanned the requested device, located the file, and will commence audio on your instruction."

"I am ready, thank you."

Jack closes his eyes as he listens to Kvellner's measured tones, interspersed with Jenny's increasingly audible weeping as it concludes.

"CASS, what is the definition of a pro-dromal phase of schizophrenia?"

"It is defined as the incipient or initial period of schizophrenia. Do you want me to compile a comprehensive list of symptoms for this illness?"

He runs both hands through his hair and squeezes the back of his head as he answers "no".

"Fuck it! Fuck it! Fuck it!" he repeats unconsciously.

"Would you like me to connect you to a pornographic site of your choice?"

"Power off," he snarls, and CASS's pretty face dissolves into the grey screen.

He shuts his eyes again. He didn't sleep a wink on the return flight from Florida and his body aches with fatigue, but his racing brain denies him sleep. He reflects on the worst day of his life, almost thirteen years ago. Jenny had a history of miscarriages prior to the birth of their only son, delivered through miraculous advances in modern gynaecology. Jack remembers the baby's very first cry in the labour ward; while the obstetrician and all the nurses broke into spontaneous applause to welcome the new arrival.

The tiny body looked so fragile, yet the infant sucked so hard when placed against Jenny's breast for the first time that Jack knew it would thrive. Jenny seized his hand and squeezed it as she said: "It was all worth it, Jack! I swear to God it was all worth it, just for this moment." He felt a dam burst from behind his eyes, kissed her on the forehead and thanked God for having answered their prayers.

Jenny had revelled in her new maternal role. She breezed through regular breast-feeding, nappy-changing routines and sleepless nights with joyous enthusiasm. When the baby was ten months old, however, Jenny's mother became terminally ill. She volunteered to look after her mother at home in her final months, so Jack and Jenny moved from their crummy apartment to their present home. Jack was apprehensive about the transition but his wife cajoled him – "There is a lovely garden for him to play in at the rear," she'd said invitingly.

Jack opens his eyes and wishes he could erase the memories as they roll relentlessly like a cinematic juggernaut. Jenny's mother insisted on erecting and decorating a Christmas tree that year, even though she was painfully aware it was to be her last. "Life goes on" was her motto as she adorned the interior of the house with sprigs of berried holly and strings of scintillating tinsel. Her grandson's cot lay at the foot of his parents' bed in an upstairs room. Jenny liked to drift to sleep while listening to the soft music of his breathing as it whistled through his tiny nostrils. It was still dark when she awoke on Christmas morning and clambered out from under the duvet. She crept to the foot of the bed and smiled as she knelt over the cot and gazed at the dim outline of her baby's face.

Her knuckle brushed tenderly against . . . a stone-cold marble cheek.

Instinctively she reached down, picked him up and pressed his little mouth to her ear. But the only sound she heard was that of her own scream. Jack awoke and wrenched the curtains from their rails, permitting a nascent fiery dawn to invade the room.

"Oh, Jesus, he's dead. Sweet Jesus!" she wailed over and over, cradling the baby's head as she paced frantically to and fro. Jack caught one glimpse of his son's rigid blue cheeks and grabbed his cell to call 911. Two paramedics arrived within ten minutes; Jack raced ahead of them up the stairs to guide them. They found Jenny, slouched on the floor in one corner of the room, rocking the stiffening corpse of her baby boy beneath her tousled blonde hair. She had ripped off her bra and clasped his lifeless lips against her breast. The paramedics dropped their equipment with a dull thud, stopped, looked at one another and shook their heads in dismay.

Jenny refused to countenance his body being interred in the cemetery. She sought and gained her mother's consent to bury him under the white oak tree in the garden. Beneath its spreading vermilion and orange foliage Jack dug out a neat grave with a small shovel.

Four people stood around that black abyss on the morning of the funeral, gazing into its depths through a fine drizzle of rain. Jenny and her dying mother clung to one another, supported only by the collective weight of their grief. An elderly priest, an old family friend, officiated at the ceremony. His voice quavered as he intoned the liturgies; his arthritic fingers struggled to separate the dampening pages of his Bible as he read. The old cleric nodded at last to signal Jack he was finished speaking. Each took an end of the tiny, snow-white coffin, knelt down and lowered it reverently into the moist earth. Jenny moaned inconsolably as Jack lay on the wet grass, reached down and placed a single red rose on the lid. When he stood up, he stooped and grabbed a fistful of clay, raising his hand and motioning to fire the sod into the grave with pure rage. But the clay sifted through his fingers and drizzled, soft as the rain itself, on the coffin below. He so wanted to tell the priest that God was merely a Santa Claus for adults, but simply asked the old man "Why?" "Some questions defy answers, only faith and compassion for one another enable us to endure," he responded, with a paternal squeeze of Jack's shoulder as he departed. A few weeks later, a small white marble cross was delivered. Jack laid it flat on his son's grave and pressed it down firmly to inset it into the still-fresh clay. He wept as he read the inscription: *"Here lies Christopher Andersson. Died on his first birthday 12-25-2026."*

The bearded Iraqi raises his eyes to the clear blue sky and seems to part the heavens with his cry, *"Allahu akhbar! . . . Allahu akhbar!"* A seething mass of wounded humanity envelops him as it surges towards the hospital entrance. The echoes of his desperate entreaties are drowned in a wail of ambulance sirens and staccato cracks of gunfire. The camera seems to shudder as it pans away and the director's voice segues into Jack's own as he orders, "Stop rolling . . . just stop!" He awakes with a startled gasp in the gloom of his tiny study and wishes it was all just a nightmare.

He gets up from his armchair and wanders back again through the empty house to the rear window of the kitchen. As he looks out, Jenny is still carefully cutting away at the same patch of grass with her tiny scissors. Josh is sitting, slumped against the base of the oak tree with the visor of his cyber-helmet lowered, his mouth agape and his head swinging from side to side as if he's chanting to himself. Jack glances at an old-fashioned wall-clock ticking above the kitchen door – it reads five after ten in Roman numerals. He lumbers upstairs and collapses onto his bed with a groan as the memories overwhelm his weary mind.

After Christopher died, Jenny sank into a deep depression. Her therapist recommended she spend as much time as possible out of doors in the sunshine; gardening has proven therapeutic value, she'd advised. So Jenny spent spring, summer and autumn "ploughing my new demesne" as she put it – Digging, raking and weeding; planting new flowers; tending the lawn and manicuring the tufts of fresh grass as they sprouted around the white marble cross. By August her late mother's neglected flower-beds were transformed into a riotous blaze of colour. Even when State water–use restrictions were introduced that same month, Jenny purchased gallons of bottled drinking water and poured them liberally on the browning lawn and parched flower-beds. Jenny's mood seemed to improve in tandem with the garden as it blossomed.

"It's perfect, honey," Jack said, strolling around the perimeter of the lawn one day; "it's just like one of those Impressionist paintings, a Monet or something." She leaned forward with one foot mounted on a spade and grinned back at him. "There is only one thing missing here, Jack!" she said, surveying all her handiwork with a lazy sweep of her eyes.

"I know, honey. I know. But we are goin' to fix that soon!" he winked with a broad smile.

Jack and Jenny held hands as they sat in a chic Manhattan agency, listening intently to the attorney's every word. "People make mistakes, Mr and Mrs Andersson, and in this country a woman has two choices if she becomes pregnant but already has an existing child – abortion or adoption. Either way, business is booming on both fronts. But do not be under any illusions; if you want a son with superior grade genetic quality – it will cost!"

"My mother passed away recently and I was the sole beneficiary," said Jenny excitedly. Jack glowered at her naivety, but the adoption attorney simply shrugged indifferently before continuing.

"Every one of this agency's prospective adoptees is subject to comprehensive and extensive genetic screening. You must understand, however, that while certain medical conditions such as Huntingdon's disease or cystic fibrosis, for example, can be definitively ruled out, we can only furnish you with statistical analysis of the probability of the child subsequently developing major illness. Similarly, certain behavioural and intellectual traits can be only loosely determined. The human genome is not a geological survey map but medical research and quantum computers do provide us with a better compass."

Jack and Jenny held hands again in an adjoining office as the genetic analyst sifted through their documentation. She stopped, arched her brows, looked up and nodded at them as she examined a letter of recommendation from the Catholic cardinal of New York. She spent a few more minutes poring over their file then turned to her computer screen and nodded sagely before she spoke.

"There is a baby boy, due early November. He will have sallow skin, brown hair, green eyes and an ectomorphic somatotype . . . that is to say, he will be of slim build," she clarified with a smile. "His parents' social background is categorized as 'superior' and I have to admit this boy has a very handsome genome, Mr and Mrs Andersson," she added with a skittish grin.

"Do you want to bid or buy, Mrs Andersson?" asked the attorney.

"What is the cost to secure adoption of this particular boy?" said Jack.

The attorney leaned back but kept his eyes trained on Jenny.

"A boy like this . . . mmm . . . we know he is going to be beautiful before he is even born. And with his family background and superior type genome, well, you can appreciate his natural parents are conscientious and want to ensure a comfortable upbringing for him." He pauses before he commits.

"The price is fifty thousand dollars, plus our commission of twenty per cent and legal fees of twenty-five per cent."

Jack's jaw dropped but Jenny didn't even blink as she heard the figures.

"That boy is mine, sir!" she said, pointing her finger at him.

"I am delighted for you, Mr and Mrs Andersson; I am sure you will have a son to treasure," he answered, rising to his feet and shaking their hands vigorously.

"There is only one minor condition, however!"

"What's that?" snapped Jenny anxiously.

"His parents have stipulated the boy be named Joshua Augustine . . . Andersson of course, in this instance."

Jenny relaxed with a cheerful sigh. "I couldn't have chosen better names myself."

Jack remembers vividly the day they collected Josh from the hospital and took him home for the very first time. That evening, Jack sat on the sofa watching TV, with his arm draped behind Jenny's neck, while she cooed at tiny Josh and nuzzled into him on her lap. An infrared image of Hurricane Lucy flickered on screen as it tracked northwards through the Gulf of Mexico; the angry red-and-white vortex, whipping counter-clockwise around its cruel eye. The picture morphed and crystallized into a monstrous, swirling maelstrom of solid white cloud as the correspondent cut in.

"Meteorologists are describing Lucy as an unprecedented Atlantic weather system. It is estimated at six hundred miles in diameter, with predicted maximum sustained wind-speeds of almost two hundred miles per hour. The power of this tropical cyclone has been supercharged as it crosses over the still warm waters of the Gulf, and its centre is currently making landfall on the Mississippi coastline. The National Hurricane Center has classified Lucy as a devastating Category Five superstorm on the Saffir-Simpson scale."

The news-anchor paused and waited to be connected to a Biloxi resident who had stayed put, determined to brave the tempest.

"Wilma? Can you hear me, Wilma?"

Her voice crackled in response as she breathlessly described the chaos outside through the cracks of her boarded-up windows.

"Lord have mercy on my poor soul! The eye of Satan himself is cast upon us this day."

"Rest assured we are all with you in this time of ordeal, Wilma."

"Oh, my God!" she yelled. "I can see something surging in the distance like a great white wall."

"What is it, Wilma? What is it?"

"Oh, sweet Jesus . . . Oh, merciful God, spare me!"

"What is it, Wilma?"

"Death's a comin' . . . death's a comin'."

"Tell us what it is, Wilma?"

"It's the sea . . . it's the sea!" she screamed.

The connection went dead and a look of horror spread across the news presenter's face.

"*Thalatta, thalatta*," he said in a quiet but distinct voice, "but now we flee from the sea. I can but quote Herb Morrison's famous words on witnessing the Hindenburg disaster. Oh, the humanity!"

The news director quickly cut to commercials as the presenter visibly strained to maintain his composure. Jack turned to Jenny, who was gazing, oblivious to the unfolding tragedy, into Josh's emerald eyes and thought:

"Welcome to the crazy world, kid!"

EIGHTEEN

THE PLANE BANKS LAZILY to the right over the vast metropolis of London as Jack looks out of his First Class window. The glass edifices of the Square Mile shimmer in the September haze, their windows like tiny silver cubes liquefying in the heat. Air traffic volume is light, and ten minutes later the captain lands the Boeing Dreamliner 818 and welcomes the passengers to London Heathrow. As the plane taxis towards the terminal, a young, pretty hostess leans over and whispers into Jack's ear.

"Could you please remain seated, sir, until all the other passengers have disembarked?"

"Sure . . . Valerie," he smiles, glancing at her lapel badge.

He waits patiently for ten minutes until he senses a shadow looming over him.

"Papers and genetic ID please, Mr Andersson," commands a voice in clipped tones.

Almost instinctively, Jack is on his feet and reaching inside his suit, rummaging for his wallet. He hands it over to a severe-looking, mustachioed man who is eyeing him suspiciously.

"I got some more papers in my hand-luggage in the overhead compartment."

"Thank you Mr Andersson," the man requests with a cursory nod.

He painstakingly scrutinizes the documents before producing a cheek swab.

"Open your mouth please."

A further five minutes are spent performing a twin iris scan while waiting for genetic ID verification via a hand-held analyzer.

"We're clear," the man says at last, speaking into his right cuff and escorting Jack along the aisle to the rear of the aircraft. Both are descending the airstairs when a large black limousine pulls up on the tarmac in front of them. Two figures emerge from the front of the vehicle and open its rear doors simultaneously, inviting in Jack and his security escort, who is now bounding down the steps.

"Welcome to the UK," he says in a frosty tone, followed by a limp handshake, before they are both whisked through the scorching streets of London.

The car sweeps past a set of security gates at the end of a short street and halts abruptly outside a Georgian-style house. As if the scene has been rehearsed a million times, the rear doors of the limousine swing outwards, synchronized perfectly with the yawning open of the building's jet-black front door. Within seconds, Jack is ushered across its threshold, and feels he is instantly transported back into an alien time and world.

"Oh," he remarks aloud to his security escort, "now I know how that Yankee felt arriving at King Arthur's court."

His palm glides over a polished mahogany handrail as he begins to ascend a grand staircase. Serried ranks of engravings and pictures of former prime ministers appear to mock at his winding ascent. At the top of the first flight of steps stands a tall, debonair figure, with arms folded, sporting a rictus smile and an insouciant air. Jack doesn't need an introduction, but his host insists on the formalities of protocol as he stretches out his hand.

"Welcome to Number Ten, Mr Andersson. I am Sir Marius Toynbee."

"I am honoured to meet you, Prime Minister, sir," he answers, reciprocating the firm handshake.

"I spoke with Eli earlier this morning, and he asked me to convey his best wishes to you. Please – walk with me."

Toynbee seems to relish acting as an historical guide as both wind their way through labyrinthine corridors, opulent staterooms and a series of grand offices. Jack loves his educated English accent. It is charming yet authoritative – *mellifluous is a good description,* he thinks.

"Forgive me, Mr Andersson, but my quarters are somewhat Spartan in contrast to the rest of Number Ten," the PM says apologetically as they finally enter his private chambers. Jack admires the ornate coving on the high ceiling and the gilded period chairs clustered around an impressive antique desk. *Typical British understatement,* he remarks to himself, sinking into the plush velvet base of one of the gilded chairs.

"Well, Prime Minister, I am conscious that our time is limited, so permit me to get straight to the point. How and when did your political relationship with Eli start?"

Toynbee chuckles to himself as he begins.

"To be strictly accurate, I first encountered Eli through his book, *The Long Childhood.* His conception that civilization, in historical terms, was metamorphosing from relative infancy to adulthood in the technological blink of an eye . . . was for me a personal revelation . . . Also his conviction that all political actions should be conducted and judged *sub specie aeternitatis* – that is to say, under the eye of eternity. Furthermore, he elucidated for me a fundamental truth in respect to human perceptions. Ultimately, as Nietzsche himself wrote, there are no facts in the human psyche – there are only interpretations. In our modern world, the media manufactures metaphors into myths that crystallize into public opinion. These myths become realities in the human consciousness – rational truths are merely fortuitous accidents."

"Climate change of course being a prime example," nods Jack, pouncing on a pause.

"Exactly! It never ceases to amaze me how society has such confidence in its scientific and technological prowess, yet takes such an inordinate amount of time to accept what climatologists have been predicting for decades. Even at this juncture, GeoNova's political fortunes are contingent upon the vagaries of extreme climatic events, or the outcomes of so-called 'Wet Wars' over precious hydrological resources straddling international boundaries. And of course Big Carbon likes to muddy the waters, funding disinformation campaigns and promises of geo-engineering solutions. Imagine: they propose introducing aerosols of sulphuric acid droplets into the stratosphere, to adjust the Earth's heat balance."

He stops and rolls his head from side to side bemusedly.

"This policy is myopic – intellectual and behavioural revolution is the sole guarantor of the life-support system that is Gaia."

"I agree, Prime Minister, but how can you encourage older people, whose views are more entrenched, to change? Particularly in view of your more liberal attitude toward euthanasia."

"With grave difficulty I'm afraid," Toynbee answers, rolling his head again. "I acknowledge many of the older generation in particular view Eli as a quixotic figure; tilting at windmills as he barnstorms around the globe. But a huge electoral chasm has developed along the demographic age-profile. The younger generation is GeoNova's natural political dynamo, as it justifiably feels that it has been betrayed – ecological treachery, as Eli calls it. There is also growing resentment between the generations in light of the fact that human longevity is increasing. Why should a twenty-five-year-old worker finance the pensions of centenarians, who have themselves jeopardized the future of posterity?"

"Yes, you're right; it doesn't seem fair," says Jack.

"This is a pressing and contentious economic issue. Is it any wonder that the young support policies encouraging euthanasia to reduce the burden on our exchequer?"

"You paint a rather depressing picture, Prime Minister, sir, if you will pardon me saying so. Perhaps we need space for hope."

Toynbee sits back in his chair, head tilted back and eyes raised, as if searching for an answer on the ornate ceiling.

"Well, Jack, GeoNova as a movement has been phenomenally successful in the geo-political theatre. We have control of governments in most Western nations, Russia, and recently, India. Ultimately, political influence resides with a very limited number of people. History has taught us that, in general, whole nations don't go to war; egocentric leaders do, however. But this concentration of power can potentially have very significant benefits. GeoNova, under Eli's stewardship, has invested billions in GM food programs, green power generation, and eco-disaster relief, to name but a few. The heads of all GeoNova party national governments are de facto Roberts appointees, and can be dismissed at his whim. From GeoNova's inception, he has envisioned a type of single world government in conventional democratic clothing, under his auspices."

Two loud pings cause Toynbee to stop, root an earpiece from his shirt pocket and clap it to the side of his head. Jack is grateful for the interruption and rises to his feet to relieve the post-flight cramps in his legs. Toynbee gestures with a circular motion of his hand, for him to remain and just amble around the room at his leisure.

Jack's attention is quickly drawn to a large, framed photograph of Eli addressing a crowd, mounted on the wall opposite. He is standing erect, in a classic Roberts pose, back arched slightly, with his long arms extended in an expansive "Y". His piercing gaze is focused on the heavens, but he is the cynosure of his audience's eyes. Alongside the photograph is a framed and autographed copy of his famous Lincoln Memorial Address, entitled "I Have a Dream Too." Jack puckers up his lips as he reads the text, and remembers the first time he heard the speech, as he himself sweltered under the Washington sun.

> In the beginning God said: "Let man reign over the fish of the sea and over the birds of the air; over the beasts of the field and every creature that creeps upon the ground."

We were the Lord's anointed. Granted dominion over this island Earth, this bountiful paradise. For millennia we proved worthy of our stewardship of this Promised Land. Nature was worshipped as our Mother and provider. But slowly and insidiously we now seek to subjugate her.

We rape her oceans.

We toxify her skies.

We poison her land.

We butcher beasts in their billions.

We are masters of this Earth but crown ourselves kings without a kingdom. Mother Nature is slow to anger but will be devastating in her wrath. . . .

Three score years ago, on this very day, a man stood here on this very spot and told the world he had a dream. I too have a dream. We are many nations, many colours, creeds and diverse ideological persuasions. But we are one species under one God. We are citizens of one planet, and human compassion must be our unifying religion. . . .

The greatest moral weight ever thrust upon the shoulders of mankind is anthropogenic climate change. It is an existential threat greater even than the prospect of global thermonuclear war. Global warming is pernicious; it is relentless; but we can stabilize its effects if we choose to change. We must choose to be victorious in the great ideological battle between hyper-capitalism and sustainable environmentalism. Climate change is ultimately a moral issue – it is a moral and categorical imperative that we modify our behaviour! Mankind has endured a long childhood – it is time civilization grew up and faced the burdens and responsibilities of adulthood. . . .

From this day forth, I pledge my gospel of wealth will

be to alleviate climate-induced human suffering. To lead humanity away from the rocky path to perdition and toward greener pastures. Brothers and sisters – we have a world to win back. Man willing . . . Man willing . . . we will worship at the altar of Gaia as of olden times. . . .

"Mr Andersson . . . Jack!"

"Oh, pardon me, Prime Minister. I was engrossed reading that speech. I apologize."

"It is quite all right. Such eloquent oratory is meant to inspire and enrapture, is it not?"

"Yes, it still does," Jack states, scanning the words a second time.

"There is a political adage that advises one should campaign in poetry and govern in prose; but poetry has always been the soul of Eli's rhetoric. Please, let us be seated again." He gestures with an open palm.

But Jack is rooted to the spot, transfixed in horror, as he gapes at a second photograph. Its subject is an emaciated African child, lying with its face half-buried in the cinnabar-tinctured soil. The one eye that is visible is staring blankly at the camera, and swarming with flies feasting on its glazed moisture. A tiny wisp of red powder, captured by the lens as it emanates from a single nostril, indicates that the body still breathes life.

In the background, surveying the scene, skulk two vultures with their large, triangular beaks opened menacingly. Their beady eyes are watching, and waiting for the desiccated dust to finally settle under the nose of the clearly dying child.

"That is horrific!" says Jack, clapping a hand over his mouth.

"That picture was taken two months ago in drought-stricken southern Sudan. The region has received scarcely any precipitation in the last five years. Images such as this consistently remind me of why I entered politics, and joined that march to Washington in August, 2023."

"I was there too, Prime Minister – purely in a journalistic capacity, but I was deeply moved nonetheless."

"Please, Jack," he gestures a second time, encouraging him to sit.

"Thank you, sir," he answers, as they resume their seats.

"I walked right alongside Roberts at the head of the column of protesters on that fateful day," continues Toynbee. "I had only recently been appointed chief of GeoNova UK's political operation, and this march was an international media event. Undoubtedly, a series of extreme climatic phenomena that summer was supplying incontrovertible evidence of man-made climate change, and contributed to the multitudes that turned out. President Goulding keenly understood the powerful symbolism of the sixtieth anniversary of King's celebrated speech. Therefore he ordered the march to be restricted and military cordons placed all over Washington."

"Yeah, I remember them. But how did Eli break the main cordon to get through to the Lincoln Memorial?"

"Well, as I am sure you remember, there was a stand-off for an hour between the protesters and the military. Then the commanding officer ordered his troops to fire just over the heads of the crowd, to encourage it to disperse. Tragically, one of the protesters had a small child on his shoulders, who was fatally shot through the throat. Eli was livid. I watched him studying his iPad for two solid minutes. That is precisely how long it took him to obtain all the personal background he required about the army commander on the ground. Then he strode up to the barrier and asked to negotiate with . . . a Colonel Harrison, I believe. The two men met briefly, but the officer was adamant in not permitting the throngs to march through, in spite of Eli's pleas and fears of further bloodshed."

Toynbee pauses and caresses his right temple affectedly with his right middle finger.

"I have never revealed this story to anyone, and I can only believe it because I witnessed their exchange of words.

"'Do you want me to tell you the day you are going to die, Colonel?' Eli said.

"'Is that a threat, Mr Roberts?' he responded.

"'No, it is not a threat.'

"'Well then, are you God, or what in hell do you mean, sir!'

"Then Roberts took one step forward and towered over Harrison as he spoke.

"'Your mother suffered terminal pancreatic cancer. Your father is probably presenting with symptoms of early-onset Alzheimer's disease, and you require daily cardiac medication.'

"The officer was absolutely flummoxed.

"'How did you obtain that information?!' he protested.

"Eli tapped his own forehead and said: 'I have your entire genome mapped and analyzed within the confines of my head. I can predict the date of your demise with ninety-five per cent accuracy. Do you wish me to divulge your death-date . . . Colonel?'

"Harrison looked aghast; he reeled and wilted at the prospect of hearing it. He quickly summoned his lieutenants and informed them their orders were rescinded, and to allow all the marchers through to avoid further spilling of American blood."

"That is quite a story, Prime Minister," says Jack, making a faint whistle and arching his brows in astonishment.

"Yes, Eli is quite a remarkable individual," he answers absentmindedly. "Of course, he doesn't perceive himself as a purely political animal, so much as an educator – 'Human history becomes more and more a race between education and catastrophe' – that is his favourite quote from HG Wells. It is certainly a peculiarly apt quote, in light of prevailing circumstances, most particularly apropos the situation in China."

"Yes, Prime Minister, the assassination of Kun Wei was a setback for GeoNova there."

"Oh, that is a complete understatement, Jack," Toynbee replies, an attenuating smile belying a note of irritation in his voice. "Eli is convinced that Kun Wei was the only individual who could accomplish GeoNova's political objectives in China. In fact, he considers that history will judge his martyrdom more significant than the murders of JFK in Dallas or Archduke Ferdinand's on the eve of the First World War."

Toynbee suddenly stands up and begins to pace about the room. He halts in front of Eli's framed Washington address and flings his arms up despairingly.

"China is a disaster, Jack! We have absolutely no political presence there, and the Chinese government is intent on exhausting its extensive fossil-fuel resources into the atmosphere. They say they are investing billions in geo-engineering research to stabilize atmospheric conditions . . . but this is like giving extra morphine shots to a terminally ill patient. This is just . . . just . . . "

Toynbee takes a deep breath, as if conscious of his increasingly animated expressions of opinion. He leans forward, steadies himself, and places both hands on the wall, one either side of the framed speech. He reads the final words of the speech aloud.

"'We must rediscover that civilization is an aggregate so much greater than the sum of its parts. Oh, yes, ladies and gentlemen, I have a dream too . . . my dream is of eight billion minds to think as one; eight billion hearts to beat as one, and eight billion souls to believe in one. And, so help me, God – I am that One!'"

Toynbee concludes with a passionate flourish, almost reliving the moment he first heard the stirring words. He wheels askance and taps his chest, just over his heart, as he turns.

"You know, GeoNova has over a billion subscribers on the Cloud. I firmly believe that with the advent of quantum computers we are on the cusp of achieving a singular global consciousness. And when we do, history will wake us up from this nightmare and deliver us from our own evils."

"But what about the essence of the man? What is Eli, the man, really like, Prime Minister?"

"I cannot give you a satisfactory answer to that question, but I will tell you this, Mr Andersson. An English public-school education still teaches one to be stoical and I am not a man given to expressing strong passions in public. I have wept twice in my lifetime, that I can remember – the occasion of my mother's funeral and the very first time that Eli Roberts looked into my eyes."

Toynbee stops and reflects before flashing a gleaming smile, endeavouring to restore a reserved façade.

"Forgive me – I am being somewhat maudlin."

"That's . . . eh—"

Jack is interrupted by the sound of the door behind him, creaking open a fraction. A greying head appears discreetly through the gap.

"Pardon me, Prime Minister. You asked me to inform you of the Russian ambassador's arrival."

"Thank you, Mr Secretary," he answers, glancing at his watch. "You may tell him I shall be with him in five minutes."

"Thank you, sir," the other replies with practised politesse and a courteous nod before closing the door.

"Well, at least Russia is something of a success story for GeoNova, sir," ventures Jack.

"Yes, of course. There were potentially dangerous disputes over the exploitation of Arctic resources; which could not have been diplomatically resolved unless we gained political supremacy in Russia itself, Canada, Scandinavia, and Greenland. Political control in Russia has also facilitated the ongoing migration of several peoples northwards to Siberia, to escape glacial meltdown in the Himalayas. Who would have imagined that Solzhenitsyn's former 'Gulag Archipelago' would be designated an Eco-haven?"

"Maybe Marx was right after all – history is tragedy the first time and farce second time round."

"Ah! Excellent point," Toynbee concedes with a generous chuckle. "Of course, the fall of communism at the end of the twentieth century was a seismic shift in geo-political terms. According to Eli, it was a philosophical triumph for market fundamentalism that fuelled a hubristic bubble of hyper-capitalism, especially in the United States. I suppose one could describe it as a Cold War victory that sowed dragon's teeth, that helped propel us towards our current predicament."

"Yes, I think you're right. I think we can only put these events into context 'under the eye of eternity', as you said. The recent past is kind of remote, when you think about it, sir."

"I could not agree more," he answers, glancing at his watch again.

"Just one more thing – do you know anything about Roberts's childhood?"

Toynbee shrugs vaguely.

"No, he is very reticent on that subject. Although I pressed him on it once, he just described his youth with a single word – '*short*'."

"It seems strange, Prime Minister. There are a million books and articles about him, yet his childhood is undocumented; there is virtually zero information on it."

"I am sorry, Jack, not to be able to enlighten you on that period of his life."

"I have to admit, sir, it's a real struggle for me to get a clear picture of Roberts even as an adult."

"Yes, that's understandable. He is a very complex man."

"You've known him a long time. Is there anything else you can tell me to try and capture the essence of the man?"

Toynbee looks sympathetically at Jack.

"Mmmm . . . he did say something to me once that might be of some use to you in a biographical context."

"What's that?" says Jack, bending forward eagerly.

"He told me about the Roman generals who celebrated their triumphs riding a chariot through the streets of Rome. For that day alone they were venerated as gods by the Senate and the people. But, just in case the general allowed the occasion to overinflate his ego, a slave always rode with him in the chariot, whispering the words 'Remember you are just a man.'

"'Marius,' Eli said to me, 'I want to be more than just a man. I want to be a revolutionary idea. What greater triumph is there for any man beyond that?'"

Jack gives Toynbee a puzzled look.

"Yeah, that's an interesting perspective."

"This biography must be quite an undertaking for you. A journey is perhaps a suitable metaphor. I sincerely hope I have aided you on that journey nonetheless."

"Thank you, Prime Minister, sir. It's been a real pleasure."

NINETEEN

"Steelman . . . "

"Good evening, sir. I have some good news for you."

"What's that?"

"Client number fifty-two is flying to Britain for a conference on Friday, so you'll need to stay in London a couple of extra days. It'll save you a long flight to Australia in the future to interview her."

"But I . . . but I," Jack falters and breathes, long, slow and hard. "Sure, it makes sense," he says at last.

"Great! A lucky break I guess you could call it. I'll text you all the requisite details soon as I've arranged the meeting. Thank you, sir."

Franklin disconnects and Jack is left listening to static while he ponders over his next transatlantic call. Eventually he takes his normal cell from his pocket, flips it open and calls out the name distinctly: "Jenny Andersson".

Her response is practically instantaneous, despite the distance.

"Hello, Jack."

"Hi, honey! How are you?"

She seems to hesitate briefly before she answers.

"Fine, okay, I guess. The garden keeps me busy."

"And Josh?"

"Eh . . . he keeps me busy too, now that he has no school to go to."

"Any luck with other schools that we applied to yet?"

"Only one school contacted us and said they would consider him, subject to an interview. They've arranged an appointment for us this coming Friday."

"*Shit*," he breathes into the phone.

"What's wrong?"

"Listen, honey, I'm sorry. Something's come up and I can't make it home until after the weekend."

Jack can almost feel her heavy sighs huffing against his burning cheeks.

"Well, that's just great! . . . just great, Jack. Josh is driving me nuts, being at home all the time. I *never* get a break from him, and along comes our one-and-only chance to get him a place at school this fall and you blow it."

"I'm really sor—"

"Oh, that's just peachy, Jack. But I suppose we need you to keep earning all this money just to pay for his pills!"

He closes his eyes as she abruptly disconnects, and thinks the static sounds sweet by comparison as he listens to it for the longest time.

Jack strides along the hotel corridor, mentally ticking off the door numbers as he passes, until he arrives at room 568. He double-checks the details and time of the appointment on his cell, before rapping on the door twice with the knuckle of his middle finger. A woman's voice calls back softly.

"Come in, Mr Andersson; the door's not locked."

He opens it and enters a luxurious suite. A middle-aged woman is perched on a satin-covered stool, applying her make-up in front of a gilded mirror. She turns and stands as Jack's approaching reflection looms into her view.

"Hello, Jack. I am Meredith Steinitz."

"I am pleased to meet you, Dr Steinitz," he says, returning her delicate handshake.

"Please, let's drop the formalities. You're not in Number Ten now. 'Merry' is just fine – a good name for a psychiatrist, don't you think?"

"Oh! I'm sorry; I didn't realize you were a psychiatrist. There was absolutely no bio on you on the Cloud. I really don't know anything about you."

"That is hardly surprising. GeoNova doesn't like to advertise my services," she says with a grin.

"Are you employed by GeoNova?"

"Yes, I provide mental health advice to their various government leaders."

"Including Roberts?"

"Of course!" she shrugs matter-of-factly.

"Is he a client of yours?"

"I don't like to use the term 'client' in his instance. You could say my role is . . . shamanic. I am somebody with whom he shares the intimate journeys of his life's experience; I prefer to think of it that way."

"Wow! I'd love to be a fly on *that* wall."

"Now's your chance," she laughs. "Ask me whatever questions you want and I'll answer them frankly. Elijah wants *you* of all people to know the truth about him."

"Sure. Fine by me."

"May I suggest, Jack, that you lie down on the bed here," she says, patting its covers. "I sense it will make it more comfortable for you to absorb it, if you stretch out and close your eyes."

Jack looks incredulously at her disarming smile but feels an immediate rapport. A scene from the movie *The Graduate* rolls into his mind's eye. He winks comically as he asks, "Are you trying to seduce me, Mrs Robinson?"

"Do you want to be seduced, Mr Andersson?" she shoots back, sitting on the stool again and crossing her legs as she does so with a cheeky smile.

Jack bursts into laughter and falls onto the bed. He pulls a pillow under his head, shuts his eyes and thinks "Merry" is just a perfect name for her.

"Elijah loves the movies. The cinema is where modern heroes were born; even now actors are still referred to as 'stars'. Science fiction is his favourite genre, as it has no imaginative constraints. He once told me that there is nothing more powerful than the human imagination – it can travel beyond the known universe and back again in the flash of a neuron. Einstein's theory of relativity does not apply to the potential of human thought."

"What's his favourite sci-fi movie?"

"An old one from the nineteen fifties, titled *Forbidden Planet.*"

"I never heard of it. What's it about?"

"Its premise is quite intriguing actually, from a psychological perspective. The story is loosely based on Shakespeare's play *The Tempest*, except it takes place on a far-off planet. It tells the story of a mighty civilization called the Krell, who invent a machine that can convert pure thoughts into physical form. It is a supreme, creative technological achievement. Yet, in a single night, that civilization is completely obliterated."

"How?" asks Jack, raising his head from the pillow.

"Monsters from the id."

"What?"

"The Krell forgot that they themselves had evolved from primitive origins. Their brains still retained archetypal nightmares deep in their primeval unconscious. Inadvertently, their supermachine gave physical form to, and energized, these terrors, which ultimately destroyed them."

"Don't tell me the Pentagon's working on this id machine?"

"No," Steinitz laughs, "but I do want to tell you a story from Elijah's childhood that resonates with that movie. He didn't really settle down anywhere when he was a child; it was a kind of peripatetic existence for him. But one time he was living out in the country, somewhere in West Virginia, I think, for a couple of years. He spent time strolling around the fields and fishing in the local river when he wasn't at school. Then, one day, he arrived at the riverbank and discovered all the fish were dead; just floating with their mouths open. It was some chemical or toxic spill upstream that caused it. Elijah told me when he saw the fish that he imagined he really saw whales. They were singing the saddest songs from the mournful depths of the oceans of memory. 'That river was my stream of consciousness, my Anna Livia Plurabelle,' he said. 'And when I cried into my great blue bedroom that is the sky, I knew it was too small to contain all my tears. I suppose those fish were similar to the Krell, in that their entire ecosystem collapsed within hours.'"

"Interesting," muses Jack aloud. "Give me the boy and I will show you the man, as the Jesuits say."

"Yes, it was a formative experience for him." She pauses before continuing. "It was probably his first experience of bereavement – but he would prefer to use the term 'epiphany'."

"You mean a sort of religious revelation?"

"Close your eyes and relax. I need to tell you about one of Elijah's dreams, because he specifically requested that you relate it in your book."

 He buries the back of his head on the pillow again and exhales gently as he prepares to listen.

"Sure, Merry. Fire ahead."

"Elijah dreams of a great plain filled with all humanity, the living and the dead generations, columned and ranked in billions – like a giant phalanx, stretching out beyond the horizon. A 'spirit' of purest white light glides over the multitudes thus arrayed; always moving and never ceasing in its eternal quest. After a search of four and a half billion years, the light approaches, stops and hovers over Elijah. The crowds begins to murmur the revealed name of the now oscillating light-being, until their whispering becomes a chant: '*Summum Bonum . . . Summum Bonum*.' Elijah steps forth and an angel descends upon him, until the two become one. He describes it as feeling like his entire body is being consumed by fire or electricity. But his mind is ice-cold, and a small, still voice echoes in his head above the sound of the chanting.

"'You are these words made flesh,' it says. 'Now dwell amongst us and show us the light.'"

Jack sits up with a gasp as Steinitz finishes recounting the dream. "What is *Summum Bonum*?"

"It means 'supreme goodness'. It is an epithet often ascribed to God himself."

"Has Roberts got some kind of a god or messiah complex?"

"Well, that is not a term in clinical use, but certainly he is conscious that he is an exceptionally gifted individual, probably even the most powerful and influential leader in all of history. But even notable historical figures need to aspire to something greater than themselves. Men dream of princes; princes dream of kings; kings dream of emperors; but emperors dream only of divinities. Elijah dreams of the Roman emperor Caesar Augustus – '*primus inter pares; pax Romana; pax Americana; pax Mundi; axis Mundi*,' as he described it to me."

"Sorry, Merry, I didn't do Latin in college. You've lost me there."

"Elijah views himself in a GeoNova context as first amongst equals, pursuing peace, not just for America but the entire world. But he knows he is the fulcrum, the axis upon which the fate of humanity depends," she explains patiently.

"Like Atlas bearing the burden of the globe on his shoulders?"

"Yes, that's a good mythological analogy."

"How can a single mind cope with that *awesome* responsibility?"

Jack is propped up now, with one elbow on the pillow, staring right at her as he eagerly anticipates her response.

Steinitz runs both hands through her hair and tosses her head back coquettishly. She narrows her smiling eyes and nods lightly in Jack's direction.

"I posed that exact question to him and this was his answer: 'Everybody has profound difficulties coping with this modern world. It is almost as if our natural neurochemicals have become inadequate and cannot adapt to our crazy lifestyle. Maybe we're just trousered apes; addicted to alcohol, drugs and anti-depressants, to sustain us in our artificial jungle instead of a real one, as Nature intended.'"

"That doesn't answer my question, though. How does *he* handle the stresses, the pressures of high office?"

"Elijah told me that the world is tiny compared to the universe – but the vastness of outer space itself is tiny compared to the complexity and infinitude of the inner space that is his mind. It is that thought, and that thought alone, that anchors his sanity – it is that single, harmonious realization that reconciles his mind with reality."

"Mmm . . . does Roberts believe in God?"

"No! He definitely conforms to the modern psychiatric consensus, in viewing Him as a sort of reductio ad absurdum – a figment of our collective imagination. To some extent, our idea of God abrogates human responsibility for our own destiny. It is of course a fundamental principle of GeoNova's philosophy that Man must be an active agent in his own salvation. Not that!" she says, raising her eyes and gesturing towards the heavens with outstretched arms.

Jack stretches out his own arms as if subconsciously mimicking her actions and stifles a yawn.

"What about Eli and Eleanor and their daughter's suicide?"

"Oh, you *know*," she says, with surprise.

"Yes, I interviewed Mrs Roberts and she told me the truth about Clara's death."

"It was shortly after that tragic event that I first met Elijah. He was racked with guilt and constantly argued with his wife, who desperately wanted to conceive another baby. But he insisted on making a symbolic statement to the world and refused to father another child. Subsequently they divorced and she became a recluse, living in that old house in the middle of nowhere; spending her days in perpetual mourning."

"A feisty lady though!"

"Oh, yes; a very erudite lady and an ideal intellectual foil for Elijah.

He is still a very attractive man, yet he has only ever loved Eleanor. All his affairs with other women have been on a purely cerebral basis; there has never been any physical involvement with any of them."

She pauses briefly, and her omnipresent smile seems to tighten with concern.

"I suspect he is a very lonely man. He knows he will never encounter another woman like Eleanor *ever* again."

"That doesn't make sense, Merry. The world's got plenty of attractive, intelligent women that he could meet."

The psychiatrist rolls her head dismissively.

"Perhaps one day you will understand . . . You know, Elijah recently said to me that life without love is like staring into an abyss – too long without it and the abyss begins to stare back at you."

Jack sits up and levers himself towards the edge of the bed, to be closer to Steinitz.

"Jesus Christ, Merry! Is this the same guy with the nuclear launch codes?"

She fires a fierce glare at him but quickly relaxes the contours of her face into a reassuring expression.

"Have you ever seen the movie *The Day the Earth Stood Still*?"

"Yeah, long time ago. But I hate those crappy black-and-white movies."

"Do you remember the story, Jack?"

"Yeah, some alien guy in a flying saucer lands in Washington and wants to save the world. Him and his giant silver robot. Gort; wasn't that the robot's name?"

"Yes."

"I bet Eli likes that movie?"

"Sure! I suppose he identifies with the alien Klaatu, who has come to Earth to try and prevent humanity from destroying itself. Gort, of course, was his omnipotent machine that had the power to destroy worlds – a kind of interstellar policeman. But the really clever part of the story is that the robot is actually the master, not the servant of Klaatu."

"Oh, yeah!" exclaims Jack. "I remember one of the characters saying some gibberish to stop Gort from annihilating the planet after the alien is shot. There were three words in it, but I forget them."

"Me too, but all I know is Elijah parallels 'Gort' with Mother Nature, capable of wiping out civilization as we know it, if we don't behave, so to speak."

Jack scratches his head and squints with one eye before he poses his next question.

"Sorry, this is gonna sound crazy but I *have* to ask. Some conspiracy theorists reckon Eli must have supernormal powers to have achieved all he has; and there is zilch information on his life before he was eighteen. He's like the man who fell to Earth in that other old alien movie of the same name. I mean: he's an enigma, isn't he?"

Steinitz claps her hands on her knees, throws her head back and laughs heartily at the notion. Her laugh lapses into a schoolgirlish giggle as she shakes her head incredulously.

"You can rest assured that Elijah Roberts is every bit as human as you or I. Sure, he doesn't talk much about his boyhood; maybe it was too traumatic for him – I don't know; we rarely discuss it. But he is *definitely* from this world," she scoffs.

Jack quickly changes the subject to conceal his embarrassment.

"What about nightmares; does he have any?"

"Well, I'm not really a devotee of Freud's oneirocritical approach – that which seeks significance in the interpretation of dreams. But certainly the sea, or being overwhelmed by the sea, would be a recurring feature of his nightmares."

"Yeah, that figures; it's a *waking* nightmare for lots of people now."

"What's *really* bothering you Jack?" the psychiatrist asks out of left field.

"Excuse me?"

"I said what's *really* bothering you? There's a question you're afraid to ask me."

"What do you mean?"

"I've a sense about these things. Come on – it's not every day you get a free consult with a good psychiatrist."

Jack pauses. Thinks what an understatement "good" is in her case.

"Yeah, you're right. Listen; let me ask you something. I've done quite a few interviews for this book. All the people I've spoken with are all quite brilliant. I mean really super-smart individuals. I'm no idiot, but I find them a bit intimidating. They make me feel so . . . so ordinary, I guess. . . . "

" . . . and you feel somewhat out of your depth?"

"Yeah. I do."

"Well, that's quite an understandable human reaction. But let me tell *you* something. Highly intelligent individuals tend to live their lives from the neck up. Frequently they think of their bodies as a mere appendage – a vehicle to carry their brains around. Quite often there's a disconnect between head and heart that manifests itself in all kinds of psychiatric disorders. It's my job to keep these people psychologically grounded. Remember they're just ordinary human beings after all."

"Mmm . . . you mean their emotions are out of sync with their minds."

"Sure."

"I've a son like that you know."

"Yes, Josh is exactly like that."

Steinitz glances at her dainty, old-fashioned gold watch.

"Oh, sorry! I have a business appointment in an hour. I'm being picked up in fifteen minutes."

"I thought it was a conference?"

"In *my* line of work, euphemisms abound," she grins knowingly.

"Yeah, I can imagine."

"When is this book of yours scheduled to be published?"

"Sometime just prior to the next election, in November next year, I guess."

"Yeah, that would make sense; Elijah's official biography is destined to be a best-seller. He'll probably do a free-launch on the Cloud to help get himself re-elected – he knows perfect electoral timing is more important than profit."

"I think he has a real battle on his hands this time round, don't you?"

She nods mutely in agreement and frowns.

"I want to tell you something before we're done. Have you ever heard of a novel by the Irish author James Joyce called *Finnegans Wake*?"

"As a matter of fact I have," he states with a hint of pride.

"That is Elijah's favourite book you know. He says it is the only feat of literature that has ever truly challenged his intellect. Even though I believe he knows it off by heart, he used always keep a copy of it under his pillow; just like Alexander the Great did with his copy of the *Iliad*; recounting the great deeds of his hero Achilles. I think . . . "

Steinitz has broken off in mid-sentence. She rises, and walks past Jack who is lying on the bed again, with his elbows splayed out and hands supporting his chin.

"Excuse me, Jack; I need to use the bathroom."

His eyes follow her across the room. Suddenly, she halts and turns towards him, gesturing to him to follow her as she does so. He frowns back.

"What?" he says quietly.

She coughs twice, signalling with her eyes this time for him to follow her, before disappearing into the bathroom. Within seconds he is staring at her bemusedly across the marble-tiled floor.

"Close the door after you," she whispers.

"Are you trying to seduce me again, Dr Steinitz?" he jokes.

But she doesn't even twitch a facial muscle in reaction to his effort to break the tension.

"I want to show you something."

She produces a battered old leather-bound book and flips it open to the last couple of pages.

"Read the text where it's underlined," she says, handing the book over.

The words echo around the bathroom as he reads them out loud from the yellowed pages.

"'Thinking always if I go all goes . . . and is there one who understands me?' What is it, Merry? What's wrong?" he says staring at her deadly serious face."

"I'm scared, Jack!"

"Scared of what?"

"Of Elijah," she whispers. "He has lost his faith in divinity and now he's losing his faith in humanity. What will there be left for him to believe in now, only insanity."

"I don't understand, Merry; you're not making sense."

"I am really good at what I do, but fifty per cent of the time it is based solely on intuition; a kind of sixth sense. You've got to help him win this next election because I don't know what's going to happen if he loses it."

"You're scaring the bejesus out of *me* now, Merry. What in hell are you talking about?!"

"Look at the title of the book."

He closes it over and gazes at its worn front cover – it is a copy of *Finnegans Wake* by James Joyce.

"That is Elijah's very own treasured copy he has had since he was a kid. He gave it to me the last time we spoke. He has stopped reading the book. God! This means something . . . it means something. I don't know what, but it terrifies me."

All at once, they find themselves in each other's embrace. Steinitz is trembling and blinking hard under the harsh glare of the bathroom lights as she leans back and stares into Jack's eyes.

"Make sure it's a great book, Jack, and be strong for Josh, won't you," she says, before kissing him hard, once on the cheek.

"I will, I will," he replies, mystified.

Three thunderous thuds resounding on the hotel room door make them clench and tighten their mutual embrace.

"Dr Steinitz . . . Dr Steinitz!" booms a man's voice from the corridor.

"They're here already," she whispers, directly into his ear. "You go answer it and tell them I'll be along in five minutes."

"Sure, okay."

"Goodbye, Mr Andersson," she says slowly, summoning a wry smile before returning to her stool to finish off her make-up.

Jack grabs the handle and quickly swings the door open. A human giant seems to fill the whole door-frame and confront him with his massive bulk. He is wearing an immaculately tailored metallic grey three-piece suit. Jack gazes up open-mouthed at his chiselled features and impassive countenance. Reflective silver wraparound Raybans give him a sinister air to complement his menacing bearing. Jack can't help but focus on the bulge of what he assumes is a weapon, concealed under his jacket.

"Hey, Merry, can you tell Gort here to step aside and let me out?" he shouts, staring up at his double reflection in the hulking figure's shades.

She laughs as she finally remembers the quote from the movie and calls it out loud and clear. "*Klaatu barada nikto.*"

The massive figure steps to one side and Jack slips past him and hurries down the corridor.

As he walks, he googles the movie *The Day the Earth Stood Still* on his cell; it is based on a short story called *Farewell to the Master*.

"This means something . . . this means something," he keeps repeating to himself, with a rising sense of unease.

TWENTY

JACK FROWNS AS HE SPIES a small white box perched precariously on the edge of the kitchen sink. He picks it up. There's a silver foil container peeping out of it. He draws it out. It is half full of tiny white pills. He recognizes the brand name printed on it as that of a common anti-depressant medication; but the prescription label affixed on the box reads "Jennifer Andersson".

"Shit!" he hisses under his breath.

Then he stares at the gallons of bottled drinking water neatly stacked under the rear window of the kitchen, which faces out onto the garden.

"Shit!" he mutters again as he struggles in vain to recall the last time it rained.

He approaches the window and gazes out over the lawn; it reminds him of a gold-and-green patchwork quilt as his eyes scan across it in search of Jenny. His vision is obscured by the oak tree but he adjusts his stance and locates her; hunkered down in a distant flower-bed. He steps out into the sunlight and is greeted by a sea of colours, ebbing and flowing like a living kaleidoscope around the perimeter of the lawn. Out of the corner of his eye he notices a little boy, kneeling at the edge of the grass and examining the centre of a large sunflower. Jack wanders towards him across a sun-dappled stretch of lawn under the white oak tree.

"Good morning, Josh."

"Good morning, Father," he replies without even turning his head.

"Do you like the sunflowers?"

"*Helianthus annuus* is my favourite flower. They are heliotropic and worship the sun as it journeys across the sky; just like the Aztecs and Egyptians used to. The florets within the cluster are arranged in an interconnected spiral pattern typically oriented to the golden angle of one hundred thirty-seven point five degrees. The number of left and right spirals are a successive Fibonacci sequence typically ranging from thirty-four to fifty-five . . . although they can vary from eighty-nine to one hundred forty-four in very large specimens."

Jack stands back with eyes downcast and his arms tightly folded as he shakes his head in bewilderment. He gazes at the fiery orange-yellow blooms arrayed before him; swaying their heads sympathetically with the gentle breeze.

"Can you not appreciate that they are simply just beautiful . . . like van Gogh did?"

Josh stands, turns to his father, and looks through him with a sphinx-like stare that seems to verge on utter contempt.

"Van Gogh made his sunflowers with lead chromate but God created these from earth, sun and water. That is why he cut his ear off and committed suicide – because artists can't compete with God."

Jack throws him a single disparaging look and marches off towards the rear of the garden.

Jenny cocks her head to one side as she hears the rustling of dry grass behind her. She stands and turns to face her husband.

"Hi, honey," he says softly.

The lineaments of her face are frozen into a doleful scowl. Her hair is dishevelled and looks bleached by the relentless sun. She wears no make-up and her skin seems as dry and weather-beaten as the browning lawn. Jack spills the words out thoughtlessly—

"Jesus, honey, you look like shit!"

She narrows her bleary eyes and retaliates with a murderous glance.

"We need to *talk*, Jack!" she hisses.

They stand glaring at one another across the kitchen table.

"I'm sorry, *okay*? I was *forced* to stay in London a few extra days."

"Yeah, sure, Jack," she replies acidly, turning away and flicking the ash from her cigarette into the sink behind her.

"Yes," he protests, "Franklin asked me to stay in England and do a second interview."

"Who was she?"

"I can't tell you that – it's confidential . . . Wait a second . . . how did you know it was a woman?"

"I went through your luggage first thing this morning before you got up. I noticed *lipstick* on the collar of one of your shirts before I threw it in the wash. You been screwing around, Jack?"

"*What!*"

"You heard me."

"No . . . no, honey; you're gettin' completely the wrong end of the stick here," he laughs. "It was just a harmless peck on the cheek."

"I don't think it's the least bit funny; in fact, that pink smudge was smack on the nape of your neck – like it was a passionate embrace."

"Listen, Jenny, I can't really explain, but . . . "

"Don't even *bother* trying," she interjects with another indignant flick of her cigarette ash into the sink.

He leans forward, placing his outstretched fingers on the table, and watches as her upper body seems to quiver in a light haze of smoke. She should be weeping but he knows the medication restrains her tears.

"Honey, I know you're in a sad place right now and that it's really just those pills talking."

"What do you mean?"

"Jenny, we've been through this before."

"I don't understand."

"I saw the *pills* you're taking," he shrugs. "Why didn't you tell me?"

She quickly averts her furious gaze and casts her sullen eyes towards the garden.

"It's not like the last time, Jack," she says abstractedly; that was a bereavement, but *this*, this is a living death – I swear this kid is a fuckin' nightmare twenty-four-seven! It's like he has a computer search engine in his brain and it *never ever stops!* And he refuses to take his medications for me now. I just can't cope with him on my own any more."

Jack buries his face in his hands for a couple of seconds. He looks up and skirts around the table with his arms outstretched to embrace her. But she folds her arms and stiffens her stance to stop him in his tracks.

"I'm sorry, honey. I should've realized this might happen when Josh couldn't get back to school."

"Yeah."

"*Listen!* I have a sensible idea. Why don't we get someone to help you look after him – like an assistant; I mean we can afford one now, right?"

"You mean like Miss Alvarez?"

Jack snaps his fingers and his eyes widen at the prospect.

"*Exactly!* She's only working part-time in the school. We could employ her full-time on a decent salary. What do you think, honey?"

"Great idea, Jack! She's young, she's attractive, and I can sleep in the spare room."

He raises his eyes to the ceiling and takes a deep breath.

"You're forgetting, Jenny, that I am abroad for two months straight come January and February, working on this book."

She sucks hard once on her cigarette and exhales a steady stream of smoke before stubbing it in the sink behind her.

"Well, that's something I can *really* look forward to," she says, lighting up another cigarette.

"How many of those things are you starting to smoke a day now?"

"Ten . . . twenty maybe," she shrugs nonchalantly. "They help calm me down."

"Sure, honey?" he notes with concern.

"Twenty . . . forty . . . sixty – it doesn't make any difference," she shrugs again. "Doctor says my genome checks out okay to smoke like a chimney."

"Crazy, isn't it?" Jack says with a baffled shake of his head. "Who'd have ever imagined doctors would be advising *some* people that they are not susceptible to any ill-effects from smoking?"

"Yeah, yeah."

"Listen, honey, I've been thinking about something. . . . "

"*What!*" she answers tartly as he hesitates.

"I'm thinking maybe, when this book is finished, we should sell up and move to Canada . . . or even Greenland."

Jenny screws her nose up in total disgust as she takes a fresh drag of her cigarette.

"*Jesus Christ!* Isn't it bad enough me having a *nut* for a son without being married to one as well!"

"Afternoon, Cass."

"Good afternoon, Jack."

"Any messages for me?"

"Sure! I have two video clips recorded; one of them with priority two status."

"Okay, Cass, play *it* first," he orders, settling back into his leather armchair.

A sombre-faced man from the National Weather Service appears on screen and speaks in gravelly tones.

"This is a hurricane warning issued for eastern New York state for Saturday, October One. Hurricane Eve – Category three status potential; expected landfall zero nine hundred Eastern Time. Preparations to prevent loss of life and property advised. . . . "

Jack grimaces as the announcer continues, and the projected track of the storm system is vividly illustrated in a whirling mass of blood red and pus yellow. Snaking its way along the Eastern seaboard and skirting the outer banks of the Carolinas before veering viciously north-eastward and barrelling towards Long Island.

"We're going to get all the rain we need come the weekend," Jack muses ruefully as the clip concludes.

"Are you ready for the second vid?" chirps CASS.

"Yes, thank you."

The face of a woman, a uniformed nurse, appears on screen. She squirms uncomfortably on her chair and fidgets with her hands as she begins to read out a prepared script to camera.

"Message for Mr Jack Andersson from Professor Sol Weiseman who sadly passed away September twenty-first." She clears her throat self-consciously before proceeding.

"I have lived long enough to know that even the greatest future eventually becomes the past. To know that Man is merely a trespasser into Eden; slowly being evicted now by Lady Nature. Nevertheless my departed spirit will pray for the future of Gaia. May the Lord bless you in writing this great book and preserving the legend of Eli. And remember: all the greatest stories are written in the stars. Goodbye, Jack Andersson, and God bless you and your son."

Jack feels a lump in his throat as he imagines the old man delivering the words himself; dressed in his crispest white shirt and blackest bow tie and welcoming death.

"Goodbye, Sol," he whispers faintly but CASS still picks up the sound.

"Do you want me to send a response to Professor Weiseman?"

He stares back incredulously at her effervescent smile, and just for once wishes she were mortal.

"Jenny fell axes, Jenny fell axes," Josh is panting excitedly.

"Huh, what?" answers Jack sleepily, stretched out on a sofa.

"Jenny fell axes, Jenny fell axes," he repeats, tugging at his father's upper shirt-sleeve.

"Jenny fell on an axe? What are you talking about, Josh?"

Josh thumps him once, hard, on the upper arm, and Jack is on his feet and chasing after him out into the garden. He finds Jenny slumped over, clutching the base of the tree for support. The high-pitched wheeze of her breathing fills the garden and echoes desperately around its walls.

"*Jesus*; honey, are you *okay?*" he says, kneeling beside her now.

Her face and neck are flushed a bright pink and she scarcely has the strength to raise her bloodshot eyes to acknowledge him. She is vainly trying to scratch her stomach with limp, wayward fingers.

"I think you've had too much of the sun, Jenny. I'll help you inside and run a cool bath."

"No . . . no . . . no," she wheezes.

"Come on, honey," he urges, "you'll be okay in a while. It's just a little sunstroke is all."

"No . . . no," she keeps repeating breathlessly.

"No! No!" shouts Josh at the top of his voice. "The patient is exhibiting symptoms of stridor, hypotension and angioedema." He bends down quickly and lifts up his mother's blouse to expose the reddened flesh of her abdomen.

"Urticaria!" he is shouting, pointing at a rash of fresh hives over her navel.

Jack stares back blankly at him at first, before a flicker of recognition makes him spring to his feet and shout into his cell.

"Cass! Medical emergency – place a nine-one-one to this address."

"It's okay, Jack," she coolly responds. "I summoned an ambulance as instructed seven minutes and thirty-five seconds ago, and informed the paramedics on board of the precise nature of the emergency. I am currently monitoring their progress en route, and ETA is approximately three minutes."

"*What?*" he replies, stunned. "Who instructed you to make the call?"

"Josh did."

For the second time in his life, Jack guides two paramedics through his home.

"My wife is over there . . . under the tree," he gasps, pointing across the garden.

The younger of the two races across the lawn, reaches her, and cups her swollen, ruddy face in his hands.

"Mrs Andersson . . . Mrs Andersson, can you hear me?"

"I think I'm dying!" she cries with a lazy roll of terrified eyes.

The older paramedic catches up with his colleague. They work feverishly, checking her blood pressure, pulse and respiratory function, before placing an oxygen mask over her mouth and examining the ugly weals now emerging all over her body.

They are nodding simultaneously as if tacitly concurring in their diagnosis.

"We'll need to give your wife a shot of epinephrine *now* and continue treating her in a hospital environment, Mr Andersson," says the older of the two.

"What's wrong with her?"

"We suspect your wife has had an adverse allergic reaction to some trigger or other . . . does she have a history of severe allergic reactions?"

"*No, none – ever!*"

The paramedic reaches into a small green holdall, pulls out a plastic bag and rips it open.

He checks the label on the barrel of a syringe filled with clear fluid before jabbing the needle into the back of Jenny's thigh.

"Is she going to be okay?"

"Yes – we should be able to stabilize her condition."

Josh comes skipping over from the sunflowers while they prepare to place Jenny on a stretcher. He stops, picks up a half-eaten apple on the ground and tosses it to his father, who catches it two-handed.

"Zzzz . . . Zzzz . . . Hymenoptera kissed mother on the lips . . . Zzzz," he drones.

"Thought so – insect sting," nods the younger paramedic.

"Is this Josh?" queries the other, frowning at the boy and raising a sidelong brow at Jack.

"Yeah."

"Your son?"

"Yeah."

"A real bright kid, Mr Andersson. He knew exactly what was happening when we spoke with him on the emergency channel. Even had the correct medical term for it."

"What *is* the term?" he inquires anxiously.

"Anaphylaxis."

"What?"

"Anaphylaxis – it's a severe hypersensitive reaction."

Jack stares open-mouthed at his green-eyed son, and the words echo in his head.

Jenny fell axes . . . Jenny fell axes.

Jack looks around the hospital waiting-room then checks the time on his cell. He sighs impatiently; it's been four hours since Jenny was admitted. In the interim, Josh has devoured every printed word in sight: from magazines and brochures to medical leaflets and warning notices.

"*Bored!*" he complains, sitting restlessly beside his father, twiddling his fingers rhythmically.

"You're a great kid. I'm proud of you, Josh," he says, running a paternal hand through the brown hair.

"Aaoww! . . . aaoww!" His son recoils, supersensitive to the fingertips combing his scalp.

"Sorry, Josh, I forgot. You know, you were here in this hospital before when you were a baby. Want to hear about it?"

The boy slowly turns towards him and intercepts the launch of the story with a withering look.

"Andersson, Joshua A., admitted eighteen twenty-two Rosalind Medical Center, Thursday, August fifteen, twenty thirty. Temperature: spike one zero four point seven Fahrenheit. Diagnosis: febrile convulsion initiated by middle ear infection."

Jack presses his own head back hard against the wall and remembers how scared he was when Josh got sick. He wonders if his son will ever be capable of loving anyone *so much* in his whole life. He closes his eyes and thinks of Cass.

"Mr Andersson," calls a voice, "you can see your wife now."

Jenny is propped up on a mound of pillows. Her eyes are bleary and bloodshot, and her face and neck still flushed bright pink.

"Hi, honey," grins a relieved Jack, kissing her tenderly on the forehead. "You gave us quite a fright."

"Yes, doctor says there are lots of new, weird insects flying around in the heat," she says softly.

"Yeah, he told me when I spoke with him just now. We're not accustomed to the different venom, he said. What's the word? It's more . . . v-v-v . . . "

"Virulent," blurts Josh impatiently. Jack ignores him.

"How do you feel, Jenny?"

"Oh, I'm just drained," she groans. "After I got stung it felt like I was dying; then I fell in the garden . . . then I fell . . . " Her voice weakens to a vacant whisper.

"Sure, doctor said the adrenaline surge causes your blood pressure to plunge; makes you feel like it's the end of the world."

"Yeah."

"He says you should be released come Thursday."

Jack pats her consolingly on the forearm. She looks up at him and then over at Josh, both standing at her bedside. Her eyes brim with tears that catch the beams of twilight as they seep through the window of the room.

"What's wrong, honey?"

"It's the garden. I felt it, I felt it – it's *dying!* It dies a little *every* day."

"No! It's just the fall coming."

"Yeah, maybe, but it arrives later and later every year now."

"Ain't it great?" says Jack. "Soon we'll have no winter at all."

TWENTY-ONE

"I STILL THINK WE SHOULD leave, Jack," Jenny pleads.

"There's no point now, honey. The freeways are like parking lots. Every train, plane and bus is booked up. There's a mass exodus of people fleeing this storm."

"My point exactly," she says with arms stretched wide.

"No! Doctor said you're not fit to travel yet. We're going to have to brave this thing out." He glances at the clock above the kitchen door. It reads five before eleven in old-style Roman numerals. "Anyway, I've a guy coming any minute to board up the windows. A professional guy; he says we'll be fine so long as we take the right precautions. Can we go through the list one more time?"

"Okay," Jenny meekly concedes with a long sigh.

Jack picks up a sheet from the table, entitled "Hurricane Preparations" that CASS has conveniently printed out.

"Top up with groceries," he states.

Without a word Jenny goes to a series of cupboards and opens them to reveal shelves packed with food.

"That's non-perishable, ready to eat stuff, right? Canned meats, fruits, etcetera? Nothing requiring refrigeration, you understand?"

"Yeah," she replies wearily.

"Fresh drinking water?"

She doesn't even bother to glance at the gallons of water stacked at the rear of the kitchen.

"Next dumb question," she answers churlishly.

He bites his lip.

"Flashlights?"

"Yeah."

"Portable radio?"

"Yeah."

"What about the potted plants in the garden? Have you put them in the garage?"

"Yeah. Don't forget to put the trash away in the garage too."

"Oh, yeah, thanks for reminding me, honey."

Jack hears a long ping from his cell.

"I'll get the door," he says. "Probably my guy anyway."

"Jack Andersson?" queries a well-built, rough-hewn man in denim overalls.

"That's me. You must be . . . ?"

"Fred Koznicki; howdy," he smiles broadly in return, doffing his cap and thrusting out an awkward right hand. It feels exactly like sandpaper.

"Nice vehicle you got, Fred," says Jack, admiring the large silver van parked in his driveway.

"Yeah, reckon I can afford a better one though after Eve blows over," he winks. "Never been so busy in my life!"

He pauses for a second or two.

"Mind if I start measuring up your windows now?"

"Go right ahead, Fred."

The workman takes a few paces back and draws out a small device from his belt. He points it towards the front of the house. Within seconds he has scanned all the windows and determined their precise measurements.

"Joe!" he calls out in a gruff voice. A head pops round, like a little bird, from the open doors at the back of the van and a young man in overalls approaches.

"Fetch the laser-saws and program in these numbers," Koznicki orders, handing him the device.

Jack leans against the frame of his front door with arms folded, and watches as the two set to work. They lift out a sheet of plywood and lay it on the ground, before each dons a pair of goggles. Jack maintains a safe distance as the orange-tinged light from the laser-saws effortlessly carves through the material. Fumes from the freshly scorched wood assail his nostrils. But the loudest sound he hears is the distant barking of a dog and the bird-song of his near-abandoned neighbourhood. Within a few minutes, there are five neatly cut rectangles of plywood numbered and laid out on the driveway.

"Number one, upper floor on the left," indicates Koznicki as his apprentice scurries to remove a ladder from the van roof. He angles it against the wall and scrambles up towards the window with monkey-like agility. His boss hands him up the sheet marked "#1" and within moments it is inset snugly into the window-frame.

"Four barrel bolts, Mr Koznicki, sir," says Joe from the top of the ladder.

One by one, they are handed up to him as he perforates the wood with a laser-drill and secures them. Finally, he burrows four holes into the corners of the concrete window surround and slides over the bolts.

"Number one done," he announces.

Jack is still gazing at the men's clinical efficiency as they work on number five.

"You ever seen a hurricane, Mr Andersson?" queries Koznicki, wiping a lather of perspiration from under his cap.

"No, Fred, only on TV."

"Shit," he laughs. "I saw one once when we were vacationing one time in Mobile. Man, it was scary and it was just a *Two*. Make you believe in God it would. And this thing is even bigger!" He gestures at a cloudless sky.

"You can take your gear through the garage to the back yard to do the rear windows," says Jack quickly.

Five minutes later and Koznicki is measuring them with his hand-held device.

Josh looks up from inspecting the sunflowers and eyes him with suspicion; but he's sufficiently intrigued by the scanner to warrant a tentative approach.

"This your son, Mr Andersson?"

"Yes, Fred."

"What age is he?"

"Josh is eleven."

"Eleven years, three hundred and twenty-six days," the boy corrects his father in a robotic voice.

"A fine looking boy," comments Koznicki, with beads of perspiration glistening on his brow and accentuating a frown.

"Yes, I have my mother's exterior and my father's interior."

The workman stares momentarily at Josh and then gives Jack a sympathetic look from under the peak of his cap.

"We'll be done in a half-hour or so."

"Thanks, Fred. Cash okay, I assume."

"Cash is just fine," he says almost bashfully, as he watches Josh skipping back towards the sunflowers.

Josh puts his hands over his ears and buries his head in his mother's armpit as they sit on the sofa watching the TV screen. Jack paces around the sitting-room, and barks again at the TV to increase the volume. The storm outside roars incessantly. The wooden shutters seem to inhale and exhale as the wind bellows intermittently down the chimneys. And the rain sounds like a blizzard of bullets, strafing the walls and roof of the old house.

"The New York metropolitan area has a population in excess of twenty million," states the news presenter in sombre tones. "And there is not a single resident of the Big Apple who cannot be overawed today at the magnitude of this rapidly developing disaster engulfing their beloved city. We are given to understand that a huge storm surge is currently funnelling through the right-angle bend between New Jersey and Long Island, into the city's harbour. FDR Drive is submerged;

Battery Park tunnel is swamped beneath ten feet of water; all Lower Manhattan roadways are inundated. We have reports of major flooding from Coney Island in Brooklyn, Hoboken and Jersey City. Both Newark and LaGuardia airports are submerged. . . . ”

Jack hangs his head in disbelief as the presenter breathlessly reams off a list of flood-stricken areas. Jenny lights up another cigarette, closes her eyes and gently strokes Josh's hair.

"I can't believe this is happening!" exclaims Jack, pointing at the scenes of utter devastation unfolding in vivid colour on the screen. "This isn't real . . . it's simply a disaster movie."

"No!' asserts Jenny, puffing her cigarette. "It's really happening. It's like the end of a phoney war or something."

"Or the end of the world!" shouts Jack animatedly.

Another voice cuts in from the TV audio.

"We scientists predicted a hurricane like Eve could happen. Sea levels along the New York coastline have risen by over a foot in the last thirty years. We have advised successive administrations of the necessity of constructing flood barriers between Staten Island and New Jersey; the entrance to New York harbour and across the upper East River on the north shore of Queens. This was a catastrophe waiting to happen – just like Katrina in New Orleans in twenty-o-five and Lucy in twenty twenty-seven, except on an exponential scale. This is a huge disaster in terms of loss of life and destruction of property!"

Jack stops and shoves his hands into his pockets. He shudders as he listens to the howling hurricane and the rain cascading on the roof and walls. He thinks of all the eco-disasters and ensuing human anguish he has witnessed on TV over the years. The black faces from drought-stricken sub-Saharan Africa. The brown faces fleeing the flooded deltas of Bangladesh. The sunken yellow faces cowering under vicious typhoons in the Far East. The olive-skinned faces migrating northwards from the Mediterranean to escape the "eternal summer" of 2034. The broad red cheeks of weeping Inuit as they abandon their melting, sacred hunting grounds.

Jack stares bug-eyed at the screen; the rolling interviews with tearful New Yorkers who are scarcely comprehending the destruction of their streets and buildings. The faces are nearly all white, but every one is bewildered and terrified.

"I remember Nine-Eleven," cries an old man, his hand trembling and pointing towards the sky. "But *we* did this . . . *we* did this!"

The wind is screaming like a demented banshee and tearing furiously at the wooden shutters. The timbers of the house creak, groan and shiver like an old sailing ship churning through a foam-curdling ocean. A flash of lightning starkly illuminates the tiny gaps between the sheets of plywood and the window-frames. Rolls of barrelling thunder quickly follow, their reverberations splintering the sky as if it were a crystal sphere shattered into innumerable fragments.

"Oh, my God!" wails Jenny, pushing Josh to one side and leaping to her feet from the sofa. "We can't stay in here, Jack!"

"Let's go to the study!" he yells. "There are no windows there."

The three run and squeeze themselves into the tiny room. Jenny curls up tight into the armchair and Josh throws himself on top of his mother, clutching at her flank with sheer terror.

"Chicken Licken . . . Chicken Licken," he says in response to every clap of thunder.

Jack crouches behind the chair and sinks his finger nails into the black leather.

CASS's beatific expression glazes over them from the screen opposite.

"Jesus Christ, Jack, would you ever change that bitch's emotional settings!" snaps Jenny.

"CASS, what's the up-to-date on Eve in this location?" he asks, disregarding his wife's request.

"Well, I am constantly collating data from the National Hurricane

Center and other meteorological sources. Current indications are that Eve has achieved maximum intensity with sustained wind-speeds of one hundred and twenty miles per hour. However, it will be downgraded to a Category One in this vicinity in approximately two hours. And storm surge or flooding is not anticipated at this elevation."

"Okay, CASS," says Jack.

"Would you like me to connect you to a news channel of your choice?"

"No, thank you," he answers. "I've seen enough already."

One hour later and the three are still huddled in the confines of the study. There is a loud *bang* from the street outside, the lights flicker in the room, and CASS's face fades from the screen. They are plunged into darkness. A single, piercing scream echoes round the tiny room.

"Josh!" shouts Jenny as she realizes he is gone from her lap, and hears him opening the door.

"It's okay, son," shouts Jack. "It's a power outage – I have a flashlight somewhere in the kitchen." He's struggling to remain calm. He gropes his way beyond the door of the study and feels his way along the walls.

"Josh . . . Josh!" he calls loudly, competing with the tumult of the raging storm. A flash of lightning briefly illuminates his route and he hastens towards the kitchen. A blast of air rapidly fills the house, rattling the roof as the rear door of the kitchen opens.

"Come back, Josh!" roars Jack at the rectangle of grey light gaping through the doorway as the boy bolts into the garden. Suddenly, Jack feels as though he has stumbled into a speeding locomotive, as the clock is swept off the wall above and strikes his face. The Roman numerals on its dial seem to swirl and dance inside his head as he staggers and hurtles headlong into the hell outside. The wind swells his clothes like billowing kite-sails, and the horizontal torrent washes away the blood pouring down one side of his face.

"Oh, my God!" he groans. "The sky is falling down."

He peers through the fingers of one hand and scans the wrecked flower-beds. He finds Josh, kneeling, stark naked, beside the remnants of the sunflowers. He is pressing his lips against a once-mighty flowering head as if trying to resurrect it with the kiss of life. The series of snapped stalks looks like a row of freshly slaughtered golden chicks, their necks wrung by a callous, invisible hand. Jack runs up from behind and grabs the bare flesh of the boy's right upper arm.

"Come back inside, Josh – now! You're in great danger."

But the boy turns instantly, wriggling and sliding from his father's damp grip. His soaked, bronzed body glistens under successive arcs of lightning as he splashes through a streaming trough at one edge of the lawn. Jack races after him, running parallel to submerged and ruined flower-beds in his frantic pursuit. The small, naked figure almost collides with the wall at the bottom of the garden. It doubles back, and careers wildly in the direction of the oak tree. Jack darts across the lawn to intercept it, lunges at it, misses, and falls flat on his face into the sodden clay.

"For God sake, Josh!" he roars, struggling to raise himself from the ground. Then he sees the boy, standing ramrod straight, in defiance of the tempest, beneath the flailing limbs of the tree. His head is extended back fully and the wind is whipping his wet hair to a frenzied mop. His arms are thrust out as a pair of tongs, beckoning towards the louring sky. Jack gazes open-mouthed at the massive coils of black cloud swirling around every horizon in a vicious, airy vortex.

"Ouroboros!" howls Josh. "Cry havoc, let slip the gods of war."

The heavens seem to split with pulsing white streaks and forks, rending the clouds asunder.

"Look, Father, at how the ichor flows through their veins."

Jack looks on, awestruck, as if the coruscating bolts of lightning seem to electrify and animate the boy, enabling him to orchestrate the entire scene.

"Mjollnir – the mighty hammer of Thor falls!" roars Josh as deafening crashes of thunder boom overhead.

"Ullhodturdenweirmudgaard . . . Thingcrooklyex . . . " the crazed boy descends into a litany of incomprehensible gibberish.

"The boy is insane, Jack!" screams a voice from beyond the sound of the wind. "I swear to God he's insane."

"No, Mother! These are thunder-words; the language of the gods; to wail the tale of Ragnarok and Götterdämmerung."

"Josh – go inside now!" orders Jack as his wife flings herself into his arms.

The child slowly turns to face his parents; his green eyes seem to vitrify as yet another bolt of lightning irradiates the skies.

"I am Satan, I am Christ!" he screeches. Then he raises his left arm and points with his index finger at the base of the oak tree. Its bole has careened over to one side, tearing a yawning wound into the brown earth, whence the storm has wrenched it. The dark and densely tangled roots are clearly exposed.

"Look yonder, Mother, Father. Little Lazarus is rise again from the Land of Nod east of Eden. Like Captain Ahab tethered to Moby Dick, he ascends from the heart of hell to spit his hate at thee. Yea – e'en the dead shall know no end to Man's war upon the elements."

"Oh, sweet Jesus!" shouts Jack.

"No! . . . No! . . . No!" caterwauls Jenny, clawing the air as if to yank an imaginary curtain across a scene of unadulterated horror.

One end of a tiny, white wooden box is visible, snared in a network of dark roots under the half-felled tree.

"I want to see my brother's bones!" Josh calls out, running towards the coffin and starting to clamber through the exposed undergrowth.

Jack and Jenny tear after him, and each grabs a bare ankle before the boy's legs disappear completely into the freshly hollowed ground.

"No!" he squeals as they drag him backwards. "Earth's kiln has enamelled his skeleton – I want to witness Christopher's bones."

His fingers claw despairingly to prise open the lid of the coffin, but Jack thrusts one hand in amongst the roots, finds the boy's head and hauls him out backwards by the hair.

"Aaaoowww!" he yelps as his bared torso and buttocks are scratched and bruised during his brutal extraction. Jenny clamps her hands onto the child's shoulders and digs her finger-nails into the flesh. She stands him up and swivels his body violently to meet her manic gaze.

"You're a demon-child!" she shrieks. "The Devil doesn't have a brother!"

She slaps his face savagely, once upon the right cheek. The boy hardly blinks as he slowly turns his head and offers his left cheek. She wallops it with the same hand and equal savageness. He stands fast and reflexively angles his flaming right cheek towards her, but she hesitates, before collapsing onto her knees in front of him. Jack is on his knees too, nursing his bloodied nose. They are both oblivious to the driving deluge, the howling hurricane, the blinding lightning-bolts and exploding thunderclaps. They watch as their precious boy arches his saturated body back slightly and zeroes his green eyes on the fiery zenith. Josh points his left index finger accusingly, first at his mother and then his father, and finally himself.

"We are the terrors from Mother Nature's id. Us! – the monsters that detonated doom – the harbingers of our own destruction! Thus spoke Zarathustra."

Jack springs to his feet, runs up behind his son and seizes him with both arms in a vice-like grip. He sweeps the boy up over one shoulder and carries him back towards the house.

"Let me go, Father!" Josh screams hysterically.

"No!"

"Let me go!"

"No!"

"Release me!"

"No!"

Suddenly, the boy frees one hand, reaches around and punches his father squarely on the nose. Jack cries out and instinctively raises his own hands to cradle his bloodied face, dropping his hysterical cargo in the process.

"Thrice you deny me, Father – dare not touch me again!"

Jack makes a rush to recapture him, trying to corral him into one corner of the garden.

"*Noli me tangere!*" the child clamours, evading his half-blind father's windmilling arms with surprising athleticism.

"Stop, I command thee; or I shall shatter the rock of your mind with one Word."

"Go on, Josh – you just fucking try!"

The boy stops dead, plants his feet into the ground and squares his body into the gale. His arms akimbo and hands clamped over his bare hips.

He bellows the word from the bottom of his lungs.

"*Steelman!*"

"You fucking freak . . . you fucking freak!" Jack roars in blind fury. A rip tide of adrenaline courses through his veins and swells his hammer-fists as he lunges.

He aims for the boy's chin, but at the last second lowers his swing and punches him mercilessly in the abdomen, poleaxing him. The boy doubles over onto the ground, writhing in agony and seeming to suffocate with convulsions of pain. He is retching, and finally vomits before heaving a series of panicked gasps. Jack circles the crumpled figure in predatory fashion, casting him intermittent baleful glances from the corners of his eyes. Blood streams from his nostrils and eddies around the cruel twist of his upper lip.

"Where the *fuck* did *you* hear that word?" he snarls.

"Auric . . . Auric told me."

"Auric?"

"The pen . . . the gold pen."

"What?"

"Engraved . . . the word," the helpless boy is panting.

"You son of a bitch, you unlocked my safe!"

"Yeah."

"There's a ten-digit security code – How did you get it?"

"Saw you once . . . pressing the buttons . . . I was only a baby."

"What?"

"I remember things . . . Everything . . . Everything."

Jack rushes forward, seizes him by the throat with one hand and raises him to the tips of his toes. He stares into the child's bulging eyes as he tightens his grip and starts to throttle him.

"I could end you now! . . . Whoever or whatever the fuck you are!"

The raging storm abates briefly as a rancid sun blinks through a break in the phosphorescent cloudscape. The peals of thunder roll away to the horizon. Josh collapses to the ground, clutching his Adam's apple and choking in great gulps of air.

"Jenny!" cries Jack again and again as he searches the house once more with a quivering flashlight. He tries calling her cell again but the network is down. Two days later and he is still plaintively calling out her name inside his aching head as he trudges around the perimeter of the storm-racked garden. The early morning sun is rising in the east, as a tepid orange disc is greeted by a merry chorus of bird-song. Their sweet strains are interrupted by a pinging sound echoing across the almost deserted neighbourhood. It takes Jack a few seconds to orient himself before he realizes it is his own cell ringing, and grabs it.

"That you, Jack?" queries a voice, nervously.

"*Hello.*"

"*Jack* . . . it's *me.*"

"Is that *you*, Robbie?"

"Yeah . . . Jack, she's here."

"*What?*"

"Jenny's here with me, and she's safe."

"How did she get . . . ?"

"She walked through the hurricane to get here. She has a few minor cuts and bruises from flying debris, but apart from that she's physically okay."

"Can I speak with her?"

There is a long pause before Robbie responds.

"I think she has had some kind of mental breakdown. She keeps saying something about Josh being the Devil . . . said she saw something truly horrific, but wouldn't tell me what it was. She doesn't want to talk to you. Anyway, I gave her some sedatives and she's asleep in bed."

"Well then, you have her exactly where you always wanted her, haven't you!" shouts Jack.

"That's not fair!"

"You're right . . . it's incredibly unfair. Jenny just wants half my money and Josh out of her life."

"You know she's depressed, don't you?"

"That makes two of us!" fumes Jack, before disconnecting with an angry click.

Then he strides back towards the house in a rage.

He hears Josh's voice calling out after him in a loud whisper. He halts and whirls around menacingly but fails to see him. The boy is lurking somewhere in the garden. His tone is almost chilling as he rasps the words.

"Cain and Abel. Cain and Abel."

TWENTY-TWO

"How long until we reach GeoNova Iceland?"

"Approximately ten minutes, Mr Andersson," answers the uniformed young brunette sitting opposite him in the train.

"Incredibly smooth and quiet for a vehicle travelling at four hundred miles per hour, isn't it?" remarks Jack as the train bullets silently across the barren landscape.

"This is a Maglev; it is suspended above the track by superconducting magnets. It's a completely frictionless mode of transport . . . Electric, naturally."

"Oh . . . Maglev . . . Icelandic word, is it?"

"No, it's English," she chuckles. "It is derived from the words 'magnetic' and 'levitation'."

"Right," says Jack, scratching his head.

"Of course, all the electricity requirements of the island are geothermally sourced," she quickly continues, sensing his embarrassment. "We are fortunate, here in Iceland, to be situated only twenty kilometres directly above a superheated column of molten volcanic rock. It is the cleanest and greenest energy available, radiated right from the Earth's core. Once we radically improved the pre-existing power generation technologies, the island became a natural choice as an eco-colony."

A vast complex of huge domes soon heaves into view, contrasting bright white against a dark moonscape of background.

"Wow!" gasps Jack at the sight. "That is *impressive*. I've been to GeoNova HQ in the Mojave, but this is . . . this is truly *enormous* in scale . . . it's awesome."

"Yes," the woman opposite nods energetically in agreement. "It's scheduled for completion next summer. We fully expect to be able to accommodate a hundred thousand personnel on this site alone."

"How many eco-colonies does GeoNova have now?"

"We have twelve sites completed in the Northern Hemisphere and four more still under construction: two in Greenland, one each in western Canada and Siberia. In the Southern Hemisphere we have three sites finished in New Zealand, Chile and Madagascar, with two more colonies to be completed in Antarctica."

Jack stares at her, marvelling at her fluent factual grasp, rhyming off the locations and scarcely drawing breath as she does so. He glances at the badge on her lapel to remind himself of her name, and then frowns at her brown eyes.

"You're not Icelandic, are you, Vanessa?"

"No," she smiles demurely. "How did you know?"

"It's your eyes – they're not blue. Where are you from originally?"

"I'm from Switzerland."

"And how does a pretty Swiss girl end up working in Iceland, of all places?"

She blushes and combs the fingers of one hand through her brown hair.

"I was head-hunted by GeoNova from the University of Zurich to work as both a language teacher and a translator. I specialize in French, German and Russian, although English is of course our standard corporate language."

"How many languages do you speak?"

"Oh, please, Mr Andersson . . . you're embarrassing me," she says, her cheeks flushing a brighter pink this time.

"No, please, Vanessa. Go on, tell me. How many?"

She hesitates with a sharp intake of breath.

"I speak twelve languages fluently . . . and I am reasonably proficient in a further ten."

Jack whistles lowly in admiration.

"How do you keep all those words, pronunciations and grammatical rules in your head?"

"It's nothing really; just a job like any other . . . a vocation, you might say, in my case. Elijah Roberts, for example, speaks numerous languages. You never see the President with a personal translator, do you? Even when he's negotiating with the Chinese."

Jack shakes his head and grins at her.

"No, but as you admitted yourself, you were specifically targeted and hired by GeoNova."

"Yes, but I was subject to standard corporate recruitment procedures and genetic screening."

"Are all its employees specially chosen, Vanessa?"

She averts her eyes briefly before returning to his gaze and quickly changes the subject.

"Is this your first time meeting Tor Magnusson?"

"Yes."

"Mmmm . . . you may prepare yourself, Mr Andersson."

"What do you mean?"

"I can promise that you will never encounter another human being like him. Sometimes he is strangely terrifying or comfortably reassuring; sometimes both at the same time. He likes to play mind-games I think. He has a certain presence that seems to alter your state of consciousness. I can't really explain it precisely. . . . "

Jack looks quizzically at her as the Maglev finally arrives at its destination.

An electric monorail system with silver gull-winged pods, similar in design to that at GeoNova HQ in California, transports Jack to the heart of the complex. He is escorted by two security officers to a heavy steel door. It glides back slowly to reveal a spacious office. A tall, impressive-looking bald man is standing within, and appears to be holding court with half a dozen seated subordinates, who nod mechanically in accord as he addresses them. The standing figure sees Jack's entry into the room and gestures with one hand to dismiss his audience. Within moments, they are all filing past Jack and obediently exiting the office, leaving the two alone. Tor Magnusson approaches, and towers over his visitor as he shakes his hand. He has a charmless smile but stunning sapphire eyes that seem to possess an almost hypnotic quality.

"Good morning, Mr Andersson. Please . . . take a seat."

"Thank you, sir."

Magnusson remains standing, his hands clasped to his hips and his chin held high. *The epitome of vanity,* thinks Jack, *like an outsized caricature of Mussolini.*

"I want to begin by showing you something."

A large computerized screen is quickly illuminated at one side of the office.

"Observe," he says, pointing towards it. "This is a map of Iceland. Here is the capital Reykjavik in the south-west, and our base some seventy kilometres due east of it." Both locations are conveniently highlighted in flashing amber as he continues. "But I would like you to focus on the geological structure of this island. Do you see these lines illustrated here in blue?"

"Yes."

"Do you know what they are?"

"No, I'm afraid I don't."

"These are seismic fault-lines, Mr Andersson. This island is situated on top of two gigantic tectonic plates that are slowly but surely separating from one another. To the west is the North-American plate and to the east the European plate. Eventually, they will cleave this entire island in two. I like to use this geological phenomenon as a metaphor for the relationship between Roberts and myself."

"I don't quite understand," says Jack, shaking his head perplexedly. "You were until quite recently the President's Science Advisor and a *personal* friend as well."

"True, but our opinions became too divergent. So you might say he re-assigned me; granted me my own private Viking fiefdom, here in the Land of Fire and Ice. A fundamental difference in emphasis emerged between us. Eli believes he can actually save humanity by bending nine billion people to his will and altering their behavioural patterns. But this is a totally unrealistic prospect, despite his tremendous achievements thus far. I am of the opinion that mankind will wipe itself out in some calamitous nuclear holocaust within the next few years." Magnusson stiffens and widens his stance as he glowers down at Jack.

"It is inevitable, is it not?" he remarks coldly as he shrugs.

"Well, I suppose it's always a possibility."

"No, he says, raising his voice insistently, "you *must* accept that it is the genetic destiny of *homo sapiens* to self-destruct."

"It is?"

"Oh, yes. I have studied the human genome extensively. As you are probably aware, I received a Nobel Prize for my work in genetics. We have performed scientific miracles to conquer many cancers with retroviral therapies. Cure complex diseases such as Huntingdon's using synthetic genes. Alleviate famine with advances in GM agriculture. There are three billion letters in the human genome that we can cut, paste and splice, much like a computer programmer can. The field of genetics, allied with the tremendous power of quantum computers, has revolutionized science and our comprehension of what it means to be human. We can effectively rewrite every chapter of the Book of Life, but we cannot alter human nature itself. That leopard will *never* change its spots or that tiger its stripes. Genes are recipes for proteins, you understand. Proteins perform almost every chemical, structural, and regulatory function in the body. But some behavioural attributes are pleiotropic . . . meaning there are multiple effects from a broad variety of genes that defy adaptation. To tamper with the DNA code would be futile and even more dangerous. . . . ”

Jack sits rigid in his chair and listens patiently as Magnusson continues to expatiate on his pet subject. The man completely dominates the room, as he paces panther-like to and fro, but never once takes his eyes off Jack; who feels totally and utterly unnerved, much as he felt when he first met Eleanor Roberts.

“ . . . Of course the theocons object to these triumphs of bio-engineering, as inimical to divine design. They describe GeoNova’s global genetic screening programs as laissez-faire eugenics; but how else are we to determine the very best that humanity has to offer? Huh, Mr Andersson?” He stops at last directly in front of him, and plants his legs colossus-like on the floor. He is but a few feet away.

“Well, Mr Magnusson, I don’t think we need get involved in ethical arguments. I basically just want to interview you about Eli Roberts and find out what kind of a man he really is.”

The towering figure glowers at him.

“You want my true opinion of the man?”

“Yes, this is exactly what I need to write the President’s biography.”

“I don’t envy you your task. Eli is a spinner of webs and every strand of them a tightrope. It must be like trying to write a biography of God himself. How many volumes would that fill?” he smiles almost sympathetically. “But, to answer your question specifically, it is my opinion that Roberts is a megalomaniac – he enjoys power for its own sake. Look at what is happening in the world around us: climatic catastrophes; ocean acidification; glacial melting; bio-diversity levels are in free-fall; carbon dioxide levels in the atmosphere are still rising alarmingly . . . the catalogue of eco-disasters continues unabated. Yet Eli persists like a man possessed, even though he knows in his heart of hearts the world is a lost cause. Do you know why?”

“I always thought Roberts cherished humanity and genuinely wanted to save it.”

“That is precisely the problem. He has too much of a conscience

. . . he is excessively altruistic. Too much of a messiah complex per-haps, as I'm sure his psychiatrist told you. No?"

"I'm sorry. I'm not at liberty to discuss . . . "

Suddenly Magnusson strides forward and grabs both arms of Jack's chair. Jack can feel his hot breath on his face as he bends down and stares directly into his eyes.

"What did Meredith Steinitz tell you in the bathroom, Mr Anders-son?"

"Whaaat?"

"What did she tell you? Our sensors couldn't pick it up."

"Nothing . . . I swear."

"You're lying, Andersson. You know it and I know it."

Jack senses his heart pounding and feels a strange, overwhelming compulsion to confess the truth under Magnusson's penetrating gaze. He fights manfully not to reveal the psychiatrist's fears.

"Tell me, Andersson!"

"Steinitz is scared . . . she's terrified, and thinks Roberts will do something terrible if he loses the next presidential election."

Magnusson quickly snaps his body back up and readopts his rigid stance.

"Mmm . . . this makes complete sense," he says, rubbing a hand over his bald head. "You know what's going to happen when he loses it, don't you?"

"No, I have no idea," Jack answers breathlessly.

"The world is growing weary of the dream of Eli. Humanity is sapped of the requisite energy of will to alter its behaviour. It is inevit-able that 'Big Carbon' will regain power in America, with its vacuous promises of geo-engineering solutions. Eli and GeoNova will lose ac-cess to the vast military and civil resources currently at their disposal."

Magnusson is perspiring now as he starts to pace over and back again. The beads of sweat glisten on his pate and begin to trail into rivulets down the sides of his face.

"I . . . I think . . . I think you should know, Mr Andersson, that Roberts intends to take his own life if he fails to secure a second term."

"I don't believe it! . . . That's incredible," Jack says, jerking his head back in shock.

"*Believe* me! My sources are extremely reliable."

"You mean this book of mine is going to be some kind of suicide note?"

"Yes, assuming he loses. He is quite concerned as to his legacy. This biography will be his *apologia pro vita sua* – the justification for his life's work. You have an awesome responsibility, when you think about it. Of course, you have probably asked yourself a thousand times why you were chosen as the author. You know why. Don't you?"

Jack's face lights up in anticipation as he answers falteringly. "No . . . no, I simply have no idea why I was chosen."

"Oh, Mr Andersson, this project is so much bigger than you. You really have no idea, do you?"

"No," he says, staring back vacantly.

"Would it surprise you to learn that Roberts and your little boy are kindred spirits, as it were?"

"What are you talking about? *That's impossible!* They couldn't be."

"Think about it," says Magnusson, stroking his chin pensively with one finger. "You are the father of an extraordinarily gifted boy in Josh; he has perhaps a mind in a billion. He possesses an unparalleled genius for language, for information retention, processing and synthesization. Roberts displays the very same intellectual prowess. I firmly believe that you were chosen as the author of this biography because of your unique insight into this type of mind."

"No, you don't understand, Mr Magnusson . . . my son . . . Josh has Asperger's Syndrome."

Magnusson folds his arms and casts him a dubious look.

"That is an all-too-familiar diagnosis in the psychological field of gifted children. Let me surmise that schizophrenia or obsessive-compulsive disorder have also been diagnosed in this instance."

"Yes," answers Jack curtly.

Magnusson folds his arms more tightly and lifts his eyes towards the ceiling in disgust.

"All the symptoms your son presents with are merely exaggerated anxieties. And the more powerful his mind becomes, the greater the imaginary fears it is possible for him to conjure up. Fear dominates his cognitive patterns, defining his experience of what it means to be human."

Magnusson pauses and nods to himself with a hint of self-satisfaction before continuing.

"You know the earliest work in world literature is the Epic of Gilgamesh from ancient Mesopotamia. It recounts the deeds of the eponymous hero and his pursuit of immortality. Thanatophobia, the fear of death, is a theme that haunts the ages, infecting our religious ideologies with promises of eternal bliss. Our modern obsession with preserving youth, worshipping youth, is rooted in this most primitive of fears. . . . "

"I don't understand. What has any of this got to do with Josh?"

Magnusson's face softens, rendering an impression of benevolence.

"The fear of death is not something that can be understood by the rational mind. It can only be experienced by the core emotional aspect of our being."

He grips Jack lightly by the arm and gestures towards a small door at the rear of the office.

"Come, Mr Andersson. Let me show you how to cure your boy."

Jack struggles to keep pace with Magnusson's rangy stride along a dark corridor. Soon, however, the two emerge, blinking in the sunlight, on the surface above the vast underground complex of GeoNova Iceland. A sleek, silver jetcopter is parked to one side of a small airstrip. Magnusson strolls towards it and opens the passenger door.

"Please make yourself comfortable," he says with an encouraging pat on the seat.

Jack climbs aboard and buckles up. The cockpit is tiny and scarcely seems able to accommodate Magnusson's bulk as he squeezes into the pilot's seat.

"Man and machine as one," he grins at Jack.

A curved bank of computerized displays quickly illuminates the inside of the craft with an eerie greenish glow. Jack closes his eyes as he hears the engine rev up and the rotors beginning to hum. The world falls away from beneath his feet as they ascend. The jetcopter swoops low and fast over the landscape like a bird of prey. Magnusson doesn't even seem to have physical control of the flight as he intermittently calls out orders to the autopilot, which reacts instantly to his verbal commands. Jack is amazed by this feat of hands-free flying, as if the pilot is exercising control through the power of his mind alone.

"Iceland is a geological marvel, you know," Magnusson says, pointing down at a series of boiling, sulphurous pools of water bubbling up from the earth and geysers spewing out jets of steam high into the cold air.

"I love Iceland," he continues. "It provides living proof of the power and restiveness of Mother Nature. And of course the island's remoteness has facilitated the evolution of a genetically pure population, which is ideal for scientific study."

The vast rocky plains stretching out below seem like the surface of an alien planet to Jack.

He is pleased to see lush, green landscape appearing on the horizon.

Magnusson indicates a rocky outcrop on top of a small hill. He orders the autopilot to reduce speed, and the craft begins to circle it.

"This is Thingvellir, the site of the world's very first parliament, dating back to the tenth century. Viking chieftains met here to discuss and resolve their differences."

"A very ordinary place for the birth of a great democratic institution," replies Jack, raising his voice over the drone of the engine.

"Agh! There is nothing great about democracy," Magnusson answers gruffly. "Partisanship is too polarizing nowadays and nothing ever gets done. Politicians can't see any further than the next election. The possibility of wielding real power and implementing effective long-term policies is being sabotaged by regular popularity contests. But that's no way to fix this broken world – only a benevolent dictatorship can do that."

"Is that how you manage GeoNova Iceland?" Jack asks guardedly.

Magnusson slowly turns his great bald head and addresses him sharply. "Our mission is to change the world. Only a tyrant like a Hitler or a Stalin or a Mao Tse Tung can ever hope to achieve it. How else should I run the operation here, hmm . . . or Roberts run the world, for that matter? One must keep one's satellites in orbit with a firm gravitational pull," he says, flexing his left fist.

Jack is transfixed by the cold, piercing blue eyes that dominate Magnusson's sombre mien. The pupils are like tiny pinpricks, burrowing into Jack's forehead.

"I'm sorry. I'm sorry . . . " he hears himself apologizing over and over as if hypnotized by some magnetic force.

All at once Magnusson's mood appears to change, heralded by an almost deranged-sounding series of guffaws.

"Of course you know who the greatest dictator of all is? Don't you?"

"Napoleon . . . Caesar . . . Genghis Khan . . . No?" ventures Jack.

"Why, God himself of course! Worship the Lord your God and serve him only. You shall have no other gods before me! The very first edict from the mountain-top, Mr Andersson. Imagine if heaven was governed as a parliamentary democracy . . . eh?"

Magnusson elbows Jack playfully in the ribs but only gets a muted grunt in response.

"Just imagine hosts of angels wittering interminably about Creation. Why, the Big Bang would just be a damp squib!"

The jetcopter hovers over a narrow, rocky gorge that stretches to the horizon.

"This is the seismic fault-line I was telling you about earlier, the one that is slowly but surely tearing this island in two," says Magnusson. "The demarcation line between two mighty tectonic plates. . . . Are you afraid of death?"

"What?"

"Do you fear death?"

"Yes, of course. Is it not the ultimate fear for everyone?"

"That is precisely the reason you must conquer it to truly embrace the world. The span of human life is but a single tick of a cosmic clock. You must learn to look death straight in the eye and not flinch . . . as I have."

Magnusson commands the autopilot to switch off, and lays his large hand on a joystick in the centre of the console in front of him. He pushes it forward and descends into the narrow chasm. The engine thrums more loudly as its vibration echoes between the sheer sides. The rotors whir perilously close to the rocks as the cockpit darkens.

Jack feels his entire body go rigid with terror.

"What are you doing?" he roars.

Magnusson blithely ignores him as he accelerates the jetcopter along the length of the gorge, expertly manoeuvring the aircraft with his fingertips caressing the joystick. The computer screens in front of him are all blinking red with speed warnings and proximity alerts. The shriek of alarms reverberates around the cockpit, warning the pilot of extreme danger.

Jack presses his hands hard over his ears and clenches his eyes shut. He feels completely disoriented, almost as if he is riding bareback on some giant metallic insect that is oblivious to the danger.

"I'm dizzy . . . I'm going to throw up. . . " he groans.

"Look death square in the eye!" orders Magnusson, "and learn to embrace that fear."

"You are insane!"

"No, I'm not insane! On the contrary, I am in complete control of the situation. Flying without fear of death is a liberating experience . . . Seizing life by the throat and saying 'Yes!' to it – just as Nietzsche preached," he laughs maniacally.

"Stop!" pleads Jack. "I'm scared."

Abruptly the craft ascends into the clear blue sky and sunlight floods in through the cabin window. A relieved Jack opens his eyes and glances at Magnusson's imperious countenance. There is not a bead of perspiration on the man's brow as he stares fixedly ahead.

He rotates the joystick and pirouettes the jetcopter through 360°, pushes the stick forward and descends, accelerating as he does so.

"No! . . . No! . . . not again!" cries Jack in terror.

But the pilot is deaf to his desperate pleas and starts to hum to himself as he weaves his way along the narrow chasm.

For the next hour, Magnusson does not utter a single word or even glance at his passenger. He repeatedly performs exactly the same acrobatic aerial exercises with a dexterity that seems to defy the laws of physics. Jack feels as if his entire body has sweated out every drop of adrenaline in his system. He is totally exhausted, and yet a strange sense of calm pervades his mind. Despite the horrendous nature of his experience he no longer has the strength even to think of death.

Magnusson suddenly snaps his fingers and jolts him out of his trance-like state.

"Is the fear gone now, Mr Andersson?"

"Yes," he answers drowsily.

"Repeated exposure to one's innermost fears will eventually reduce levels of anxiety. It is a basic principle of human psychology. This is how you must treat Josh. You understand now, Jack, don't you?"

"What . . . what are you saying, Magnusson?"

"You must recalibrate the boy's state of consciousness."

"How?"

"Get him to confront his fears. Put him on an airplane. Take him to the Grand Canyon and put him standing on the edge and staring into the abyss. Switch his bedroom light off at night . . . anything . . . anything, to save that boy and show him he has nothing to fear, not even his inner demons."

"Why are you so interested in my son?"

"Your boy has a profound talent. The world needs this boy. Geo-Nova needs this boy. I cannot bear to witness such a mind go to waste under your supervision. Either you resolve the boy's imaginary psychological illness soon, or I promise I will intervene myself!"

Magnusson fires a fierce glare at him; an eye-lock so invasive that it seems to drain Jack of the will to even question the implicit threat, and somehow cow him into abject submission. There is something utterly sinister, cold and ruthless about those sapphire eyes – a look that brooks absolutely no opposition, thinks Jack.

The two zoom over the barren Icelandic landscape in sullen silence as they return to GeoNova. Jack leans back and imagines the entire island floating on a sea of molten rock.

He thinks of volcanoes and geysers and boiling pools. He glances surreptitiously at the pilot's now-flushed face, and knows that Tor Magnusson's mercurial temperament is perfectly suited to the land of Fire and Ice. And deep down, he feels a peculiar blend of animosity and admiration for the man – a man with that rare quality of living without fear.

TWENTY-THREE

WALTER FRANKLIN IS SITTING in Jack's living-room, watching him pacing around the mahogany table. Franklin occasionally shakes his head vigorously in response to his angry words.

"Who the hell does Magnusson think he is? . . . Threatening my son like that . . . 'I'll intervene myself . . . this project is so much bigger than *you*,' he told me . . . arrogant, fascist son of a bitch is what he is! And another thing . . . this code-name 'Steelman' has been compromised. I saw the word written as the last entry in Clara Roberts's diary . . . it was etched into the gold pen Sol Weiseman gave me as well."

Jack pauses and scrunches up his nose.

"Josh knows the code-name too," he sighs. "He saw the goddam pen, even though I had it locked away in my safe . . . something smells here, Walt! Something rotten, yet another slimy maggot burrowing beneath the Beltway, I suspect. I don't know what it is, but I'm fed up being treated like an idiot."

Franklin raises a palm in a pacifying manner but to no avail.

"I've lost my wife. My son is seriously mentally ill, and this book is becoming overwhelming . . . It's not easy living here on my own with a kid like Josh, you know."

Franklin's patience suddenly snaps.

"For God's sake, Andersson, would you just shut up already! Just shut up and listen. Okay!"

Franklin sweeps a hand through his thinning grey hair before continuing.

"Whenever you're working for a guy like Eli Roberts there are always things going on in the background. Things or events that you either can't or don't need to know about. But the bottom line is you

234

have undertaken a task to complete the President's biography and you have been handsomely paid for it in advance. Very handsomely! And don't tell me you were under any illusions before you cashed the cheque either," he says, wagging his finger. "There is no hidden agenda here. It's just a book to help him get re-elected. You make it sound like there is something sinister afoot."

"Damn right there is."

"What are you talking about for Chrissake?!"

Jack stops in his tracks and glares at Franklin.

"Almost everybody I've interviewed has mentioned or enquired after Josh. What's so special about him, Walt?"

"What do you mean?"

"Magnusson said my son had some special talent."

"Sorry, Jack, I've no idea what the man meant, although I know he's constantly scouting for high IQ individuals to recruit at GeoNova. Perhaps that's what he meant."

"You worked with Magnusson, didn't you?"

"Sure."

"What was he like to work with?"

"Let me tell you that Tor Magnusson is one of the most competent and savvy political operators I have ever met. He was the only one of Roberts's inner circle who would dare go mano a mano with him. I swear, to watch those two go hammer and tongs at one another across the cabinet table was like having a ringside seat at a heavyweight boxing contest. Both of them utterly fearless and each convinced of their own superiority of opinion. A pair of intellectual prize-fighters, that's what they were, but they had tremendous respect for each other, despite their differences."

"So how come Roberts effectively exiled him to Iceland – literally left him out in the cold? Magnusson's away from Washington; he's been removed from the centre of power now, even though he's still working for GeoNova."

Franklin leans back in his chair with an exaggerated shrug of his shoulders.

"That's politics – one day you're the best of buddies with some guy and the next day you're slitting his throat."

"No, Roberts and Magnusson were friends for years. There's something you're not telling me, Walt!"

"What the hell is this, the Spanish Inquisition?!" he protests.

"What happened between Roberts and Magnusson – some huge ideological rift, wasn't there?"

Franklin shifts uncomfortably in his chair and leans forward with elbows placed on the table. His fingers are tightly clasped and he raps both thumbs nervously together in an unconscious rhythmical movement.

"It's irrelevant," he answers with a dismissive shake of his head.

"Then why are you so reluctant to tell me?"

Franklin rises from his chair and fixes Jack under his steely gaze.

"I don't like wasting my time responding to questions you know the answer to already."

"What do you mean?"

"Magnusson told you himself. He has lost faith in the democratic system. Big deal . . . he is hardly alone in being disillusioned with it. We've had a crisis of governance for decades in this country. The political process is paralyzed and Congress is constantly gridlocked. Legislation to tackle climate change is getting delayed for years . . . and frankly, we don't have the time to procrastinate any more. America just isn't able to make decisions unless every lobbyist's opinion and every financial interest is pandered to and ultimately accommodated. Compromise means everyone's gotta be seen to be a winner. And that's the primary objective of modern politics – to never appear to be a loser, and get re-elected at all costs."

"So Roberts is no different from any other President in being desperate to get re-elected, is he . . . and what does your boss think of democracy then?"

Franklin purses his lips.

"Considering the alternatives, democracy is the least bloodiest option."

"But it doesn't work any more," smirks Jack in return.

"But don't you see how GeoNova is bridging that democratic deficit? We're so close to achieving single-party domination of global politics that we *will* be in a position to transform the world. That's the difference between the politics of the near future and the moribund system we are going to leave behind. The structures of real political power are going to be rationalized and executive decision-making centralized. The world is going to be governed as a single entity, rather than a disparate group of nations vying with one another for economic and military supremacy."

"Have you *any* idea, Walt, just how *crazy* this all sounds . . . huh?" says Jack with a sarcastic grunt.

"Sure I do."

"What?" answers Jack quickly, surprised at the candour of the reply.

"Is it any *less* crazy than what people are doing anyway – destroying life on the planet? But you mark my words: Elijah Roberts is not a man to be underestimated, not for one second. Believe me, if there's any chance of saving this insane world then he's the only guy capable of doing it. The last, best hope for humanity, that's what the man is!"

The two stand in awkward silence.

"What about the code-word?" asks Jack at length. "It means something, doesn't it?"

"Don't worry about it. It means nothing."

"You're treating me like a goddam idiot again. How can the very last word that Roberts's daughter wrote *not* mean something . . . not be *significant* somehow."

"Anyone ever tell you you've an overactive imagination, Jack?"

"Anyone ever tell you you're a lousy liar, Walt?"

"Hey, you just watch your mouth! I said the name means nothing . . . nothing at all, understand?" he says, raising his voice.

Franklin's face is haggard and grey despite his temper. His eyes dart about the room, unwilling to return Jack's reproachful look.

For a split second, Jack detects a look of fear in those eyes. He suddenly remembers the crazy jetcopter ride in Iceland . . . thinks about Magnusson and the conquest of fear . . . how to teach Josh. . . .

"Tell me what 'Steelman' means, or I swear to God I'll stop writing this book."

"You want to play games with me, Andersson?"

"It's just a simple question."

"Don't fuck around with us or . . . "

"Or what, Walt . . . ?"

"I'm warning you to back off."

"You *threatening* me?"

Franklin steps back; loosens his tie and grimaces. He pulls his cell out of his inside breast pocket.

"Vespazzi!" he barks into it. "Get your ass in here now!"

A few seconds later and the burly figure of Tony Vespazzi bounds into the room.

"You okay, Mr Franklin?" he enquires coolly in a deep baritone voice.

"No, Tony! I want you to grab a hold of this gentleman here and shoot him in the head on my count of five," he answers, calmly indicating an incredulous Jack.

Vespazzi swivels on his heels, extends his right arm and locks his hand up against Jack's throat before he even has time to move. He presses his left forearm against Jack's chest, and muscles him back tight against a wall. The agent draws out his handgun, waits for his victim's next gulp of air, then shoves the barrel into the opened mouth.

"One . . . two . . . three . . . four . . . " Franklin calls out and then pauses as Vespazzi readies to squeeze the trigger.

Vespazzi frowns at his boss.

All the while, Jack can feel the heavy muzzle of the gun clacking against his teeth. The force of it being rammed in has split the corners of his mouth and he can taste the blood. His eyes are riveted on his would-be killer but the words of Tor Magnusson are resounding in his head – "Look death straight in the eye and not flinch." He lets his body go limp and doesn't even countenance the thought of his imminent demise.

"Will I kill him, sir?"

"Do you reckon he's scared, Tony?"

"No, sir! This one don't scare so easy."

"That will do, Tony, thanks," he says at last, dismissing him from the room with a lethargic nod.

Franklin flashes a malicious grin at Jack as he watches him wiping the blood from his mouth with the back of one hand.

"You just remember who you're working for, Andersson. You terminate this contract and you're signing your own death-warrant."

Jack is rubbing his Adam's apple. Feels like he has just swallowed a golf ball.

"Well, sorry . . . to . . . disappoint you . . . but I don't frighten . . . as easily as I used to," he gasps. "I'm entitled to know . . . what does 'Steelman' mean?"

Franklin hesitates and starts drumming his fingers against the surface of the mahogany table as he ponders his response.

"Okay, okay, I'll level with you. It's quite an innocent explanation," he says at length. "It was the nickname that Clara Roberts gave her father."

"What!"

"Can you imagine what it must have been like for that little girl, growing up with a man like Eli Roberts for a father? She rarely saw him – and even when she did, he came across as an austere and aloof figure. Poor kid felt she wasn't loved, so she took her own life but pinned the blame on Eli with her final entry in her diary. A man of steel, that's how Clara perceived her father; cold and tough as the metal itself."

Franklin pauses briefly, arches his brows and winds his head wistfully.

"Roberts was consumed with guilt over his daughter's suicide," he continues; "it was horrific for him having to live with that responsibility on his conscience. It damn near killed the man . . . that's why he had to see Steinitz. . . . " His voice trails off into a whisper.

"Yeah, I know; she told me."

"Imagine a twelve-year-old kid taking her own life. I mean it's unthinkable. You'd do anything to stop your only child even *thinking* about the prospect, let alone *doing* it; wouldn't you, Jack?"

"Sure, of course I would."

"Well then, you better start acting as if you mean it!"

"What are you talking about?"

"It's high time you forced Josh to overcome his anxieties; otherwise he's going to end up overwhelmed by this world, just like Clara Roberts was. And *we* can't let that happen. Tor Magnusson is not a man given to idle threats, so you do *exactly* what that man advised you to do – don't *fuck* with him!"

Franklin dons a fawn cashmere overcoat and screws a matching hat onto his head. He cuts a dapper figure as he superciliously struts past a speechless Jack and exits the room.

Jack hears the click of the front door opening and then Franklin's voice echoing in the hallway.

"Hello, Josh."

"Good evening, Mr Franklin," the boy answers in a tremulous voice.

"Don't be scared, son; you'll be okay," he answers in a sympathetic tone. "We'll help you. You know who I work for, don't you?"

"Yes . . . you work for God."

Jack can hear Franklin's laugh reverberate.

"Yes, I suppose I do in a way."

"Vespazzi is a comical name."

"It's a great name, isn't it?"

"It's Italian for wasp."

"Is that so, Josh?"

"Yes, Mr Franklin, it's an excellent name for a killer," he says coldly.

Jack hears the door bang shut and Franklin's footsteps fading into the distance.

Josh is standing at the living-room door, watching his father still staunching the blood oozing from the corners of his mouth with the back of his hand. A crop of freshly ripening bruises is appearing on both sides of his throat now.

"I warned you before, Father – a single glance from God could kill you."

Jack plunges yet another little candle into the smooth orange frosting on the cake. He strikes a match, cups it in his hand and starts to light each one in turn.

"*Happy Birthday Josh*" is delicately written in black calligraphic script atop its surface. For as long as he can remember, Josh's birthday cakes have always been orange – his favourite colour. He thinks back to a time when his son actually had lots of other kids to celebrate his parties with. Thinks how the numbers have dwindled over a few short years as his social behaviour gradually deteriorated.

A frightened little boy: lost somewhere in a fathomless mind, become an island unto himself . . . slowly sinking in a sea of words . . . too paralyzed with fears to stop himself from drowning.

"Ouch!" cries Jack, feeling a burning sensation in his palm. "Goddam match!" He strikes up a fresh one and soon all twelve candles are flickering, casting a faint amber glow around the kitchen.

"Shall I extinguish them now, Father?" whispers Josh from behind him.

Jack nods his assent. The boy leans forward and gently snuffs out each one in short, measured breaths. Jack hands him an envelope when he has finished.

Josh opens it and stares disbelievingly at a ticket he is now holding in his trembling hand.

"Happy birthday, son!" says Jack, wryly.

"Canada?"

"Yeah, you're flying to Ottawa with me next week. I have an interview to do there."

"No! Miss Alvarez will stay here and supervise me, same as when you went to Iceland."

"No, this time you're coming with me."

"But I don't want to die in the sky."

"We're not going to die, Josh."

"Everyone dies in the long run and the sky is a big location. Scared we might get lost in it."

"Maybe it's time you learned not to be scared."

The boy walks nervously around the kitchen table, muttering to himself and making intricate circles in the air with his left index finger. He stops directly in front of his father and kneels before him, raising his moist green eyes up imploringly as he does so.

"Don't make me go," he whimpers over and over, clasping his hands as if in prayer.

Jack looks at him sceptically, and intuitively knows this melodramatic pleading is just a re-enactment of some film or literary scene the boy has seen or read. He grabs him by the shoulders and hauls him up to a standing position.

"You're just playing games with me, Josh! All these fears . . . these phobias . . . Asperger's and schizophrenia are just delusions . . . nonsense created by your own imagination, tuning into catastrophic thoughts all the time. Switch the channel, Josh . . . change frequency, challenge your fears and you'll eventually conquer them. It's all just a big lie you've created inside your head."

The boy closes his eyes and rubs his temples in frustration.

"You don't understand my mind!" he cries loudly.

"Take your mind off your mind and start living in the real world, Josh!"

"The mind is a place unto itself; it can make a heaven of hell or a hell of heaven."

"Yeah, and you have chosen *hell* for yourself."

"No, Father – hell has chosen *me*," he sobs. "Hell has chosen *me*."

TWENTY-FOUR

VIKTOR BRONSTEIN SINKS BACK in his chair and sticks his legs out straight on the desk in front of him, before crossing them at the ankles. He places both hands behind his head and twiddles his feet as if to better admire his own reflection in his highly polished shoes. Two damp patches of perspiration darken the armpits of his light-blue, tailored shirt. He's wearing an old-fashioned set of red braces; Jack thinks they make him appear faintly ridiculous. But he has a supremely confident air, the pompous self-assurance of a man who cares little for others' opinions or sensitivities.

"You recording this interview, Andersson?"

"Yes, sir, I record all my interviews," he answers, holding up his cell.

"Switch it off!" Bronstein snaps.

"Excuse me?"

"Switch that device off. I don't want this conversation recorded."

Jack frowns quickly, shrugs his shoulders and presses off the power button.

He searches in his jacket pockets for a pen, without success.

"Have you a pen I could borrow, sir, for writing notes at least?"

"No, I stopped using those things years ago. When I started out in law school the best advice I got was to think a lot, say little and write down nothing, because more people incriminate themselves using their pens, not their tongues. A pen is a deadly weapon," Bronstein declares. "Every lawyer knows that," he adds humourlessly.

"Well then, I guess I'll just have to rely on my memory."

"Yes, but I don't want anything I say to you about Roberts attributed to me as a source, understood?"

"Sure, okay," sighs Jack, grim-faced. "Where did you meet him first?"

"Scott Reshevsky hired me to work for GeoNova Finance soon as I finished law school. I was there a few months when Roberts invited me out to lunch one day . . . outta the blue.

"I'd never met the guy before. We talked for twenty minutes and then he told me he was firing me from the company. 'You're too idealistic, kid, to be working just for money. I want you working for *me*,' he said; 'I need you working to change the world.' He told me he was appointing me head of the legal department of GeoNova's political wing, with a team of sixty lawyers under me. I was twenty-six years old at the time."

"That was some career move . . . a helluva responsibility at that age."

Bronstein adjusts his feet on the desk once again and admires the reflection in his shoes.

"Not really," he remarks casually. "Einstein did all his best work at the same age. Age is irrelevant – talent and motivation are all that matter."

"What cases did you work on with Roberts himself?"

"Most of them were quite technical – trying to get legislation passed to combat climate change; licences for green power generation and the construction of nuclear power plants, et cetera. Of course, stuff like that was getting held up for years in the courts with appeals. It was only when climatic disasters became more frequent and GeoNova gained political traction that the judicial system and Congress were forced to depart from their customary glacial pace. Even then, though, it was too late – years too late; we were just tinkering around with Kyoto protocols and trading carbon credits. International laws and treaties are only as robust as the general will to observe them, and capitalism, unfortunately, is blind to everything except profit. Many corporations have more power, influence, and money now than whole nations. . . . "

Bronstein pauses and slides his thumbs up and down the inside of his bright red braces. He cocks his head and squints with one eye closed at Jack.

"Marx was even more prescient than even *he himself* could possibly have imagined – capitalism is rapidly destroying us – a '*dégringolade*' as Roberts calls it," he adds with a sardonic curl of his upper lip.

"What about the change in the wording of the oath of office? You worked with him on that case; removing reference to God from the presidential oath; didn't you?"

"Yes," Bronstein answers sharply.

"Why was it so important to Roberts to pursue it? I mean: he lost the Christian Right vote soon as he declared the grounds for his objection to the oath."

"Strange thing is, most people completely misunderstood Roberts's position. They assumed he was an atheist, even though he is a man of deep religious conviction. But not in the orthodox sense of the word. His legal argument was a lot more subtle than most people realize."

"Yeah, it is the human idea of God that is important not his *actual* existence, isn't it?" interrupts Jack, eager to impress Bronstein.

Bronstein slowly gets up from his chair and walks languidly from behind his desk to his office window. He stands with his legs apart, thrusts both hands in his pockets, cocks his head again and gazes out from his tenth-storey office at the city of Ottawa below.

"You won't get too far in a court of law with that line of reasoning. That's an ontological argument, not a legal one. Listen, and I'll try and keep my explanation simple for you, Andersson," he says, with his back still turned towards him.

Jack looks at Bronstein's figure silhouetted and framed by the square office window against a background of angry sky. The posture seems arrogant, contemptuous of the world below and beyond. Jack loathes his lecturing tone.

"You step into a witness box, and the first thing the court wants to know before you testify is whether you believe in God or not. You could have previous convictions for rape or murder but the jury is not allowed to know that because it would prejudice their verdict. However, the system compels you to swear an oath to God, or give an affirmation instead if you don't believe in Him. If you're an atheist and act according to your convictions, you must choose the latter. And if there's God-fearing Christians on the jury . . . well then, you're as guilty as the hell you're going to as far as they are concerned. But Roberts refused to swear an oath or give an affirmation either; he argued the courts weren't entitled to drive a coach and four through the privacy of his own conscience. He said swearing an oath on the Bible was just an 'anachronistic charade'. I remember the first time he uttered that phrase in court, he was sentenced to three months in jail for contempt. But he fought his case right up to the Supreme Court. I told him he was committing political suicide; but I was wrong – his poll ratings went up instead – the electorate enjoyed the novelty of a politician defending the truth of his own convictions against a corrupt system.

"That case hinged upon a point of archaic legal tradition that should have been resolved within a few days; instead, it took years and millions of dollars! It's ridiculous it takes so long and has become so expensive to achieve judicial reform. I mean, God has no place in a courtroom since the end of the twentieth century at least."

Bronstein pauses, turns from the window and casts his eyes towards the ceiling.

"Roberts hates the law, you know; *hates* it almost as much as *I* do."

Jack regards the lawyer with a confused expression.

"Well, I suppose it's a necessary evil, sir, isn't it? Necessary for civilization, is it not?"

"And civilization is the ruination of the planet . . . is it not?"

"Well, that's not the law's fault?"

"Oh, but it *is*, if you think deeply about it."

"How so?" queries Jack.

"We seem to live our lives under the illusion that the law can legislate for the totality of human experience; that it can somehow control the worst excesses of our base nature. We have spent years continually amending and expanding these laws. Yet all we have ended up with is a gargantuan ideological thought-construct so arcane and unfathomably complex that justice becomes serendipitous. Roberts likens the law to geological strata: accumulated layers of juridical concepts compressed to an abstraction, paralyzed under the immense weight of its own contradictions. With all these rules and regulations and red tape, we have bound up our collective psyche in some Kafkaesque, dystopian nightmare . . . and condemned humanity to a state of intellectual inertia . . . where quantum algorithms have effectively superseded cognitive function."

Jack blinks slowly, as if to remove a film of glaze from his eyes. He can feel the lines on his forehead furrowing into a puzzled frown. Why can't Bronstein just keep his explanation simple, as he promised?

Bronstein tilts his head back and looks down along the length of his nose.

"You're not keeping up with me, Andersson," he says, noting his mystified expression. "I'll have to make it simpler for you. What's eighteen multiplied by twenty-seven?" he asks, snapping his fingers as if anticipating an instantaneous answer.

Jack mouths the numbers in response. He struggles to calculate the answer quickly in his head.

"Come on, it's easy; it should be child's play!"

"Four hundred and eh . . . eh . . . "

"Four hundred eighty six," Bronstein growls impatiently. "You're a little on the slow side with your mental arithmetic?"

Jack reaches for his cell and inputs the sum to confirm the lawyer's answer. He nods and then glances with a hangdog expression at Bronstein, who is now leaning over him, looking askance at the screen on the cell.

"What's the point in doing mental arithmetic anyway when you've got one of these? I find it a lot more reliable than my brain."

"That's my whole point, Andersson – the electronic calculator was just the thin end of the technological wedge. Once upon a time people were quite adept at performing mathematical operations in their heads. But they gradually lost that skill because they stopped practising it. Primitive computers just did basic mathematics and code-breaking, but they evolved and ultimately gained control over our entire socio-industrial and military complexes. With the development of quantum computing, the vast sum of human knowledge became instantly accessible, an infinite stream of free information to all users. Can't you understand the adverse psychological consequences of this for mankind?"

Jack leans back and smiles wryly to himself. He can't help but visualize Cass's exquisite face. Thinks how he can seem to cope with life without Jenny but feels it would be unbearable without Cass. . . . "A surrogate wife for you, Father, and the only mother I will ever need," Josh had told him recently; "at least she will never desert us."

"What do you mean, *adverse*?"

"I mean the human mind has capitulated to artificial intelligence. The majority of people can no longer make even the simplest decisions or calculations without it. They are too lazy to even exercise their memories any more, because all the information they need is at their instant electronic disposal. As you admitted yourself, why bother doing mental arithmetic when you have an electronic calculator? The logical inference from that argument is: why bother learning facts, languages, anything at all, when it is available on the Cloud? The human brain has practically evolved into a data receiver; unable to process the ceaseless stream of information that bombards it. Bound up in silicon chains is what we are!"

Bronstein turns away quickly and resumes his seat. He swings his feet up onto the desk again then starts to rock the soles of his shoes to and fro like a pair of windscreen wipers.

"Humanity is doomed!" he says, tugging and snapping his red braces against his chest. "Everybody knows it but nobody really *believes* it," he announces with a self-important jut of his lower jaw.

"Does Roberts believe it too?"

"Ah . . . it doesn't make any difference what Eli thinks. He is not going to get re-elected anyhow. In twelve months, GeoNova's political influence in America will decline and . . . "

Bronstein stops abruptly and quickly swings his legs back off the desk. He stands and straightens himself up as if to attention; fixes his tie and adjusts his diamond cufflinks.

"Good afternoon, sir!" he says, with a single, deferential nod.

"Good afternoon, Viktor . . . Mr Andersson."

Jack recognizes the distinctive voice immediately. He turns and stares in amazement at the towering figure of Tor Magnusson standing directly behind him.

His intense blue eyes flash past Jack and pin Bronstein under their inscrutable gaze. He speaks coolly but authoritatively.

"I have reviewed sections two and three of Article Seven in the proposed constitution. The directorial powers referred to in section three must be expressed in more explicit terms, specifically in paragraphs one and four . . . also you omitted to mention the recently completed New Zealand colony in the final paragraph of section two . . . the wording of this paragraph is also unnecessarily abstruse – simplify it." Bronstein nods intermittently in acknowledgement of his opinions. "Yes, sir" . . . "Of course, sir" . . . "We will make the requisite amendments immediately, sir," he is saying in obsequious tones. He fumbles for a key in his pocket then reaches down, unlocks a drawer from behind his desk, and pulls out a gold pen and a thick file. He gets increasingly flustered as he thumbs furiously through its pages, struggling to find the relevant documents.

"Sorry, Mr Magnusson, sir, I have sections two and three here in front of me now," he says at last, panting. Jack grins as he watches Bronstein and listens to the staccato scratching of his pen. He reminds him of a snivelling little schoolboy, embarrassed at all the mistakes the teacher has pointed out in his homework. Magnusson speaks for ten minutes solid, detailing a litany of objections and suggested corrections. He never once hesitates or resorts to notes or takes his icy eyes off the lawyer, not for a single second.

" . . . I warned your people before, Viktor, this constitution of ours must confer dictatorial status on each colony leader. They must wield greater executive power than mere gauleiters or satraps waiting for the emperor's bidding – understood?!"

Magnusson has punched the air angrily to emphasize his point. His arm is still outstretched as he suddenly switches attention away from Bronstein and stares intently at Jack.

"Is the boy with you? Did you put him on the plane as I instructed?"

His giant fist is still hanging in the air, like a sword of Damocles, directly over Jack's head.

"No, sir! I . . . I couldn't persuade him; he was too afraid!" he answers, almost cowering in his chair as he looks up.

Magnusson's cheeks flush crimson.

"Then you did not act according to my instructions!"

Suddenly, he brings his clenched fist crashing down on the head below.

But Jack feels no physical sensation, no pain; no whoosh of rushing air, nothing.

"What! . . . What is this?" he shouts, leaping to his feet in astonishment.

Magnusson folds his arms and stands toe to toe with him now. His great bald head glistens with a film of perspiration. "Time for me to intervene on the boy's behalf!" he snaps in a menacing tone.

He wags his index finger, there is a gentle click and Magnusson vanishes into thin air.

Jack turns instantly to Bronstein.

"What the hell just happ—?"

"*Deus ex machina.*"

"What?"

"It's a hologram – a god from the machinery, you might say."

"But it's so . . . so *realistic* . . . it's incredible."

"Yeah, GeoNova scientists only recently perfected the technology. Roberts uses it regularly now to chair conferences with the eco-colonies. He doesn't even need to step out of the Oval Office to attend them. When you think about it, there's no real difference between being virtually present and actually physically present. Is there?"

"You mean the President can appear at any location without actually *being* there."

"Sure! As long as you've got the latest holographic imagers installed and set at the correct frequency. The President gave a public lecture in Harvard last month and only his entourage knew he wasn't physically present. The audience or the media didn't notice any difference."

"But . . . that's *fraud*."

Bronstein stiffens his stance as if stung by the word.

"I can assure you, Roberts didn't contravene any state or federal laws. In fact holographic technology is greener and infinitely safer than having to travel around the world in person. The President's life is under constant threat – and this is an ideal security arrangement to minimize the chances of assassination. We don't want Roberts succumbing to the same fate as Kun Wei in China."

"But it's a trick, a false image!" blusters Jack indignantly. "You're fooling people . . . it's just plain *wrong!*"

Bronstein hooks his thumbs inside his braces and runs them from the top of his shoulders to his waist, snapping the straps as he does so.

"I'm a lawyer; I'm not interested in right or wrong," he declares. "This type of dualistic thinking, reductive reasoning and childish clinging to absolutes is the root cause of the collapse of civilization.

Even our goddam computers have progressed beyond binary codes to qubits. You haven't studied your Nietzsche; have you? How can you write a book on Eli Roberts if you haven't grasped the basics of Nietzschean philosophy?"

"Listen, Bronstein, I came here to do an interview, not undergo a cross-examination."

Bronstein strolls to the window, raises his arms straight above his head and leans against the glass. His back is turned to Jack. He inhales deeply and emits a sharp sigh.

"It would have been better if you'd taken the boy as instructed."

He hesitates.

"I need to tell you something . . . it's a rumour . . . hearsay, you understand . . . but I feel compelled to tell you. Kun Wei was murdered with a few hundred nanograms of the radioactive element polonium two hundred ten. A tiny amount laced in his coffee. Once ingested, the poison invaded every single cell in his body, one by one. Only a few atoms are sufficient to slowly disintegrate their vital structures. It was an excruciating and unimaginably cruel death for him. It took him weeks to die."

Bronstein sighs heavily once more and his voice deepens.

"Polonium two hundred ten is virtually impossible to obtain commercially and prohibitively expensive to manufacture. Despite GeoNova agents conducting an extensive investigation, they could never establish exactly who the perpetrator was. However, it gradually became apparent that Kun Wei was eliminated by rogue elements within the party. Whoever killed him was making a statement, a *de facto* challenge to Roberts's authority. Only one individual within the party was considered fearless enough to defy Roberts, ruthless enough to commit murder and clever enough not to get caught. . . . "

Bronstein clears his throat once, affectedly, and his voice reduces to a whisper.

"Eli naturally couldn't air his suspicions publicly, he couldn't even confide in his inner circle. The prime suspect was '*reassigned*' but still retains an extremely powerful position within the party organization. Make an enemy of that man and I guarantee you that he will be your last. Am I making sense, Andersson?"

Jack slumps back down in his chair. He asks himself a question he hasn't posed for some time: *Why me? Why me? – it's something to do with Josh – something to do with what the boy knows or is capable of understanding . . . Magnusson, a man without fear . . . possibly a murderer!*

"Is my life . . . in danger?" he asks tentatively.

"Probably," answers the lawyer, turning from the window. "I think only you have been contracted by Roberts to write this biography of his . . . a nobody like you would more than likely be dead already! He's keeping you under his wing, as it were; protecting you from Magnusson. . . . "

Bronstein repeatedly clicks the top of a gold pen he is holding. He clicks it quickly and noisily as if to deliberately bring it to Jack's attention.

"I thought you said you stopped using a pen years ago?"

"This is an exception," he says, reverently stroking the gold shaft with his fingers. "It's a present from Eli. I am sure you have one too."

"Yeah, I got one all right."

"Well, as I said, Roberts is protecting you," he winks knowingly.

The lawyer returns to his desk and carefully replaces the thick file in its drawer. Then he slides the gold pen into a small black box, puts it in the same drawer and locks it again.

What, Jack thinks, *is so important about the pen?* "Josh calls the pen Auric," he says, fishing for more information. "I don't know why exactly?"

"It's from the Latin for gold," says Bronstein. "But of course we both know that what these pens contain is worth a lot more than gold . . . worth even more than polonium two hundred ten!"

"Yeah, sure," lies Jack, clueless. "Mightier than the sword, as they say."

"Most lethal weapon of all, Mr Andersson."

TWENTY-FIVE

"THE THOUGHTS IN MY HEAD won't shut up!" roars Josh, his voice hoarse from constant screaming. He grabs his hair and pounds his fists furiously against the sides of his head.

"Please make them be quiet, Miss Alvarez! Make them stop!" he screams. "Oh, I can't stand it . . . I can't stand it any more . . . please, I'm begging you."

He flings his arms around her in desperation and buries his head in her bosom.

"Ssh . . . ssh, Josh," she whispers reassuringly. She hugs him and massages his scalp as if trying to erase his overpowering thoughts. His screaming dies down to a series of short, shuddering breaths, interspersed with sobs.

"Ssh . . . ssh . . . Josh," she says softly. "Thoughts can't hurt you; they can't hurt you . . . they're not real. Ssh . . . they're just things that happen in your mind – nowhere else."

The boy clenches his eyes shut. Starts to shake uncontrollably and clutches Alvarez's body even tighter. Panic overwhelms him yet again.

"But what if they are true? What if the thoughts are true?" he wails, "Oh, my God . . . oh, my God!"

"Calm down, Josh. Take your medication and I promise you'll feel better . . . please!"

He releases her from his grip and staggers back with a look of sheer horror frozen on his pallid face. His legs seem to buckle under the weight of some abhorrent realization; a thought so appalling it is too much for his body, let alone his mind, to bear. He crumples to the floor, clasps his arms over his knees and tucks them firmly under his chin.

"I want to be a fetus again . . . a fetus again," the boy moans. He shoves his left thumb into his mouth, clamps his teeth on it and sucks hard.

Juanita Alvarez stares at Josh in bewilderment. His body now rocking over and back like a helpless giant infant. Her ears are still ringing from the boy's high-pitched screaming.

"CASS!" she calls out.

"Yes, Juanita," the computer responds, pronouncing her name in perfectly accented Spanish.

"Connect me with Mr Andersson."

"Robert or Jack Andersson? Please specify."

"Jack!" she snaps back impatiently.

Her face quickly appears on Jack's cell-phone screen.

"What time will you be back?"

"Are you okay, Juanita?" he answers, noting the alarm in her voice.

"Not really; Josh is extremely upset. He has been screaming most of the day. I've never seen him behave like this before."

"CASS, relay me a live feed on Josh!" he orders.

The computer focuses in on the boy, who is now sitting under a table. Still rocking back and forth, sucking his thumb. Jack sighs as he watches the scene.

"I'll be landing shortly, Juanita. I should be home by cab in a couple of hours."

"I'm sorry; I don't know what has caused this. Perhaps he just misses you, perhaps his mother."

"Yeah, I'm sure you're right."

Jack disconnects abruptly and feels his heart sink to the pit of his stomach. Tor Magnusson's imposing figure looms into his mind's eye and his authoritative tones dictate to his inner voice.

"*I warned you . . . Franklin warned you . . . yet you lacked the will to carry out my instructions . . . now I must intervene on the boy's*

*behalf. But don't be afraid . . . I taught you a lesson once on the con-
quest of fear, remember; to look death square in the eye and don't
flinch; even if I kill you slowly as I did Kun Wei . . . one microscopic
cell at a time!"*

Jack recalls seeing an image of the dying Kun Wei on television,
his face bloated and hair all fallen out. The public was told he had an
inoperable brain tumour, but now he knows the truth of it. What a
cruel death! Cruel, yet aesthetic in its execution. Anybody capable of
inflicting such a death was more than a mere murderer – they were
an artist.

Juanita Alvarez opens the front door as soon as she hears the cab
pulling up outside. Jack thrusts a fistful of notes into the driver's hand
and grabs his luggage from the boot. He runs up the driveway.

"Where is he?" he shouts.

"In the kitchen."

He brushes past her.

"He hasn't moved since I called you. Not an inch in two hours," she
says, following him into the kitchen. "It's as if he is paralyzed."

Jack stops dead in his tracks and stares at the figure sitting on the
floor under the table. The boy has his arms wrapped tightly around
one of the table legs, clinging to it as if his life depended on it. Every
muscle of his body is taut with terror and his facial features are frozen. All except for his eyes; blinking, long and slow like those of a
petrified animal, dazzled by onrushing headlight beams.

"I've seen this type of thing before sometimes . . . but not with children," says Alvarez. "I think it's called an acute psychotic episode. He
might need to go to hospital."

Jack gets down on his haunches and caresses Josh's cheek. The boy
doesn't respond to his father's touch; he just sits there like a statue.

"Something must have happened to trigger this, Juanita," he says,
his tone unintentionally hostile.

"But I did *nada*, nothing, I *swear* of it!" she protests. "He hasn't taken any medication for me since you went to Ottawa a few days ago. I tried to give him pills but he just kept spitting them out. That's why he's like *this*," she says agitatedly, pointing at the boy.

"You said he was screaming all day. When exactly did he start?"

"Sometime this morning . . . maybe ten . . . ten thirty perhaps; I'm not sure?"

"Where was he at the time?"

"What?"

"What room was Josh in when he started screaming?"

"I don't know. The scream seemed to come from every room."

"But he must have *said* something to you about what upset him."

"*Nada*, nothing," she repeats, tearfully this time. "Please, it's not my fault, Mr Andersson."

"I'm sorry, Juanita . . . I didn't mean to suggest that it *was* . . . I'm sorry."

She brushes the tears from her cheeks with the back of her hand.

"Your son is a very sick little boy, you know," she sobs. "I pray to God every day for him."

Jack stands up and looks down at the still-motionless figure under the table. He clucks his tongue a few times, wondering what to do. After a few seconds he bends down, grips the boy by the arms and drags him out from under the table.

"What's wrong, Josh? Come on, tell me!" he shouts.

But the boy continues to sit on the floor, totally unresponsive, his body maintaining its catatonic posture. Jack snaps his fingers loudly, directly in front of the boy's eyes – still no reaction; slaps him hard on the cheek – still no response.

"He is psychotic, I tell you," pleads Alvarez. "Don't hurt him, Mr Andersson!"

This must be Magnusson's doing, he tells himself, perfectly timed to coincide with my arrival home from Canada. "I must intervene on the boy's behalf," he'd said. Not a man given to idle threats, Franklin had warned. How or what the fuck could Magnusson possibly have done to traumatize the boy . . . ?

"Cass!" he calls out suddenly.

"Welcome home, Jack," she chirps. "Had you a pleasant trip?"

"Was Josh in the study with you this morning?" he continues brusquely.

"Yes."

"What time exactly?"

"Ten thirteen to ten eighteen."

"What were you showing Josh when he started to scream?"

"I'm sorry, Jack. I am not at liberty to answer that question."

"Why not, Cass?" he demands.

She seems to hesitate, the timbre of her normally cheery voice lowering a few octaves as she replies.

"Security protocols prohibit."

Jack recalls Cass using precisely the same technical terminology before: the time she refused to compile the report for Kvellner on what material Josh was accessing on-line. Robbie came over to try and fix her but had to call one of his tech-buddies for assistance . . . Jack struggles to remember his name . . . he'd said something about an uncrackable ciphertext in a rogue program. Said he'd seen it only once before, while doing contract work for the Pentagon. . . .

Jack is nodding to himself, contemplating, slowly unpicking the knots in the warp and weft of his tangled mind. The Pentagon; the government, Magnusson, Cass, Josh.

"Yes, of course," he groans.

"That's it! That *has* to be it," he mutters under his breath.

Magnusson has been communicating with Josh all the time using Cass . . . that's how he knows so much about the boy . . . even knew he kept his bedroom light switched on at night. Jack squats down on his haunches again and cups Josh's cheeks in his hands. He stares into his glazed, green eyes.

"Tor Magnusson; you know the man, don't you?" he asks calmly.

Still the boy retains his vacant gaze.

"Tor Magnusson got Cass to show you something that scared you; didn't he?"

Jack grips him by the shoulders now and gently shakes his still rigid frame.

"Tor Magnusson, he . . . "

The boy blinks back in recognition, slowly at first, then flickers his eyes quickly as if startled from a deep sleep.

"Tor Magnusson, you know him?" Jack says, raising his voice.

Josh nods twice in affirmation.

"I'm sooo scared, Dad . . . soooo scared," he whispers. He reaches up with both arms and clasps them around his father's waist.

"Need to tell or I'll explode . . . gotta tell someone."

"Tell *what*, Josh?. . . tell *who*?"

The boy squeezes his father's waist even tighter and presses his face into his abdomen. His words are muffled.

"Kvellner . . . Kvellner, maybe he can stop the voices . . . oh, please, Dad. I'm so scared!"

Jack paces the kitchen nervously as he argues into his cell.

" . . . but the boy is willing to talk to you *now*, Doctor. He wants to see you tonight."

"I'm sorry, I'm not in my office," insists the voice at the other end of the cell. "You'll have to contact my secretary in the morning to arrange an appointment."

"But he's going crazy on me; what am I to do?"

"As I told you already, your son is having acute psychotic episodes because he stopped taking the medication I prescribed. In my opinion, judging by the symptoms you describe, the child needs to be admitted to a hospital. Me just talking to him is not going to resolve *anything*."

"But you don't understand, Doctor . . . I can't explain it to you . . . it's an emergency."

"Listen, Mr Andersson, I'm sorry but I can't help you in this instance other than to advise you to take him to hospital. Okay?"

"But there are possibly other lives at stake here."

Jack can hear Kvellner quicken his breathing in exasperation at the other end.

"Well, if *that* is the case it is a matter for the police," he says firmly.

"But Josh is willing to talk *now.* . . . "

"Look, I'm sorry, okay? I'm sorry. I can't help you . . . Goodbye."

Kvellner terminates the connection abruptly.

Ten minutes later and the psychiatrist calls back, full of apologies for his previously off-hand manner.

"I'll see the boy immediately, Mr Andersson, *sir!*" he is saying with artificial sincerity.

There is an indeterminate edge to his voice; it sounds at once apprehensive and angry. *What,* Jack wonders, *made the guy change his mind so quickly?*

"Thank you, Doctor. I appreciate it's very short notice," he says, looking at his watch. "We should be in your office about ten thirty."

Edvard Munch, *The Scream*, 1893

William Blake, *Ancient of Days (God Creating the Universe)* c. 1794

TWENTY-SIX

KVELLNER LEANS FORWARD in his office chair. He is constantly patting his neat silver hair and nervously adjusting the gold-rimmed spectacles perched on his nose. His twelve-year-old client refuses to sit down, simply traipses over and back in an agitated manner in front of him. Josh doesn't want any relaxing music for this session; doesn't want to imagine liquid gold filling up his body from the tips of his toes to his head. The boy has a hunted look about him, the psychiatrist thinks.

"What do you want to tell me, Josh?"

"Yeah . . . yeah . . . Doc," he says anxiously, "I'm still formulating the words but they're not coming. Difficult to think straight if emotions are crooked."

"Try thinking in terms of pictures inside your head, instead of using complicated words."

"Okay . . . okay . . . okay."

"Then just describe the pictures using simple words."

Kvellner waits patiently for a few seconds as the boy still paces to and fro.

"Have you got a picture in your mind you can tell me about now?"

"Yes."

"Good, now describe that picture for me. Keep the words simple, okay."

"There is a bald figure standing beside the railings on a bridge. I don't know if the creature is a man or a woman or an alien. Its face is switched on, like one of those amber light bulbs from olden times; or an inverted pear or a bulbous skull. The hands are covering the ears and its lidless eyes seem to radiate electric agony of soul. The creature's body is thin and wispy like a spectre. I think the head is too heavy for its body, like in the story I wrote – *NoBody*. Oh, and the mouth . . . the mouth is toothless and tongueless, cavernous yet speechless, madness and hellness, black-rimmed and petrified in its eggness. There is a black river under the bridge. No, it's the sky I think . . . Mmm . . . Yes, that's it, the sky and the Styx are swirling together, flowing beneath the bridge. The sky is violent orange-yellow and ver-milion bands. . . . "

Kvellner recognizes the scene the boy is detailing as that of an old painting by Edvard Munch from the nineteenth century.

"You're describing an *actual* painting, Josh, called *The Scream,*" he interrupts.

"I know," the boy retorts. "Every psychiatrist should have a print of it hanging in their office," he says without irony. "It's got all my favourite colours in it."

"Why is the figure in the painting scared, Josh?"

"I guess it's probably terrified of being alive, Doc . . . because it can't look death square in the eye and *not* scream."

"Is that how you feel? Like the figure in the painting, I mean?"

"All the time! All the time!" he cries. "It's like I'm trapped in the universe, watching all the stars and galaxies being snuffed out one by one. Until it's just me left alone in eternal darkness . . . me and eternity . . . a nothingness of being, until time itself expires."

"What does it all mean, Doc?" he asks mournfully, his lips quiver-ing. "What could human life possibly mean if even the stars have to die?"

"Is *this* what you came here to discuss with me so urgently?" Kvellner says, raising his voice, "to discuss your existential angst. I don't think so! I think you're playing games with me, aren't you? You've been playing games all your life, haven't you? Pretending you are suffering from Asperger's syndrome and now schizophrenia? You can't maintain this charade – this front – any more. I know a lot more about you than you might think, Josh Andersson!"

The boy stops; he chews his lower lip and twists the fingers of both hands together. The tears hang heavy in his eyes, almost forcing him to lower his gaze.

"Tor Magnusson contacted you straight after my father called this evening. He threatened you, told you I was busting to tell someone like you . . . a mind expert . . . what I know, what I am capable of knowing. Why did I never figure it out until now? Why? . . . Why? . . . I've known it since I was five, yet never realized what I was doing . . . it's *impossible* . . . it's all so *impossible*. I must be insane and sane at the same time!"

"You know this man Magnusson?"

"Yes."

"You know he is a friend of the President?"

"Yes."

"Does your father work for the federal government?"

"No, he works for the President and Mr Franklin."

Kvellner grimaces, inhaling and exhaling sharply through his nostrils as he does so. He hooks his thumb and forefinger under the collar of his shirt and undoes the top button.

"What did you come here to tell me, Josh? Is it something you discovered about government affairs . . . something you found out that scares you?"

"Not supposed to talk about it," he says in a tremulous voice. "Roberts must win the next election or else. . . . "

" . . . Or else what?"

The boy looks away. He clenches his left hand into a fist, puts it into his mouth and bites hard on it.

"Scared . . . so scared," he cries repeatedly.

"Come on, Josh," urges Kvellner. "It's high time you put your fears into words. Time to tell me what you feel and what you know."

"But it's not just *what* I know, Doc! . . . It's *how* I know!"

"What do you mean exactly?"

"The voices in my head tell me things . . . secret things . . . disgusting things . . . frightening things!"

"Do the voices tell you to do things?"

"No," the boy answers quietly.

"How many different voices do you usually hear in your head . . . three, four, five maybe?"

The boy gulps as if the answer is stuck fast in the hollow of his throat.

"Th . . . th . . . thousands."

Kvellner looks at him incredulously.

"You're playing games with me again," he says. "Aren't you?"

"No, Dr Kvellner, I swear I'm telling you the truth. I sometimes can't believe it myself. And I . . . I don't blame you for doubting me because you won't find my condition listed in any of your manuals."

"Do you *really* consider yourself unique . . . a somehow unprecedented case in all the long history of psychiatry?"

The boy starts to sob; tears trickle down his cheeks and slide around the corners of his quivering mouth. But soon the words begin to flow, spilling out involuntarily, like his tears.

"I . . . I remember my first day at school like as if it happened five minutes ago. I remember everything, Dr Kvellner. All my experiences, thoughts and emotions, still as fresh, still as vivid *now* as the exact moment they *actually happened*; no matter how long ago. It's like my brain is a computer that stores all my memories and every single one of those memories can be retrieved instantaneously by my preconscious mind and transmitted into my conscious mind. *Everything* I have ever heard or read I can remember . . . entire books . . . dictionaries . . . encyclopaedias . . . cloud-sites . . . conversations . . . *everything!*"

The boy hesitates.

"What was so special about your first day at school?" Kvellner asks.

266

"That's the first day I realized I was different from the other kids; realized that I was way smarter than they were, and that I simply couldn't communicate with them at their inferior intellectual frequency. I was so bored in class I kept pestering Teacher with questions about particle physics, even though I knew the answers already. I liked to watch her face turn pink. I remember she asked us to draw a picture . . . to draw a picture of whatever we wanted. She walked around the class trying to help each kid with their colours and stuff. Most kids just drew cats and dogs, flowers and houses, trite subjects. When she came to my desk, she leaned over my shoulder and frowned at my sheet, peculiar-like, kinda consterned.

"'What are you drawing Josh?' she said.

"'I'm drawing a portrait of God,' I told her.

"'But NoBody knows what God looks like.'

"I shrugged and said right back at her – 'Well, when I'm done with my picture, Everybody will know what God looks like.' Then she got pinker and angrier and shouted at me not to be so smart. I told her I couldn't help being intelligent. Then she became red angry; she grabbed my picture, crumpled it up and missiled it into the bin. After her face reverted to calm white, she gave me a fresh sheet to draw on. But I just left the sheet blank . . . drew nothing at all on it . . . not even a squiggle. A few minutes later teacher came back and leaned over me again. She whispered an apology into my ear for shouting at me earlier.

"'Do you like my new portrait of God?' I asked her friendly. 'Is it an improvement?'

"'But it's still blank! . . . There's nothing there, Josh,' she said, standing up straight and throwing her hands up in the air in frustration.

"I remember looking at her and seeing how tiny her mind was. I looked around at all the other children in class and knew how tiny their minds were too. And I hated each and every one of them, despised them and eclipsed them with my asymmetrical intellect . . .

wanted to make satellites of them all . . . capture them in orbit around the centripetal coruscating sun of my mind. Because their imaginations were so limited, I could understand them, was certain I might even control them like little automatons. . . . "

"What do you mean . . . control them or understand their minds?" interrupts Kvellner. He removes his spectacles quickly with one hand and squints at the boy as he poses the question.

"It's difficult to explain, Doctor . . . ever since I was a baby I've . . . I've seen images in my head . . . you know, playing like a movie or something. The images were black and white at first, fuzzy too, but when I was five years old they changed to colour. Then, as I got older, the words arrived. Nouns first, then the verbs and adjectives . . . a sort of commentary or soundtrack playing alongside the movies inside my head. It was like . . . it was like very slowly tuning in to a TV or radio station – the reception getting clearer as time went by. . . . "

Kvellner looks perplexed as he listens to the boy. What, he wonders, is so abnormal about this? A very young child learning to interpret the world through a constant series of words and images.

The boy notices the psychiatrist's puzzled look.

" . . . I'm sorry, Doctor. I'm not clarifying this abnormality well," he says. "I wasn't just interpreting the world through a constant series of words and images. . . . "

It's getting late, Kvellner thinks. I wish the boy would get to the point.

" . . . I know it's getting late, Doctor, but . . . but I need to tell you a story to get to the point."

The boy raises his big green eyes as if there were lead weights hanging from their lashes. He stares directly at Kvellner.

"Will you promise not to tell my dad the story?"

"Why, Josh?"

"Because if you tell him he won't be able to love me any more, that's why!" he cries. "He'll *hate me*, just like my teacher and the other kids at school *hated me*. He'll be afraid of me for ever if I tell him. Everybody would be terrified if they knew what I can do, even you, Doctor! I didn't want anybody to discover my 'curse-gift' . . . that's why I pretended to have Asperger's . . . I felt safe behind that syndrome . . . acting out according to its classic symptoms . . . easing the burden of my existence. Skulking scared on the outskirts of my Byzantine mind was I, desperate to avoid exploring its labyrinthine centre. . . . "

"Just tell me the story," Kvellner says impatiently, sensing the boy might retreat from the brink of confession.

"I remember sitting in class one day. Teacher started asking us a bunch of history questions – stuff we'd done already, so I knew all the answers. I kept putting my arm up and snapping my fingers to get her attention. She warned me to stop but I couldn't. I so wanted to impress her and all the rest of the kids with all the knowledge stuffed in my head. I remember her standing up straight with her hands on her hips and a venomous expression. She didn't move her mouth but I could still hear her speaking distinctly: 'Shut up, Josh Andersson . . . shut up, you freak!' Then she smiled peculiar and asked me some ridiculously obscure historical question about the Peloponnesian War. I didn't know the answer. She continued smiling at me, waiting for the answer she knew would never come. All the other boys and girls were silent. I could feel their eyes burning like molten iron rain in my brain. I felt humiliated, 'cos I *so* wanted that answer, Doc . . . I *so* wanted that answer. So I stared at the teacher, and suddenly I could see it like a reflection in the mirror of her soul . . . heard it like an echo in a cave.

"'*Brasidas . . . Spartan general; Died Battle of Amphipolis, Four Two Two BCE,*' I blurted out.

"The teacher started to totter on her pointy heels as if her ankles were turned to Jell-O. She seemed to have to grab the edge of her desk to maintain her balance. I watched her wilt and felt a momentary surge of pride knowing that I could do what God alone can do. But then I felt her rage . . . her overwhelming rage inside of me . . . and my head filled hot with mayhem and my body cold with fear. . . . ”

Kvellner is shaking his head in disbelief as he listens. The boy is playing games again, he thinks, imagining that he can *actually* read minds. The voices in his head are definitely symptomatic of schizophrenia; maybe some kind of manic disorder as well.

“ . . . I used to think the voices in my head were my own but now I know they belong to other people . . . hell is other people, Doc – just like Sartre said it was.”

“But it’s not possible . . . it isn’t physically or psychologically possible, Josh!”

“But don’t you understand, Dr Kvellner – quantum computers can do it to a very limited extent; translate simple human cognitive patterns into images. And what’s a computer but a series of codes just like the genetic sequences in every cell in our bodies and brains.”

“But computers are not human, Josh; they are inanimate.”

“All matter is inanimate, Doctor . . . all living matter is constructed of inanimate atoms selfishly reproducing their arrangements. Human life is simply a tragicomic accident . . . atoms becoming conscious of their temporary molecular structures.”

Kvellner watches the boy still pacing over and back across the room. He struggles to counter the logic of his twelve-year-old patient’s arguments. He stands up and walks over behind the boy and puts one hand on his shoulder to stop him.

“You have a really *wonderful* imagination!” he tells him. “So wonderful I’m not surprised you feel scared of it all the time. But this gift of yours . . . this ‘curse-gift’, as you call it . . . it’s just not possible . . . it’s just a figment of your powerful imagination.”

The child turns and fires a fierce look at Kvellner.

“You never even noticed, Doc, did you?”

“Noticed what?”

“Noticed that I responded to some of your thoughts without you being consciously aware of them . . . that's caused by the ossification of your neural architecture – the pathways in your neocortex becoming less plastic."

"I don't understand what you mean."

"Think of an animal . . . any animal, Doc."

Kvellner frowns slowly, and thinks of a jumping kangaroo.

The boy stares at the psychiatrist's forehead and twitches a half-smile as he utters the word.

"Kangaroo."

The psychiatrist stands back, aghast; horrified that the child could have read the thought; could *actually* breach that most holy of citadels and invade the inner sanctum of his consciousness. His heart begins to pound and his mind starts to race. He holds his hands up against his forehead, hoping that they will physically prevent the boy from scanning his mind. Josh is smiling now, effortlessly reading every one of Kvellner's racing thoughts.

"It's okay. Try not to be scared. I can't *control* your mind . . . I can only perceive your *conscious* thoughts, not your unconscious ones."

"My God . . . my God!" gasps Kvellner, turning away quickly and striding towards the door. *The boy's father must know . . . he deserves an explanation for his son's behaviour*, he thinks.

"Don't tell him, Doctor . . . please don't tell him . . . If you do . . . if you do . . . I'll tell your wife Gretta you've had sex with your secretary, Miss Chang. It was during a conference in Dallas in July, wasn't it? I saw her thinking about it one day in the office."

Kvellner stops at the door and turns viciously, as if to instantly deny such a scandalous allegation. He stands still for a few seconds, his cheeks flushed with embarrassment. How can you conceal *any* secrets, he thinks, from such an omniscient mind? Governments would pay billions . . . He glares at the boy; stares at the handsome features of his sallow face; a countenance that seems to radiate a beguiling innocence. But the eyes . . . those eyes . . . the psychiatrist thinks; such eyes as can dissect the innards of the human soul know more of evil than of good.

Josh is sitting in the passenger seat as his father drives home from Kvellner's office. They haven't spoken a word to each other since leaving it.

"What did you tell Kvellner?" asks Jack eventually.

"Nothing," the boy replies sullenly.

Jack gives him a dubious look.

"Hmmm . . . whatever you said you scared him witless. Was it something to do with what Tor Magnusson showed you this morning?"

Josh turns his head away.

"Was it, Josh?"

"Pull over, Dad. I need to tell you something," he says quietly.

Jack spends a few minutes looking for a place to park. He finds one in the near-empty car-park of an all-night diner. As soon as he pulls up, he orders the vehicle's on-board computer to switch off the ignition and kill the headlights.

"Well, what do you want to tell me?"

"I don't think anyone will understand . . . Nobody will understand."

"Understand what?" Jack growls impatiently. "I've had a goddam long day!"

"I remember when you and Mom gave me a present of a globe for my third birthday. All those lines of longitude and latitude crisscrossed on it looked like the bars of some spherical cage. I wondered what kind of animal lived inside that cage. I imagined it must have been black and orange because that was the colour of the inside of the Earth when it bled through volcanoes. It must be a tiger, I thought, and every time it roared, the Earth shook and that's how earthquakes happened. . . . "

"What's this got to do with Magnusson?"

"Magnusson sent me a video clip this morning. It showed him clutching a rifle, and standing over the body of a tiger. One he had hunted and killed, himself – he'd boasted it was probably the last one left in the wild. He was laughing as he said it. He'd blown the animal's head clean off with a single silver bullet. Then he told me there was a tiger inside Everybody . . . and that that beast could never be tamed because Nature wouldn't allow it. . . . "

Jack is shaking his head and frowning, wondering why the contents of the video so frightened his son. Footage of the slaughtered animal might be upsetting for the boy, but hardly terrifying . . . scarcely enough to justify his extreme reaction.

Josh looks at his father and knows he fails to appreciate the significance of the story. He doesn't blame him for not understanding it; doesn't blame him for not remembering all the details of his interview with Magnusson in Iceland.

"Magnusson told you already, Dad. Don't you remember? . . . 'We cannot alter human nature itself. That leopard will never change its spots or that tiger its stripes.'"

"Yeah, I vaguely recall him saying something like that . . . I have it recorded anyhow."

"It's time, Dad . . . time I showed you what it all means. To tell you the truth about Elijah Roberts and what Steelman really is. . . . "

TWENTY-SEVEN

A FLIGHT ATTENDANT GREETS THEM at the top of a stairwell connected to the front of the aircraft.

She scans their irises with a small hand-held device, Jack first, then Josh. She smiles broadly as she confirms their identities and directs them to their First Class cabin seats. Josh looks anxiously into the cockpit and his heart sinks as he walks past. The cockpit is tiny and there are no seats or windows. He sees a man in blue overalls standing on the floor of the cockpit. The man is pointing a quantum scanner at an array of on-board computers. He speaks coldly, using a strange kind of English, as he converses with the computers. *Obviously conducting a series of standard preflight checks in technospeak – what a soulless language,* the boy thinks. His father had warned him that many airlines no longer use human pilots, especially for short-haul flights like New York to Charleston, West Virginia. "It makes perfect sense," he'd said. "Computer control is superior to human control – it's safer and more cost effective. An air accident has never, ever happened with a computerized pilot."

Even human air-traffic controllers are becoming obsolete. Surgeons and dentists, too; their raw skills of manipulation lost, their precious human craft slowly ebbing. What phrase, Josh thinks, did Professor Weiseman use? Yes – "The hand is the cutting edge of the mind." But the mind is blunted now, destroyed by a product of its own creation. Like the mighty Krell, as Steinitz said, "their civilization obliterated in a single night" by a machine. Bronstein expressed similar opinion in mental terms – "Quantum algorithms have superseded cognitive function." Roberts, Josh decides, is right to do this; it's the most humane plan in the event of him losing the next election – to ride the

Trojan horse. *Roberts is not the first to think of the idea but now we have the technological means to achieve it. To win quickly without widespread slaughter in the great war to save humanity from itself....*

"Come on, Josh, time to sit down and buckle up. We'll be taking off in a few minutes," his father tells him with a heartening smile. "This aircraft is capable of travelling at Mach Two, you know. We'll be in Charleston in twenty minutes. Are you nervous?"

"No, Dad," the boy replies as he straps himself into his spacious First Class window seat.

There is a gentle sucking sound as all the automatic doors of the aircraft are simultaneously closed, sealing the hollow tube of the delta-winged craft. The plane taxis to its takeoff position. The powerful engines start to whine as the aircraft accelerates along the runway, yet strangely, there is scarcely a shudder inside the cabin. Takeoff is as smooth and efficient as if it were the gentle wing-beats of a hummingbird enabling its ascent.

I can't believe Josh is taking this so calmly, Jack thinks to himself. *Something has changed in him . . . as if the fear has died inside him. Like what happened me after that crazy jetcopter flight I had with Magnusson . . . .*

"Would you like a drink, Mr Andersson?" asks a young, blonde flight-attendant. She is wearing a bright red uniform with a tight fitting short skirt and a low-cut white blouse.

"Yes," he answers quickly, "I'll have a scotch."

The attendant presses a button on her trolley and pours the drink directly from it into a crystal glass.

"Would you like some ice in it?"

"Yes, thank you."

She hands the tinkling glass to Jack, smiling at him as she does so.

Ooooh, she is so sexy, he thinks.

"Would your little boy like a drink?"

"Josh, would you like something to drink?"

"Sure, okay I guess. I'll have an AppleFizz."

The attendant searches in her trolley and takes out a bright green aluminium can; it is shaped exactly like an apple. She pulls a metal stalk off the top of the can with her bright-red painted finger-nails and inserts a straw through the froth oozing out of the hole.

"There you go, young man," she says, leaning forward slightly and across Jack to give the boy his soda. *Nice perfume*, Jack remarks to himself, hurriedly sipping his scotch. *Must be the air-conditioning that makes her nipples stick out like that under her blouse . . . No! Wait a sec . . . she's not wearing a brassiere. Mmmm . . . I could tear that blouse right off and suck those tits . . . lick her navel while she claws those nails into my back. . . Yeah, rip her panties off and screw her so hard she wouldn't be able to walk for a week . . . Christ, just imagine it!!*

He watches her sashaying down the aisle, her swaying hips seeming to caress the sides of every seat before she stops and bends down to attend another passenger. *Ooooh! . . . That ass is so tight. I wonder does she like . . .*

"Dad!"

. . . Doing it like a dog . . .

"Dad!!"

Even just a blowjob.

"Dad!!!"

"Yeah! . . . What is it?"

The boy's face is bright pink as he stares at his father.

"Do you miss Mom?"

Jack drives the hire car at a snail's pace through a maze of dirt-track country roads. He's been driving for three hours solid since leaving the interstate west of Charleston. The overgrown verges begin to encroach more and more onto the road now, brushing the sides of the car occasionally with tall blades of brown grass. It is early December, yet many of the fields in the surrounding countryside still look burned up.

"You sure you programmed the correct co-ordinates into this thing, Josh?" asks Jack, indicating the navigation system . . . "Computer here thinks the fields round here should be green!" he adds sarcastically.

The boy shrugs sullenly.

"Thirty-five minutes approximately to your destination," calls out a female voice from the navigation system speakers.

"Hell! This better be worth the trip, kid. I can't see what could be so important that you need to show me, here in the middle of the boondocks."

The boy still fails to react.

Jack glances over at the figure sitting in the passenger seat beside him; oblivious to the fact the boy is preoccupied with his own father's thoughts.

Why doesn't he say something? You shouldn't have done it, son. Why did you do it? Pretend to be sick and make your own mother crack up and pack up and away. Do I miss Mom? I'll never forgive you for this, Josh . . . for what you did to me and Jenny.

The boy chews his lower lip and looks over at his father.

"I'm sorry, Dad. I'm sorry. I couldn't help it."

"Sorry for what?" he answers, frowning

"Sorry for being me . . . sorry for being me, I guess."

One half hour later they arrive at their destination. It is a small town. The buildings lining the main street are quaint but have long since lost their old-world charm. They appear shuffled together, like an untidy deck of tobacco-stained, dog-eared cards. The middle of the asphalt surface of the road has fissured in jagged lines; crumbled into a hotchpotch of ashen-grey gravel and potholes at its edges. There are battered hulks of old cars strewn around, their paintwork all faded to a near-universal, dirty white. The few pedestrians plodding on the pavements all seem old and stooping under the weight of the sun. The unforgiving sun that bleached the colour from their lives; dried up their rivers and shrivelled their crops.

Jack pulls up to the kerb in his shiny new rented car and gets out.

"Excuse me, sir!" he calls to an old man.

The old man turns and looks at him suspiciously. One of his eyes has a cataract; like a silver coin for an iris. He regards the new car suspiciously with the one good eye. His face is wizened and his voice sounds husky and dry as he speaks.

"You from the guvment?"

"No, sir!"

"Well, you must be a rich son of a bitch driving that machine!"

"No, sir. It's a rental."

"New York, ain't yah! All the young folk round here moved to the cities, ya know. Not enough water this year even to keep the goddam birds from gettin' thirsty, never mind livestock and crops. I remember when I was a young feller, why I . . . "

The old man groans on for a couple of minutes about his youth; farming . . . pride in them fields . . . life-giving land . . . flies buzzing and birdsong . . . He's forgotten his initial suspicions and just wants a sympathetic ear.

"Excuse me, sir . . . eh, I'm looking for a Mrs Emma Lee van Groot," interrupts Jack. "Where would I find her?"

"Mrs van Groot, did ya say?"

"Yes, sir."

"You sure you're not from the guvment? She don't much relish talkin' to guvment types."

"Well, not really," Jack answers heedlessly.

"Hang dammit! I knew it. . . . "

A child's voice suddenly calls out from behind the two men.

"Excuse me, Mr Stephenson, sir," Josh is saying timidly, looking directly at the old farmer as he turns towards him. "Mrs van Groot is expecting us."

The old farmer stares in amazement at Josh. He goes up to him and rubs the boy's smooth-skinned sallow cheeks with the gnarled knuckles of one hand. He ruffles his brown hair with the other.

"Young feller . . . it's a young feller! . . . Long time since I seen one . . . how are ya, young feller?" he is croaking, with tears silvering the corners of his eyes.

"I'm fine, sir, thank you. I'm sorry your fields are broken but we're going to fix them. You mark my words, Mr Stephenson; we're going to fix them."

The old man smiles with a mouthful of crooked yellow teeth as if he's been waiting years to hear those very words. He coughs; sounds like his lungs are full of rattling old chains.

"I sure miss working 'em, son. Ya fix 'em real good, won't ya?"

"Sure."

"Mrs van Groot lives over her son's barber store on the left," the old man indicates with a trembling finger. "I'm seventy-five, ya know, and that woman taught me at school. Must be near ninety now, old Emma." He coughs again as he turns away and shuffles aimlessly down the street.

"How in hell did you know that guy's name, Josh?" asks Jack.

"Easy," he quickly replies. "Cass has National Security profiles and pics of all the citizens here. I simply memorized them."

The barber's body is so corpulent that it looks like a collapsed pyramid of flesh from his neck to his waist. And his red-and-white chequered apron is stretched so tight across his chest and the folds of his massive stomach. . . .

He must need it to stop his guts spilling out, thinks Jack.

Humpty-Dumpty, Roly-Poly Roland, thinks Josh.

"You're late, Mr Andersson," complains Roland van Groot.

He doesn't even bother to look up from shaving his sole customer; concentrates on his blade, furrowing neat tracks through the grey lather on the wrinkled leather face beneath him. *Recycled water makes the shaving-foam dirty*, thinks Josh.

"Momma! Those gentlemen you're expectin' are here to see ya!" the barber bellows, still bending over his customer.

There is a shuffling sound from above the ceiling, and after a minute the old woman's footsteps echo down a wooden staircase. The barber stands up straight at last, and looks lazily over at Jack and Josh. His eyes bulge like a reptile's over a set of slimy jowls, and he tugs at his greasy dewlap as he focuses his gaze on the boy. He nods leadenly as if in recognition of somebody he once vaguely knew but hasn't met in a long time.

Emma Lee van Groot fumbles with an ancient set of iron keys before she finds the correct one. The lock on the old schoolhouse door resists a couple of turns then yields with a slow *clunk*. She creaks open the door. A warm breeze whistles through a broken window at the far end of the single classroom, even though the air is still dank with the smell of stale books. Half a dozen low tables are stacked together to one side of the room and small children's chairs are strewn about the floor. The old teacher rummages now through the drawers of a large wooden desk.

"I know the attendance register is here somewhere," she is muttering. "You ain't gonna believe me otherwise . . . ahh, here it is!"

She places a large book down on the desk, opens it gingerly, thumbs slowly through its yellowed pages, stops at one, runs a hooked finger carefully along the edge of it and finds the name she is looking for. She turns the book around and slides it across the desk towards Jack and Josh, her bony finger pointing proudly at the name.

Elijah Hunt Roberts

"How long was Roberts a pupil here?" queries Jack.

"I taught him for two years. He left when he was around Josh's age."

Jack sniffs the air and looks around disparagingly at the near-derelict classroom.

"Humble beginnings for such a great man," he says. "What was he like as a child? Super-smart I suppose."

"A little unnerving, to be honest – the smartest and the saddest child I ever taught."

"How do you mean, Mam?"

"Elijah never smiled . . . never had any friends. Other children, including my Roland, shunned him. They were afraid of him but never told me why. Children sometimes have a sense about other kids that adults don't have. I can't really explain it. *I* was afraid of him too in some ways."

Jack frowns at the elderly teacher. How could she, he thinks, have been afraid of a little boy?

"Tell my father!" Josh urges. "Tell him, Mrs van Groot. He needs to know."

She breathes in deeply and sighs heavily; closes her eyes as she speaks.

"I don't know why he scared me so much. Elijah just sat in class reading books all day. He had more knowledge and wisdom in his head than I did; maybe that's why. He seldom spoke to anyone. But when he did speak, there was a kind of significance to it – a meaning beyond mere words. He told me once he loved words more than people: 'You could put all the words in a dictionary and define them all from A to Z, but you couldn't do the same with people.' Elijah seemed to lack emotions, or if he did show 'em, he acted as though he had learned them from a dictionary – not *felt* them as regular people do. There was something cold and automatic about him, like a robot or something."

The old lady rises slowly from behind the desk, shambles to the broken window and looks out at the parched landscape. Her back is turned to Jack and Josh and she speaks haltingly.

"I think . . . I think that Roberts was somehow abnormally intelligent. Almost as if it was an illness of some kind, ya know. Kinda like that line between genius and madness, except maybe he had one foot stood either side of it. I can't be sure . . . but I suspect he had some sort of . . . some sort of . . . "

Van Groot turns from the window. The paper-thin skin of her neck is almost translucent in the sunlight. She gazes at Josh and smiles with thin, purple lips.

"Some sort of what, Mam?"

" . . . autistic disorder, Mr Andersson," she answers, still gazing at the boy. She has exactly the same expression as her son Roland had when he first looked at Josh.

"Oh, Christ!" groans Jack. "No . . . No!"

"There's quite a physical likeness in fact," she says. "I remember Roberts being a very handsome boy."

"No . . . no," Jack continues to groan repeatedly, holding his head in his hands. He goes to the middle of the room and delivers a flying kick to one of the chairs. It bounces across the floor, clatters against the stack of low tables and hits off the wall above it.

"Fuck it . . . Fuck it!" he roars.

"You little cunt!" he roars, rounding on Josh. "Hadn't the balls to tell me yourself . . . Joshua Roberts! Got this sweet old dame to do it for you. This is a *conspiracy* . . . just a big *fucking* game to all of you."

"It's not *my* fault . . . it's not *my* fault!" wails Josh. "You always knew you were not my genetic father, so what difference does it make?"

"Absolutely right, young man," says van Groot sharply. "Rearing the son of a great man ought to be a privilege not a burden, Mr Andersson. You should be proud of him; you should love him. Once you signed your name on the adoption papers you promised to love that boy, irrespective of who his real parents were."

"But he's the son of Eli Roberts, don't you see . . . Christ!!" protests Jack, still pacing the room and gesticulating angrily.

The old lady smiles endearingly as if trying to placate a truculent pupil.

"All the more reason to love him," she says.

"Love *him*?" Jack shouts, pointing an accusing finger at Josh.

"Unconditionally . . . Mr Andersson."

Van Groot waits for Jack to regain his composure before continuing.

"Eli didn't have a father around to love him. His mother was a little strange too; sort of intense, didn't talk to local folk much nor leave her house much either, except to go to church on Sundays. She got friendly with Father Joe Noone, who was an elderly Jesuit priest who retired here. Even though Mrs Roberts was a quiet soul, she always liked to argue about religion. She was passionate about it and so was Father Joe, who being Irish, I guess was always up for a good argument. Sometimes they'd be at it for hours, shouting at each other 'til they were hoarse. Folks around here thought they were plain crazy. Eli said according to the dictionary he was embarrassed; he wanted the two of 'em to stop carryin' on so . . . neither of them was clever enough to clinch the argument, he'd said. But he was goin' to settle it himself . . . so he did."

"What did Eli do, Mam?" says Jack.

The old lady smiles sweetly before continuing, almost a twinkling in her eye as she gazes continuously at Josh . . . remembering . . . remembering the boy Elijah.

"Well," she answers, "Eli himself got real friendly with Father Joe. I suppose in a funny way the old priest became a mentor for the boy, and being a Jesuit he was a very learned man. I caught Eli one day in class reading a copy of *Ulysses*. I don't know much about that book but I knew it wasn't appropriate for a twelve-year-old so I confiscated it. Father Joe came to see me afterward in school and him mad as hell shouting: 'Dare you woman interfere with that boy's education; *I* gave him that book. Damned philistine hillbillies, all of you! That boy is a genuine genius, you know that . . . a genius parading his pearls before swine.'

"I reckoned the old priest was losing his marbles, so I gave the book back to Eli, to keep the peace, so to speak. Just as well – Father Joe died not long after – heart gave out so far as I can remember."

The elderly woman stoops and opens a drawer behind her desk. She takes out a sheaf of browning pages, their edges curled with age and stapled together in one corner. Even the staple is rusty. She blows a film of dust off the top page and then hands the sheets to Jack.

"What's this?" he says.

"It's a play."

"A play?" he frowns.

"Yes, a script that Eli wrote for Father Noone. He gave it to him shortly before he died."

"Why?"

"I wanted to show you what Josh is capable of doing. What he is capable of writing even at his age. Father Joe told me after he read it that it clinched the argument, defined the madness of his inner struggle. Even the Dublin accents, the idioms were authentic in the play, penned with a Joycean ear he'd said. 'The boy is a genius,' he kept repeating on his deathbed . . . 'That boy has read my rotten soul like a book. I am numbered, numbered, weighed divided; I face death alone and am afraid.' He gave Eli an old leather-bound book, you know, in his will. I can't remember the name of it."

"*Finnegans Wake*," says Josh. "Remember, Dad; Merry Steinitz showed it to you already."

Jack stares at the boy in disbelief and thinks of the old priest lying on his deathbed. "That boy has read my rotten soul like a book," he'd said.

The dry earth crunches underfoot as Jack and Josh meander through the undulating coppered mosaic of countryside. The odd corroding shell of a tractor dotting the landscape is silent testament to its former fertility. Weeds are growing thickly along the wild hedgerows, and are sprouting in rust-coloured patches among the tall blades of arid grass in the middle of the fields. There is no buzz of insects or bird-song or sound of any other living thing. Mother Nature has stayed the hardy hands that once tilled the soil and coaxed life from it for generations.

"It's along the western edge of the next field," says Josh.

His father nods. He hasn't spoken to the boy since they left Emma Lee van Groot back to her son's shop. They trek alongside a hedgerow for another five minutes, before Josh raises his hand and points to a shallow ravine running parallel to the hedgerow.

"This is it," he says.

"What the hell is it?!" snaps Jack.

"It was a river."

"You took me all the way here to show me a dried-up river bed?"

"Yes."

Jack folds his arms and looks along the length of the ravine, searching for anything of significance.

"Waste of time!" he mutters.

"Don't you remember, Father? Steinitz told you about Roberts when he was a little boy. He used to go fishing in this river. Then one day he came here and all the fish were dead – poisoned by a toxic spillage. Elijah said he imagined the fish were actually whales, singing the saddest songs from the mournful depths of the oceans of memory. Don't you remember, Father?"

"Yeah, I remember. You must have listened to all my recorded interviews?"

"Yes, I memorized them all."

The boy looks up at the sky. Twilight is fast approaching. He lies down on the bank of the ravine and pats the ground beside him.

"Lie down beside me, Father, and together we will watch the stars come out. I know the name of every one of them."

"It's getting cold. I'm heading back to the car."

"No, Father! The steel men march here, yet you do not see them," the boy says gravely and points towards the western horizon where the sky is spreading a golden orange.

Jack shields his eyes and squints at the setting sun.

There is a line of tall electricity pylons in the next field. The waning sunlight filters through their latticework and silhouettes their superstructure stark black against the backdrop of sky. Long cables are threaded through the heads and arms of the pylons as they stretch into the distance.

"These are the steel men," says Josh.

"What? What do you mean?"

The boy cannot look him straight in the eye; he just gazes at the setting sun as he speaks.

"Steelman is a quantum computer virus. It has been engineered by GeoNova scientists to attack and destroy electrical generation control systems worldwide. It is set to be activated in the event of Roberts failing to get re-elected. It is the final solution to ecological Armageddon. . . . "

"But that will be an end to civilization . . . nuclear war will break out."

"No, this virus will pull the plug on the world in a matter of hours. You can't launch any weapons if the computers don't work."

"But society will break down . . . anarchy . . . It's not a bloodless . . . Jesus Christ . . . Christ!"

"I know, but it's a lot cleaner than an inevitable atomic holocaust if we continue on our current trajectory. 'Steelman' is entirely logical, efficient, and humane in many ways. . . . "

Jack presses his palms against his cheeks in horror as he listens,

286

amazed at the boy's cavalier attitude and matter-of-fact tone. The boy seems so remote, so removed from the enormity of such a diabolical act.

" . . . Roberts got the idea from the plot of that old movie *The Day the Earth Stood Still*. The world is so integrated, now that we have the means to implement it and terminate a mighty civilization in a single night. Mankind deserves such a demise. Just like the Krell in *Forbidden Planet*, we have forgotten we are creatures and not gods."

The night is moonless and freezing cold. Jack is lying on his back on the bank of the ravine staring at the heavens. The longer he stares into the starry abyss, the more he feels himself drawn towards it; as if the sky is a bottomless black chasm and the stars twinkling pin-pricks of hope illuminating its depths. He thinks of Roberts and all the lights going out across the world as it plunges into a new and terrifying Dark Age, but that the stars will still shine steadfast nonetheless.

Josh is lying on his back on the slope of the ravine about twenty metres away from his father. He contemplates the profusion of Creation above – the view into the soul of eternity – the high, wispy cloud of the Milky Way. Imagines the aeons it takes for light to travel to Earth from other galaxies. Closes his eyes and reaches out with arms wide towards the stars. Plucks handfuls of them like grains of sand and sprinkles them delicately on his forehead with his fingers.

"I anoint thee with the treasures of the cosmos," he murmurs to himself. And he feels his body glowing as if it is energized with stars.

He stares unflinchingly into the universe, and knows that even it, too, will one day perish.

TWENTY-EIGHT

ALL MY SINS

by

Elijah Hunt Roberts

A Play for Everybody and Nobody

CHARACTERS

Father Joe:	An elderly parish priest.
Father Tom:	An young parish priest.
Vera:	A female parishioner known to Father Joe.
John:	A male parishioner known to Father Joe.
May:	A female parishioner known to Father Joe.
Penitent:	An unknown male.

WE HEAR PEOPLE IN A PEW, QUEUED FOR
CONFESSION. LOW MURMURS, PRAYERS,
INTERSPERSED WITH BENEDICTIONS FROM FATHER JOE.
THE SOUND OF A WOODEN BOARD BEING DRAWN
ACROSS A CONFESSIONAL HATCH.

1. VERA: (*low*)	Bless me, Father, for I have sinned. It's been six weeks since me last confession. (*beat*) I'm still losing me temper with me husband, Father. But his drinkin's just a burden on the whole family.
2. FATHER JOE:	I know, I know. Mm . . . mm. The drink's a curse on many's a marriage and family.
3. VERA: (*low*)	I'll soon be left on me own to cope, Father, the way things is goin'. The boys have just finished their exams and sure the girls, well, they all *had* to leave home. You know the story yourself, Father.
4. FATHER JOE:	Ah, too well, Vera. Too well.

5. VERA: (*low*)	Ye'll say a prayer for me, Father?
6. FATHER JOE:	I will of course, Vera. Have faith in the Man Above to look after you in the long run. (*beat*) Now! The blessings of Almighty God upon you, and say a rosary for your own failings.
7. VERA: (*low*)	Thanks, Father. God bless you.

SOUND OF WOODEN BOARD BEING DRAWN ACROSS
THE CONFESSIONAL HATCH.

8. JOHN:	Bless me, Father, for I have sinned. It's been, eh, eh, five months since me last confession. (*beat*) I took the Lord's name in vain four times. I had impure thoughts, eh, eh, eh, six times I think. Yeah, yeah, and I, I, eh, I . . .
9. FATHER JOE:	Well, what else, my son?
10. JOHN:	Eh, I abused meself once, Father. That's all, just the once!
11. FATHER JOE:	Hmm, I see, I see. And are you truly sorry and seek forgiveness for those sins you have committed?
12. JOHN:	Yes, Father.
13. FATHER JOE:	Those impure thoughts and actions

can be the ruination of many's a good mind. I know myself it's not easy for a single man like you, John. But you must resist the temptations of the flesh that Satan lays before you. And seek redemption in the eternal truth and goodness that are the teachings of Christ our Savior. (*beat*) Now! A rosary a night for the next week and three more Our Fathers for good measure. In the name of the Father, Son and Holy Spirit I absolve thee. Amen.

14. JOHN: Thanks, Father.

SOUND OF WOODEN BOARD BEING DRAWN ACROSS
THE CONFESSIONAL HATCH.

15. MAY: Bless me, Father, for I have sinned. It's been over a week now since my last confession. (*beat*) Our Robert's in trouble again, Father. He's up again for thieving in court. I know he did it, Father. He's as guilty as the hell he's goin' to end up in. Those bleedin' drugs rob a soul of all reason. He won't come to see ya, Father. I kind of, ye know, have to seek God's forgiveness on his behalf. Ye know what I mean, Father.

16. FATHER JOE: Ah, May! He's a big boy now. He won't find salvation through his mother's

	intercession. Tell him to get Mass on Sundays or talk to one of the younger priests here.
17. MAY:	Ah, Father, I'm wastin' me breath on him. I've told him a t'ousand times, if it wasn't for me faith in the Man Above I'd have gone crazy years ago meself. Could ya not see him yourself, Father?
18. FATHER JOE:	No, no, May. My pastoral days are long over.
19. MAY:	But sure none of the other priests go visitin' either.
20. FATHER JOE:	Now, now! We're all busy doing Our Lord's work in our own way, May.
21. MAY:	Sorry, Father. (*beat*) Will ye say a Mass for me?
22. FATHER JOE:	I'd be glad to. Your usual time next Sunday, May.
23. MAY:	Oh, that'd be grand.
24. FATHER JOE:	Now keep the faith and you shall be rewarded in the kingdom of heaven everlasting.
25. MAY:	Bless ya, Father. No penance today?

26. FATHER JOE:	No. No prescription today. Your problems are penance enough, May. Now go, and God bless you.
27. MAY:	Thanks, Father Joe.
28. FATHER JOE:	Oh, May, (*beat*) any more for confession?
29. MAY:	No, Father, I was the last one. Yer day's work is done.
30. FATHER JOE:	Great. Thanks, May.

HE STARTS TO WHISTLE SOFTLY BUT STOPS.
PENITENT SELF-CONSCIOUSLY CLEARS HIS THROAT.
WOODEN SLIDER IS DRAGGED BACK.

31. FATHER JOE:	Sorry. Forgive me. I didn't realize there was someone else still there.
32. PENITENT:	Bless me, Father, for I have sinned. It's been many years since my last confession.
33. FATHER JOE:	(*pause*) Well! What ails you, my son?
34. PENITENT:	I think I've committed a murder, Father. Well, in a manner of speaking.
35. FATHER JOE:	No! In plain speaking, my son. You might be under a privilege here, a

confessional seal, but you have an
overwhelming spiritual obligation to
tell the truth under God. Do you hear
me now?

36. PENITENT: I have killed my faith in God, Father.

37. FATHER JOE: You mean you've lost it.

38. PENITENT: No, Father, I mean I've murdered it;
                     literally with my own bare hands.

39. FATHER JOE: Sure how could you possibly do that?

40. PENITENT: Turning pages, Father. Pages and pages.
                     Death by a thousand cuts, death by a
                     million pages. I've studied books on
                     philosophy, theology, cosmology,
                     Christianity, ethics. You name it,
                     anything concerning religion.

41. FATHER JOE: And the Good Book . . . the Bible?

42. PENITENT: Of course, Father. Hundreds of times
                     maybe. Sure I know it practically
                     verbatim.

43. FATHER JOE: Good man, good man. And what did
                     your common senses tell you after
                     studying it?

44. PENITENT: Honestly, Father, I didn't taste one drop

of distilled essence of pure truth in it, from Genesis to Revelations.

45. FATHER JOE: Aw, come on, my son. You must have seen something in it.

46. PENITENT: No, Father. No color, not even black nor white. Just gray. Shades of gray, infinite gray.

47. FATHER JOE: So the Bible didn't speak to you *per se*.

48. PENITENT: Oh, I'm sure it did, Father. But all I heard, after building my huge, intellectual Tower of Babble was a mass of confusion and contradictions. Just like the ancient architects themselves.

49. FATHER JOE: And what did you feel? What did you feel inside your head and in your heart?

50. PENITENT: My head told me I must be as wise as Solomon for all my accumulated learning, but my heart told me I was on a fool's errand. (*chuckles*) You might say, Father, I felt the wisest fool in Christendom.

51. FATHER JOE: And what about your sixth sense?

52. PENITENT: What do you mean, Father?

53. FATHER JOE:	Your faith, your faith, that bedrock of belief we all need in something infinitely greater than ourselves. The greatest thought we can possibly think. God.
54. PENITENT:	Faith, huh! What is faith but an ideological straitjacket, a mental anesthetic, a comfort blanket to quieten our inner demons.
55. FATHER JOE:	Wrong! Wrong! my friend. Profoundly wrong!
56. PENITENT:	As a poet might once have said, Father, I squeezed the almighty book into a ball and rolled it toward some overwhelming question. I sought an inner promised land but found only a desolate, gray wasteland.
57. FATHER JOE:	(*exhales long and slowly*) Do I know you?
58. PENITENT:	I'm not sure, Father.
59. FATHER JOE:	No, I can't say I recognize the voice just off. You know, I must admit the Bible can be a bit confusing sometimes, but you must remember Man was merely inspired as an imperfect writing instrument to convey the word of God our Creator.

60. PENITENT:	I agree, Father, but do you not think he could have left a less ambiguous legacy? God might not play dice but he's a genius at Cryptic Scrabble and cross words.
61. FATHER JOE:	God doesn't play dice. Didn't Albert Einstein say that?
62. PENITENT:	Oh! His most famous quote.
63. FATHER JOE:	Well, then. Even the greatest scientific mind in history believed in Almighty God.
64. PENITENT:	Oh! I've read lots of books on science too, Father.
65. FATHER JOE:	Did you now? (*resignedly*) I'm sure you found them illuminating.
66. PENITENT:	Oh, indeed, Father. In fact the more I read and discovered, the less room I found in my heart of hearts for God. You've heard of the expression the god of the gaps, haven't you, Father?
67. FATHER JOE:	Ah, sort of.
68. PENITENT:	Well, all those natural phenomena that we can't understand in the universe around us we attribute to God's

handiwork – the gaps in our knowledge, so to speak. Well, science progressively and relentlessly just keeps plugging those gaps and—

69. FATHER JOE: —and rationalizes God out of existence.

70. PENITENT: Precisely, Father.

71. FATHER JOE: Ah, don't talk to me of scientists. Philistines gnawing at the roots of the Tree of Knowledge, the Tree of Life itself. All I know is that God created the universe, everything. That God is ultimate truth. That the Bible teaches us how to go to heaven, not how the heavens go – 'tis not a work of science.

72. PENITENT: But at least science seeks empirical truth, not some transcendental, ethereal notion that can never prosper under serious scrutiny.

73. FATHER JOE: Listen to me, my son! You have not looked deep enough or well enough to find Our Lord. But I warrant you this: you will find Him between the end of the telescope and the bottom of the electron microscope. Every law of physics, every star and galaxy in the cosmos, every molecule, every atom, every subatomic particle bears *His*

hallowed hallmarks, and moves in accordance with his magisterial ordinances.

74. PENITENT: Bravo! A veritable quantum leap of faith, Father. But what of mortal Man himself? Is he not just a convenient molecular arrangement we call a body, a brain, a consciousness? Same elements as those stars and galaxies. We are literally stardust. *"Remember thou art dust and unto dust thou shalt return."* You've uttered it over a thousand coffins yourself, Father.

75. FATHER JOE: Ah, but you must acknowledge the human mind is infinitely greater than the sum of its parts. 'Tis such a sophisticated and brilliant construction that only God himself in his omnipotence could have conceived it. (*beat*) Think about it: here are you and I with probably a century of memories between us, and yet we can scarcely scratch the surface of our own consciousness let alone another's.

76. PENITENT: Yes, Father, it's fair to say we can never truly know another human being. Life is ultimately a solitary experience to which we are all condemned.

77. FATHER JOE:	No! Not if you have a soul or a heart humble enough to embrace and accept the grace of Our Lord Jesus Christ (*beat*) as I have. (*beat*) God created us in his own image. We took all the greatest of human virtues and crystallized them into a paradigm of goodness, an apotheosis of perfection we called God. We grasped our greatest fear, found a panacea and resurrected ourselves into sublime immortality. (*exhales long and slowly*) You are indeed poor in spirit, my son. Maybe, like so many nowadays, you have a surfeit of worldly goods to stock your barren vaults.
78. PENITENT:	No, Father. No, you misunderstand me entirely. I'm not one to carry my convictions in my wallet. I'm not one to sacrifice the sweat of my labors on the altar of consumerism. (*beat*) A more potent, brand-new religion than old Catholicism, though, and finer cathedrals too, whose doors are always open. No, Father, I do not seek to crucify Christ on a cross of gold.
79. FATHER JOE:	Well, what do you seek then?
80. PENITENT:	I seek to crucify Christ on a cross of pure intellectual reasoning. To nail Him

to the cross again and again with the weightiest tomes I can possibly carry.

81. FATHER JOE: You can intellectualize all you want but the Gospel's teachings are still as relevant today as they were two thousand years ago. Even the civil law, which we must observe, has the basic tenets of Christianity enshrined within it. A moral framework, an ethical blueprint inspired by Christ's divine message.

82. PENITENT: Not at all, Father. (*beat*) Don't console yourself with the fiction that the daily pronouncements from the bench are the secular equivalent of what you spit from the pulpit on Sundays.

83. FATHER JOE: (*puzzled*) What!

84. PENITENT: I see the law of this land become a tangled, primeval forest, where I cannot tell the wood from the trees nor discern justice from the laws. And the lawyers, those fawning sycophantic snakes, their moral spines shattered by the sacks of silver heaped upon their backs. They are simply high priests in the temples of justice, who have taken silken robes for your own cloth ones. (*beat*) And what of you, Father? (*beat*)

Holy man! You and your theological ilk! Are you any better than amateur philosophical assassins like me or are you just as capable of unspeakable abuses against humanity's innocents?

85. FATHER JOE: Ah, ah, of course there's some corruption in any profession.

86. PENITENT: The corruption of the best is surely the worst.

87. FATHER JOE: Ah, but a few grains of sandstone doesn't mean the Parthenon's not made of marble.

88. PENITENT: It's not just the edifice, Father. The whole foundation is crumbling.

89. FATHER JOE: (*exhales long and slowly*) It's a long time since I heard such anger and cynicism as yours seize a human heart. Do you not feel any remorse or guilt, my son?

90. PENITENT: Guilt! Guilt is the grease that oils this two-thousand-year-old creaking machine.

91. FATHER JOE: It's still not too late for you, my son.

92. PENITENT: Too late for what, Father?

93. FATHER JOE:	To turn back.
94. PENITENT:	And go where?
95. FATHER JOE:	Where you came from? You obviously came to a fork in the road that is your life's path. You, of your own volition, your own God-given free will. have chosen the road to hell. This life can be a severe examination of many's a Christian's conscience but 'tis infinitely superior to follow salvation's surer path to the Pearly Gates than the rocky road to perdition.
96. PENITENT:	Tell me, Father, you will agree with me when I say God is omnipotent?
97. FATHER JOE:	Yes.
98. PENITENT:	You will agree with me when I say God is omniscient?
99. FATHER JOE:	Yes, of course.
100. PENITENT:	He is all-seeing, all-knowing, all-powerful, a perfect prophet?
101. FATHER JOE:	Granted.
102. PENITENT:	So God already knows if I am going to pass or fail this divine test that is life?

103. FATHER JOE:	Yes, yes.
104. PENITENT:	Then why bother conduct the test if He already knows the results? Your beloved doctrine of free will is rendered meaningless, flying in the face of his perfect foreknowledge.
105. FATHER JOE:	No! No! Free will is sacrosanct. 'Tis always *your* own choice which direction, which route, to undertake.
106. PENITENT:	And what of genetic predisposition?
107. FATHER JOE:	What! What pseudoscientific sophistry is this?!
108. PENITENT:	Some people are imperfectly programmed, more inclined to alcoholism, insanity, criminality. (*beat*) This test is inequitable. It is manifestly unfair. Some of us are not just destined to fail, we are designed to fail.
109. FATHER JOE:	(*breathes slowly and loudly*) Tell me, my son, why did you really come to see me? To listen to you, you could engage in theosophical disputation with a conclave of cardinals. (*beat*) Why confess to me . . . me, a humble parish priest?

110. PENITENT:	What better place to seek the truth but in the heart of a humble man?
111. FATHER JOE:	What truth, what question? Spit it out, man.
112. PENITENT:	I seek absolution for the greatest sin of all.
113. FATHER JOE:	What mortal sin? What dreadful deed?
114. PENITENT:	Perpetuating the lie that is God to my children; a Santa Claus for grown-ups. The true taint of original sin is not from some serpent tempting a woman to take a bite out of a fruit a million years ago. (*beat*) Oh no! Oh no! The real crime is peddling the same flawed mythology down through the generations. What is religion but merely a cultural expression? We Catholics are no more right nor wrong than the Muslims, or Hindus, or Buddhists, or a thousand other brands. How do we know *we're* right? I can almost picture the sign atop the Pearly Gates: No Irish need apply. (*beat*) Admit it, Father Joe. Admit you're wrong.
115. FATHER JOE:	No! No! The Roman Catholic faith is the one true faith.

116. PENITENT:	Pride, passionate and pompous pride in the piety of your own self-righteous religion. Well, Hubris solicits Nemesis, and never was she welcomed with such open embrace yet the coldest kiss. So here I am, Joseph Noone. Father No One; Nobodaddy!
117. FATHER JOE:	(*mild anger*) Who are you? Who in God's name are you?
118. PENITENT:	I can be your greatest friend or your most mortal enemy.
119. FATHER JOE:	You're spinning riddles to me now!
120. PENITENT:	Well then, I'll make it plain, if I have to slaughter your entire herd of sacred cows.
121. FATHER JOE:	(*softly, pathetically*) No, no, no.

BELL RINGS IN BACKGROUND. IT RISES IN
INTENSITY AND SYNCHRONIZES WITH EACH OF
FATHER JOE'S NO, NO, NO'S.

122. PENITENT:	I am weary of your pedantic liturgies.
123. FATHER JOE:	No, no.
124. PENITENT:	Your canonical contortions.

306

125. FATHER JOE:	No, no.
126. PENITENT:	Your Eucharistic obsessions.

BELL CONTINUES TO RING.

127. FATHER JOE:	No, no.
128. PENITENT:	And celibacy. The queerest brand of sexual deviancy is most assuredly abstinence.
129. FATHER JOE:	No, no.
130. PENITENT:	(*shouts*) There is so much Devil in the detail that God can never prevail!
131. FATHER JOE:	No! No!
132. PENITENT:	Admit it, admit it, renounce.

BELL STOPS.

133. FATHER JOE:	Sweet Divinity, this is not a confession, 'tis an inquisition. Who will rid me of this turbulent penitent?
134. PENITENT:	Don't you dare condemn me. Me! A tormented soul maddened with the wrong of it all. Do you know, Father Joseph Noone, in all the forty-three

307

long years of your vocation (*shouts loudly*) it . . . has . . . all . . . been . . . a . . . waste . . . of . . . fecking . . . time.

135. FATHER JOE: (*angry*) Whaaaat?!

SOUNDS OF FATHER JOE EXITING CONFESSIONAL IN A RAGE.

136. FATHER JOE: (*shouts*) Come out, come out, ya feckin' pseudointellectual savage, ya sacrilegious scoundrel! Get out of that confession box or I'll drag you out myself and dump you in the gutter. Where I pray that the heresies in your head may be sluiced to the sewers and dilute a billion-fold in the broad Atlantic. (*beat*) Get out, I say, before I rip your door from its hinges to witness the face of blasphemy incarnate. (*beat*) To hell! I'm opening thy door.

SOUND OF DOOR BEING YANKED OPEN.

137. FATHER JOE: Oh, Christ! Oh, Christ! Oh, Jesus Christ! You can't be. You cannot be . . . gone . . . disappeared. There is Nobody in here. (*sobs*) *Mea culpa, mea culpa, mea maxima culpa!* Forgive me, Lord, for I have sinned. Cast out a poor sacrificial scapegoat beyond the

confines of this your holy church. Oh, wise the sage said Man never does evil so completely, so cheerfully, as from religious conviction. Into thine hands I commend my guilt, O Lord, to cleanse this, my *rotten* soul!

SOUND OF APPROACHING FOOTSTEPS.

138. FATHER TOM: Joe, Joe, what's wrong? I heard an unmerciful commotion. Are you all right, Joe?

139. FATHER JOE: Father Tom. Did you see him, Tom?

140. FATHER TOM: Who? Who?

141. FATHER JOE: A man fleeing the church.

142. FATHER TOM: No, no. I didn't see anybody. I was just fixing the sacristy for tomorrow morning's Mass when I heard this shouting and roaring. (*beat*) Sure we'll go to the front door and have a look outside if it'll calm ye.

143. FATHER JOE: Yes! Yes!

SOUNDS OF TWO MEN EXITING CHURCH.
SOUND OF WIND AND CROWS CAWING.

144. FATHER TOM: God, it's freezing out here. I can't see anybody, not a soul. You must have

nodded off in the confessional and had a nightmare.

145. FATHER JOE: Maybe, but I'm truly awakened now.

146. FATHER TOM: Wait a minute. What's that?

147. FATHER JOE: Do you see him, do you see him, what?

148. FATHER TOM: No, Joe . . . It's just some graffiti.

149. FATHER JOE: What?

150. FATHER TOM: Look! The writing on the wall. (*beat*) Next the doors.

151. FATHER JOE: What does it say? Is there a message?

152. FATHER TOM: Godrip.

153. FATHER JOE: Godrip. That's a queer name. Who in hell's bells is Godrip?

154. FATHER TOM: 'Tis, 'tis, 'tis, 'tisss . . . Ah, it's God R.I.P. There's your lost sheep, Joe.

155. FATHER JOE: I fear 'tis not the sheep that is lost but the shepherd as well.

156. FATHER TOM: Och! Is there no edifice safe from desecration by those vandals, those pagan barbarians?

310

| 157. FATHER JOE: | Come on, young Tom. Quickly now. Help me close the big doors for the night. |
| 158. FATHER TOM: | Right, Joe. |

SOUND OF DOORS CREAKING.

159. FATHER JOE:	Push now. These old doors are getting harder and harder to close. (*very breathless*)
160. FATHER TOM:	Are you all right, Joe? You're puffing a terror. You look as though you're in a bit of pain?
161. FATHER JOE:	Aw, I'm all right. Just a touch of angina. I'll be all right.
162. FATHER TOM:	Mind yourself, Joe. Perhaps you'd want to get somebody to examine that sick heart of yours.
163. FATHER JOE:	Methinks I already have, Tom. . . .

DOORS CLOSE WITH AN ALMIGHTY BANG,
OVERLAID WITH BREATHLESSNESS.

It must have been agony for old Noone to read that play, thinks Jack. What a neat twist – the old priest listening to his own confession the whole time and not realizing it. No wonder he thought Roberts was a genius. How could a twelve-year-old kid possibly write something like that? Have such a mature insight into the human condition? Jack looks at the subtitle on the front cover of the yellowing manuscript he is holding – *A Play for Everybody and Nobody*. The words seem vaguely familiar.

"What was the title of that story you wrote, Josh . . . remember the one Miss Alvarez asked you to write?"

"*Nobody,*" he replies.

"Have you read this script?"

"Yeah."

"What does it mean . . . *A Play for Everybody and Nobody?*"

"It's the same subtitle as Nietzsche's book *Also Sprach Zarathustra – A Book for Everybody and Nobody* he called it."

"What did he mean by that?" Jack says, arching a brow.

"What Nietzsche meant is not important; it is how you interpret it that is," the boy answers with an impertinent shrug.

"What does it mean to *you* then, Josh?"

"I think you've got to see all arguments in the round. Like Zarathustra standing on the mountain-top and looking at all the angles. Everybody thinks mostly in straight lines from A to B because it's easier. But you got to think in circles from A to Z; methodically get as many points of view as possible to determine the best decision. Nietzsche thought that way. Roberts thinks that way too . . . thinks in circles – except the circles don't have any circumference."

"How in hell can you make your mind up about *anything* if you keep thinking in circles without diameters?"

"Because when you make up your mind, it is only at a specific point in time – it doesn't have to be for ever. Everybody forgets that. Nobody wants to change their opinions and admit they might have been wrong. They're like autos without reverse – stupid!"

Jack looks at Josh and wonders whether he loves or loathes the boy.

"It's okay, Dad."

"What's okay?"

"It's okay to hold contradictory views on people and things."

"What do you mean?"

"It's okay to love someone and hate them simultaneously – to accept humans are a mixture of good and bad parts, like a curate's egg."

"Ain't that the truth," Jack answers wearily.

"Yes – but we must overcome our human nature to survive – to ensure our future."

Jack winces as he hears the word "future". Remembers the suicide note Clara Roberts left to her mother Eleanor – "*like a lamb to the slaughter – born without a future,*" it read. "*Steelman*" *was the very last entry in her diary. Magnusson said Roberts will take his own life too if he doesn't get re-elected . . . he obviously doesn't want to live with the consequences.*

Josh looks shocked. *Magnusson must have scrubbed that section of his recorded interview with Father,* he realizes.

"I'm going to help you write this book, Dad. Going to help you get Roberts re-elected come November. I'll go with you on your trip in January and February. Visit every eco-colony on the planet and interview all the directors if we have to. But we must help get him re-elected because I don't want him to die . . . I don't want Eli to die, you understand. *Not ever.*"

TWENTY-NINE

FOR THE FIRST TWO MONTHS OF 2040, Jack and Josh Andersson do a grand tour of GeoNova's network of eco-colonies. They zig-zag across the globe from Canada to Greenland to South America, Antarctica, New Zealand, Siberia, Madagascar and Scandinavia. All the sites are in remote locations but are massive in scale. Each one is an independent, self-sufficient operation, they learn, effectively governed by a "director" with autocratic powers. All directors have been solely appointed by Roberts. Roberts likes to consider himself *primus inter pares* – a first amongst equals – but his appointees share no such illusion. Several of the directors interviewed describe Eli in almost divine terms: his spiritual presence, his uncanny intuition, the concise manner in which he can articulate his global vision to a near-infallible argument. The director of the Swedish eco-colony spoke of him with particular passion. "You have travelled the world, Mr Andersson . . . visited *all* the colonies . . . flown over many nations now governed by GeoNova . . . Roberts is more than a mere man . . . all these works are surely the product of no *ordinary* human intellect but that of a *gottlich* mind . . . a supreme intelligence . . . a steel soul and an iron will to power!"

Josh meets all the directors too. He talks to them privately, while Jack is guided on extensive tours of the various colonies, after his *own* interviews have concluded. At first Jack thought it so ridiculous – a twelve-year-old boy conducting interviews with the upper echelons of GeoNova – practically usurping *his* position as researcher for Roberts's official biography. But not a single eco-colony director objects to being questioned by the boy. They act as if they have always been expecting him to arrive, and therefore when he does, they welcome him with open arms, yet a solemn enthusiasm that verges upon reverence.

"I must be about my Father's business," the boy informs them. "We must be prepared to murder the child within us to become men, for I am sent by the prophet Elijah before the great and terrible Day of the Lord comes." And each director understands precisely what the boy means – for the Day of Judgement cometh with election in November – *Vox populi vox Dei.*

THIRTY

WALTER FRANKLIN SITS IN FRONT of a bank of computer screens mounted on his White House office wall. There is an anxious face on every screen in front of him for this morning's election briefing for the GeoNova hierarchy. Franklin himself looks gaunt; the long months of a gruelling election campaign are taking their toll.

"Well, boys and girls! What can I tell you," he says, with mock cheerfulness. "The latest poll numbers indicate the President is thirteen per cent behind Mendez, with three weeks to go. Last week, the gap was eleven per cent – any suggestions?"

Franklin is confronted with a series of glum, disillusioned faces and a burning silence.

"Come on, people!" he exhorts them, banging his fist upon his desk. "I'm not ready to give up this fucking fight for a measly thirteen per cent. This is Elijah Roberts we're talking about; you gotta have faith in the guy and what he symbolizes . . . what he is capable of doing. . . . "

"Walt . . . Walt," interrupts a voice. "None of us here are idiots. You know we can't swing this thing around, barring a miracle."

"No better man than Roberts to perform miracles!" Franklin responds in a jocular tone, in the vain hope of galvanizing his troops.

"Our policies were too ambitious," says the same voice. "People are tired of ecological austerity measures."

"Yes . . . people would rather die than change. Let the turkeys vote for Christmas," says another.

"No . . . no, our mistake was the President embarking on holographic electoral campaigning," chimes in yet another. "People think they're voting for a ghost . . . a spectre of a man. How could Roberts have hoped to get re-elected if he insisted on staying in the White

316

House most the time? Make no mistake about it, this is the most serious crisis that has ever threatened the GeoNova movement. It is not beyond the bounds of possibility that if we lose America it would jeopardize our political bases in many other countries. The entire party structure could crumble, and with it the dream of Eli, and the last best hope for humanity to save itself."

A palpable air of despondency pervades the room after the last speaker's comments. They have all privately conceded for months that the election would probably be lost. All hoped their political fortunes would somehow change; that Roberts's genius would somehow triumph. But, as time progressed, their hopes have slowly evaporated. They can all sense that something is awry with Roberts; an uncharacteristic absence of will; a recognition that power no longer weighs so lightly on his titanic shoulders. And as the election fast approaches, the certitude and magnitude of defeat become stark in their minds. Like a monster that slumbers in the depths, lurking, waiting patiently, to surface inevitably from the cold darkness. The end of an era beckons – Roberts who has stood astride the global stage like a colossus for years, will shortly be rendered a political dinosaur in a single day.

Franklin scans the disconsolate faces on the dozen screens in front of him; feels his eyes stinging and his heart pounding. His voice is filled with passion as he rises to his feet from behind his desk.

"We simply can't allow this to happen. We've got a world to save, not just a President. We are letting our destiny be dictated by events. We need something immediate, something radical to turn the tide in our favour. It's long past time we created our own *events* to enable this President get re-elected."

"What are you saying, Franklin?"

"Roberts has a plan to change the game."

"What kind of a plan?"

"An *event* I hope will restore *your* faith in him; an *event* that will restore the faith of the American people and the entire world in him."

The faces on the computer screens seem to form one collective frown.

Franklin folds his arms and eyes them all with the poise and panache of a man convinced he can snatch victory from ignominious defeat.

"One o'clock tomorrow, Eastern Standard Time. Keep your eyes on the screens and your hands together in prayer. We're goin' to win this thing . . . So help me, God, we're gonna win this election!"

Jack Andersson glances at his old watch. It is almost noon. Josh has been in the Oval Office now for almost three hours, alone with the President. A throng of people are congregated outside the Oval Office, waiting to meet Roberts. They talk in whispers and nod gravely, check the time on their cells or the clocks on the wall. Their faces are solemn, many of them tired and red-eyed. Jack had expected the White House to be abuzz, with staffers rushing around, feverishly organizing the day's electoral campaigning. But the atmosphere is thick with gloom, almost funereal.

Do they all know about Steelman? Jack wonders. Surely *some* of them must know.

Jack looks at the array of clocks on the wall opposite, displaying the times in London, Beijing, Tokyo, Sydney, Rio de Janeiro and a host of other cities.

Will time stop ticking everywhere simultaneously? Atomic clocks won't function any more – they need electricity. Cellphone networks will fail too. The lights will go out all over the world. Industrial production . . . computers will cease. . . .

"Jesus!" Jack mutters to himself as he is gripped by the terror of his thoughts becoming reality. Since Josh told him about Steelman all those months ago, he has surprisingly grown used to the idea. Consoled himself with the fact that civilization existed for millennia before electricity was harnessed; that global warming would be arrested and mankind's future ensured. There was something so magnificently simple about Steelman's execution that rendered it positively beautiful. Like a silver bullet shot straight through the heart of human folly or a Gordian knot the size of the world severed with a single sword-stroke. But as Election Day approaches, and Roberts's prospects of re-election diminish rapidly, the sheer horror of Steelman is chiselled in sharper relief in Jack's mind. Millions will surely die from starvation, disease . . . social order will break down in advanced countries . . . money, machinery, factories, hospitals . . . everything will come to a halt! Chaos will ensue.

"Sweet suffering Jesus!" mutters Jack, squirming in his seat and wiping a film of sweat from his brow.

"You got an appointment to see the President . . . Mr . . . eh . . . Andersson?" asks a young man, peering at the ID clipped to the breast pocket of Jack's brand-new suit.

"Yeah . . . I was supposed to see him at nine a.m."

"Hell!" groans the young man, "I was supposed to have a briefing with him and the campaign team at ten fifteen. Sorry! I'm Mike Lasker," he says apologetically, extending a hand. "I'm the President's campaign manager."

"Yeah," nods Jack, standing now and shaking his hand, "I recognized you." He pauses. "Things ain't looking too good, Mike."

Lasker smiles tightly through clenched teeth before he answers.

"Don't underestimate Roberts . . . not for *one* second. We got three whole weeks to turn around this election. This guy has never lost a fight in his entire career, dammit. And he is sure as hell *not* going to lose one on my watch!"

"Damn right, Mike! That's the spirit!" says the man behind him now, clapping a hand on his shoulder. "You tell him!"

"Walt! . . . Walt, how am I supposed to run a campaign if I can't even consult the President this morning?" Lasker turns and complains.

Franklin purses his lips into a surly expression.

"Who in hell is *so* important that they demand over three hours of the President's time?" Lasker continues bitterly. "One of the secretaries told me she thought it was just a boy . . . a boy, for Chrissakes!"

"Don't worry about it, Mike."

"What?"

"I said don't worry about it. Did you come up with any new campaign slogans?"

"Yeah, yeah, the team thought we might tackle Big Carbon with 'What will your sales profit you if you lose the whole world? Reckon it's a runner, Walt?"

"Not bad but nah … 'sins' is better than 'sales'. Climate change is a moral issue. Sins has got more of a biblical ring to it too. The President prefers that."

"But . . . "

"Enough already. He'll buy it, Mike."

"You sure?"

"Trust me. I know the man better than—"

Franklin suddenly claps his hand to one ear.

"Yes, sir!" he answers promptly "Right away, sir . . . okay, fifteen minutes at most, Mr President."

Franklin lowers his hand and looks at Jack.

"The President will see you now. You've got fifteen minutes with him, Jack."

The Oval Office is not what he had envisaged. The famous light-blue carpet with its signature presidential eagle has been replaced with one of green and orange, the trademark colours of GeoNova. There are no American flags in the room, only GeoNova ones. The walls are adorned with framed photographs of Roberts addressing massive crowds . . . copies of his speeches, receiving the Nobel Peace Prize . . . Roberts triumphant in London, Moscow, Paris, New Delhi, all the major capitals where GeoNova has attained political supremacy. It is as if the office is testament to the power of one man alone. A man who bears the burden of the world on his shoulders yet relishes every moment of the moulding of it to his almighty will. Where, thinks Andersson, is America here?

"*America in absentia*," calls out a lofty voice. "I am a true citizen of this world."

Jack squints at a window from where the voice seems to emanate. The rays of the noon sun are shining through it. The golden shafts of light silhouette a mighty head. It appears as though every hair on that head tapers into a series of liquid amber beads, offering a scintillating halo effect. Roberts consciously positions himself so, like a sunflower, although Jack doesn't know it. The man is enormous, six foot eight at least, not overweight but a solid block of a man nonetheless. He strolls from the embrasure of the window, past his desk and towers over Andersson, who is standing awestruck in the middle of the office floor. It is the eyes; those mesmerizing cobalt eyes that seem to look in to your soul and comprehend . . . know what it is to be human and divine, thinks Jack. The two men gaze at each other for a few seconds.

Jack starts to weep. He feels overwhelmed by Roberts's numinous aura; feels intimidated and unworthy in the presence of such genius – and madness.

"I wish I believed in God," he cries stupidly . . . "wish He would come and save us from Steelman."

"*Vox populi vox Dei* – the voice of the people is the voice of God!"

"But people don't understand . . . you're going to destroy everything."

"No – this is an act of salvation, Mr Andersson."

"How? . . . How?" he whimpers. "It is an act of evil."

"It is beyond Good and Evil."

"What do you mean?"

"Acts of God . . . Acts of Satan . . . Acts of Men. The only distinction drawn within this trinity is one of interpretation, not agency."

"I don't understand . . . I don't . . . "

"Was it a crime to drop atomic weapons on Hiroshima and Nagasaki?" asks Roberts coolly.

"I suppose so," Jack answers timidly, his mind a fog of confusion.

"I don't agree. Hundreds of thousands died but millions of lives were ultimately saved, as it hastened the end of World War Two."

Jack nods mutely in agreement.

"Was the Holocaust a crime?" asks Roberts with a smile.

Jack staggers back at such an inane question then quickly remembers Sol Weiseman posing precisely the same question to him when they met. He recalls the old professor remarking what difference did it make for all those Jews to die – they were destined to live in eternal bliss anyway – their journey was merely accelerated. Maybe the old man knew about Steelman – he came across as being strangely excited, even though he was dying.

"Would the modern state of Israel have been founded if it were not for the world's sympathy in the aftermath of that Holocaust?" Roberts continues. "Steelman will be a return to the Promised Land, to the Garden of Eden. What matter how much blood is spilled in the process so long as the human race survives? This planet will be uninhabitable within a century if eco-transformative plans are not implemented. Steelman will at least be a form of *controlled catastrophe* that will maintain Earth's viability as a living organism. And although Steelman may appear subjectively monstrous to you, history will judge it objectively as the greatest act of compassion ever performed. . . . "

Jack shakes his head incredulously as he listens to Roberts's justification. The President speaks with an icy air of detached authority, speaks with utter conviction but never resorts to histrionics. His long arms hang loosely by his sides and his legs are planted firmly in a wide stance. His back is arched slightly and his head cocked. Only his lips move as he speaks. The body language betrays nothing . . . nothing except his resoluteness in defiance of the world. This is the worst breed of a man imaginable, thinks Jack – a zealot who professes himself a moderate, a murderer who proclaims himself a saviour, a Satan who masquerades as a Christ.

" . . . if the people reject me then they vote for their own crucifixion as well as mine. . . "

Jack frowns at Roberts, and all at once feels a profound pity for him.

" . . . what nobler cause than a man to sacrifice his life for his country when that country be the world itself . . . Is it not courageous?"

"*Courageous* . . . ?" exclaims Jack, puzzled.

"*Yes, courageous!* Is it not the bravest of human attributes to know that we will die, yet consider our lives worthy of the living? To perhaps know the date of our death, yet fill the intervening days with glorious purpose. Live each day as if our demise were merely an abstraction."

"Is it true, sir . . . true that you will take your own life if . . . ?"

"It is not a taking but an offering, Mr Andersson."

Jack plunges his hands into his pockets, closes his eyes and lowers his head.

"I couldn't do it, sir . . . I couldn't write the book," he confesses meekly.

"I know. I always knew. Did you seriously expect a man of your modest intellectual talents to accomplish such a task?"

"So why did you ask me?"

"To facilitate the collection of information."

"*What?*"

"You recorded all your interviews. You enabled Josh to meet all the eco-colony Directors and to gauge their commitment to Steelman, and loyalty to me."

"I was just a pawn then?"

"Not even a pawn. Merely a conduit, Mr Andersson."

"So you wanted Josh to write your biography all along?"

"Correct. Joshua will write my biography. Joyce asked the question at the end of *Finnegans Wake* . . . 'Is there one who understands me?' That boy, and that boy alone, is capable of doing it and I have therefore revealed my innermost mind to him this very morning. Only his unique intellect can ascend beyond the *Zeitgeist* and create the timeless legacy I require. The boy has a Third Eye."

"What do you mean, a Third Eye?"

"A Third Eye . . . The Eye of Horus . . . Omniscient eyes of the Sun and Moon."

"I don't follow you, sir."

Roberts pauses now and folds his arms across his chest. He hesitates, as if debating whether to keep his own counsel. Jack senses his discomfort; he feels his knees trembling and his hands shaking as he waits for Roberts to speak.

"There are certain privileged individuals who have a wondrous talent . . . a divine intuition, you might say. It is a talent that *I* myself possess and have cultivated over many years. Kun Wei had the gift . . . Merry Steinitz too, which makes her a quite brilliant psychiatrist, and of course Eleanor. But Joshua's talent is even more prodigious. It is unique in that both his natural mother *and* his father were endowed with it. You could cogently argue that that boy is *the* greatest advance in human evolution . . . a genetic triumph that God himself would envy."

"What are you talking about . . . a *gift*? What *kind* of a gift?"

Roberts turns and ambles gracefully towards the sunlit window. He halts and turns once more to face his visitor. The sun is shining directly behind his head again, forcing his visitor to squint at him. The outline of his massive frame seems to shimmer in the golden rays of the sun. And his eyes shine forth a piercing electric blue, like lustrous gemstones of lapis lazuli set into an ebony effigy. Jack can hear himself gasp. He feels his legs giving way and his knees sinking into the carpet. He clasps his hands together to stop them from shaking.

"I have never divulged this to anyone, but . . . but I can . . . I can read minds. Primarily preconscious thoughts, you understand, mainly those thoughts that present themselves to the conscious mind. But Joshua will soon be capable of penetrating the subconscious mind. And even God himself cannot do that. So forgive him his apparent madness; it is but a reflection of the dark depths of his experience of the human condition."

Jack hears himself calling out in a melancholy tone. "Are you a god or a man?"

"I am both."

"What?"

"The line between divinity and humanity is contiguous to that between sanity and insanity."

Roberts pauses.

"You have something to give me, Mr Andersson?"

Jack rises to his feet now and reaches inside his jacket. He pulls out a cheque and holds it up high for Roberts to see all the zeroes on it.

"I don't deserve this."

"No . . . not *that!* A letter . . . the letter Eleanor gave you from my daughter Clara."

"Yes, I'm sorry. I have it here. I'd plain forgotten."

Jack takes out a sealed white envelope addressed "*To Daddy*". He holds it out in his trembling hand as Roberts approaches. The President stops a few feet in front of him.

"Open it, Mr Andersson, and read it to me."

"But . . . it's private . . . it's just for you to see . . . it's a suicide note."

"Open it, Mr Andersson."

He fumbles open the envelope and unfolds the single, cream-coloured page inside it. He is looking at a verse written in Clara Roberts's neat, delicate script. Her final words to her mother, Eleanor, come back to him – "*Like a lamb to the slaughter – born without a future.*"

"Read it aloud to me," Roberts orders.

Jack glances at him and takes a deep breath.

"The Tyger . . .

"When the stars threw down their spears
"And water'd heaven with their tears;
"Did he smile his work to see?
"Did he who made the Lamb make thee?"

Roberts fingers the corrugations of his brow as he listens to the verse. Inhales sharply at the end of each line as if bludgeoned by their import.

"Oh wait! There's something else in the envelope here, Mr President."

Jack carefully pulls out a blood-red, coal-eyed paper poppy and holds it up high.

There is a protracted silence before Roberts responds. His voice is choking with emotion.

"I remember the morning all those fish died in the river. I remember crying all that day and weeping under the stars that night. And then I gazed at the long line of those electricity pylons and I felt Fate's hand upon me. 'Steelman' was conceived at that very moment . . . But Clara had the third eye. She saw the project in my mind . . . my poor daughter couldn't cope with the prospect . . . couldn't handle her abilities. Oh, Clara . . . Clara . . . my sweet darling daughter . . . my sacrificial lamb!" he exclaims.

Jack looks at the giant of a man breaking down and sobbing like a child in front of him. He instinctively wants to reach out and touch him, to comfort him, to assuage his obvious guilt over his daughter's suicide. But Roberts stiffens his posture, regains his composure and stands proudly in defiance of the world again.

326

"Give me the letter!" he commands, thrusting out a hand.

Jack places the letter, the cheque and the paper flower gingerly on Roberts's palm.

The three sink through it and float slowly to the floor.

"You . . . you're a hologram . . . a hologram!" exclaims Jack in horror. "You're not real!"

Roberts looks at him indifferently.

"I am currently in the Situation Room with Joshua. It was not convenient for me to meet you *physically*."

"But . . . but?"

"But what, Mr Andersson?"

Jack simply stares silently at him, his mouth agape.

"My corporeal presence is irrelevant – only the *idea* of me is truly important. But I want that *idea* to be magnificent – Man and myth combined in the memory of mankind – but only a mighty book can achieve that."

All at once Josh appears, seeming as if to materialize from the sunlight itself. He is standing directly in front of Roberts with his back towards him. The President lays his hands affectionately upon the boy's shoulders.

"*Ecce puer,*" he declaims. "Behold the boy who will sanctify my name in the mouths of men unto the ages; a supreme literary artist who possesses the courage to transcend the *Zeitgeist* and address the Übermenschen; a boy singularly worthy of penning a New Testament for a New Age. A boy who will ensure my voice will speak louder and clearer in death than in life."

There is a distinct click and Roberts and Josh's images instantly disappear.

Jack is staring into the empty space that remains. For some curious reason he thinks of Jenny. She seems a distant memory now – like a mental hologram – as if she *never physically* existed. As if sixteen years of marriage do not matter; only the *idea* of it does now. He turns to look at the Oval Office, and feels the rays of the sun streaming through the windows and warming his face. He remembers making love to Jenny for the very first time . . . how he misses her body . . . how alone he is in this great place . . . how memories can wound but ideas can kill. How complete his humiliation is.

Jack wept.

THIRTY-ONE

THE SILVER DOORS of the Situation Room slide back silently. Roberts has to stoop as he enters.

"*Atten . . . tion!*" barks a marine standing guard inside.

Some dozen military personnel simultaneously spring to their feet and wait for the President to assume his seat at the head of a large table.

"What's the problem, General?" he says calmly, settling into his customary green-and-orange leather chair.

General Benko remains standing as his colleagues resume their seats.

"Mr President, *sir!*" he begins. "At thirteen ten Eastern Standard Time, Military Intelligence received reports of a vehicle explosion in central Jerusalem. First reports indicated a number of civilian casualties . . . eh, the latest intelligence suggest . . . " He motions his head towards a subordinate.

"Twenty-two dead and more than a hundred injured now, Mr President, sir, according to Israeli military sources," replies Colonel Santini.

"Thank you, Colonel!" snaps Benko.

" . . . But that's the least of our problems, Mr President. Initial analysis of the scene of the explosion indicates elevated levels of radioactive nuclear isotopes; specifically those of caesium one thirty-seven and cobalt sixty. The Israeli government has issued a mass civilian evacuation order for central Jerusalem. We suspect their military is mobilizing for war, Mr President, pending confirmation that the source of the explosion was indeed 'a dirty bomb'."

"Of Islamic terrorist origin, I assume, General," says Roberts.

"In all probability, sir!"

"What scenario has the Pentagon quantum-modelled for this eventuality?"

"The Israelis won't consider it as a purely terrorist act. The Israeli government will treat it as a declaration of war by proxy by the entire Arab world. We anticipate that their air force will strike Mecca and other sites sacred to the Muslim faith within a timeframe of twenty-four, perhaps forty-eight, hours. Probably deploying tactical nuclear devices as they would deem it a proportionate response. It is inevitable that the Iranian military will launch a massive strategic nuclear counter-strike on the state of Israel itself. . . . "

"We have the graphics ready now, General, sir!" interrupts a young lieutenant, tapping furiously at the monitor in front of him.

Roberts intimates with an abrupt movement of his left hand that he doesn't wish to witness Armageddon played out on the large screens covering the walls of the Situation Room.

"It's okay, I get the picture already," he says solemnly. "Have we summoned the Israeli ambassador?"

"Yes, Mr President," a voice answers smartly. "She's on her way. ETA five minutes."

There is a protracted silence. Every pair of eyes in the room is riveted on Roberts. His head is tilted back and his chin juts upwards as he gazes impassively at the ceiling and deliberates. The air is dank and heavy now with the odour of perspiration. All those seated lean forward eagerly with elbows pressed against the table as Roberts prepares to speak.

"This is the dreaded dawn of the age of nuclear terrorism. Man has crossed the Rubicon and left a river of fire in his wake," the President declares. "You may advise the Joint Chiefs that I am ordering all our forces to DEFCON Two with immediate effect. . . "

The hushed room is suddenly transformed into a scene of frenzied activity as the order is speedily communicated along the chain of command.

Walter Franklin enters, panting.

"Mr President . . . the Israeli ambassador . . . she's here . . . in your office."

"Madame Ambassador."

"Mr President."

"I presume you have some communication from Prime Minister Spellman to convey to me. He has refused to respond to my calls and has deactivated the holographic receiver in his office."

"The situation is very fluid, Mr President. But he will address the nation of Israel first."

"And tell your people what?"

The ambassador is a petite frame of a middle-aged woman. Roberts is standing, looming over her, glowering at her with a fierce intensity. His physical presence is intimidating.

She hesitates before answering. Then starts to read in a faltering voice from a prepared script she is holding in trembling hands.

"The sacred soil of Jerusalem has been desecrated . . . a crude but highly radioactive bomb detonated . . . We are bound by our covenant with God to strike at our enemies for such an act of abomination . . . an eye for an eye . . . the Jewish people will not acquiesce to a second Holocaust. . . . "

"And who have you identified as *the enemy* in this instance?" demands Roberts.

"We are entitled to retaliate, Mr President. The American people would not stand idle at such gross provocation either."

"Who have you identified as directly responsible for this atrocity?"

"Our response will be proportionate and our choice of targets equally symbolic as the holy city of Jerusalem."

"Yes, I know," answers the President angrily. "You intend to destroy the Kaaba in Mecca, thereby provoking a nuclear conflagration with the Arab world. Is that what you want?"

"Our enemies have chosen to cast the first stone."

"You *still* have not answered my question, Madame Ambassador. Who do your government hold accountable for this act of terrorism?"

She looks at Roberts and her eyes well up.

"I have two sons; one in the military and one in Mossad, you know."

"I know, Marta," he says in a low voice.

"Our security agencies are entirely satisfied, even at this early stage, that al-Hussein is the man responsible. He has planned this for years, but we have never been able to precisely locate him and eliminate him. We know he operates from a deep bunker somewhere in Damascus. That is all. . . . "

All at once the ambassador breaks down and starts to sob.

"Oh, Eli, this is the *end!* Spellman is battling to control his generals already. I spoke with my son on my way here. They want to devastate Damascus, Eli . . . this will be Armageddon, I swear . . . this is the *end.*"

Roberts is back in the Situation Room. He paces over and back along a bank of computer screens, glancing at each one in turn.

"The Iranians are mobilizing their armies *here*, *here* and *here*, Mr President," says an officer beside him, pointing at various locations on one of the monitors.

"We are picking up increased aerial activity in Saudi airspace," reports the young lieutenant. "Just Saudi patrols at the moment, Mr President."

"The Chinese have put their Second Fleet on the Black Sea on maximum alert, Mr President," says Colonel Santini.

General Benko is standing beside a computerized monitor displaying a map of Israel. His face is marble-white as he listens intently to the voices being broadcast through the monitor's speakers.

"The Israelis have closed their airspace to all civilian aircraft and our satellites are picking up IDF radio as reporting . . . well . . . well . . . "

"Well, *what*, Benko?!" barks Roberts.

"Combat operations to commence in twelve hours, Mr President."

For the next five minutes Roberts stands motionless with his eyes closed. He doesn't utter a sound as he is bombarded with a barrage of intelligence from his advisors. The shrill, tremulous voice of Lev Spellman can be heard now in the background, addressing the people of Israel. A series of frantic calls from several world leaders are blinking red and stacking up on a telecommunications hotline as the Prime Minister's speech concludes.

Roberts opens his eyes lazily. When he speaks it is in measured tones.

"Gentlemen, this situation does not lend itself to a purely military solution. It is imperative to pursue unorthodox strategies to resolve this crisis.

"I want Air Force One prepared for take-off – Wheels-up in exactly one hour.

"I also want a special-ops team on the ground within six hours at the al-Rashid refugee camp in Damascus. Walt here will provide you with all the requisite operational details."

Roberts turns swiftly to exit the room.

"Where are you going, Mr President?" queries an astonished Benko.

"I am flying to Jerusalem, General."

"*What!*" he gasps. "Are you *insane*, Mr President? America needs you in Washington."

"Yes, General. But the world needs me in Jerusalem."

Prime Minister Lev Spellman is on his feet in his command bunker beneath Tel Aviv. The scene around him is chaotic as the army ratchets up its war machine. His General Staff is crowded about him, harassing him, haranguing him with various doomsday options. Spellman holds his head in his hands as they shout at him to strike Teheran and Riyadh and Damascus immediately. General Attazada, the diminutive army chief, is the most hawkish of all the officers. The corners of his mouth foam with venomous spittle and his voice rises to a shriek.

"You cannot betray weakness, Prime Minister, in this hour of our destiny! If we fail to strike immediately we risk a pre-emptive nuclear strike from the Iranians."

"This is an overreaction, General. A small group of terrorists set off a dirty bomb and a chain of events that could lead to the total destruction of Israel. It is *not a proportionate response!* You are giving our enemies justification to annihilate us."

"Hatred of the Jewish people *is* sufficient justification for our enemies."

"No! No!" roars Spellman. "We must confine our military response to the destruction of Damascus, so as to ensure al-Hussein and his command structure are both taken out."

Attazada looks at the Prime Minister with a bemused expression and then breaks into a hollow laugh, quickly mimicked by his coterie of subordinates.

"And do you think, Prime Minister, that the Arabs will accept the levelling of the Syrian capital and the martyrdom of three million of their brothers as a fair price for twenty-two Israeli lives?"

"I don't know . . . I . . . "

"Agh, you are weak, Lev. This is a day for soldiers not politicians."

"How dare you address me in such a manner?!"

A red phone rings beside Spellman. He snatches it and presses the receiver to his ear.

The voice at the other end is breathless.

"Prime Minister."

"Yes!"

"We are tracking an aircraft fast approaching our airspace over the Mediterranean . . . It is failing to obey repeated requests to alter course. We have dispatched fighters to intercept it."

"You have my authority to blow it out of the sky if it enters our airspace."

"But Prime Minister, sir – the aircraft identifies itself as Air Force One."

"*What!* Have you confirmation of this . . . ?"

"The White House informed us thirty seconds ago that President Roberts intends to land at Ben Gurion within fifteen minutes."

"*Mein Gott . . . mein Gott!*" exclaims Spellman. He clasps the telephone receiver tight to his chest and inhales sharply.

"Roberts is on his way *here*," he announces to his General Staff. "He intends to arrive at Ben Gurion in the next fifteen minutes."

Attazada crinkles the lower lids of his sharp-set eyes and flares the thin nostrils of his aquiline nose. He seizes the phone from Spellman's grasp and thunders into the receiver.

"AF One denied permission to land . . . repeat: denied permission to land."

"Yes, General," acknowledges the voice at the other end.

The connection remains open and the exchange between the control tower and Air Force One is put on speaker and is clearly audible to all in the bunker.

"AF One, this is TLV Tower – permission denied for landing – repeat permission denied for landing. Acknowledge."

"TLV Tower, this is Air Force One. We will obtain clearance after we land. Over."

"Repeat . . . don't understand . . . repeat, AF One?"

"We will obtain clearance after we land. ETA thirteen minutes. Over."

"You are not authorized to land; understand, AF One . . . not authorized. You have illegally entered Israeli military airspace."

"I have AF One on visual," cuts in another voice. "Target locked and weapons armed. Please advise."

"*General . . . General . . .* what to do?!" shouts the Air Traffic Controller.

Attazada pauses.

"Don't be a fool, General!" says Spellman viciously, stabbing his finger towards him. "We cannot murder Roberts, and *you know* it. The eyes of the world are upon us."

Attazada seems to freeze as if he cannot stomach to hear himself countermand his own orders.

Spellman quickly grabs the red phone receiver back from the general.

"Tᴌᴠ Tower . . . Permission granted for AF One to land. Repeat AF One permission to land."

The general stares scornfully and seethes silently at his Prime Minister, who is admonishing him now.

" . . . Thus Elijah returns to Israel from the sky. We dare not set his chariot aflame or our people shall burn once more in the holocaust to follow – understood!"

For the next hour an acrimonious debate rages unabated in the command post under Tel Aviv where all await Roberts's arrival. The tension between the political elite and the military top brass is becoming unbearable. Spellman can sense with every passing minute that he is losing his grip on the situation. Aaron Attazada may be a hot-headed maverick, he thinks, but that does not diminish the forcefulness of his personality or the persuasiveness of his arguments. One tough, tenacious bastard who retains the unswerving loyalty of all his troops and nicknamed the "Hammer of Palestine" for his brutal suppression of the "great Intifada" of 2025.

"He is coming!" echoes a loud voice around the bunker.

The room's occupants turn as one. Time itself seems suspended as everybody trains his gaze on a large panel indicating an elevator's long descent.

"Have you ever met Roberts, sir?" queries the general's adjutant.

"No."

"They say his eyes are like the Gorgon Medusa – a look that can turn men into stone."

"What if one is made of granite already?" the general quips laconically.

His adjutant smirks, and patiently watches the panel as it indicates the elevator has finally reached basement level. There are faint voices in the distance beyond the bunker's blast-proof door now; the sound of a bounding stride along a corridor, distinct from the rush of feet trailing behind it, striving to keep pace. A muffled commotion of anxious voices is soon heard directly outside. The bunker door yawns open with a metallic groan and Elijah Roberts lopes into the hushed room. Its confines accentuate his already imposing height and immensity of frame. The sheer physical size of the man elicits a collective gasp from all within the bunker. Roberts's eyes appear to flash like lightning as he surveys the scene. And a booming thunder seems to fill his throat as he trumpets in perfect Hebrew.

"O hear ye, sons of Zion! Ye shall make waste the land of David upon this very day, lest ye be subtle as serpents and wise as Solomon. Albeit the earth quakes beneath thy feet, smite not thine enemies with thy weapons but with thy wits. Let I, Elijah, be thy shield of Abraham and thy sword of Joshua, to slay those that have defiled holy Jerusalem. Let I alone visit vengeance upon al-Hussein, so that when I strike him, the world shall fear my name as the Lord."

The General Staff and the politicians look first to each other with amazement and then back at Roberts. They are utterly confounded by his rhetoric.

"What are you proposing, Mr President?" asks Spellman.

"GeoNova is aware of al-Hussein's precise location, five hundred metres under Damascus. We can eliminate him with a surgical strike within a matter of hours."

"Wait . . . wait," protests a senior air-force officer. "To destroy a bunker at that depth requires deploying a weapon of such magnitude that it will destroy half the city anyway. War is thus *inevitable* in our opinion."

"Not with the advanced technology we have at our disposal. The weaponry we intend to utilize will inflict no collateral damage."

"This is ridiculous!" answers the same officer. "It is not possible to destroy *such* a target, at *such* a depth, in an urban environment without widespread civilian casualties. *Impossible*, Mr President!"

A number of officers are nodding in agreement with their colleague, simultaneously shrugging their shoulders and muttering between themselves.

"But if my forces are capable of it, gentlemen; if we can kill al-Hussein and his fellow-jihadists holed up in their bunker, *without* causing wholesale destruction. If we can punish those terrorists directly responsible for this monstrous act then war can possibly be averted. You must remember, gentlemen, that many in the Muslim world proclaim al-Hussein as a *Mahdi*. His death would be hugely symbolic, a demonstration also of the might of American support for Israel, and foremost – a restrained, proportionate, non-nuclear response that denies Iran and the Saudis sufficient justification to attack you."

The mood in the bunker has suddenly changed. Spellman is nodding enthusiastically, as are his cabinet ministers and advisors. The military officers react more sceptically, but from what Roberts can read of their minds, they are becoming less inclined to conduct a nuclear offensive.

Attazada alone remains obdurate in his convictions.

"Mr President," he says, "you do not understand the mentality of the Arab as I do. He dreams solely of the destruction of Israel. Today we must prove to him it is a nightmare. We must aggressively defend every boundary of the land that God gave us."

"God does not create nations, General. Man alone drafts maps with his blood and—"

" —and we Jews have sacrificed much blood, Mr President, to preserve every line on that map. We will not be felled like Goliath of old by little boys with their crude weapons."

"There are too many Goliaths ranged against you, armed with the power of the atom. You court your own destruction, General."

Attazada jostles his way through the throng of people now semi-circled around Roberts. He strides up to the President and comes to a halt directly in front of him. The diminutive Chief of staff is dwarfed by his towering height, but stands undaunted in his shadow. He turns to address his fellow-officers, and the politicians he detests so much. For five whole minutes he holds the entire room in thrall, reminding his audience of the overwhelming superiority of their nuclear arsenal. Emphasizing with repeated punches of one hand against the palm of the other of their moral obligation to the state. Accusing Spellman and his political cronies of rank cowardice and abandoning their duty on this "day of destiny". Telling them that the army will be the salvation of Israel, as it has always been from time immemorial. The admiring officers break out into spontaneous applause at his fiery tirade. Spellman is livid at his "rancorous runt" of a ranting general and roars at his military.

"When all you have is a hammer then everything you encounter is a *fucking nail!*"

The bickering and sniping begin afresh between the General Staff and the politicians.

Roberts raises a hand to try to restore order, but to no avail; he knows the hawks are gaining the upper hand. All at once he seizes Attazada by his epaulettes and spins him one hundred and eighty degrees to face him. He flicks him around so quickly that he knocks the maroon beret off his head. The bunker falls silent at the sight of this manhandling of such a senior officer.

Elijah glowers into the general's eyes. Senses he cannot dissuade him at a rational level but must plumb the depths of his soul to engage his emotions.

"You are a true son of Israel, Aaron," he says, as was your brother Ehud."

"What?"

"Remember your elder brother Ehud. Remember the day he teased you about your stature and you fought him like a lion. You fought him in the house, you fought him in the yard, and you fought him in the garden until he climbed a tree to escape your wrath. You clambered up the same tree and fought him in the branches until poor Ehud fell and broke his neck. Tell me, Aaron . . . tell me not a day passes that you do not think of your brother, who lived and died in that wheelchair you condemned him to. Tell me, Aaron, that not a day passes that you do not wish you had desisted, had somehow stayed your hand."

"*Enough!*" shouts Attazada angrily, tearing himself away from Roberts's grip. "This is of no consequence whatever!"

"And your mother on her deathbed, holding your hand as you watched the sun set over the Negev. She told you that she was proud of you, proud that you were a brave soldier and destined to be a hero. But her last words were that 'sometimes heroes are those that choose *not* to act.' Perhaps opting *not* to fight is the most courageous deed of all, she'd said. And you solemnly agreed . . . *Aaron!*"

Attazada jolts back in astonishment. He is twisting his head from side to side and asking Roberts under his breath, "How can you know this? . . . How do you know this?"

He bends down now and picks up his beret from the floor. For just a few seconds it looks as if he is burying his face in the beret before replacing it firmly on his head. All in the room recognize from his demeanour that his granite façade has cracked. Roberts can feel that the consensus has swung in his favour, and doesn't waste time in putting his plan to a vote.

"Well, gentlemen, will you sanction my proposed operation?"

All of them raise their hands, except for Attazada and his adjutant.

Roberts promptly flips open his cell phone.

"Walt! We are *green* on 'Apex'. Repeat – we are *green* on 'Apex'."

Ygor Lozitsky gazes across Damascus from his vantage-point on the flat roof of the American Embassy. He presses a button on his infra-red binoculars and homes in on his target. The GeoNova GPS micro-satellite his binoculars are synced with focuses the image crystal clear in his eyepieces, even though it is night. Lozitsky notes the target range illuminated in vivid green to one side of the lens.

"Seventeen hundred sixty-three metres," he grunts to himself.

He pulls out the lit cigarette that almost perpetually dangles from the left corner of his mouth and blows little curlicues of smoke into the breeze. There are voices behind him, most whimpering and weeping in Arabic. Others are yelling abuse in American accents.

"Ya fuckin' Muslim scum!" chides one of the Special Ops soldiers.

"Mohammed's bastards!" screams another.

Lozitsky turns and looks at a group of about a dozen males that have been rounded up by Special Ops. All are wearing traditional, white Arab robes; all are either blood-stained, piss-stained or shit-stained. Lozitsky approaches one of the prisoners.

"Will you help us find Khalid al-Hussein?" he asks him quietly in Arabic, a fresh cigarette hanging from the corner of his mouth.

"*Allahu Akhbar! . . . Allahu Akhbar!*" the prisoner repeats over and over, dropping to his knees now and begging for mercy.

"This man is of no use to us," says Lozitsky apathetically. He signals to Tony Vespazzi with a single raised eyebrow.

"We must encourage the others."

Vespazzi grabs the terrified prisoner by the hair. He locks a giant hand around the man's throat to stop his screaming and half-drags him to the edge of the roof. Draws out his pistol and shoots him in the face, before tossing his body like a rag-doll into the compound far below. There is a muffled thud.

"Nighty-night, Abdul," he calls out in a metallic voice as he peers over the edge of the building to inspect his handiwork.

Lozitsky is interrogating the rest of the prisoners all the while. He tugs at their beards and stares into their brown eyes, his voice never rising beyond a calm whisper.

"Will you help us find Khalid al-Hussein?" he asks each in turn.

They all shake their heads in despair. All save one. Lozitsky has found his man, but reasons that he requires further persuasion to guarantee his co-operation. He takes the cigarette from between his lips, and flicks some ash onto a youth cowering in the midst of the detainees. The youth is thirteen, maybe fourteen, years old. Other than twin tear-tracks, his cheeks are completely caked with blood and grime. Lozitsky signals Vespazzi with a raised eyebrow again. One of the older men from the group of prisoners screams out as Vespazzi seizes the boy.

"Please, no . . . please, no, I beg you. He is my son! . . . my son! Please, I build mosque for you . . . I build mosque if you not kill him . . . please kill *me* . . . kill *me* if you happy."

"Any you guys wanna mosque?" calls out a soldier to his colleagues. No one laughs.

The boy walks stoically at first in front of Vespazzi as if he is resigned to his fate. They reach the roof's edge and the boy kneels and bows his head.

"*Allahu Akhbar!*" he cries valiantly. Vespazzi pulls out his gun and pauses . . . pauses just long enough to hear the boy break down and sob and beg for his life.

He pulls the trigger.

The bullet shears the top of his victim's skull half off.

Vespazzi looks at the remnants of exposed brain still spurting blood. Views it casually almost, as if he had just peeled back the lid of a can of ripe tomatoes. The boy's father is distraught, wailing into the night sky before lashing out at his captors with flailing arms.

"Put that wretched animal out of his misery," commands Lozitsky, indicating the man with the butt of his cigarette.

"Yes, Colonel," answers a soldier. He grabs the man by the beard and jabs his weapon into the howling mouth.

"Nighty-night, Abdul," he says as he slowly squeezes the trigger.

Lozitsky looks coolly at the prisoner he noticed earlier, the one who did not shake his head when questioned about the whereabouts of al-Hussein.

"What is your name?" he asks, addressing him directly.

"Naseem."

"Will you help us now, Naseem?"

Naseem looks nervously at the terrified faces of the remaining prisoners. They seem to nod their assent in concert.

"Yes, I help . . .I help . . . I help very much," he stutters.

"You are familiar with the layout of the bunker al-Hussein is hiding in . . . Yes?"

Naseem nods vigorously.

"Come with me, then!" Lozitsky says gruffly.

Lozitsky taps the keys quickly on his holographic keyboard. A large, three-dimensional holographic image of the al-Rashid refugee camp materializes next to his computer. Naseem looks at it in amazement.

"This is the area . . . yes?" queries the colonel.

"Yes!"

"And this is the building under which Khalid al-Hussein has his bunker . . . Yes?" he asks, pointing at an unassuming ramshackle of houses.

"Yes."

Lozitsky taps at his keyboard again, inputting the precise co-ordinates of the building.

"Vespazzi!" he yells, "bring me the case!"

Tony strides across the embassy roof with a small aluminium briefcase chained to his wrist. He lays it down beside Lozitsky and decrypts its security code with a quantum scanner. The Colonel stubs out his latest cigarette and opens the briefcase carefully. There are ten small silver objects on a magnetic grid inside it, arrayed in a triangular pattern. Lozitsky dons a pair of black gloves, each with a network of electronic circuits woven through its fabric.

"What the fuck are *they*?" asks Vespazzi, picking up one of the silver objects and examining what appear to be tiny wings and legs on it.

"Don't touch!" shouts the Colonel. "You fucking ape."

"Hey, watch your mouth, Rooskie."

"Polish . . . Polish . . . I'd shoot you if you were one of my soldiers."

"What the *fuck* you talkin' bout?"

"Agh . . . you agents are taught to kill slowly, one at a time, with your pea-shooters." Lozitsky remarks scornfully, plucking the silver object from Vespazzi's fingers and replacing it on the magnetic grid. "But me . . . I kill many, qvickly."

The Colonel turns to his keyboard. He taps a few keys and the metallic objects rise gracefully into the air, maintaining their triangular formation and hovering now. Naseem and Vespazzi's eyes widen in astonishment.

"These are artificial insects. Seven of them are armed with an anti-matter-based explosive. The other three, one at each vertex of the triangle, are equipped with cameras," explains Lozitsky. "I can manipulate their flight sequence using the holographic display here."

He runs a gloved hand over a holographic image of the insect array and manoeuvres them into position with dexterous, minute movements of his fingers. He dons a headset.

"Apex launched," he announces into his mic as he taps his keyboard.

The little swarm of insects flies silently towards its target. Within two minutes it is at the heart of the al-Rashid district, wending its way through a warren of streets and alleyways. Its progress is detailed on the holographic image of Damascus.

"Is this the building, Naseem?" asks Lozitsky.

"Yes . . . left here, and one hundred metres on the left, there is entrance."

"Is this it?"

"Yes."

"Fuck, I've lost one!" shouts Lozitsky, springing to one side and reconfiguring the holographic array with his electronic gloves.

"Slow down . . . slower," says Naseem, fingering his beard nervously.

Nine insects are inside the building now. The lead insect's camera scans a large room with only a single door leading off it. The door is closed.

"The elevator to the bunker is beyond that door."

"Fuck it anyway!"

Lozitsky detaches one of the insects from the array and tries to negotiate it through a keyhole in the door. It gets stuck.

"Key must be in the fucking door!" he says in exasperation.

He has no choice but to land the insects on the floor and try and have them crawl through the gap under the door. He succeeds in squeezing six of them through, but there is only one remaining now equipped with a camera. Lozitsky reconfigures the swarm into a perfect triangle and the insects take wing again.

"Elevator . . . elevator twenty metres to the right!" says Naseem.

There are a number of armed men milling around outside the elevator doors. The Colonel stops his little swarm in mid-flight and slowly guides it towards the ceiling. It hovers silently above the guards' eye-level. He waits patiently for the elevator doors to open . . . ten minutes . . . fifteen minutes . . . twenty minutes. He glances anxiously at a power indicator level blinking on his computer monitor and talks into his mic.

"Fifteen per cent left . . . thirteen per cent power."

Suddenly the doors open and two men step out. Lozitsky accelerates the insects into the empty elevator.

"Come on . . . come on," he mutters to himself as the elevator remains motionless for a couple of minutes. The doors eventually close and the elevator begins a long descent.

"Eight per cent power left," answers Lozitsky to a desperate voice coming through his headset.

"Six per cent . . . thirty-two metres to the bunker now . . . five per cent."

Lozitsky tears off his headset in frustration and flings it one side.

The elevator finally comes to a halt and its doors glide back.

"Is this it, Naseem? . . . Is this the bunker?"

"Yes . . . yes."

The camera on the lead insect scans the interior of the bunker and feeds the images to Lozitsky's computer. There are seven men inside, drinking tea and watching a news channel on a large screen. Each face is instantly matched to the computer's database of Islamic terrorist suspects.

"I see him . . . I see Khalid . . . I see the *Mahdi!*" cries Naseem.

The Colonel taps a red key on his holographic keyboard and there is a single dazzling flash on his screen.

"Checkmate," he announces coldly.

He takes off his black electronic gloves and pops a fresh cigarette into the left corner of his mouth. He picks up the headset he tossed onto the ground earlier. There is a cacophony of voices emanating from it, all screaming for information.

Colonel Lozitsky lights up his cigarette and blows little curlicues of smoke again into the night air. He dons the headset and adjusts the mic to avoid the cigarette dangling from the corner of his mouth.

"Apex successful . . . targets terminated."

Naseem is ecstatic now. Waving his hands jubilantly and praising the colonel for his "magic".

"*Loshky akhbar . . . Loshky akhbar,*" he repeats ad nauseam.

Lozitsky looks at him and permits himself a thin smile.

He signals Vespazzi with a single raised eyebrow. . . .

The footage of al-Hussein's assassination is broadcast across the global news networks within a matter of hours. Roberts addresses the Knesset – the Israeli Parliament. He praises Spellman and Attazada for their calmness and restraint in responding to such an evil provocation. Warns other terrorist cells that they will be similarly hunted down and destroyed using this revolutionary technology developed by GeoNova.

"We will seek you, we will find you, and we will kill you," he declares.

The world breathes a collective sigh of relief and thanks God for Elijah Hunt Roberts.

Walter Franklin is standing, arms akimbo, in the Situation Room, watching Roberts's speech being aired live from Jerusalem. Keenly aware of what a damn close, near-run thing Apex has been – brinkmanship of the first magnitude. A gambit only a fuckwit or an Einstein could conceive and execute. Franklin glances at the President's poll ratings climbing on a separate screen. His rugged, craggy features crack into a smile as broad as the Grand Canyon.

"Hallelujah . . . hallelujah," he murmurs to himself. "You've saved the world, Eli."

THIRTY-TWO

FOR THE NEXT FORTNIGHT, Roberts's poll numbers continue their upward trend, until he is level with his election rival, Antonio Mendez. The President is feted as a hero on the campaign trail for his role in successfully resolving the Middle East crisis. Political pundits consistently compare him with JFK and *his* handling of the Cuban missile crisis of 1962. The GeoNova media machine goes into overdrive, subtly likening their candidate to a second Messiah who returned to Jerusalem and saved the world once more. Even the Christian fundamentalists, who revile Roberts, pore through their Books of Revelation, and detect more of the Jesus than the Lucifer in the man. But a few days prior to Election Day, on 6 November, the incumbent's numbers dip two percentage points below Mendez. It is almost as if America has wearied of the age of the global eco-warrior and wants "Big Carbon" back to resuscitate its flagging economy.

Jack Andersson awakens early on the morning of polling day. He knows *exactly* what is at stake if Roberts loses the election and can think of little else but the terrifying consequences. *Maybe people deserve Steelman*, he broods, *for forsaking their eco-crusading hero and ignoring climatic disasters. Maybe avoiding environmental apocalypse is simply too high a sacrifice to pay for the pleasures of the present.* Jack props himself up on a pile of pillows and looks at the time – five thirty – polling booths open in the east in ninety minutes. Knowing he is too tense to fall back to sleep, he orders the television on. He rubs his eyes at the image of an old house as it appears on the screen. He has seen this house before somewhere, nestling in a copse of trees, at the foot of a mountain.

"Breaking news this election day, ladies and gentlemen," announces a voice. "Breaking news this hour . . . Eleanor Roberts . . . former wife of President Elijah Roberts . . . *is dead*. Her body was discovered in her bedroom at her home in the West of Ireland, where she retired to, some fifteen years ago. Irish police authorities are refusing to comment on speculation that she may have taken her own life but have confirmed that foul play is not suspected. . . . "

Jack is stunned as he watches, selfishly wondering how this event will influence the minds of the voters. There could possibly be a groundswell of sympathy for the President that might swing the result of the election in his favour. Eleanor knew all about Steelman and couldn't have timed her suicide any better if she had wished to thwart its actuation. *Wonder if it was an overdose of sleeping pills, like her daughter Clara?*

Jack blinks at the images flashed up on the television monitor of Eleanor as an angelic, nubile young bride. She doesn't look remotely like the spiteful vixen he remembers interviewing some eighteen months previously. The grief over her daughter's death destroyed her, broke her feisty soul, and almost drove Roberts himself insane with guilt.

Jack leaps out of bed and walks quickly to Josh's bedroom. The boy is wide-awake. He looks at his father standing in the doorway.

"My birth mother is dead, isn't she?" he says.

"Yes."

"Do *you* think it was suicide?"

"Yes, Josh. I think she was a very troubled woman."

"No, Dad, Elijah had his wife murdered and made to look like suicide. You know the President is perfectly crazy, don't you?"

"No . . . no . . . he wouldn't do that."

"Not even to get re-elected and save the world from his own insanity? You don't know the man as I do, Dad. The man is a monster . . . believe me . . . a monster!"

Jack flits from one room to another all day, doing housework and vainly trying to distract himself from the election coverage. Every TV monitor in the house is tuned to a news channel. All ballots are now cast electronically, so the election results come in thick and fast as soon as the polling booths close in the east. Every time a state votes for Roberts, Jack lets out a whoop as if his team has just won the Superbowl. Josh seems totally uninterested, and spends most of the day conversing with Cass in the study. Mendez polls well with the Hispanic communities; Roberts scores well with GeoNova's youth base in the cities. The election race gets tighter and tighter the further west it progresses. By early next morning it becomes obvious that California's massive Electoral College vote will decide the issue. Jack can feel his heart pounding as he waits for the announcement of the result. He doesn't want to be alone as he watches it, so he rushes into the study and stands beside Josh, who is seated in the leather armchair. He squeezes his son's hand lightly and requests Cass to display a news channel. The news anchor's voice is breathless with anticipation.

"Ladies and Gentlemen . . . Election Twenty Forty is shaping up to be one of the most exciting and fascinating electoral battles in decades. All hinges on the golden state of California, for which we will have the result in just a couple of minutes. Final thoughts on the outcome, Art?" she says to an electoral pundit beside her in the studio.

"Oh, this is just *way* too close to call. California's large Hispanic population should give Mendez the edge I think. But GeoNova's youth constituency has also increased in the last few years. Yesterday I'd a said Mendez was a shoo-in, but the overnight news of the President's personal tragedy has certainly swung events in his favour. If you were to put my back to the wall though I'd still reckon Mendez will shade it."

The news anchor suddenly claps her hand to her earpiece. "Sorry, Art . . . the result is coming through any moment . . . any moment now."

She pauses as the result is fed into her ear-piece.

"Say again . . . confirm those numbers, please."

She stares straight at the camera as she calls it out loud and clear. "Ladies and gentlemen; the state of California votes for *GeoNova!* Elijah Hunt Roberts retains the presidency. I repeat: Roberts ret . . . "

Jack cannot contain himself – jumping up and down and punching the air exultantly with both fists, shouting ecstatically about the momentous turnaround this election has been.

"We're saved, Josh . . . Thank God almighty we are spared Steelman!" he yells, bending down now and kissing and hugging the boy with relief. The scene on the computer screen switches from the news studio to the Yankee Stadium in New York, where Roberts is preparing to deliver his victory speech. The stadium is a sea of waving green-and-orange GeoNova flags and banners. The applause, cheering, chanting and singing reaches a crescendo of "Four more years . . . four more years . . . " mixed with the corporate anthem, *Bitter Sweet Symphony*. Mark, the news correspondent on the ground, has to shout to make himself heard.

"Unbelievable scenes of wild jubilation here . . . drama worthy of Hollywood . . . a sensational victory for Roberts. . . . "

His commentary is drowned out by a volcanic roar as the multitude erupts in ecstasy. And tens of thousands of green-and-orange helium balloons are released into the night sky to signal Roberts's arrival on stage.

The President is positioned now on the podium, patiently waiting for his audience to quieten down so he can address it. He raises both arms in a giant "Y" and stretches them towards the night sky. He fans out his fingers and almost seems to touch the stars with their tips. His mighty head is tilted back and his mesmeric eyes are zeroed on the zenith.

"I am Elijah Hunt Roberts. I am going to reclaim the Promised

Land and you're all coming with me. Together we're going to change the world . . . I swear we're going to change the world."

Even for a man of such commanding confidence and consummate calmness, Roberts appears ill at ease on this occasion. There is a film of perspiration on his forehead and his voice begins to quaver. He arches his spine as if the better to reach for the stars, but just keeps falling backwards, and collapses onto the stage. His bodyguards and aides instinctively rush towards the President and surround him.

"Oh, my Lord!" cuts in the studio anchor, "I think something has happened the President. Mark, Mark . . . can you tell us what's happening?"

"I can't see . . . eh, there's people all around him . . . it's chaotic down there . . . wait a second . . . don't see any blood. His bodyguards are carrying him from the stage . . . eh, maybe he's just fainted; maybe exhaustion . . . I dunno . . . I dunno . . . maybe something terrible's happened."

Jack turns to Josh in horror.

"What's happening? . . . What the hell is happening, Josh?"

The boy looks at him with tears in his eyes and just keeps repeating, "Say farewell to the Master . . . say farewell to the Master."

Then he holds up a gold pen and unscrews the top off it. He appears to pull something out of it now with his finger-nails. Jack can hardly see it at first, but catches sight of it glinting in the light – it is a tiny hypodermic syringe. Josh rolls up his sleeve quickly and jabs himself in the arm with it.

"What are you doing, Josh? . . . What the hell *is* that?"

"I'm sorry, Dad," he says sotto voce. The eyes roll back in his head involuntarily and he starts to stagger out of the study, before collapsing unconscious on the floor. Jack rushes to him and desperately tries to revive him, slapping his cheeks and loosening his clothing. He feels for a pulse at the side of his neck and checks his breathing; they are both becoming faint.

"What have you done, son? . . . What have you injected yourself with?" he pleads despairingly. He lifts up the boy's limp frame and carries him through the kitchen and out into the rear garden to get him some fresh air. But Josh remains unconscious. Jack checks for a pulse again in his neck but can't detect one. He checks the pulse on his wrist but still can't find it. He reaches behind Josh's head and brings the boy's mouth up to his ear to listen to his breathing.

"He's dead . . . he's dead!" screams Jack, "Oh, Jesus, he's dead!"

He dials 911 a few times on his cell but it is constantly engaged.

"Oh, Jesus, he's dead . . . my little boy is dead again," he wails.

Jack lays Josh down on a couch in the living-room. He caresses the boy's beautiful face and tousles his silky brown shock of hair.

"Why? Why?" he moans pitifully, hugging the boy and kissing his cold cheeks.

Pale orange shafts of sunlight seep through a window and cast a golden amber glow over the room. Jack glances at a TV monitor and sees Elijah Roberts's face fill the screen. The voiceover is lugubrious in tone.

"President Elijah Hunt Roberts, forty-ninth President of these United States of America, pronounced *dead* at seven fifty-three this morning. Although the precise cause of his death remains unclear, it is believed the President was the victim of a suspected chemical or nerve-agent attack at Yankee Stadium. An unknown number of others also attending the President's post-electoral victory celebrations in the stadium have either lapsed into a coma or died. . . . "

There is an almighty crash. The front door of the house bursts open. Half a dozen armed agents storm into the living-room. They haul Jack away from Josh and restrain him at one end of the room. A huge, bald man enters and goes towards the boy, who is stretched out on a couch. He kneels, and takes something from inside his jacket and administers it to the boy.

"Come on, my son," he says, tapping him gently on both cheeks with his large hands. "Time to wake up, Joshua . . . time to wake up, my boy."

After a minute there is the sound of a short cough, and the giant figure stands up and claps his hands with relief.

"Come to my arms, my beamish boy," he announces in a loud voice.

Josh rises groggily to his feet and embraces the man with arms trembling. The man lifts him up, hugs him and cradles him in his arms before carrying him from the living-room, through the kitchen and out into the garden. They are followed now by a distinguished looking group of uniformed GeoNova personnel.

"Will you hold the Bible for me, Joshua?" asks the man, stopping at the half-uprooted white oak tree, still dominating the centre of the garden.

"Yes, Father."

A small crowd has filed out to the garden and is assembled now under the spreading vermilion foliage of the tree. A man in black robes steps forward and places a small burgundy velvet-bound book in the boy's outstretched palms. He nods solemnly at the tall, bald man, standing beside the boy and turns to the crowd.

"Ladies and Gentlemen, we are gathered here this morning to witness a man take an oath. It is the dawn not only of a new day but also of a new era. May the Lord forgive us our sins and preserve the peace for posterity. Amen."

The tall man comes forth and lays his left hand reverently on the Bible. His voice booms across the stillness of the morning air.

"I, Tor Magnusson, do solemnly swear that I will faithfully execute the Office of President of the United Colonies of GeoNova, and will, to the best of my ability, preserve, protect, and defend the Constitution of these United Colonies of GeoNova . . . So help me, God."

There is desultory applause from his audience; some of the crowd are in tears. Others approach Magnusson, tentatively shake his left hand and wish him luck. Tyler Kincaid, CEO of GeoNova Industries, congratulates him lukewarmly.

"I sincerely hope you will be a worthy successor to your brother Eli," he tells him.

Magnusson bends down now and whispers into Josh's ear.

"Your day will come too, my son; and when it does, *carpe diem, carpe mundum*. Seize the day, seize the world."

The boy gazes at the eastern horizon as he responds. "Fear not, Father! When my day comes the scales will fall from my eyes and I shall outstare the face of the noonday sun."

The small crowd troop back through the house and within a minute they are gone. Josh gives Jack a sidelong glance as he walks past him, accompanied by Magnusson. The boy halts a few seconds and gazes at Tony Vespazzi through moistened eyes before finally leaving.

Jack and the agent are alone now.

"This is a *coup*, isn't it, a goddam *coup d'état*?" Jack protests.

Vespazzi draws out his gun, locks his hand up against Jack's throat and pins him against a wall. He jams the muzzle of the weapon into his victim's mouth. Curls his index finger around the trigger and squeezes it a fraction. He hesitates; shoves the gun further down Jack's throat until he starts gagging. The agent doesn't seem to know whether to shoot him or asphyxiate him.

"I can't do this . . . I can't do this *shit* no more. Everyone's going to die anyway," he cries. He pulls the gun out of Jack's mouth.

"*What?*" croaks Jack.

Vespazzi rubs a cuff across his sweat-spangled brow and breathes heavily.

"This is a category five shitstorm, Andersson. Steelman is not just a computer virus. It's a fuckin' nano-virus designed to get everyone to fall asleep, 'cept they never wake up. The artificial bees is the vector."

"What?"

"Everybody's going to Morningtown, even the kids, 'less you got the antidote."

"It's in the gold pens, isn't it?"

"Yeah . . . yeah . . . I ain't got nobody, Andersson. No wife, no kids . . . nothing, *understand*," Vespazzi sobs.

He reaches into his jacket pocket, pulls out a gold pen and gives it to Jack.

He walks away a few paces, stops and turns.

"Only one person left I gotta kill, and he ain't even worth the slug," he cries.

A few seconds later, Jack hears a single shot ring out from the kitchen.

The networks are reporting power outages and multiple fatalities within the hour.

Jack Andersson is sitting in his study with Vespazzi's gun in one hand and the gold pen in the other, watching events unfold. He thinks about losing Josh and Jenny and Christopher. He wonders whether Eli Roberts is really dead at all, or if he will be resurrected in one of the eco-colonies somewhere.

"Cᴀss!" he calls out.

Her beautiful face appears on the screen in front of him with her crystal-blue eyes and champagne smile and curly blonde tresses.

"Can I help you, Jack?" she asks cheerfully.

Jack Andersson raises his gun and aims it right between her eyes.

"Goodbye, Cᴀss," he says.

EPILOGUE

"I am the Lamb of God cometh to take away the sin of the world. Lord have mercy on me."

Those were the final words spoken to me by our founding father before Gaia was cleansed of humankind, almost in its entirety. The brutal Soviet dictator Stalin (whose name literally translates as "man of steel") allegedly said that the death of one individual is a tragedy, millions a statistic. I seek no solace in that quote; derive no comfort from its kernel of truth. But I can think of no finer epitaph for our Saviour: Elijah Roberts.

My brothers and sisters, some of you, on this fiftieth anniversary commemoration, have expressed great remorse and a tremendous burden of guilt over Steelman. Indeed, some describe it as the most heinous crime in history; an avoidable cataclysm. But I am not here to pass moral judgement on an event that was beyond good and evil. I am not here to condemn it or condone it or argue that it was the triumph of the Übermenschen to impose Nietzschean ideals. No – each and every one of us must interpret it subjectively, in the privacy and quietude of our own conscience.

However, I shall say this; Steelman was the birth pangs of a new world from the diseased womb of the old. It was unquestionably a renaissance. And it is incumbent on this generation, via GeoNova, to strive to be the greatest that humanity can possibly be. That is the debt we owe the old world. And perhaps . . . perhaps the noblest aspiration through which we may seek atonement for the sacrifices of the past.

Elijah told me that he spent his boyhood studying the lives of great historical figures. As a child he marvelled at how they gained, wielded and maintained their immense powers. Those heroes he'd sought to emulate, however, were still "prisoners of history" and "slaves to the Zeitgeist", he'd said – all their majestic empires ultimately collapsed from within. Thus it was true also of twenty-first century civilization – "An Empire of the Mind", a Noosphere as Elijah called it. The advances in artificial intelligence helped foster a collective global consciousness, but to the detriment of individual human cognition. Quantum computing in particular accelerated the divorce of human consciousness from the stark realities of our nature. In short, we drifted into allowing computers do our thinking for us while we indulged our basic physical appetites.

But the elite at GeoNova realized, as Nietzsche preached, that we must transcend our own human nature, our orthodox moral framework – indeed our own history – to survive; that the price of saving humanity had to be its near eradication.

For my own conscience's sake I seek consolation in the thought that nine billion people falling asleep for ever was the most humane of inhumanities. But my heart feels like a lead pendulum nonetheless whenever I reflect upon it.

It is an enduring characteristic of the human condition, and most particularly our highly intellectualized society, to denigrate emotionality. Our philosophers routinely argue that rationality is subservient to our emotions. They are still enamoured of the idea of the perfectibility of Man. To some extent I feel we have become too ultra-rationalist a society, at the expense of compassion. I believe the time is ripe, however, to adopt a more holistic approach.

Let me tell you, brothers and sisters, that I was a cold child to my adoptive parents. I was so infatuated with my intellectual powers, so entranced by my own mind, so narcissistic, that I was incapable of expressing love for anyone but myself. It was a time of great emptiness. A void only acknowledged and filled by the arrival of my own children. Not a day goes past that I don't seek my adoptive parents' forgiveness for the pain I caused them.

I suppose what I'm truly trying to say is that reason and passion complement each other. They are both good servants in equal standing, whose fusion constitutes our human spirit, our human soul.

For reason without passion, and passion devoid of reason, render our existence joyless and inert.

Perhaps the same principle is applicable to our notion of rationality and irrationality.

Perhaps we must accept that the line between logic and lunacy is oft times not merely indeterminate, but indeed invisible.

Knowing that my father, Tor Magnusson, was not a religious man, I asked him once why he chose to swear an oath on the Bible the day Steelman was launched.

"Son," he answered, "when I was a little boy, I gazed at all the stars in the vastness of the heavens, and felt afraid. When I became a man, I realized my mind was bigger than the universe and I felt even more afraid. But it was the thought of God, the idea of God, the dream of God alone that harmonized outer space and inner space for me. Only then did I discover the sustenance of sanity.

On that note: May God bless you, and God bless these Federated Colonies of GeoNova on this auspicious day.

Joshua Augustine Magnusson
3rd President of the Federated Colonies of GeoNova

November 7, 2090